"Pa," Emma had called, running across the deck, surefooted as any of her brothers. "Pa, I've got some hot stew for you, and corn bread, too."

Manny turned and saw a sudden gust of wind catch the grappling hook. "Emma! Duck, girl, duck!"

But she hadn't heard, and the vicious curve of iron grazed her arm, laying it open to the bone. The bucket of stew had spilled across the deck, mingling with the blood spurting from her wound.

They'd made a tourniquet of a filthy rag lying nearby and carried her ashore. The only reason they took her to young Doc Morgan was that his office was closer than old man Broderick's. "Will she lose her arm?" Manny demanded after Joshua treated her.

"No. And the scar will be barely noticeable in a couple of years."

Manny had eyed Joshua with suspicion then. After all, he was young and cocksure, and doctoring was always chancy, everybody knew it. "You certain 'bout that?"

"Absolutely sure," Joshua assured him. "You were quick with the tourniquet, and you got her here in record time. Emma will be fine. Take your daughter home now, Captain Silva. I'll call in on her and change the dressing tomorrow."

And it had seemed to both Emma and Joshua that tomorrow would never come, never be soon enough. For they'd looked at each other while he stitched her arm, and their eyes had spoken, and love had been born without either of them able to control it. And both were frightened and a little ashamed, because she was a child of fifteen and he was an old man of twenty-five.

THE MORGAN WOMEN

Beverly Byrne

BANTAM BOOKS
New York • Toronto • London • Sydney • Auckland

THE MORGAN WOMEN

A Bantam Book / August 1990

ISBN 0-553-28468-1

Published simultaneously in the United States and Canada

PRINTED IN THE UNITED STATES OF AMERICA

RAD   0 9 8 7 6 5 4 3 2 1

BOOK
ONE
1915 — 1924

EMMA

1

Gulls cawed and swooped and screamed overhead, their gray and white plumage enflamed by the early setting sun of December. Joshua Morgan watched the gulls while leaning against the door of a filthy hovel and taking deep breaths. How he needed the draughts of cold salt air at this moment. His throat, his lungs were fouled with the stench of deprivation and disease.

Once this part of Gloucester had been the site of the main defense of the superb harbor spread in front of him. In this year of 1915 local people still called the area on the north shore of Massachusetts the fort, but now it was home to the families of the Italians who worked on the fishing boats. From here Joshua could see the great fleet anchored a quarter of a mile away. Every trawler in the fleet was steam driven now, the days of working sail ended.

Joshua was a man in love with progress and he did not mourn the past—not the clippers and windjammers and whalers which the trawlers had replaced, nor his boyhood home behind him out of sight on Eastern Point—least of all that. The point was another world, a world studded with the houses of the mighty who had made great fortunes from the sea.

Yankees most of them—those first-comers who scented the riches to be gleaned on this jut of land on Massachusetts Bay called Cape Ann—and bloodsuckers all. They amassed fleets of boats, and grew rich and fat on the bounty of the ocean and the carcass of the town they had made. They determined the shape, the very bones of the place, building for themselves magnificent coastal mansions with sea views and large, lush gardens.

After the Yankees grew wealthy, they brought in the Portuguese, and sent them to sea in their stead. These days it was men whose parents and grandparents came from Portugal who captained the boats, some of them even owned one or two. Over the years they had claimed for themselves the hills north of Gloucester's Main Street, and made smaller houses and smaller gardens. Lastly the Italians arrived, and what was left for them were the most dangerous and dirty and poorly paid jobs in the business of harvesting the sea. It was the Italians who lived in the shanties hastily erected in the fort.

Joshua was just thirty, a big man, broad shouldered and slim hipped, with a thick head of black curly hair and green eyes that crinkled at the corners each time he smiled. Despite the fact that he was married, the daughters of Eastern Point sighed over him, and some of the wives as well. Joshua ignored them because he loved his wife, and because he was preoccupied by the plight of the girls and women who lived in the fort. He wanted to help them, was trained to help them, but usually he could do little against the twin foes of ignorance and poverty.

On this winter evening he watched the gulls and thought about these things until a small boy appeared at his side and tugged on his sleeve. "Mom's awake again," the child said.

Hearing the woman moan then gasp, Joshua turned quickly and went into the house.

It had only two rooms. Rosa Tecci lay in the frontmost, in a bed that had been pulled close to the coal stove and its smoke-blackened chimney. The table which normally held what food there was for her brood of ten had been scrubbed clean and covered with a white sheet. All the tools of Morgan's trade were laid out on that sheet—scalpels, swabs, bandages, even one of the new stethoscopes. They seemed to him a pitiful arsenal against the agony of the woman in the bed.

She was terrifyingly thin despite the swollen abdomen of her full-term pregnancy. Her pinched, sweat-soaked face looked as if it had seen sixty years, not a mere twenty-six. "How are you feeling, Rosa?" Joshua wiped her forehead with a wet towel.

"Very bad, Doctor. I no think I can stand it. Is two days already, no?"

Joshua nodded, raging inwardly at the sight of her, and choked with frustration. "Don't try and talk, Rosa. Save your strength."

As he spoke she arched her frail body and screamed through the duration of another contraction. Morgan whipped back the covers, praying there would be a sign that birth would come soon, but once more his experienced, probing fingers found nothing. The infant's head wasn't yet in the birth canal, and until it was, he could do nothing except monitor the terrible contractions and the rising fever and the weakening pulse.

"Joe," the woman said weakly. A man who'd been lurking in the shadows appeared. "Joe, you get Father Roncaldi."

Joe Tecci wasn't an immigrant; he'd been born in Gloucester, he spoke without his wife's pronounced Italian accent. "Don't say things like that, Rosa. You ain't gonna die. Doc Morgan's here. He knows all the new things from Boston. He ain't gonna let you die. Stop talking stupid."

His gruffness was a mask for his terror and his pain, his wife knew that. "*Si, va bene,*" she muttered through clenched teeth, "but you get me the priest. *Per piacere,* Joe . . ."

Tecci's eyes sought out Joshua's and asked the question he would not put into words: Is it true that I need a priest to come and give the last rites to my wife?

Joshua swallowed hard, then nodded. The other man stared at him for a moment, and turned white when he read the death sentence written on the doctor's face. Then he cursed softly under his breath and headed for the door.

Morgan followed him and put a hand on his shoulder. "It's only a precaution, Joe, to give Rosa peace of mind. She's young and a fighter. And I'm doing everything I can."

Tecci nodded, then hurried out.

A few seconds later Rosa had another contraction. Joshua checked again. This time he felt something. Not the head, a foot—a breach presentation, he'd had plenty of experience with those. Thank God, at last he could do something. "Push hard with the next contraction, Rosa. We're winning. This little critter's finally decided to be born. C'mon, girl, push. You can do it."

He was only peripherally aware of Joe Tecci returning

with Father Roncaldi; he paid no attention when both men took up a position at the head of the bed. He scarcely realized that the ten Tecci children had trooped in from the small room in the rear and knelt somewhere behind him. He heard the droning litany of their prayers to the Virgin, but he was consumed by the struggle for life going on beneath his hands.

Blinking the sweat out of his eyes, Joshua ignored the rivers of it pouring down his back and making his shirt stick to his skin. "Push! Bear down, Rosa. Good, again. Come on, push!" He felt her struggle to respond to his commands, felt the ripples of effort from her exhausted, quivering muscles. It seemed to go on forever, but it was only minutes later when, with a last mighty heave, he pulled the baby into the world. It was a boy, bruised and purple and silent. No time for the stethoscope, he held the tiny body to his ear. Yes! Yes by God, there was a faintly discernible heartbeat.

Fast now, it all had to be so fast. . . . Joshua shoved his finger into the infant's mouth and swabbed away the choking mucous. He snipped the cord expertly and clamped both ends, then held the child by its ankles and smacked it sharply on the buttocks. Nothing happened. The sound of the rosary continued behind him. He slapped the baby again, and three seconds later the infant let out one lusty cry.

"He's alive, Rosa," Morgan cried triumphantly. "You've a fine son and he's alive."

"She's gone, Doctor," the priest said softly. "Rosa's gone to God." He moved forward, stretching out arms encased in the black cassock of his trade. "Here, give me the boy. You look ready to drop." The cleric reached for the child with one hand and for a clean blanket with the other. "Don't blame yourself, son," he murmured softly. "God decides these things, you're only his instrument."

Joshua bit back a reply and bent over Rosa. The priest and the fisherman were laymen, they might be wrong. Maybe she wasn't dead, only in shock. He grabbed the stethoscope and put it to her breast, moved it all over, pressed his sensitive fingers to her wrists and her temples. Nothing. The effort of that last great contraction, her enormous struggle to push as he'd told her to, and a heart wearied by ten live births and three miscarriages in eleven years—it had all been too much. He sighed and closed her eyes with his blood-stained fingers and drew the frayed blanket over her face.

The gesture communicated the reality of their mother's death to the watching children. Several of them began to cry, with the controlled desperation learned from their particular experience of life. The sound of his children's quiet sobbing roused Joe Tecci from shock. He rose from his knees and approached the doctor. "If I sent Rosa to the new hospital to have the baby, like you said, would it've been different?"

Joshua shook his head. "No, probably not. I'm sorrier than I can say, Joe. She was just too tired. Too worn-out with all her pregnancies."

"It's my fault," the man muttered. "After the last time, when she lost the baby after four months, when there was so much blood and pain, I swore I wouldn't touch her again. We both swore to the Virgin. Only . . . it's my fault," he repeated.

Father Roncaldi was still holding the newborn. He stepped closer and thrust the baby into his father's arms. "It's nobody's fault, Joe. It's the will of almighty God. Here, take your son. New life. Life goes on, that's God's will too."

Joshua Morgan looked at the priest with loathing.

Captain Manny Silva paid a visit to his daughter while Rosa Tecci was busy dying. "Where's Josh?" he asked when she let him in. "I brung you some cod steaks for his supper."

Emma Silva Morgan took the newspaper-wrapped package from his hand. "Thank you. Josh isn't back yet from delivering a baby down in the fort."

Manny grunted. "Too damn many babies born down in the fort. That's the trouble with them wops."

Emma didn't reply, she knew full well the animosity between the Portuguese who had been here for three generations and the immigrant Italians. She had grown up with that prejudice, and with another sort unique to her family. "Do you have time for coffee, Pa?"

"Yeah, sure." He sat down at his daughter's kitchen table and watched her ladle heaping spoonfuls of coffee into a jug and add hot water. Made it the English way, just like her ma. Looked like her ma too. The same red hair. The same blue-green eyes, the color of the sea, just like Jessica's had been. Damn, it was too late to choke up over Jess. She'd been dead going on three years. "Put that fish in the ice chest, girl. Don't go letting it spoil and givin' it to Josh and sayin' I brung it."

Emma carried the package to the new wooden icebox. She knew her father too well to be offended by his tone. "Thanks again, Pa. We'll have the cod for lunch tomorrow if Josh doesn't get back in time tonight."

"You do that. And Bess said to tell you to drop by sometime soon. We hardly see you these days."

"I'll try and come next week." Bess was her sister-in-law, the wife of the oldest of Emma's four brothers. She had three children, and they all lived with Manny in the big house where Emma herself had been born. In the Silva family that house was a legend as well as a legacy. It had been made possible by Jessica's dowry.

Emma's mother was the daughter of a shipbuilder who owned a prosperous yard in Bristol, England. She met Manny when, as a young man hungry for adventure, he gave up fishing and went to sea in an enormous square-rigged windjammer, one of those behemoths fighting steam for dominance in world trade.

Jessica's family was appalled at her choice of husband, and they cut her off without a penny. But an uncle had slipped her a purse containing fifty guineas just before she sailed off to America. Manny had wanted to use some of it to purchase decent quarters for his bride—the windjammer had such luxuries available for a price—but she refused, and won for herself a disastrous crossing in a dark, airless cabin deep in the hold.

The trip was hugely successful from the point of view of the captain. His craft was driven by the storms and gales on which the tall ships thrived, and she docked in Boston after just three weeks. Jessica emerged thin and pale, her lovely eyes dark shadowed, and she never went to sea again, but the fifty guineas were intact. They provided the down payment on a fishing boat for Manny, so he could forego the long voyages which would separate him from his wife, and a house on Friend Street overlooking the harbor.

Manny was thinking of that now. "Got yourselves a nice place here, you and Josh. Though I don't know why he had to build it way out here in Annisquam."

"It's close to the hospital, Pa." Emma poured his coffee and added sugar and milk. "I baked a nice sponge this morning, have a piece."

Another little quirk Emma had picked up from Jess. She always said sponge, not sponge cake. Girl had all her mother's fancy ways. Please God it wouldn't become a source of trouble and grief between her and her husband, like it had with him and Jess. "Haven't got time. I just came by to bring you the fish and see how you was doin'."

"I'm fine, Pa. Josh too."

"You sure? You're not pinin', stuck way out here by yourself?"

Emma smiled. "I'm very sure."

"Right, then I'll be goin'."

She went with him to the door and waited until he'd gone down the path and let himself out the gate, then waved a final good-bye and went inside. Manny hesitated a moment, looking at the gray-shingled saltbox house Morgan had built for his daughter. Nice. And Emma was a lady, not like the rest of them. Jess had got her way in the end, at least about the girl. Too bad she didn't live to see it. "You'd have been proud of her, Jessie," he muttered. "Right proud."

It was nearly eleven when Josh returned to the little house in Annisquam. Emma took one look at him and was wise enough to ask no questions. He was trembling with fatigue and he smelled of whisky. "There's hot coffee, darling. Would you like some?"

He nodded and slumped into a chair. She brought it to him, along with a bottle of brandy they kept for special occasions. Josh laced the coffee with the spirit and drank it down quickly. The grandfather clock chimed in the hall. The clock was a memento of Josh's childhood home, but it sounded unnaturally loud in this small living room. It didn't have the resonance it used to have in the front hall of the great house on Eastern Point. Josh glanced at it. "I'm going to bed. I'm sorry, but I'm just too exhausted to talk."

Emma kissed his forehead. "You don't have to talk. And I'll come up with you." She helped him undress and tucked him in like a child.

Tired as he was, he couldn't sleep. A few minutes later

he was conscious of her slipping into the bed beside him. He reached out and took her hand. "Rosa Tecci died. There wasn't a damn thing I could do."

"What about the baby?"

"Alive. A boy. Now Joe Tecci has eleven motherless kids to worry about."

"Go to sleep, Josh darling," she said softly. "We'll talk about it in the morning."

Her voice and her presence soothed him and he rolled over and slept.

The December sun was high when he woke, and he started guiltily and groped for his watch, worrying about his office and his patients. Then he realized it was Sunday and sank back into the warm bed with relief. Emma was gone. She was always an early riser, even on Sundays. Joshua reached out his arm and touched her pillow. Blessings on you, Emma, he thought. How had she gotten to be the wise one when he was ten years older? God alone knew, but she was.

After drifting between sleeping and waking for another half an hour, Josh rose and went to the window to look down on the tiny winterbound garden. Like the house, it was small and new and still raw. The trees were mere saplings whipping in the wind, and the earth was bare where someday there would be flowers. While he watched, Emma appeared from the direction of the kitchen door. For Josh the garden was transformed by her presence.

Bundled against the cold, she worked on wrapping a young apple tree. Even her heavy winter coat couldn't disguise the tall, slim grace of her. Her long red hair was wound into a heavy chignon at the nape of her neck. He thought about the way it looked in the privacy of their bedroom when it hung free and became a shimmering cape that covered her shoulders. Now, pulled back, it showed off the perfection of her high forehead, her generous mouth, the sculptured brows arching over her incomparable eyes. Josh remembered the first time he'd looked into Emma's aquamarine eyes with their pale, opalescent irises. She'd been a child, only fifteen, but he had thought he might drown in those eyes. He still did.

She turned just then and saw him in the bedroom window and smiled and mouthed some words he couldn't make out. Josh shook his head, and she disappeared. A few seconds later he heard her feet tripping lightly up the stairs, then she was with him in the bedroom, arms around his neck, head tucked into his shoulder, smelling of the outdoors and the subtle scent of violets that always seemed to accompany her.

"Good morning, Joshua darling. The water for your bath is hot and waiting, and the pancakes will be ready before you're out of the tub."

He hugged her. "Need a bath, do I?"

Emma wrinkled her nose. "I think so."

He shivered slightly. "Very well, I shall bear it like a man." He'd never had an aversion to baths until he had built this cottage and came up with the bright idea of making a separate bathroom in the upstairs hall. It still seemed a sensible, if not bright idea—except for one small oversight. When he had decided against open fires with all their mess and installed a furnace in the cellar, he'd overlooked the matter of heating the bathroom. With no radiator the bathroom would be freezing this morning.

Emma knew what Josh was thinking. She laughed. "I cheated. I've put an old hip tub in the kitchen by the stove. You can talk to me while I fix your breakfast."

"God knows what Joe Tecci will do now. Just take the oldest girl out of school and make her a mother at nine, I suppose. What else can he do?" Josh squirmed in the tub, pulling his long legs closer to his chest. "It's such a waste. Thirteen pregnancies in eleven years. My God, we're like animals. Worse! Animals only mate in season."

Emma took the sponge from his hand, soaping his back and loving the breadth of it, the way the muscles of his shoulders rippled beneath his skin. "Do you think women have a season too? A special time when they can conceive? Professor Schoener said something about that."

She was thinking as much of herself as of Rosa Tecci and the other women of the fort. Josh knew it. They'd been married ten months and there was still no sign of starting a family. "I don't know," he said. "Neither does Professor Schoener yet. That's one of the things his research is supposed to find out."

"Josh, do you ever regret not taking his offer?"

"No," he said too quickly. He could hear his own defensiveness and knew she'd heard it too. He reached for the sponge. "Here, give me that. Listen, Emma, we've been all over this. I want to be a country doctor, a general practitioner. I admire Schoener and I owe him an enormous amount, but I don't want to be a fancy Boston gynecologist. I want to help women like Rosa, not kowtow to society ladies with imaginary ills."

Emma moved to the stove and flipped over the bacon frying slowly in the big iron spider. The good, smokey smell filled the kitchen. "All the same, it might be better to do more research. Better for Rosa, God rest her soul, and the other women like her."

He'd thought of that, too, thought of little else for the three hours before he came home last night. Alone in his office with a bottle of bourbon for company, he'd gone over all the arguments for the hundredth time. Now he shook his head, half in disagreement with her, half to indicate that he didn't want to discuss it further, and climbed out of the tub and wrapped himself in a huge towel. "I'll eat before I shave, if you don't mind. I'm ravenous."

Emma bided her time. She was good at it. She'd grown up on Gloucester's wharves, and she knew that you had to wait for the fish to start running before you could hope for a catch. The way she had waited until she was old enough to make Joshua Morgan marry her.

When she first saw him it was 1910 and he'd just returned from medical school and a stint in a Boston hospital. He opened a little office on Main Street and hoped the local people would learn to trust him, despite the peculiar circumstances which made him neither one of the ordinary fisherfolk nor a legitimate member of the ruling gentry.

One summer day a few weeks after Josh went into practice, Emma's father and her brothers had been working on their boat. They were cleaning and painting, doing the endless chores that occupied them whenever they were in port. She'd gone to bring them lunch, glad of the opportunity because she loved the sea and the trawlers. Jessica hated her to be among them, but she'd been especially rushed that morning, so she sent Emma to the boat with lunch for Manny and the boys.

"Pa," she had called, running across the deck, sure-footed as any of her brothers. "Pa, I've got some hot stew for you, and corn bread too."

Manny turned and saw a sudden gust of wind catch the grappling hook. "Emma! Duck, girl, duck!"

But she hadn't heard, and the vicious curve of iron grazed her arm, laying it open to the bone. The bucket of stew had spilled across the deck, mingling with the blood spurting from her wound.

They'd made a tourniquet of a filthy rag lying nearby and carried her ashore. The only reason they took her to young Doc Morgan was that his office was closer than old man Broderick's. "Will she lose her arm?" Manny demanded after Joshua treated her.

"No. And the scar will be barely noticeable in a couple of years."

Manny had eyed Joshua with suspicion then. After all he was young and cocksure, and doctoring was always chancy, everybody knew it. "You certain 'bout that?"

"Absolutely sure," Joshua assured him. "You were quick with the tourniquet, and you got her here in record time. Emma will be fine."

"Sometimes after a wound like that there's fever," Manny insisted. "I seen it plenty of times."

"So have I. But that doesn't have to happen anymore. Not if the wound is thoroughly cleaned." Morgan had thought of explaining about germs and the newest theories of asepsis, but Manny Silva was unlikely to believe in microbes. "From now on," Josh said, "anytime you have an accident like that aboard, wash the wound with spirits. Anything will do, corn liquor, even wine. And use the cleanest linen for a bandage, and wash your hands before you change it. That will put an end to any chance of infection."

"What's infe . . . whatever you called it?"

"Infection. The thing that causes the fever. Take your daughter home now, Captain Silva. I'll call in on her and change the dressing tomorrow."

And it had seemed to both Emma and Joshua that tomorrow would never come, never be soon enough. For they'd looked at each other while he stitched her arm, and their eyes had spoken, and love had been born without either of them able to control it. And both were frightened and a little ashamed, because she was a child of fifteen and he was an old man of twenty-five.

For three years they didn't acknowledge their feelings,

though Gloucester was a small town and they met often, and their glances spoke passionate sonnets while their lips mouthed platitudes about the weather or the catch. Then came the day in August of 1913 when Emma turned eighteen. She waited for Josh outside his office on Main Street, uncaring of who saw them or what might be said.

"I'm eighteen today," she announced without preamble. "Are you going to ask my father for me?"

He'd gasped and felt himself go dizzy with the boldness of her, and the honesty.

"Well," she had pressed when he didn't answer. "Are you?"

"It's supposed to be the man who proposes marriage," he'd muttered, hating himself for the prim stupidity of the remark even before it was said.

"You have, countless times," Emma said calmly. "Your eyes have asked me over and over. I'd never have had the courage to speak if they hadn't."

Joshua knew she was protecting his male pride, and he sensed, dimly, the wisdom deep inside her, and knew it was more important than her physical beauty; and he'd sensed, too, her will of iron. "I love you, Emma Silva," he'd whispered, unconscious of the passersby on Main Street and hearing only her soft sigh of pleasure.

"I love you, Joshua Morgan. See my father tonight. He'll be home after sundown. He won't like it, you're not one of us. But my mother will help."

Emma had been right in that too. Jessica Silva had been a dutiful wife and mother, even after the first bloom of love wore off and the differences between her and Manny became painful. But she wanted different things, better things, for her only daughter. So she'd soothed Manny and made him agree at least to consider Joshua's suit. The next month she fell victim to the cholera that came to plague the town, and neither her will nor Josh's skills could save her and she died.

After that it took Emma two more years to wear down her father and make him accept Joshua as a son-in-law.

"You'll be wanting a heretic wedding, I expect," Manny had said finally. He was a nominal Catholic at best, and he'd not really cared about his wife's alien religion, not as much as some of the other things she did. He'd even allowed her to baptize Emma in her church, although the parish priest at Our Lady of Good Voyage had railed mightily against the sin. "I brought all the boys to you," Manny had said. "Jessie can have the girl." So now he wasn't surprised when Emma said yes she did want to be married at the Congregational Church on Congress Street. And she was, and as far as Manny was concerned that was an end to it, but of course for Emma and Josh it was a beginning. And Emma had learned the value of biding one's time.

The first month of 1916 was cold and dry, promising snow that never came. There was a ten-day period at the beginning of the month when Emma thought she was pregnant, but she wasn't sure, so she said nothing to Josh. On the eleventh her monthlies started. She felt relieved. One part of her wanted desperately to have Josh's child, another part kept saying, no, not until the other business was settled. She knew that Rosa Tecci's death had given her a piece of vital ammunition, but she wasn't sure yet how to use it. She began taking long walks and thinking about the problem.

The Morgans' cottage was the only real house on Green Street. The street itself was little more than a lane behind the small settlement that made up Annisquam Village. It petered out after a quarter of a mile, ending in a grove of pine trees that meandered down to the Annisquam River. Emma's closest neighbors were Alice and Warren Crane.

The Cranes lived in a small place close to the river. It was a deserted hovel when they took it over and while they'd done their best, it still wasn't much more. Warren Crane kept a boat moored a few yards from his home, and in season he sold bait and fished for a living. Apart from that the couple kept to themselves. They weren't Gloucester folk originally, they'd come from Newburyport ten years earlier. They'd been barely out of their teens then, and word had gone round that they had fled Newburyport because both families opposed the marriage. At first people said that Warren had gotten Alice in trouble and had to marry her, but the couple never produced a child, so that couldn't be true.

Emma was aware of the proximity of the Cranes. Sometimes Josh walked down to their place on a Sunday to buy bait for his desultory fishing, but they never seemed to leave their shack and she'd never done more than nod to either of them. So she was thoroughly startled when she literally fell over Alice Crane during one of those January walks in the woods.

She'd been gazing up into the branches of the pine trees, and the next thing she knew she had stumbled over a woman who was sitting on the ground. "I'm so sorry, do forgive me. I didn't know anyone was here."

"S'all right." Alice Crane lifted a tear-stained face. "I was just going anyway."

Emma looked closely at the other woman. Her face wasn't merely ravished by tears, it was a disaster. Her left eye was closing rapidly and she had a cut on one cheek. "You've been hurt. Please come back to my cottage, Mrs. Crane. My husband will be home soon and he can see to you."

"No, I don't need no doctor."

"But you do," Emma said firmly. "Here, let me help you up."

Alice pushed Emma's hand away. "Don't need no help. Mind your own affairs." With that she stumbled to her feet and headed off in the direction of the river.

Emma told the story to Josh that evening. He shook his head wearily. "I suppose he has a few too many and belts her one, poor woman. There's nothing we can do about it, I'm afraid."

"There must be someway to help her." Emma pursed her lips and looked genuinely disturbed.

"Sorry, darling, there isn't. If Alice Crane wants a doctor, I'll do whatever I can for her. If she chooses to keep her troubles to herself, we can't do anything but respect her wishes."

Four days later Emma was fixing dinner when there was a timid knock on her kitchen door. When she opened it, her neighbor was leaning against the shingled wall. Blood dripped from her mouth and both her eyes were swollen to slits. She didn't refer to her face when she came inside. "It's my arm. Broke, I think. If it don't get set proper, I won't be able to do my work. You said I could come, so I came."

Emma said little, just seated the other woman in the rocking chair by the stove and poured hot tea and brandy into her and waited for Josh. Fortunately he wasn't delayed. At six-thirty he came into the kitchen and by six thirty-two he was setting Alice's arm. She gritted her teeth and bore the painful process without a murmur.

"That will hold for the time being," Josh said after a few minutes. "Now we'll go down to the hospital, and I'll put a cast on it. I'm sorry, but I don't have the things I need to do the job here in the house."

"I don't want to go to no hospital. Folks'll talk."

"Nobody's going to talk," Josh insisted. "And if you don't have a cast, you might just as well not have bothered to come. That arm will heal crooked, and you'll lose the use of it for the rest of your life. Is that what you want, Mrs. Crane?"

The woman shook her head in dumb misery.

"Where's your husband?" Josh asked more gently.

"Home."

Emma moved forward. "I'll take him a bit of supper and explain what's happened, shall I?"

"Ain't no point. Warren's liquored up something fierce. Passed out cold on the bed, and he'll stay that way till morning." She looked at Emma and then at Josh, her gaze distorted by her swollen eyes, but apparently clear enough for her to see their sympathy. She opened her mouth, closed it again, then opened it a second time and the words rushed out of her; a flood of explanations made as much for herself as for the Morgans.

"Don't think poorly of Warren. He didn't used to be like this. It's the disappointment what done it. We loved each other so much in the old days. Ran away from home just to be together. Our folks didn't want us to get married, but we only wanted to be together and live our own lives. So we came down here. I know nobody thinks much of our little place, but it suits us fine. And Warren's a hard worker. We get by okay. Leastwise we did until the last couple of years when Warren finally realized I wasn't never going to be in a family way. Every month he asks me, and every month I has to say 'Yes, I got the curse.' So he started drinking and pushing me around a bit. Not because he's naturally mean. It's just the disappointment, like I said."

Early the following Sunday morning Emma accompanied Joshua to the post office where there was a telephone

in the outer lobby that was kept unlocked. Even had she
not known whom he was calling, she could have guessed.
His tone of respect and affection was reserved for only
Professor Helmut Schoener. Josh looked pleased with himself when he hung up. "I want to go down to the Cranes'
place this morning after breakfast, and I'd like you to come
with me."

"Fine. Are you going to tell me why?"

"I think I know a way to help Alice Crane concieve, at
least a way that's worth trying. I talked to her some more
the night I set her arm, and I convinced her to have a
preliminary examination. I think I know what the problem
is, and I've just heard enough from Professor Schoener to
feel certain of my diagnosis. So I want to suggest that Alice
have a simple operation."

Emma flinched. "She won't like that. People like her
are terrified of surgery."

"I know, that's why I want you there. I suspect they'll
both be a little less nervous if there's another woman
present." Josh looked hard at his wife. "You don't mind
my talking so openly about birth and reproduction do you?
You don't think I'm indelicate?"

Emma stared at him a moment, then giggled. "Josh,
darling, sometimes you're the biggest fool in Massachusetts. Come on, let's go. We'll have a late breakfast. Better
to get there early before Warren has a chance to start on
the whisky bottle."

The interview was awkward and difficult. Both Cranes
eyed their uninvited callers warily. Only Josh's voice broke
the strained silence. "You see, when I examined you, Mrs.
Crane, I could tell that the neck of your cervix, that's the
part of a woman that leads to her fallopian tubes, was very
tightly closed. I think maybe it's blocked. What I'm suggesting is simple surgery to dilate it. I think that might
allow you to become pregnant."

Josh's explanation came to a faltering end, smothered by
the silence in the room. Finally Warren Crane spoke. He
was a small, wiry man with a shock of red hair and strong
arms showing below his rolled up shirtsleeves. Emma
looked at them and shuddered at the thought of his beating his wife, but he had a kind face, and his voice was
clear and pleasant enough. "I don't exactly understand a
lot of that," he told Josh. "But what I think you mean is

that there ain't no guarantee Alice will get in a family way, even if she has this here operation."

"That's exactly what I'm saying," Josh admitted.

"Have lots of other women had it?" Warren Crane demanded. "How many of 'em had a baby afterwards?"

"As far as I know, the procedure has never been tried before. It's been developed by a colleague of mine in Boston. A brilliant man. Of course it may not work, but I can't see that your wife will come to any harm if we try."

"You'd be experimentin' on Alice," the other man said slowly. "That don't sound right to me. I don't like it. Maybe it ain't so important, us havin' a kid. Maybe I jus' gotta make up my mind to that and stop thinking 'bout it so much."

Alice Crane turned and lay her hand on his arm. Despite everything there was obvious love in the gesture. "Course it's important, Warren honey. I ain't scared. I'd have the operation if Doc Morgan thinks it'll do some good. But," she turned to face Joshua, "we ain't got no money. So the whole thing's just a dream."

"Forgive me," Josh said quickly. "I thought I'd made it clear at the outset. You would be furthering the interests of medical science, Mrs. Crane. I wouldn't exactly use your husband's word, I don't consider what we're doing as experiments. But there is much to be learned from observing the procedure, and—"

"What my husband means," Emma interrupted, "is that the whole thing would be free."

Josh looked at her gratefully. They waited for the Cranes to speak. Warren cleared his throat. "We'll think it over and let you know."

A week later Alice Crane entered the Addison Gilbert Hospital in Gloucester, and two days after that Joshua dilated her cervix. Professor Schoener had intended to be present, but at the last moment he caught a bad cold. Emma was secretly delighted; she wanted Josh to have all the glory. It was bound to be a brilliant operation.

That spring, while America learned with shock that in the war in Europe the Germans had used poison gas on their French and English enemies, the Morgans and the Cranes had to admit that they'd lost their private battle. The procedure had failed. Alice still wasn't pregnant and there was no reason to suppose her any more likely to be now than before Josh operated.

At first he didn't discuss it with Emma. Then, one April night, he suddenly looked at his wife across the dinner table and exploded. "Damn! I was so sure the theory was sound."

Emma passed him another helping of chicken pie and took a deep breath. "Joshua, isn't it true that Alice's case doesn't disprove the theory? According to Professor Schoener's books there can be many reasons for infertility."

Josh put down his fork. His green eyes fastened on Emma's face. "Have you been reading Schoener's books?"

"Yes, I have to do something here alone all day. Besides, they're fascinating."

Josh shook his head. His dark hair fell across his forehead, and he pushed it away in a gesture Emma always found appealing. "What an extraordinary woman you are. I don't think I'll ever get over you, Emma Silva."

"Emma Morgan. And the important thing is that it's in your power to learn more about all women. About the problems of conception and birth. It is, Josh, you know it is. Look at what's happened these past six months. Rosa Tecci and Alice Crane are two sides of the same coin, aren't they? And if you knew more, if the research was further advanced, you could have helped them both."

Joshua rose from the table. He was very pale. "I never expected you to throw my failures in my face, Emma."

"Josh! How can you think that's what I'm doing? I'm trying to show you your destiny."

"Mine or yours? I'm beginning to realize that you lust after Boston and the grand life, Emma. Your mother's legacy I suppose, but it's something I never knew about you." He didn't wait for an answer. Josh simply turned and walked out of the room and the house.

Joshua walked for hours, drawn to the sea as he always was in time of pain. God knew, he'd had enough experience with pain, a lifetime of secret, hidden pain, covered by a crust of apparent privilege. He thought of that and his mouth tasted of ashes, but the cold wind blowing across the quiet harbor cooled his flushed skin. He'd been wrong to get angry with Emma. She wasn't rubbing his nose in failure, just pointing out a truth he already knew. His labors on behalf of Rosa and Alice were nonsense, a sop to his conscience, because he was afraid to do what would really help them and thousands of others like them.

"Research, my son," old Schoener had said repeatedly. "Research and more research, until we know why and how and when."

Yes, but such efforts had to be made in Boston. With the slick, wellborn men who were always so sure of themselves, who always knew the right thing to say. And with their equally confident women. Not that such women provided the live bodies on which to test new theories, sweet Christ, no. They simply paid the bills that supplied the money to experiment. The charity patients who filled the city's hospitals were the guinea pigs. But what of it? Most of them were dying anyway, of filth and disease and despair and constant motherhood, just as Rosa Tecci had died. It wasn't moral qualms that kept him in this backwater. It was a failure of confidence, and neither the success of his gynecological residency in Boston, nor Schoener's affection had given him the inner strength to pit himself against the men of the great city.

Morgan straddled a bollard, his long legs finding purchase on the splintered wood of the dock, and stared across the prows of the anchored boats. A whistling buoy sounded its mournful cry into the silent night. He thought of Emma. She was the stronger of the two of them, he knew that. If it wasn't for her he'd have nursed his love and his longing in silence, and watched her wed some sturdy fisherboy closer to her age and her class. He shuddered at the thought. It was hard to imagine Emma married to someone else, hard to think of himself going through life without her.

When he stood up, he discovered his buttocks had gone numb with the damp cold of the stone bollard and his fingers tingled with chill. The moon lit the ocean and if he strained he could swear he saw the lighthouse of Nahant, some twenty miles to the south. The moonlight was a path leading down the coast, leading to Boston. Joshua turned his back and walked away.

2

When Joshua got home the hands of the grandfather clock pointed to two A.M. He climbed the stairs and went into the bedroom. Emma was awake, he could tell by her breathing, but he undressed silently and didn't say a word as he lay down beside her.

This was the first serious quarrel of their married life, the first rupture of their private universe. The knowledge of that wound was a weight on his heart. Finally Josh turned to her. "Forgive me, darling," he whispered into the silken softness of her hair. "Walking out like that was terrible. We have to learn to talk out our differences."

"I'm to blame. I've been . . ." Emma hesitated over the word, but forced herself to say it. "I've been manipulating you."

"Ssh. I'm a stiff-necked idiot and I don't deserve you."

"Josh, you have to listen to me. If I don't confess I can't live with myself."

"Confess what?" He nuzzled her cheek and stroked her back and was clearly not very concerned with her reply, but Emma continued.

"I've always wanted to live in Boston. The very idea is bliss. I want to go everywhere and see everything. It's such a big world, and this is such a small town. Josh, what are you doing? You're not listening to me."

He lifted his head for a moment to say, "I'll listen later."

Then he went back to kissing the smooth skin of her breasts.

It was a slow, sweet coupling, full of tenderness and warmth and forgiveness. When it was over, Emma lay with her head on his chest, feeling his strong fingers twined in her hair and drifting between wakefulness and sleep in a landscape of pure pleasure.

"Did you really mean what you said about Boston?" Josh asked.

"That I want to live there? Yes. My parents took me to Boston once when I was nine. I promised myself that someday I'd be a Boston lady."

"Is that why you wanted to marry me?"

Emma shot out of his arms and sat up, trying to see his face in the dark. "Josh! How can you think that? I wanted to marry you because I love you. After I met you, nothing else mattered."

He pulled her back down. "I know you love me. Forget I said that, it was stupid. Go to sleep now, my sweet. We'll talk more in the morning."

But in the morning Joshua had to dash out of the house on an emergency visit to a scalded child, and it wasn't until evening that they had another chance to talk. Then it turned out to be an announcement, not a discussion. "I called Schoener today," Josh said over his final cup of coffee. "I'm to write him a letter tomorrow going into all the details, but the short of it is I asked if he still wants me to join his practice."

For a breathless second Emma felt as if her heart had stopped. "And?"

"And he does. So we'll probably be moving to Boston this summer. Emma, say something. Aren't you pleased?"

"Very," she whispered. "I only hope you are."

In the hall the clock chimed eight. "Come for a drive," Josh said suddenly. "It's not too late. I want to show you something."

He cranked up the Model-T while she put on her hat and her gloves. As she came out to join him it struck him that she would make a fine Boston lady. The car started smoothly and they drove in silence. Not until they were across the cut bridge that separated Annisquam from the rest of Gloucester did Emma ask where they were going.

"Out to Eastern Point. You've never been there, have
you?"

"No, never." She was afraid to say more. She could
sense that Josh was beginning to open doors he'd kept
closed to her.

It was completely black on the Point, no street lamps
here, only the yellow lights winking from the windows of
the widely spaced grand houses alleviated the darkness.
But Josh knew the winding roads very well. He drove them
expertly, finally turning down a crooked lane that led to a
great hulk of a mansion silhouetted against the moon. No
light showed. The curtains were all drawn. The place
looked abandoned. "Not many people live here now," Josh
said softly. "It was sold after Prissy Sweet died. The buyers
only come for vacations in the summer."

Emma sensed the tension in him. "Tell me about it,"
she said. "Tell me what it was like growing up here."

The house was already a quarter of a century old on the
Fourth of July in 1885 when the first childbirth took place
within its walls. It had been built by Captain Joshua Sweet
for his bride, Priscilla, but it was not the aging lady of the
house who took to her bed with labor pains on that Independence Day. It was her cook, Viola Morgan. Vi, too
old, was somewhat past her prime for a first child at thirty-
four. When she was certain she was in a family way and
told her mistress, Vi expected her to be annoyed. Quite to
the contrary, Priscilla Sweet was delighted.

Prissy took intense, vicarious pleasure in her cook's
pregnancy. Childless because the handsome captain was
impotent, though not a soul knew, she'd managed to keep
herself from becoming embittered. Now, when Vi took to
her bed of confinement, it was Prissy who sat beside her.
She held the cook's hand and mopped her brow, and
almost felt as if her womb were contracting and expanding
with such exquisite agony. When Vi arched her back and
moaned and gritted her teeth against screaming, Prissy
pursed her lips, too, and bore down . . . as if by exerting
enough pressure she could miraculously expel a child from
between her own inviolate thighs.

"Hold my hand, Vi, dear. Squeeze it as hard as you like
if it makes you feel any better."

Viola Morgan clung to her mistress' dainty hand. Her own was large and workaday and callused, but who was the luckier woman today? Another pain. She withstood it in silence until a great booming noise from outside distracted her from her agony. "What's that?"

"Just the menfolk celebrating the Fourth down at the harbor. Little boys, the lot of them. They love the speeches and the cannons and the pyrotechnics."

"Is William here?" It was the first time Vi had inquired after her husband. Having babies was women's business.

"Oh no, he drove the captain's new carriage to the celebrations. They'll be gone for sometime I imagine. There's to be a blind dory race and a greasy pig contest as well as the other events."

"Good," Vi said. "Then I'll be done having this baby before they get back."

"Oh no, my dear. I don't think so. I sent for Doctor Broderick, but he said it would be ages before he was needed. Probably not until tomorrow, this being your first and all."

"Meaning no disrespect, ma'am, but the doctor's wrong. This is going to be a Yankee-Doodle baby, born on the Fourth of July."

She was quite right. Viola Morgan's son was born within the hour, just as his mother predicted.

Prissy cursed Dr. Broderick's stupidity—doubtless he'd wanted to go to the celebrations too—and attended her cook as well as she could. She called an Irish maid to help, but got little practical aid from the fourteen-year-old girl. When six days later Viola died of childbed fever, Prissy wondered if it was her incompetence which had caused the tragedy. Dr. Broderick assured her it was not, but Prissy was never entirely convinced.

Her guilt was secretly more poignant because she was just a little bit glad at the way things had worked out. The death of Vi had given her an extraordinary—and wonderful—idea. "Joshua," she said to her husband after the cook's funeral, "I would like to adopt Vi's little boy."

"Adopt? Are you mad, Prissy? At our age? And the child of a servant?"

"But Joshua . . ." Prissy twisted her handkerchief in her slim fingers and didn't know how to continue. It flitted through her mind that she could insist. She could threaten

to tell the world that the wealthy and imposing Captain
Sweet was incapable of performing his marital duty. But
the thought merely flitted and was gone. In twenty-five
years she'd never insisted on anything, it was too late to
start now. She began to creep from his study.

"Hold on a moment, my dear," the captain said before
the door closed behind her. "I don't mean that you can't
do everything you like for the lad. That's clearly your
Christian duty. See he's well treated and educated according to his station. That's quite all right. It's only adoption
I'm ruling out."

And my one chance to be a mother, Prissy thought.
Aloud she said, "Thank you, Joshua. I'll see that William
names his son after you, since you're being so kind."

It was Prissy who was the boy's sponsor at the Congregational Church when the minister informed the Almighty
that the child's name was Joshua. William watched her all
during the ceremony. He saw how Mrs. Sweet clung to
the infant. She wanted him for her own, that was sure.
And why not? Vi was gone and this child she'd died
birthing could grow up like a rich man's son, if Mrs. Sweet
raised him. So be it. Soon after the christening William
left for parts unknown, and neither his son nor anyone in
Gloucester ever saw him again.

Little Josh's room was next to Aunt Prissy's, as he was
taught to call her, and his clothes came from Brown's, the
finest store in Gloucester. He went to the public school
until he was thirteen. Then he won a scholarship to Exeter. Joshua never wanted for anything while he was at the
exclusive preparatory school, and he knew that if he succeeded in his ambition to gain entrance to Harvard to
study medicine, his tuition would be paid by Captain
Sweet. But the captain also made the boy aware of other
things; he had done so since Josh was old enough to
notice.

The captain, in his seventies by the time Josh went to
Exeter, never addressed the boy by name. It was always
"you," sometimes "boy." When Joshua reached the age at
which he could expect to dine with adults, the expectation
was disappointed. On the captain's specific orders he continued to take all his meals in the kitchen. In short, he was
never allowed to forget that he was a privileged member
of the household, but not in name or reality a member of

the family. Aunt Prissy did her best to make these slights unimportant, but she couldn't provide what Joshua craved, a father's love. Through all the years of his education Joshua made no friends. He did not participate in sports or other activities. He was first a boy alone, and then a man alone.

Captain Sweet died during Joshua's junior year at Harvard. The evening after the funeral Prissy set a place for Joshua at the baronial mahogany table in the dining room of the house on Eastern Point. To please her Josh ate that meal with her beneath the sparkling crystal chandelier, surrounded by elegant silver and fine china. He refused to do so ever again. Prissy, accustomed to being dictated to by men, didn't argue.

Not until 1906 did a man appear to fill the painful gap in Joshua's life. Professor Helmut Schoener, an immigrant German, taught obstetrics and gynecology at Harvard. He took an instant liking to the earnest and brilliant student from Gloucester. Eventually the liking became something akin to love, and when Dr. Joshua Morgan began his residency at Boston Memorial Hospital under Professor Schoener's patronage, the two men were like father and son. The very fact that Joshua underwent a period of in-hospital training after medical school was Schoener's doing.

When Joshua started at Harvard Medical School, that institution was one of the very few in the nation providing any practical experience for its students. Harvard and a few other farsighted schools allowed its nascent doctors to go into hospitals and see real patients. At most other colleges of medicine lectures were the only source of learning.

Despite Harvard's advanced practices, Schoener, trained in the more demanding and rigorous European system, was appalled at the ease with which a man could claim himself a qualified doctor in America. State licensing for general practitioners had become the norm, but specialization remained an area where just about anybody could claim to be just about anything.

"You must be a gynecologist, Joshua," the professor had told the young man. "And for this you must work with me in my hospital."

Joshua was awed by the prospect. Gynecology was the

fastest growing specialty in the nation because in the 1870's a few pioneers had demonstrated that it was possible to surgically remove an ovarian tumor. When Josh began his residency under Schoener, the removal of female reproductive organs was epidemic. Ovariectomies and hysterectomies were being performed for every complaint a woman had. Was she melancholy or run-down or in a state of nerve or prone to colds and fevers? Surely, the growing army of surgeons proclaimed, an operation would cure her. Schoener's practice of gynecology was different.

"Butchers," he cursed. "They want to play with their little knives. Never do they think about why these things should happen. What is birth, Josh? Why does labor begin yesterday, not today or tomorrow? Why some women have a baby every year and others never? The same thing they are doing with their husbands, *hein*? So why sometimes a child and sometimes no child? Or two at the same time?"

The questions fascinated Joshua, too, but when his year of residency was over he amazed Schoener by refusing to remain in Boston and join the old man's practice. Instead he insisted that he was returning to Gloucester to be a country doctor.

"But for why?" the older man demanded. "Now that your auntie is dead, what is bringing you back to that place? Nothing exciting in medicine is going to happen in Gloucester, Josh. A few fishermen falling into the sea, some children with whooping cough, for this did I train you?"

"It's nothing to do with Aunt Prissy," Josh insisted.

Indeed the old woman's death a few months back had freed him to follow his inclinations. He might not have wanted to return to Gloucester if she were still alive. Aunt Prissy wouldn't have approved of the simple lifestyle he envisioned for himself.

The professor fumed. "What then? Some kind of explanation I'm owed."

Mute, Josh shook his head. He couldn't answer the question. Much as he loved and respected Schoener, the habit of a lifetime couldn't be broken. Never having had another man in whom to confide his deepest hopes and fears, Josh had failed to learn the knack. He couldn't tell the professor that he was terrified of the rich society women who made up most of Schoener's private practice, indeed, unwittingly supported his research. Or that living in Boston and playing the role of the up-and-coming bachelor doctor was beyond him. The snubs of Captain Sweet had made scars too deep to be erased even by Schoener.

"I'm sorry," was all he could say.

"Very well, Josh. Only remember, if you change your mind I will always be holding open for you the door. That is how you say it, *hein?*"

"Yes," Josh said with the smile for which he was famous among the nurses. "That's how you say it. And thank you."

If he had entertained any secret thoughts of changing his mind and taking up Schoener's invitation, they disappeared during the first year of his practice. On the day that young Emma Silva cut her arm and was brought to his office on Main Street and Josh felt himself drowning in her aquamarine eyes, she became the center of his world . . . and Boston a distant universe.

Emma had not said a word while he spoke, now she reached over and lay one hand lightly on his arm. "Thank you, it helps to know all that."

Josh turned to her, his face lit only by the moon riding high over Eastern Point. "It's helped me to tell you. But now it's behind me, behind us. We're going to Boston, Emma, where nobody's ever heard of Prissy and Joshua Sweet. Probably most Bostonians don't even know that Eastern Point exists."

She smiled and nodded. "Yes, we're going to Boston. And I'll make a prediction, Josh: Someday a lot of folks will have heard of Dr. Joshua Morgan."

All his life Helmut Schoener had been ugly. He had coarse, heavy features that belied a mind of delicacy and precision as well as brilliance, and thick curled eyebrows that met across the bridge of his nose and shadowed the kindness of his large brown eyes. At sixty-two he stood exactly five feet and weighed two hundred pounds. His legs were so short they appeared deformed beneath his barrel chest.

Schoener did nothing to improve his appearance. He ignored fashion and always wore a tall black silk top hat and a swallow-tailed black frock coat. He hadn't changed his style of dress since he left Germany in 1891. Always, as today, he walked with the air of a man who knew the impression he created, and reveled in it.

Lately he'd felt oppressed by news of the war in Europe, by the senseless slaughter the newspapers reported and by a secret fear of what might happen to him and other German immigrants if America got into it on the side of the British, but today Schoener pranced along Commonwealth Avenue, swinging his gold-topped walking stick and admiring the line of trees that bisected the long street. A boy stared, then snickered. Schoener waved his stick under the child's nose.

"Careful you should be *mein* kind, or one morning you'll wake up looking like me." He laughed loudly at the boy's horrified expression. Today he felt like laughing at everything, because Joshua was coming to Boston. Six years late, but he was coming.

Schoener crossed the intersection of Commonwealth Avenue and Dartmouth Street and headed down his own block. His office was on the first two floors of the building numbered 163, his laboratory on the third and fourth floor, and his living quarters in a small apartment under the eaves on the fifth. He had no wife and no children, had never had either, and this arrangement suited him. It wouldn't suit Joshua and his lovely Emma, however. He knew what would.

Schoener turned to mount the short steps to his front door, and glanced at the building on his left, number 165. There was a discreet "For Sale" sign in the front window. He had noticed it before, had even toyed with the notion that the house might be a good investment, but until today he'd not actually made up his mind to make an offer for the house. Now Schoener nodded and grinned broadly. Life was perfect and the fates were smiling on him.

During her growing up years Emma watched the puffing locomotives of the Boston & Maine Railroad chug into Gloucester and out again, either north toward Bangor or south toward Boston. Only once had she ever been on a train, the one time her parents had taken her into the city, but it was just as she remembered it. She smelled the same lovely, musty smell of the blue velvet seats and saw the same polished brass luggage rack overhead. Despite the cold of that October day in 1916 she pushed up the wooden frame window and leaned out.

"You'll catch a chill, darling." Josh's voice was gentle, he understood.

"I don't care. It's worth it. Oh, Josh, I can hardly believe it. We're going to Boston, to live not just to visit."

"I can hardly believe it, either. It took long enough to get it arranged."

He'd hoped to move during the summer, but there had been the house to sell and all the furniture, and the motorcar. Then old Dr. Broderick died, and Josh didn't feel he could leave Gloucester until he had found a replacement. Handling the details had dragged on and on. "No regrets about taking so little with us?" he asked Emma. They had nothing but their clothes, packed in the luggage overhead, and the grandfather clock and a few boxes of books and the like they'd sent on ahead.

"No, why should I? The house in Boston is furnished."

That was true, but Josh marveled anew at how ready she was to burn her bridges behind her. She had spent only a brief hour saying good-bye to her father and her brothers and their wives, and sworn there was no one else she needed to see before they left. Children of peculiar backgrounds, both of them, he thought. But Emma's experiences had made her strong and independent. What could he say about himself? Josh found the question unsettling. He dismissed it and watched his wife, taking pleasure in her enthusiasm.

She hung out the window for most of the journey, ignoring the wind and the cold and the disapproving stares of the other passengers. Smoke and soot from the engine blew back in her face, but Emma ignored that too. Manchester, Prides Crossing, Beverly, Salem; small towns all, not unlike the one she had left behind. No hint of what they were approaching until two hours later when they left Lynn and drew near the city. Within fifteen minutes she could see the water of the inner harbor and the smokestacks of the city skyline.

"Look, Josh, Boston."

She spoke the words in an almost reverential hush, but by the time Joshua closed his book and looked out the window, the only thing to look at were the freight yards. There seemed to be miles of them, noisy and dirty and unpleasant. "It's really a very pretty city. A shame to see all this ugliness first," he said.

"It's not ugly. Not if you think about what it means. How can there be a great city without railroads?"

Josh smiled indulgently and said no more. A black man walked through the coach calling, "Next stop Bos-Ton." He said the name as if it were two words, and added his own evaluation of the grand dame of American metropolises. "Athens of America, yes suh!"

"Hub of the world, more like," Emma whispered to Josh. "And we're going to live there."

It was a bleak, gray day, and raining. The hobble skirt of Emma's blue suit got wet and muddy when she stepped out of the taxi in front of her new home at 165 Commonwealth Avenue. She didn't care, nothing that happened today could dim her joy and sense of triumph.

She and Josh had inspected the house once before, in July. Helmut Schoener had wanted to give it to them, but they wouldn't hear of such a thing. They had sold the Green Street cottage for twenty-five hundred dollars, and that was their down payment. The professor held a mortgage for the additional eleven thousand he'd paid for the house. Today, taking possession of it, Emma didn't think about money. She danced from room to room. "There are six open fireplaces, Josh. Isn't it heaven?"

He looked at her laughing face, at her breast heaving with excitement, and decided that women were perverse. He'd taken great pride in building Emma a cottage that didn't need messy open fires because it had a coal burning furnace in the cellar, now Emma was enchanted by fireplaces. "I suppose so, if you like that sort of thing," he said stiffly.

Emma laughed. "I do, I do. Hearths can be so beautiful," she pronounced. "And this may be the most beautiful house in Boston."

Josh had to admit it was a handsome residence. Red brick with a tiled roof, it had been built like most of its Back Bay neighbors during the last half of the nineteenth century. In order to conserve the expensive land reclaimed from marsh when the area was created in 1857, number 165 was two rooms wide and five stories high.

The Morgans explored slowly, examining every detail

with care. After an hour they reached the third floor nursery. Because Schoener had purchased the house fully furnished, there were four little beds in the room. Each had its own bright yellow coverlet and lots of ruffled pillows.

"We'll have to get busy if we mean to fill these." Josh slipped his arm around Emma's waist.

"I thought we'd been busy in that department right along."

Josh tilted her chin and looked into her eyes. "It feels like I've barely started. I can never get enough of you, Mrs. Morgan."

Emma ducked out of his embrace and walked a few steps to the nearest bed and plumped the already perfectly arranged pillows. "It would be lovely, wouldn't it?" There was a wistful note in her voice.

"What do you mean *would* be? *Will be* is more like it."

"You do really think so, Josh, don't you? We've been married well over a year."

Josh pulled her into his arms. "Don't start worrying when there's no cause. I'm the doctor in this family, remember."

Josh woke early their first morning in Boston. He drew back the heavy rose-colored brocade drapes, and sun poured into the room. "Seems as if it's going to be a nice day." In the distance he could just see the tops of the trees in the Public Gardens, and between them and his house, the myriad roofs of the close-set city buildings. It looked nothing like the view of Annisquam from the bedroom window of the cottage. "I'd almost forgotten what a rabbit warren Boston is," he muttered.

Emma stretched in the big, warm bed. "Not rabbits, bees. Bees busy making honey. That's what a city is."

"For a country girl you've a lot of strong ideas about city life." He turned to her with laughter in his green eyes. "Not me, I feel like a bumpkin. Thoroughly disoriented because I don't know what patients I'm going to see today, or anything else."

"You'll be fine after your first examination. At bottom, darling, women's illnesses are the same in Boston as they are in Gloucester."

"At bottom indeed," Josh said, chuckling.

Emma turned bright red. "I didn't mean that. It was just an expression."

"Yes you did mean it." He walked over and slapped her rump. "At bottom you're a shameless hussy, and I adore you. Now, what are you going to do today? You have a cook and a maid, Mrs. Morgan. All carefully selected by the professor, so don't tell me you'll spend your time at the usual drudgery."

Emma had not yet thought much of her new role as a woman of leisure. She looked startled when there was a light tap on the door and immediately afterward it opened. "Morning, sir. Morning, ma'am. I brung your tea."

The maid bobbed a quick curtsy while she spoke. She looked about fourteen. She wore a blue dress and a white apron and a white cap, and she put the tea tray down beside the bed then knelt and put a match to the fire. Emma intently watched all this. The maid fanned the flames until they caught. Then stood up and looked expectantly at her new mistress. "Will that be all, ma'am?"

Emma was tongue-tied. Jessica had taught her daughter all manner of things that other daughters of fishermen didn't know. Never in Emma's life, however, had she even given a thought to how to instruct a servant. "Yes," Josh interposed softly. "That will be all. Except, what's your name?"

"Mary, sir."

"Very well, Mary. Mrs. Morgan and I will be down for breakfast in half an hour. Thank you, you may go."

Emma stared at the door Mary shut behind her. "There were some advantages to growing up on Eastern Point, weren't there?" she asked finally.

"A few perhaps."

"Yes, I think so." She tossed back the quilt and swung her long legs over the side of the bed. "And that decides what I'm going to do today. There's a public library in Boston, isn't there?" Josh nodded. "Good," Emma said. "I shall go there and find some books that will tell me what a mistress says to servants."

Joshua was quickly integrated into Schoener's practice. That first day the professor kept Josh by his side in his old-fashioned, book-lined office. "My friend and colleague, Doctor Joshua Morgan," he said as each patient entered.

"Doctor Morgan is joining my practice. You aren't minding he should be here while we talk?"

Inevitably the woman would glance at Joshua, then drop her eyes to conceal her reaction to his good looks. A few minutes later, when the consultation was finished, Schoener would say, "So I'm being full up next Wednesday when you must come again. You aren't minding you should see Doctor Morgan?" The woman always nodded approval of this plan.

Within a week Josh had a full quota of patients and had been accredited at Boston Memorial Hospital. The waiting time had been waived since Josh had done his residency at Memorial.

The hospital was among the city's oldest institutions, founded by one of the town's early ship owners, it continued to benefit from the man's handsome endowment. A stipulation of the trust was that Memorial Hospital must care for a sizeable number of the poor. There were three large charity wards. Perhaps the old seaman had been soothing his puritan conscience and putting to good use money largely earned from the slave trade, but nobody minded about that now. The Italian and Jewish immigrants from the nearby West End flocked to Memorial for care, and Joshua, like every doctor who admitted patients to the hospital, agreed to see patients in the free clinic for five hours a week.

The good weather held for much of October. Emma used the Indian summer to walk all over the city and get to know it. Commonwealth Avenue and Beacon Street were the two parallel roads that marked the Back Bay. Grand thoroughfares designed to show off the affluence of Victorian times, they were lined with the homes of wealthy professional men and the mansions of the fabled old guard.

Between the two avenues there were numerous cross streets—Dartmouth and Clarendon and Berkeley, and even one named Gloucester. They were filled with the shops that supplied the needs of the households on either side. Secretly Emma was delighted with the wondrous displays of foods and clothes and furnishings, and everything else a woman could think of to buy, but she examined them with a stern face. After all, she would have to deal with the merchants behind the counters, and if any of them noticed her, she didn't want them to see a gawking country girl.

She had to suppress a giggle at that thought. Imagine anyone noticing her in all the crush of busy humanity surrounding her.

"So this is good old Boston," Emma said to herself as she walked along, craning her neck to see the tops of the tall buildings. "Home of the bean and the cod, where the Cabots speak only to the Lowells, and the Lowells speak only to God." And neither of them were ever likely to speak to her, as if she cared.

She really didn't—there was too much new and exciting to see and do. Besides, she'd spent her life as a pawn in the war between Manny and Jessica, and rejected the whole notion of snobbery as a waste of time and energy. She was just as interested in the poor neighborhoods as the rich ones.

One Saturday morning she skirted the Public Garden and turned left. Behind her was the glittering golden dome of the State House, ahead was a different world. She had come to the West End, a riotous jumble of hilly streets filled with looming tenements and strange looking foreigners. Women wore long, shapeless dresses and shawls covering their heads; men were bearded and had soft black hats pulled down almost to their ears, or shabby caps tilted over their eyes. In the West End the goods for sale weren't displayed in artful arrangements behind glass, they spilled from stalls, boxes, and pushcarts. Trundled by tired-looking horses or pulled by gnarled old men, the pushcarts swayed slowly along the street and sidewalk, many seeming as if they were poised for a disastrous plunge down the steep hills.

Emma stared in fascination. "Good stuff cheap, lady," a man shouted almost in her ear. "You want a new kettle? Look, the best and only fifteen cents." He held up a battered tin kettle with a mended spout.

"No, thank you. I don't need a kettle."

"What need? Who can't use an extra when the price is right?" The man was missing most of his teeth, and his gray beard was stained yellow. His clothes consisted of countless layers buttoned one on top of the other. Most were no longer of any identifiable color, but they were all patched with a rainbow of fabrics and threads. "Cheap," he repeated. "So okay, not fifteen cents. A dime maybe?"

"No, I'm sorry." Emma turned quickly, feeling the peddler's rheumy eyes on her back. She heard him mutter something in a language she didn't know. A curse probably. She felt a small tingle of apprehension ripple down her spine and walked faster. She made one turn, then another, and suddenly realized she was lost.

"Good apples, lady." A woman placed herself directly in Emma's path. A shawl covered her head, and beneath it her shadowed face was careworn, but young. She had a baby bundled under one arm and two slightly older children clinging to her skirts. A basket of apples hung round her neck, so she could keep both hands free. "Good," she repeated. "Seven cents a half-dozen." The woman dropped her voice. "Please, lady. The children . . . They're good apples, fresh, no worms."

Emma fumbled with her purse and pulled out a dime. She pushed it into the woman's hand. "No, never mind any change. And you keep the apples."

The woman's eyes darkened. "I'm no beggar." She almost threw the apples into Emma's still-open bag, and when she walked on Emma thought she heard herself cursed again in the same mysterious tongue.

She wanted to run, but she didn't know which way to go. She looked up, twisting her head in all directions, and finally spotted the golden dome of the State House to her left. The landmark oriented her and she began walking swiftly toward it. She was almost back at the Public Garden before she noticed the butcher's shop and its sign with a six-pointed star in one corner. The sign bore strange characters that she interpreted as the numbers seven and eleven. Of course, she realized suddenly, these people were Jews. She'd heard about Jews, but never seen one.

She walked into the Public Garden and sat down on the first bench she came to. The sun was warm and the apples in her bag smelled marvelous. She was tempted to eat one, but a lady couldn't gnaw on an apple in public. She contented herself with running her gloved fingers over the shiny surfaces. Would the apple taste as good as it looked? Appearances could be so deceptive.

She thought of Professor Schoener, who was so frightening at first, yet one of the kindest men she'd ever met, after Josh. Or the apple seller, who looked so exhausted and beaten, but had a core of pride deep inside. Three children, at a glance all under four. And God only knew how many more at home. Just like Rosa Tecci and the women in the fort. While she, on the other hand . . . All the way home Emma unconsciously kept one hand pressed over her flat stomach.

In November, when she began to feel a bit more confident about her house and her servants, Emma inaugurated a custom that was to become traditional. "You must have Sunday lunch with us, professor."

"I don't wish to be a trouble to you," Schoener said shyly.

"Nonsense, you're no trouble at all. We'll be delighted. Please say you'll come."

Schoener's smile lit his ugly face. "With pleasure, my dear. I am coming with pleasure."

She'd progressed to knowing how to give orders to the cook. "Roast beef," Emma instructed. "And mashed potatoes and turnips. And don't forget the horseradish sauce."

"No, ma'am, I won't. And I'll make some biscuits. Will you be having a fish course?"

"Oh, of course," Emma said hastily. A fish course. The idea had never occurred to her. One had fish or meat, but both? Apparently so, in Boston. Well, she knew about fish. "I'll stop by the fishmonger myself Saturday afternoon."

It was a shop on nearby Berkeley Street, but she was delayed and it was nearly six when she arrived on Saturday. The man behind the counter was obviously getting ready to close and had packed away most of his fish. He tried to sell her some cod that was still in the glass case in the front of the shop. "No," Emma said. "Too ordinary. I want something more delicate. The whiting should be running now."

"None left," the fishmonger said. He looked at his customer. She was very pretty. "Come in the back, ma'am."

Emma followed him into a small room filled with a great wooden chest cooled by enormous blocks of ice. He drew out three small fish, each with a faintly green-striped body and a double top fin. "Young sea bass," Emma said. "How perfect."

"You know about fish," the man said. "I could tell as soon as you came in. These are perfectly fresh, ma'am. Don't often have them this size. Delicious."

"Yes. I'll take them. If they're not too expensive," she added hastily.

"Fifty cents for the three of them. A special price."

Emma left the shop bearing her treasure.

It was an excellent meal, but neither Josh nor the professor seemed to pay a great deal of attention to the food. "I'm thinking we must try again the cervical dilation, Josh. Even though your Gloucester lady was a big disappointment."

"Yes, my thought exactly."

"Good. So, are you having in mind a patient?"

"How about Mrs. Adams? I saw her last week. She's worried about not having a child."

Schoener glanced up, a spoonful of chocolate pudding halfway to his mouth. "*Im Himmels Willen!* Are you mad? The husband of Mrs. Adams is a rich lawyer. To such a one you cannot be suggesting a new procedure untried except once in Gloucester."

"No, I guess you're right. We'll have to find someone among the charity patients at the clinic. I'll keep my eyes open."

What about me? Emma wanted to ask. I've been married almost two years and I'm not pregnant. Why don't you try the new procedure on me?

Emma didn't say a word, though, because she knew it would make Josh furious that she couldn't follow his instructions and stop worrying.

Josh found a candidate for cervical dilation the following week. He watched the woman disrobe in the treatment room at the clinic. No modesty screen in here, he noted angrily. The poor weren't supposed to be modest. Her skin was coffee-colored and her body young and firm. He glanced down at the card she'd brought in with her, it contained her name and her medical history, but very little else. "Where are you from, Mrs. Deauville?"

"From New Orleans, suh. My Jacques and me, we came north six years ago. Jacques started as a cleaner with the railroad. Now he's a waiter," she added proudly.

"I see. Very good. And what's your problem today?" He expected her to complain of some foul discharge. That was what brought most of the women to the gynecological clinic. Usually by the time they came it was too late to arrest the yeast infection that was the primary cause. And if the origin of the discharge was gonorrhea, it was always too late. Inevitably they had given the disease to their menfolk, where it led to painful urinary disease, and to their children, who almost invariably went blind as a result.

"I ain't sick," the woman said in her soft southern drawl. "Leastwise I don't think so. It's jus' that we been married near seven years, suh. And no sign of babies." She looked away from him shyly.

"Let's just have a look at you, shall we?" Josh kept his voice calm, and let none of his excitement show. Mrs. Deauville climbed up on the examining table and Josh rang the bell for a nurse. One came in and helped him slip on the rubber gloves that had been introduced only a few years before. They were thick and clumsy, but, like scrubbing everything in the hospital with carbolic, wearing them had all but stopped the spread of disease from patient to patient.

"What's your first name?" he asked, probing as gently as he could.

"Jennie," the woman said through a grunt of pain. "And you're Doctor Morgan, ain't you? I heard some of the other ladies talking."

"That's right." He was distracted now, concentrating on the information his fingers were relaying. He didn't think to ask her what the other ladies were saying about him.

In minutes the examination was ended. "You have a tightly closed cervix," he announced. His voice was almost triumphant.

"Is that bad, Doctor Morgan?"

"Not necessarily. Listen, Jennie, until recently we couldn't have helped you, but now there's a new procedure. . . ."

Two months after Josh surgically dilated Jennie Deauville's cervix he was able to tell her she was pregnant. "God bless you, Doctor Morgan. My Jacques and me, we're gonna bless your name for the rest of our lives. We gonna ask God to bless you every night when we sez our prayers."

Within twenty-four hours talk of the success of the Schoener-Morgan procedure had seeped out of the doctors' private lounges and offices, through the ranks of the nurses, and reached the patients. Joshua Morgan was a name beginning to be spoken in tones of awe. He looked like a handsome young god, and the women to whom he ministered were quite willing to believe him possessed of divine wisdom.

In the next few weeks Joshua and the professor dilated the cervixes of four more women, anxious about their long-standing infertility, who had come to the charity clinic for help. Two showed no results, but one conceived almost immediately and the other soon after.

"Proven we're not yet," Schoener said. "But this is enough to be telling our colleagues. You must write for the *Journal of Medicine* an article, Josh."

"You should be the one to do that, sir. It's your procedure."

"*Im Himmels Warren!* From my English they have suffered already enough. No, you do it."

It was February of 1917 when Joshua submitted his first article to the *Journal of Medicine*. Trial by his peers, the thing he'd always dreaded, brought a cautious but favorable verdict. Josh realized that he'd crossed his Rubicon, he need not look back. Emma knew it too.

She lay awake nights thinking of Joshua, what he'd accomplished in so short a time. He was accepted by his patients both rich and poor, and by the medical fraternity of the hospital. Nothing seemed beyond him, at least that's how it appeared to her now. Joshua was handsome, brilliant, and the chosen heir of a man of great reputation. Every door in Boston was opening to him. But what of her?

In the still darkness Emma would clasp her hands across her empty belly and listen to Josh breathing steadily beside her. Maybe she was being silly. It wasn't as if she was being snubbed. She'd been invited three times to the Wednesday Circle, a club made up of some of the doctors' wives. They met twice a month in different homes. There was a luncheon, and then a discussion of the latest book.

It was Booth Tarkington's *Seventeen* last week. And that story of adolescence led the women just where they wanted to go, to talking about their children. Emma had sat silent and shy, feeling as if everyone secretly watched her. Once she'd glanced up and met the eyes of Deborah Wilkins. Her husband was brilliant too. An anesthetist, he was one of the first doctors to specialize in this field formerly the exclusive domain of nurses. But Deborah Wilkins was small and dried up and bitter. She had been married for years and had no children. Her gaze had seemed to Emma to be trying to draw her into a private pact, an unholy alliance of failure. She'd pulled her glance away with an almost physical effort.

Don't let me be like Deborah Wilkins, Emma prayed during the silent nights while Josh slept soundly beside her.

3

*I*n March the days were lengthening and spring was definitely coming to Boston, but there was no lightening of the news from abroad. It was all terrible and getting worse. The papers were full of lurid and frightening reports of the war in Europe, and interminable death and destruction on what they called the Western Front. People muttered about poison gas and evil, power-crazed huns. One evening Josh came home with a clumsy package. He put it in the front hall closet without a word of explanation.

Emma had an ugly suspicion about the contents of the package. She examined it the next day. Gas masks, half a dozen of them. She held them for a moment with cold hands, then shoved them back in their wrappings and slammed the door. She was afraid, afraid. Of war. And of the agony of being gassed. And of being tested as a woman and found wanting, and dying before she could change that assessment.

"You think America is going to get into the war, don't you?" she asked Josh that night.

He looked at her across the lovely dining table with its gleaming white linen and lace and silver candles—all the signs of gracious living that Emma had learned to manage—and knew that she'd seen the gas masks, and that in some secret part of his mind he'd meant her to see them. "I don't know, but it looks that way. There's our trade to protect, and all our talk about democracy and freedom. Wilson's being backed into a corner. I hope not, but I don't see what choice we have."

"Will there be poison gas?" she whispered. "Here in Boston?"

"I don't think so. It's unlikely, farfetched even. I just wanted to be prepared."

Emma nodded. "What about the professor? If we go to war with Germany, how will it be for Germans like him?"

Josh ran his fingers through his hair. "That's going to be a terrible problem, isn't it? I hear foul things around town."

"Yes, I hear them too. And there was something nasty written on the window of the German bakery on Clarendon Street."

"We'll just have to see," Josh said. "Nothing to do but wait and see."

March rushed toward April and spring. Emma took more of the long walks she loved, smelling the city waking after its long winter sleep, loving it, grieving for it when she thought of war, grieving for herself.

She tried to talk to Josh about her secret fear, the terrible one that she'd never have a child. He was gentle and reassuring, yet she never thought he really understood. He knew more about all the clinical things than she did, but he wasn't a woman, he didn't know about the despairing sense of failure.

"You're a fine, healthy girl," he said, pressing his face to her hair. "You'll have a baby soon if you just stop worrying about it."

"Maybe my cervix needs to be dilated, like Jennie Deauville and the others."

"It doesn't."

"How do you know that, Josh? You've never examined me." She felt the heat of his flush, though she couldn't see it in the darkened bedroom. "You never have, Josh," she repeated.

"Yes, I have." His voice was so low she could barely hear him.

Emma pulled away from him and sat up in the bed. "Never. Why are you lying to me, Josh?"

"Darling, listen. I . . . sometimes when we make love—" He broke off and reached for her, cradling her in his arms again. "Sweet God, how do I explain? Sometimes when we make love I touch you, don't I?"

Now both their bodies were hot with embarrassment, and she buried her face in his chest, inhaling the marvelous male scent of him, wanting to breathe in his strength. "Yes, sometimes you do."

"Well, that's not much different than an internal examination. I mean it is, of course. Totally different. But it's the same," he finished helplessly. "In a sort of way."

"All the women you examine day after day? It's like it is with us, with me?" Her voice was heavy with despair.

"Dear heaven, no, of course not. That's what I'm trying to say. It's entirely different. Only if I want to, and I did just once, well, I can get some information."

Emma was silent for many minutes. Finally Josh spoke again. "Tell you what, if it will make you feel better, see the professor. Ask him to examine you. That will put your mind at rest. I'll arrange it."

She thought of being probed so intimately by the professor, a man she thought of as family, and she shivered. Then she thought of the other two gynecologists at Memorial, Frank Rhineman and Charles West. Both their wives were members of the Wednesday Circle. If either learned the results of her husband's examination, Emma wouldn't be able to bear it. Whatever Josh said, she was convinced she was medically imperfect, doomed, barren. It remained only for some doctor to pronounce her so, better the professor than a stranger. "Yes," she whispered. "Please tell the professor I'd like it to be very soon."

Schoener beamed with delight when she came out of his examining room and joined him in his office. "Nothing is wrong, my dear Emma. Inside you are as beautiful as out. Only you are worrying too much I think. Keep yourself busy, my dear. And stop thinking every month yes, no, yes, no. Soon you'll see what a big tummy you'll have."

Emma felt faint with relief, dizzy with it, a woman reprieved from a sentence of living death. Josh wasn't in the office, it was his afternoon at the clinic. Probably they had arranged that between them, he and the professor, so she would feel more at ease.

She almost floated next door to her own house and into the library on the second floor. She sat down and stared out the window and watched dusk creep over the mansard roofs of the Back Bay.

They had taken to having a glass of sherry before dinner, tonight she didn't want to wait for Josh. She poured a small drink for herself. Every perception was heightened, the nutty wine had never tasted so delicious. She sipped it and thought about the professor's advice. Keep busy.

There were lots of ways for Emma to keep busy in Boston. There was the Wednesday Club, and the various charity boards she'd been invited to join; shopping on Washington Street at Jordan Marsh for the latest fashions, or at Raymonds' for bargains, or at elegant R. H. Stearns on Tremont Street where having a charge account meant you have arrived among the better families of Boston. Oh yes, lots to do.

Emma set down the small glass of sherry and waited for Josh's step on the stairs. Would he already know her good news when he came in? Yes, he had probably called the professor and talked about the clinical details. Maybe not, though, maybe she'd have the pleasure of telling him herself. She'd tell him about the prescription too. Keep busy, keep your mind off yourself. Stop worrying. She had to follow the professor's advice. All the activities she'd just been imagining flashed through her mind and something in her rebelled.

Some deep core of her being, formed in Gloucester at Jessica's knee and at Manny's, rejected the notion of becoming a leisured lady. She had longed to come here, made it happen, but she was still a fisherman's daughter, a country girl bred to country truths. Life wasn't a game, it was not about social climbing. It was real and difficult and to the strong went the prize.

Her hand strayed to the folded newspaper waiting by Josh's chair. Quickly she picked it up and turned to the back page. EMPLOYMENT FOR LADIES, that was the heading of the column in the *Boston Herald*. Not a full column, only half, and at first glance nothing that looked promising or even possible. A secretary had to know how to use a typewriting machine and she didn't. Becoming a salesclerk was out of the question; the job was too public, and Josh would never agree. There wasn't any quick and easy answer, but the idea had been born and she wouldn't give it up easily

The door opened and Josh came in. She could tell by his smile that he knew. Emma dropped the newspaper and crossed the room into his eager arms.

From 165 Commonwealth Avenue to Memorial Hospital on the corner of Berkeley and Beacon Streets was a distance of less than half a mile. Josh enjoyed walking it, especially on this first day of April. The hospital was a large, gracious granite building designed by Charles Bulfinch in the previous century. It had been added to in later years by architects of lesser distinction, but none of them had tampered with Bulfinch's symmetrical and satisfying facade. Josh looked at it with pleasure, then climbed the broad steps.

Inside the hospital image was of little concern, efficiency was paramount. Josh took pleasure, too, in that value. "As good as Massachusetts General," he'd told Emma months ago. "As good as any in the nation."

Josh made a practice of visiting his charity patients at eight-thirty each morning, before he made the rounds of his patients in the private wing, or his office hours began on Commonwealth Avenue.

Charity Ward three, reserved for what in hospital parlance was ob-gyn, was in the west wing on the ground floor. It was a long room and on some days there were as many as fourteen beds on each side of the narrow aisle. Space was always a problem, particularly this morning.

Josh counted swiftly, sixteen on one side, seventeen on the other. Sweet Christ, they were packed in like sardines. He looked around and spotted the head nurse. "Miss Grayson, there are far too many patients in here."

She was a woman in her sixties and had been a member of the first class to graduate from Memorial's new school of nursing in 1881. "Don't tell me, Doctor Morgan," she snapped back. "Why don't you march up and down West Street and Joy Street and Bowdoin Square and tell the poor we've no room for them."

At that moment a woman in labor shrieked and Miss Grayson hurried off before Josh could reply.

The next morning the head nurse was waiting for him at the door to her ward. She bristled from the top of her ruffled triangular organdy cap to the tips of her highly polished black shoes. Her black dress, white apron, and

cap seemed capable of standing on their own, so stiffly
were they starched. But Miss Grayson's voice had not its
usual ring of authority, it sounded almost tremulous. "Doctor Morgan, I owe you a most humble apology. I didn't
sleep a wink last night thinking of my impertinence. Please
forgive me."

"It's I who must apologize, Miss Grayson. The crowded
conditions of this ward are no doing of yours, and you
manage heroically under the circumstances. Shall we just
forget the incident?" He favored the nurse with his famous
smile.

"I will not forget it, Doctor Morgan," the woman said
gravely. "Nor your gracious and gentlemanly reaction."

A working partnership had been forged, and another
tale was added to the growing legend of Josh Morgan.

"So it's come." Josh put down the newspaper and looked
at Emma across the table in the breakfast room. "Don't
worry, darling, I don't think it's going to be so terrible for
us here at home."

"It's awful." She lifted a coffee cup with trembling fingers. "Yesterday, when I first heard the news, I was in the
grocer's on Clarendon Street. The two men behind the
counter cheered, but none of the women did."

"Men are a bloodthirsty lot, I guess. We Americans
haven't fought a major war in some fifty years. I suppose
there's a whole generation or two that think they've missed
all the fun." Josh folded his napkin and put it beside his
plate. "I have to go. Emma, you'll be all right, won't you?"

She smiled at him. "Of course I'm going to be all right.
Am I supposed to carry my gas mask when I go out
today?"

"No, I don't think so." Josh chuckled softly. "It's not
really funny except in a macabre sort of way. Because I
gave in to an impulse and bought those damned things,
we're somewhat better prepared than others." He gestured at the paper. "There's an article in there says we
have about a quarter of a million men in the army. Not
nearly enough to 'show Kaiser Bill what for,' as we're
being urged to do."

Emma stood up and moved into his arms. "Hold me,
Josh, just for a moment."

Their embrace was a good deal warmer than normal on that morning of April seventh.

Joshua was still thinking about the war when Miss Grayson met him at the door of word three. "I have what you might call a problem of diplomacy, Doctor Morgan."

"Surely we don't have any war casualties yet?"

"War? No, of course not. I'm not happy about Mrs. Cohen. She's been in labor for thirty-six hours, but her contractions are still coming only at five-minute intervals. Dilation is complete, but there's no sign of hard labor and the fetal heartbeat is getting very faint."

They were serious symptoms, but the nurse saw them every day; they didn't constitute a problem of diplomacy. "Is Mrs. Cohen assigned to a doctor?"

"Yes, Doctor Rhineman." The woman hesitated. "I believe Mrs. Cohen asked to see you," she added softly.

Ah, so that was it. Charity patients had no right to ask for any particular doctor; they took whomever was available and on the roster. "I'll just stop by and see her then, shall I? Only to say hello."

Miss Grayson smiled broadly and helped him into a white coat. "She's down the hall in the treatment room."

Josh found Sophie Cohen strapped on the table, her legs already in stirrups. She was moaning softly and her face was bathed in sweat despite the constant sponging her forehead was getting from a student nurse. "Good morning, Sophie. I'm Doctor Morgan."

The woman reached out a clawlike hand and grasped Josh's arm. "Oh, I'm so glad. They say—aagh . . ." She struggled for long seconds with a pain. Jason lay his hands on her distended stomach and probed.

"She has three children at home," Miss Grayson murmured. "No previous delivery has been this difficult."

The pain had relented for a moment. Sophie could speak again. "I ain't never had it this bad, Doctor Morgan. Can you do something? Please? My mother-in-law, she says I'm crazy to come here to have my babies, that I should have them at home. But I tell her we're in America now, and they do wonderful things in America. They have doctors like you who know how to make everything all right."

Josh started to say something soothing and meaningless, Miss Grayson touched his arm and nodded toward the autoclave which was hissing noisily. Josh looked more closely. A set of Tarnier axis-traction forceps filled the sterilizer. The special lever which would insure maximum grip on the head of the infant gleamed in the bright white light of the small room.

Josh motioned the nurse to follow him out into the corridor. "Who ordered the forceps?"

"Doctor Rhineman."

They exchanged an intense look. Josh understood the entire drama now, and why he was involved. He grunted and stepped back into the treatment room. "Let's have a proper look at her." He was scrubbed and gloved and examining Sophie Cohen when Rhineman returned.

The man was handsome in an effete sort of way, a thin little mustache and fair hair parted in the middle and sleeked back. "So I'm to have the benefit of your consultation, Doctor Morgan. To what do I owe that honor?"

Josh went on with his examination and didn't answer. The only sound in the room was Sophie Cohen's moans. "The head of the fetus isn't engaged in the birth canal," Josh said finally.

"So I've determined. That's why I'm going to use high forceps and put an end to the patient's suffering."

"A step up from a deliberate craniotomy, but only just," Morgan said softly as he peeled off his rubber gloves.

Rhineman stiffened. Craniotomy was the deliberate crushing of the infant's skull, a death sentence for the child and sometimes the mother. "In careful hands high forceps are no such thing."

"There aren't any hands in medicine that careful."

The nurse stepped between the two men. "Doctors, please." She motioned to the patient.

Rhineman moved beyond the door and Joshua followed him. "Who the hell are you to question my judgment, Morgan?" A vein throbbed in Rhineman's temple.

"Calm down," Josh said, though he wasn't a bit calm himself. "In common decency, Frank, why not a cesarian?"

"Because the woman's an orthodox Jew. They breed like rabbits. If I section her now, the scar will split during her next labor."

"To quote your words, 'not in careful hands.'"

Whatever Rhineman might have answered went unspoken as Sophie Cohen's tortured voice rent the hospital hush. "Doctor Morgan! Please, Doctor Morgan!"

Rhineman stiffened, then smiled. "Well, that seems to be the deciding factor. Have at it, miracle worker." He turned and disappeared up the corridor.

"Miss Grayson," Josh said. "Call surgery and tell them to prepare for an emergency section."

Three minutes later Joshua was scrubbing for surgery. Through the glass separating him from his patient he could see a nurse-anesthetist administering ether to his patient. An intern stood by the operating table with a stethoscope pressed to Sophie Cohen's belly. He looked worried. Josh knew he had very little time and a critical decision to make.

Frank Rhineman was an incompetent fool who got by on his looks and his bedside manner, but his comment about danger of more pregnancies after a cesarian wasn't unfounded. On the other hand, Josh had been thinking for some time of a way to virtually eliminate that risk. But he'd not yet tried it, not even discussed it with Schoener.

"Doctor Morgan . . ." A nurse stepped forward to help him into his gown and mask.

Josh shoved his arms into the sleeves and bent his head so she could tie on the face guard, one more simple thing that in recent years had radically reduced the risks in surgery. Again his eye wandered to the operating theater. High on the wall he saw the old steel jets that had been installed in 1880 for "wet surgery"—flooding the patient, the wound, the instruments, and the room with antiseptic mist. When that principle was first put forth by Lister in London, everyone said the man's talk of dangerous, invisible microbes was insane. But they came around. Wet surgery had a great heyday and was just on its way out when Josh started his residency, and antiseptic had been replaced by aseptic. With everything sterile in advance a doctor could operate in the dry and still avoid infection. A major breakthrough brought about by one man with brain and nerve.

Josh drew a deep breath and went into the theater. He'd made his decision.

Sophie Cohen was delivered of a baby girl twenty minutes later. Mother and child had an excellent chance of surviving, and Sophie's future childbearing was not at risk because of her section. Josh had not made his cut through the protective abdominal layer, the peritoneum, into the upper part of the uterus. His incision was much lower down, dangerously close to the bladder, where the uterus consisted mostly of connective tissue and little muscle. It was a procedure demanding consumate surgical skill, but done properly—and this one had been—the benefits were obvious to the eyes watching through the observation window.

Not until the operation was over did Josh realize he'd had an audience. The observation room was designed for students, but when he glanced up Morgan saw not young, slightly green faces. There were seasoned men up there. His peers were sitting in judgment on him once more. Word that he was trying something unusual must have gone round pretty damned quickly. But then, it always did. The place was a rumor factory. Well, damn the bastards, they'd seen something, hadn't they? He strode from the room, buffeted by a mixture of satisfaction and annoyance.

"That was brilliant, sir," the young intern who'd assisted him commented. "Just brilliant."

Josh merely grunted.

Within a week what they were calling the "low cervical" cesarian section was being discussed throughout the Boston medical community. A few days later Josh went to scrub for a delivery and found himself standing next to Charles West.

"Welcome, miracle worker," West said in greeting. He was a prominent obstetrician some ten years Morgan's senior, and when he added a congratulatory comment it didn't ring true.

"Thank you." Josh hoped the subject would be dropped.

West wouldn't let it die. He hummed a few bars of "Pomp and Circumstance," then intoned, "And so a new day dawns for medical science as the brilliant young Joshua Morgan invents a new procedure to save lives. . . ."

Josh didn't laugh. "I didn't invent a thing, I only modified an existing technique."

"Ah, but so publicly, my boy. So publicly."

Josh escaped to the delivery room. Ten tables stood in a row, each with its set of straps and metal stirrups for restaining women in the last stages of labor. He'd taken

Emma on a tour of the hospital when they first came, and she'd been appalled by the delivery room, saying it resembled a torture chamber.

Josh looked at it now, mentally arguing with her again. It wasn't a torture chamber. All the straps and stirrups insured the safest position for delivery. Yes, ten in a row was a bit much in terms of privacy, but dammit, they were pressed for space.

He watched a nurse strapping the legs of his patient into position. She was a private patient, not a charity case, and she'd hinted weeks ago that she wanted to deliver at home. He'd needed all his charm to persuade her that it was an outmoded and dangerous idea not to be hospitalized. Well, he'd done it, and now she was here and in labor and screaming lustily. There was work to be done. Josh strode forward.

In secret Emma ripened her idea of getting a job. She took to buying the *Boston Globe* as well as the *Herald*. The *Globe* was an upstart newspaper, but it had more employment notices than the *Herald*. She made sure she flung it into the fire before Josh came home.

She answered three advertisements for clerks. One turned out to be a salesgirl's job, and she'd already decided she wouldn't consider that. One was in a wholesale grocer's and might have been suitable, but they wanted a clerk who could also operate a typewriting machine. The third was in a seedy little office near North Station, too far to walk. If she had to take a trolley twice a day, she'd have precious little left of her eight-dollar-a-week wage. Besides, the man who greeted her terrified Emma. He looked at her as if she weren't wearing any clothes. She didn't wait to find out what kind of an office it was or what were the duties of the job, she just fled in fright and disappointment.

Finding some kind of work had seemed like such a brilliant idea. The whole notion of the independence it would give her was thrilling. Not that she really wanted to be independent of Josh. It was simply her memories—Jessica waiting for Manny to give her the housekeeping money each week, and looking grim because it was never enough—coupled with her innate distaste for the shallow females she'd met socially. A whole range of things had come together to create this ambition, she wasn't ready to give it up. Emma scoured the newspapers unsuccessfully for two days after the North Station fiasco. On the third she saw something interesting.

"Clerk required for research chemist. No experience necessary, will train proper applicant." The address was on nearby Massachusetts Avenue. Walking distance! Emma dressed carefully, trying not to let her hopes rise too high.

Howard Chemical Laboratory, she read on the placard in the foyer of the building, third floor rear. She climbed the stairs. There was a closed door with the name Howard Chemical blazoned in neat black letters, but no bell. Emma knocked timidly.

"Come in."

The voice was gruff, low, and Emma thought it belonged to a man until she stepped into the laboratory.

"Just wait a moment, please. I'll be with you as soon as I finish here."

A small, white-coated figure was bent over a workbench, a test tube gripped in long forceps in her left hand, her right busily making notes in a ledger. From behind, Emma could see only the thick tweed skirt beneath the dingy laboratory coat, and heavy black lisle stockings above very sturdy looking black oxfords. Conscious of her elegant gray suit with its border of paler gray satin and matching satin hat, Emma wondered what she had been thinking of when she had dressed. She looked like a society matron, not a woman trying to get a job.

The other woman turned. "Good afternoon, I'm Celia Howard. Can I help you?"

"I came in response to your advertisement. The one about a clerk." Emma stumbled and bit her lip, seeing disbelief in the woman's light brown eyes. And something more, a twitch of amusement around her thin lips. "My name is Emma Morgan," she added miserably, aware that she had already lost a marvelous opportunity.

"Miss or Mrs. Morgan?" the woman asked. She had iron-gray straight hair, cut almost as short as a man's. Now she pushed it away from her forehead with no regard for how it might look. "Well, are you married or single?"

"Married." Emma couldn't get her voice above a whisper. "I'm Mrs. Joshua Morgan."

"I see. Wait a moment, is your husband by any chance Doctor Joshua Morgan? Professor Schoener's protégé?"

"Yes, he is." There was something unsettling in Celia Howard's attitude. Emma's chin came up. She wouldn't brook any criticism of Josh.

The Howard woman noted the reaction and looked even more amused. "Do sit down, Mrs. Morgan." She indicated a rickety chair in one corner and perched herself on the stool beside her workbench.

The pungent smell of chemicals made Emma's nose itch and her eyes water a bit, but she ignored it. She sat down gingerly, her back very straight, her gloved hands folded primly in her lap. She had to take some initiative. She moistened her lips with her tongue. "I have no experience, Mrs. Howard, but your advertisement said you were willing to train."

"Miss Howard. Not Mrs. Never been married and don't intend to be. And I don't require experience. Just intelligence and a willingness to work hard for little pay."

"Oh, I'm quite amenable to that. And I do learn quickly."

Celia Howard eyed her visitor a moment. "Mrs. Morgan, why are you looking for a job? Forgive me, I know that sounds quite rude, but it does seem extraordinary for a woman in your position to be doing so."

Direct enough. And what could she answer? How could she possibly explain to this formidable-looking female? "I have no children," Emma said haltingly. "Very little to do all day. And I wish to be useful."

Miss Howard made a noise rather like one of Josh's grunts. "How long have you been married?"

"Two years this June."

Again that sound that was neither yes or no or maybe. "Do you have a legible hand?"

"Oh, very!" Emma swallowed hard. She had to stop speaking in exclamations. "I was well trained in penmanship in school," she added in what she hoped was a more businesslike tone.

"Where was that? Your school, I mean."

"In Gloucester. My husband and I moved to Boston last autumn. So he could join Professor Schoener's practice."

Celia Howard scrutinized her caller. She saw the country girl beneath the city slick facade, and something of the unhappiness and determination. She'd never had a woman clerk before. And her male assistants always resented her, just as the other men in her profession resented her. But the kind of women who went out of their homes to work were usually not suitable for the laboratory, neither careful enough, nor sufficiently intelligent. She got up and turned her back to her visitor, staring out the single, rather grimy window at the city. She didn't say anything for some minutes, then she turned back to face Emma.

"I despise injustice," she said with sudden ferocity. "Despise it. I love my work, and I'm the best chemist in Boston, quite possibly in America, but that—" She broke off and dismissed the topic with a wave of her hand. "Listen, if you come to work for me you must dress sensibly, not like a society matron. And you must never gossip about what happens in this lab. Nor be squeamish about ugly sights and smells. Nor fail to note with absolute accuracy the results of every experiment. That will be your job. Writing down the results exactly as I describe them. And generally keeping this place tidy."

Emma noted the change from *if* to certainty and her heart soared. "I can do all that. I'll work very hard, Miss Howard. And I do learn extremely quickly. I'm not boasting."

"Good. Neither am I. Salary's seven dollars and fifty cents a week. You can begin Monday morning at eight. By the way, I presume your husband approves?" Her brown eyes narrowed as she studied Emma's face. "Haven't discussed it with him yet, have you?"

"No," Emma admitted. "But I shall, this evening. And he will allow me to take the job. I promise."

"Hmm . . . I hope so. See you Monday at eight then." She walked all the way downstairs with Emma, and the two women didn't stop talking until Emma was out the door and on the street.

"Come for a walk," Emma said to Josh that evening after dinner. "It's still light. And really spring now that we're in the middle of April."

They strolled along the Charles River Embankment. For long stretches they were silent, not needing words to communicate their contentment in each other's company. The Harvard rowing team was practicing. Their elegant skulls darted swiftly through the water, filled with intent and dedicated young men. "I wish we hadn't gotten into this damned war," Josh said quietly. "I look at those boys and can't help but wonder if they'll soon be sent off to be slaughtered in battle."

"Why did we get into it? I still can't see what it has to do with us. Europe's thousands of miles away."

"Yes, but the whole concept of democracy is threatened. I suppose there was no alternative."

"Principles above all, yes, I see. And that's as good an opportunity as I'm going to get. Josh, I want to take a job."

He stopped and stared at her. "Did I hear you correctly? You did say a job?"

"Yes, I did. I've already found it. There was an advertisement in the *Globe* for a clerical assistant to a chemist. I had an interview today and the position is mine if I want it. I'm to start on Monday if you agree."

"But why? I don't understand. Emma, surely you have no unmet needs. And we're in Boston, where you wanted to live. Why on earth would you take a job?"

She told him, sparing no detail of her anguish over not conceiving and the professor's advice.

"I'm sure he didn't mean you should go to work," Josh insisted. His jaw was getting that set look Emma knew too well.

"No, I know he didn't. The old love, he'd never imagine such a thing. But it's right for me, Josh. I'm not the sort to spend my time at tea parties and ladies' circles. I want to do something in my own right, something to make you proud of me."

Josh put his hands on her shoulders and looked into her incredible blue eyes. "There's no room in my heart for any more pride in you, Emma, it would burst. You know that."

"Yes, I do. Perhaps what I really mean is that I want to be proud of myself."

They looked at each other for some seconds, then Emma added in a whisper, "Please, Josh."

He sighed and took his hands from her shoulders and let them hang limp at his sides. "What sort of a chemist? Who is the man?"

"A research chemist, and not a man, a woman. Miss Celia Howard. She's extraordinary, Josh. Such drive, such talent. She got a degree in chemistry from the Sorbonne in Paris, then came home for more study at Radcliffe. When she was finished no one in Boston would hire her, so she opened her own laboratory. Now she does tests for all the major hospitals, and even for the government when they want to know about the purity of foodstuffs and so forth."

"And what would you be doing?" he asked. "You don't know anything about chemistry."

Emma steeled herself not to respond to his obvious unhappiness. "I told Miss Howard that, and she says it doesn't matter. My work would be to keep her files in order and record her results. She'll train me. By the way, she was quite impressed when she realized I was your wife. She read your article in the *Journal of Medicine*."

Josh smiled for the first time since conversation about Emma's job had begun. "Don't try flattery just to get your way, you little minx." It was an attempt at lightness, but it sounded hollow.

"I shall get my way, though, shan't I, darling?"

Josh nodded. "If it's really what you want."

"It is."

They walked home, their silence now less comfortable and warm than earlier. Emma paused in the front hall to remove her hat, studying her face by the light of the lamp beside the mirror. She was flushed with happiness and she knew she looked marvelous. But how to make Joshua happy? How to keep him from thinking that her decision meant she wasn't content as his wife. That's what was behind his disapproval. That, and his basic male conservatism. Impulsively she unbuttoned the top of her blouse so the creamy skin above her breasts showed, and followed him into the living room.

"It's warm tonight, darling, isn't it?" she asked brightly. "Would you like a sherry before bed?" He turned to face her and she saw in his eyes that he sensed her mood, her wantonness.

"Whisky, I think."

She poured it into a heavy crystal tumbler, almost filling the glass, and before handing it to him she took a sip. She didn't cough, but it required an effort. "It's strong."

"Yes." He took a long swallow. "You admire strong things, don't you, Emma?"

"Yes. That's one of the things I love about you, your strength." She put her hands on his arms, lingering over the muscles beneath his fine wool jacket. "Aren't you warm? Shouldn't we go up to bed?"

"Why not?" He tossed back the rest of the drink, then followed her up the stairs, his eyes studying the curve of her rump beneath her skirt, wondering if she always swayed it in just that way.

Once in bed he turned to her hungrily, and was amazed at the speed and the heat of her response. "Emma, oh Christ, Emma! I don't want you miserable, I'm not some nineteenth-century domestic tyrant."

"Ssh, I know, I understand. Don't talk. Just love me."

He rolled on to her with a moan that was half pleasure and half pain.

A fine, misty rain drifted in the May evening, swirling in unexpected ways, undercutting the efficiency of Emma's umbrella. She turned from Huntington Avenue into Dartmouth Street, conscious of the fact that her clothes were damp and her shoes made a faint squishing sound.

She should have taken a trolley, maybe even a cab, but she was determined to be economical, economy befitted a working woman. So did her flat-heeled brogues, now singing a high-pitched whine with each step, and the tailored suit she wore. The skirt was mid-calf length, russet wool and the jacket swung in soft, loose folds. Emma's hat was small and dark, her gloves dark as well. Sensible clothes for a sensible, modern lady.

But how modern? "Are you a suffragette?" Celia Howard had demanded out of the blue that afternoon.

Emma hadn't answered quickly. Her employer of one month might sound spontaneous, even impulsive, but Miss Howard always had everything clearly documented in her quick mind. So Emma had hesitated, begged the question a bit. "I've never taken an active part in the campaign to get the vote for women, so I suppose I'm not a suffragette. But it does seem only fair. We're people after all, half the human race. Besides, look at the mess the world's in. I rather think the gentlemen could use a bit of help."

Miss Howard had replied with one of her grunts, and Emma still wasn't sure whether her answer had scored points or lost them. She knew it mattered, however. Celia

Howard's opinion was becoming very important to her. A gust of wind nearly pulled the umbrella from her hands and she was distracted.

A man was standing on the corner of Dartmouth Street and Commonwealth Avenue. He was bent under a dripping sandwich board announcing a Liberty bond rally to be held next evening at Faneuil Hall. Emma turned east onto her own block and left the man and his board behind. They'd already bought some Liberty bonds in support of the war effort, they didn't need to go to Faneuil Hall.

She opened the front door and glanced at the grandfather clock. Just after six, she'd have time to change before Josh got home. She was trying very hard to keep her working life and her role as Josh's wife separate.

Just as she started up the stairs the cook appeared from the door leading to the kitchen and the pantries in the basement. "Begging your pardon, ma'am, but I had to change the menu for dinner. On my own, since you weren't at home." The cook was a large woman, big and mannish and severe. Her expression said clearly what she thought of having a mistress who went out to work.

"Why did you have to change the menu?" Emma glanced at the clock. She desperately didn't want Josh to come in now and find her like this, standing on the stairs sodden and dripping and arguing with a servant.

"It's the gov'ment, ma'am. They say we can't have no meat tonight."

"What?"

"Yes, ma'am. It was in the paper this morning. That fellow they're calling the food administrator, Mr. Hoover, he says we can't eat no meat on Tuesdays, not until we teach the Kaiser what for. So I couldn't cook the lamb chops like you said. I ordered some flounder."

"I see. Very well, flounder will be fine."

Emma fled to her bedroom, thinking of wheatless Mondays and Wednesdays, and porkless Thursdays and Saturdays. Now meatless Tuesdays. Every detail of their menus was being dictated from Washington. "Very well, Mr. Hoover," she muttered. "The Morgans will do as they're told." She thought of the gas masks still in the front closet and shuddered.

Josh didn't arrive until nearly seven, by then she was bathed and changed and standing in the library waiting for him. But he didn't seem to notice her green silk tea gown or artfully arranged hair. He didn't even say good evening properly. He muttered something and went straight to the decanters on the long mahogany table beneath the windows and poured himself a large, neat bourbon whisky and swallowed it in one gulp.

"What's wrong, Josh?"

"It's those swine at Memorial, Rhineman and his lot. Has to be them."

Emma's heart fluttered, then began to beat a bit too fast. Please, God, not trouble at the hospital, not now when things were going so well. She couldn't bear it if they had to move back to Gloucester now. "Do you want to talk about it?"

"I must I suppose, you'll have to know." He turned to face her. "There was a meeting of the Gynecolgoy Committee today. To discuss the use of chloroform and ether during labor. Rhineman and his pals all promise their ladies painless labor but for a high price in my book—the cost to the infant. Anyway, that's beside the point, we've been having that argument since I was a resident. The thing is, they changed the venue at the last minute and notified everybody but Professor Schoener."

He gulped the last of his drink and poured himself another. His movements were jerky, displaying none of his customary grace.

Emma was relieved. It was some medical squabble, nothing to threaten the shape of their lives. "Is the professor opposed to Doctor Rhineman using anesthesia during delivery?" She made herself sound interested. Even a working wife had to be willing to listen to her husband's worries.

"Of course he is, but that's not the issue. As I said, they've been fighting about that for years. What counts is the deliberate snub. The deliberate freeze out."

"Of the professor? But why? I don't understand."

"You do, Emma, we talked about it before. Because Schoener's a German, one of those hated huns we're all so hysterical about, Memorial's going to mount its own witch-hunt and Schoener's top of the list. Never mind that he's the most brilliant gynecologist in the country. Suddenly he's just a damned hun and maybe even a spy for the enemy."

"Oh my God . . ." Emma sat down in the nearest chair, weak with anger and disgust, thinking of the man with the dripping sandwich board announcing a Liberty bond rally, of food rationing, of the lurid posters she'd seen warning people to be on the lookout for spies. "How awful," she murmured. "How perfectly awful and incredibly stupid. Professor Schoener has been here for years, he's a naturalized citizen." She added another thought, worse than those that had gone before. "Josh, does he realize? Does he know what they're doing?"

"Of course he does. He's not a fool. He's expected it right along, mentioned it to me in fact. But I didn't think it would really happen. Not this fast and this blatant." He looked up from his glass and into Emma's face. "Darling, I'm sorry, I didn't mean to make you so upset."

"My being upset is hardly the issue. What will he do?"

"Can't say for sure yet. Anyway, you're to put it out of your mind. Tell me about your day. What rabbits did the extraordinary Miss Howard produce from her disreputable hat?"

Emma drew her tongue over her lips and had a sudden irrational urge to blurt out that she'd missed her monthlies this month and might be pregnant. The dinner bell rang and she took it as a sign. Not now, not like this, and not so soon. It was very likely to be just another false alarm. She smiled at him and took his arm, and while they started for the dining room she was thinking up funny stories from the lab to keep him amused all during his meatless Tuesday meal.

Nine weeks later Professor Helmut Schoener formally withdrew from his affiliation with Boston Memorial Hospital. Josh and Emma both urged him to hang on, to fight the prejudice, but he refused. "Enough it is, I'm old and for many years I'm making disease and ignorance mine enemies. I have no time left for a new fight."

They were in his cluttered, little sitting room, sipping iced lemon tea on a glorious July afternoon. Emma found her hands trembling so she could hardly hold her glass. The professor seemed shrunken, gray with weariness and fatigue. Josh too. She had to do something. She couldn't bear to see them looking so dejected. "Listen, both of you.

I want to say something. I'm pregnant. At least I think I am."

There was a long silence, both men stared at her, then began talking at once. "Since when?" "How far along do you think you're being?" "How do you feel?" "Why didn't you say something before now?"

"Wait a minute. I can only answer one question at a time. I haven't . . . that is, there have been no monthlies since April. Right after I started working. Nothing in May or June, and I'm a week overdue this month."

Schoener insisted that she come downstairs for an examination immediately. They left Josh where he was, looking pale, and as overawed as any layman. When they returned he hadn't moved, and he stared from one solemn face to the other, finally blurting out, "Well? Yes or no?"

"Yes," Schoener said with a sudden broad grin. "Sure I'm being. Three months."

Emma and Josh fell into each other's arms, and the old man beamed on them like the paterfamilias he felt himself to be. Even at this dreadful time in his life, Emma's pregnancy after the two sterile, barren years was some consolation.

"You'll have to stop working right away," Josh said. There was a glimmer of triumph in his green eyes. It flashed into Emma's mind that it was not merely the fact of her pregnancy delighting him.

"Oh no, not yet, surely?" She turned quickly to the older man. "Professor, you're my obstetrician, don't you think I can work a few months more? I feel perfectly well, and I enjoy my job."

Schoener looked from Josh to Emma, ostensibly unaware of the undercurrent between them. "Well, darling, a little while more maybe. It was your work that relaxed you enough to conceive. Sure I'm being. So why not stay relaxed a little longer, *hein*?"

Josh couldn't argue with that. "Very well, you're the doctor," he said easily.

"No, I'm not. I can't deliver your baby, my Emma, though loving it I would have."

They'd almost forgotten the situation at Memorial, and the fact that in the present climate the professor would not now get credentials to practice in any hospital in the nation.

"Listen," Josh said. "You see Emma through her pregnancy and I'll get Charles West to take charge of the delivery. He's perfectly competent, and he's not a bad sort. I'm sure he'll understand. As for the practice, you continue to see patients as a consultant. If hospitalization is required I'll handle it."

Schoener shrugged, looking again as weary and dejected as he had before Emma's announcement. "Whatever you say, Josh. In your hands I'm leaving it. Maybe my patients too will think I'm a spy, but I'm too tired to fight fools."

4

*T*he October day on which Emma chose to tell Celia Howard she had to give up her job, was, as it turned out, the half year anniversary of her employment. Emma was astounded when Miss Howard produced a bottle of sherry and some little cakes around four in the afternoon. She hadn't said a word yet, and though almost six months pregnant, she knew her condition didn't show.

"But how did you know?" she demanded when Miss Howard announced they were taking a break for a small celebration.

"My dear Emma, I know to the minute the day you started working for me. I count it as one of the luckier moments of my existence. Six months today."

Emma flushed. "I'm sorry. I misunderstood. I've been rather preoccupied lately and I forgot the date."

"What did you think we were celebrating?" The older woman cocked her gray head and studied her employee. "Don't tell me, I can guess. You're pregnant, aren't you?"

"Yes. Five months, but Josh and the professor insist that I stop work now."

"Of course," Celia Howard said with a sigh. "I should have known it was too good to last. Serves me right for hiring a beautiful, young married woman. Nature could be relied on to take its course."

Emma felt as if she'd committed a crime. "I am sorry. I

didn't know, you see. We'd been married over two years and I'd never . . ."

"Oh, Emma, don't apologize, dear child. I'm being a selfish old spinster, as much of a harpy as my male colleagues insist I am." She crossed the room and put her hands on Emma's shoulders. "Please accept my belated congratulations. I am happy for you, Emma. Truly. It's wonderful that you're going to have a child. You mustn't think anything else."

The two women toasted each other with tiny glasses of cream sherry and nibbled on the cakes that Celia Howard had bought at the Women's Exchange. When the last crumb was gone, she looked speculatively at her assistant. "Emma, I'm probably insane to bring this up now, but . . ."

There was a moment's silence. "Yes, Miss Howard," Emma encouraged. "What is it?"

Celia Howard bit her lip, still hesitating. Finally she seemed to make up her mind. "If I'm going to say it, it better be now," she murmured. "We'll hardly see each other now that you won't be working in the lab every day." She took a deep breath. "Please forgive a flagrantly personal question. You can tell me to mind my own business if you wish. I know you've wanted a child for some time, but what about women who have too many children? Do you think they have the right to forestall pregnancy?"

"Forestall . . . Do you mean practice birth control?"

Celia Howard nodded.

Emma thought of the women she'd seen in poor districts like the West End, those shawled creatures with pushcarts and trays of apples to sell. She thought of Rosa Tecci dead in Gloucester, and eleven motherless children left behind her. "Yes, I do. If there's some safe way for them to do it."

Celia Howard nodded again. "Good for you. I agree. In fact, I consider it to be the single most important problem facing women. Not to be able to control your own body must be the ultimate injustice. Like slavery. Emma, tell me something else, what does your husband think about it?"

"Josh is very interested in the problem. It's why we came to Boston, so he could work with Professor Schoener and do research."

"I hoped you'd say that. It's why I had the courage to

bring up the subject." She put down her empty glass and stood up. "Emma, we are going to close the lab early today." She walked to the peg by the front door and took her sensible felt hat and jammed it on her head. "Well, come on, what are you waiting for?"

Emma hastened to pull on her jacket and her hat and gloves. "Where are we going?"

"Someplace remarkable, my dear. Truly remarkable."

It was a small back room behind a bookshop on Milk Street. Every surface was crowded with leaflets and pamphlets and booklets, and the whole was overseen by a pasty-faced woman somewhere the wrong side of fifty. "Emma, this is Thelma Willard. Thelma, Emma Morgan. Mrs. Joshua Morgan," she added pointedly.

"Doctor Morgan's wife?"

Emma heard the remark as a challenge, her chin came up defiantly. "Yes, that's right."

"And are you and your husband interested in our cause?" Thelma Willard demanded.

"I don't know. I have no idea what your cause is."

"Freedom, Mrs. Morgan. Freedom for women who have been enslaved by their inability to plan their reproduction. The cause championed by the greatest woman of our age, Margaret Sanger."

Celia Howard sat down heavily and pulled off her hat, uncaring of the disorderly tangle it had made of her short, gray hair. "Thelma, you're your own worst enemy. You sound like the avenging furies, and that's not likely to convince anyone. Sit down, Emma, and I'll tell you what this is all about. But before I do, I'd best warn you that Margaret Sanger's work, and ours, is in flagrant violation of the law. So Thelma and I and our co-workers are criminals of a sort. Perhaps you'd rather leave right now."

Emma drew up the one remaining chair in the room. "No, Miss Howard, I don't want to do that."

Celia smiled at her. "I didn't think you would. But before we go on, won't you please call me Celia. I don't think criminals stand on ceremony. Now, there are some facts you must know. Margaret Sanger began as a public health nurse but she always believed that the real problem for poor women was their inability to have only as many children as they wanted and could afford. She began looking for information, but in this whole nation, Emma, in this whole great country, she could find no one who was studying the problem of controlling births. So six years ago she went to Holland and learned there about the latest methods."

Emma held up her hand. "Just a moment, I don't understand. What methods?"

"I'm getting to the details," Celia promised. "When Margaret returned from Europe, she had learned about a device, a pessary or cap which covers the head of the cervix during sexual relations. For God's sake, Emma, you're a married woman, why are you blushing?"

"I'm not blushing."

"Yes, you are. Why, you're red as a beet. She is, isn't she, Thelma?" Thelma nodded.

"Well maybe I am," Emma said. "But I still want to hear the rest of the story. If such a device as this exists, why haven't I heard about it? Why hasn't every woman heard about it?"

"Because," Thelma Willard said, "it doesn't suit men to have us know about such things. We will be harder to enslave if we aren't pregnant all the time."

"Shush, Thelma. You've never been pregnant in your life, neither have I, but Emma is." She turned to Emma once more. "It's not a war, my dear. Not a struggle against all the men in the world, though Thelma sometimes thinks it is. But the cap needs to be fitted by a trained medical person, and if the poor are to have access to it, there must be free clinics. As things stand, there can't be. The fitting of such a device is absolutely illegal in every state in America—and in England, by the way. Worse, even discussing the issue is illegal. Margaret Sanger's books and newsletters have been confiscated as obscene; every public meeting she's tried to convene has been broken up by the police." She leaned back, as if the long explanation had exhausted her. "Maybe Thelma's not so far wrong, it is a war."

Emma looked around, seeing the little room with new eyes. "Is this a birth control clinic?"

"Not really, would to God that it were. We do have a nurse friend who is courageous enough to get the devices, and she sometimes fits them in her own home. We send women to her when we can." Celia reached out and drew a stack of pamphlets nearer. "But what we really are is a branch of the Planned Parenthood League. Our job is to change public opinion. We distribute things like this."

Emma thumbed through the literature; two books, *The Woman Rebel* and *What Every Girl Should Know*, and a magazine, *The Birth Control Review*. "You're telling me it's illegal to circulate these things?"

"If we send it through the mails, yes definitely. So what we do is give out our literature privately by hand. That's less clearly a violation of the law but the Catholic Church is very powerful in Massachusetts, so it's difficult to recruit people to help."

"There's that woman who sometimes comes in, Celia. You're forgetting about her," Thelma said.

"Miss Landry, yes, but she's an apostle for her own creed, it's not exactly the same thing." Celia turned expectantly to Emma. "I think it's fair to say that so far there are just two of us working here in Boston, Thelma and myself."

Emma stood up, drawing on her gloves. "I have to go now. Josh will be home soon. But there aren't two of you any longer. Now there are three."

Emma decided to walk home through the Common and the Public Gardens to give herself time to sort through what she'd just experienced and figure out how she was going to explain to Josh. She'd not gone very far when a voice at her shoulder said, "Please, I'd like to speak with you if I may."

The words had a very un-Boston lilt, and they issued from a statuesque woman wearing an unseasonable straw hat atop heavy chestnut hair swept back from a broad forehead. There was something decidedly odd, strangely stagelike, about the woman. Emma wondered if she might be a gypsy of some sort, or even a beggar. "Yes," she said tentatively. "How can I help you?"

"I think I may be able to help you." The accent was more pronounced, but Emma still couldn't identify it.

"Help me how?"

"That rightly depends on what you was asking Miss Willard and Miss Howard."

A chill crept up Emma's spine. "Flagrantly illegal," Celia Howard had said. "I don't know what you're talking about."

"Don't be feared, honey. I know that lots of ladies go to Milk Street thinking they can get help for something that already is, not something they can maybe prevent. And when they leave that place looking as worried as you, they sometimes do crazy things. Terrible, dangerous things with knitting needles or knives. I just want to tell you there's a better way. Or maybe you might not have to find no way at all. If you can see a clear path through, that's always the best."

They were standing in the middle of the walk, and it was growing dark and people were hurrying past them in both directions. Emma stepped over to one of the benches and the woman in the straw hat followed her. "You feeling all right, honey?"

"No, I am feeling very ill." She sat down. Someone had been feeding pigeons earlier, a litter of peanut shells blew about her high-buttoned boots. Emma stared at them a moment and then turned to the remarkable woman sitting beside her. "What is your name?"

"Billy-Jo Landry."

"And I'm Emma Morgan. How do you do?"

"I do just fine, but we were talking about you."

"You thought you were. Now, Miss Landry, we'd best get some misconceptions cleared away."

Her tale was told at the dining room table, in short bursts that ended each time the maid came into the room, and began again the moment she and Josh were alone. "Are you telling me," Josh said at one point, "that this odious creature from the Ozarks or wherever offered to perform an abortion for you?"

"Yes. You could say so, but not the way you mean. And she's not an odious creature."

"Emma, if you had any idea of the things women do to themselves and each other, the terrible mutilations in the most unsanitary conditions. Words fail me. And abortion is a disgusting concept. Life is sacred. I should think you'd see that, not be bamboozled by some semiliterate hussy from the back of—"

"Lower your voice, Josh." Emma served him a second helping of apple pie. "You're so busy shouting and being scandalized you're not listening to what I say. Billy-Jo Landry doesn't use any surgical procedures. She feels the same way you do about them. She uses herbs to induce a miscarriage. Claims she learned about them from her mother and her grandmother. Apparently such things are commonplace where she comes from."

Josh opened his mouth to comment, but Emma stopped him. "There's no point in going on about this, you'll have a chance to meet the lady yourself. I've invited her to have dinner with us tomorrow evening. She's bringing me some samples of what she calls her 'potions.' To test in the laboratory. She's been stalking the Planned Parenthood office on Milk Street for weeks, but she never found out Celia was a chemist."

"I thought you always called her Miss Howard." Josh looked like a small boy, sullen and disgruntled because he'd been beaten in an argument and didn't quite see how. "Is this sudden familiarity the result of your afternoon's activities?"

"Yes. Celia said it was silly to go on being formal if we were joining forces to spread word of Margaret Sanger's work. What about that, Josh? You've been ranting and raving about abortion, but surely the real issue is contraception."

"You know I agree with that. You've heard me say so often enough. But it's hard to imagine that your Miss Sanger is going to prevail against all the narrow-minded bigotry opposing her, least of all here in Boston."

"Still, someone has to try. I want to work with Celia and Thelma, Josh. Just a couple of afternoons a week in the office, sorting leaflets and things like that."

It was quiet in the elegant dining room at 165 Commonwealth Avenue. The maid cleared the table and brought coffee in a heavy silver pot. Emma poured it into delicate china cups and added sugar with little silver tongs. Finally she could bear the silence no longer. "What are you thinking, Josh?"

"I'm thinking that you look like Aunt Prissy. Not really, just that as you sit here presiding over this table you remind me of her. She never had a child, that was the great sorrow of her life. She tried to make up for it with me, but it wasn't the same. And you were desperately unhappy when you didn't conceive right away. But now we're arguing about abortion and the prevention of conception. Doesn't make much sense, does it?"

Emma leaned forward, her eyes wide in her earnestness. "Yes, darling, it does. I thought about that, too, while I was waiting for you to come home. It's all part of the same piece, Josh. Alice Crane and Rosa Tecci are sisters and their problem is every woman's problem. We have to get some control. That's why your work is the most exciting, important thing happening in medicine today." She reached out and lay her hand on his sleeve. "I want to be part of it, Josh. At least in a small way. That's why I want to work with the Planned Parenthood League."

"And if I say no? If I point out that it's illegal and you could become involved in a sordid lawsuit and drag our name and reputation into the newspapers?"

"If you say those things I won't do it," Emma said quietly. "I know I'm putting you at risk as well as myself, Josh. I won't do it without your approval. Are you going to withhold it?"

Another long silence. The coffee grew cold and neither of them noticed. At last Josh sighed. "No, darling, I'm not going to oppose you. Just so long as you don't endanger your health by working too hard. And I'll meet your Ozark lady with the man's name, and listen to her nonsense about witch's brews. But just this once. After tomorrow evening I don't want to hear another word about abortion or mad women from the hills."

"I don't think there's any magic 'bout it at all," Billy-Jo Landry said. "I 'spect there's something in the plants that has an effect on a lady's womb and makes it expel the fetus. That's the right word, isn't it, Doctor?"

"Yes."

Josh's tone was clipped, his jaw tight, and there was a thin white line around his mouth. Emma recognized the familiar signs of tension. But Josh was controlling himself for her sake. She felt obligated to voice his objections. "Josh questions the whole concept of abortion, Miss Landry. It is rather horribly close to murder. And doctors are sworn to protect life."

"Oh, Mrs. Morgan, I know that. I told you the other evening that it was best if a woman could see a clear path to birthin' the child. It's just that some can't. They want to, but they can't. That's when I know my way is better and safer than all them terrible things with knives and knitting needles and the like."

Josh leaned forward over the china and cutlery on the dining table. "Miss Landry, there are times when everyone has to face the consequences of her actions, when there is no way to avoid them. Don't you agree?"

Emma looked at the other woman and waited for her answer. Despite her accent, her voice was low and pleasant, and her arguments well thought through. She was turning out to be not at all the poor, simple hillbilly Emma had first judged her to be.

"I agree, Doctor Morgan," Billy-Jo Landry said. "But how come it's always the woman who has to face the consequences, as you put it? What about the man, don't he have responsibilities too?"

"Of course he has. But I don't think anyone is likely to find a way to cause men to bear children. Given that irrefutable law of nature, women just have to cope."

"What about rape? You think a woman should just have to cope then too?"

Josh took a long drink of iced water, then set down the goblet. "Miss Landry, this is quite the most extraordinary conversation that has ever taken place at my dinner table. I think you and I had best agree to disagree. And you ladies must excuse me. I have to return to the hospital to see a patient."

He rose and kissed Emma's cheek and nodded to her guest and left the room. Emma waited until the door had closed behind him, then grinned broadly. "Don't be fooled by his manner. Josh is a very thoughtful and fair man. You've given him a lot to consider and I know he will. Now, did you bring the samples for Miss Howard's laboratory?"

"Yes, I did. I'm quite excited 'bout that. It's been in my mind all along that somebody smart could find out what's in the herbs that makes 'em work. I never knowed Miss Howard was a scientist. Imagine a lady bein' something like that! It's hard to believe."

"You can believe it. Celia Howard is the smartest chemist in Boston, man or woman. If it can be done, she'll do it, I promise you." Emma rose from the table. Almost overnight her pregnancy had become obvious and she was starting to move awkwardly. "Let's have our coffee in the library, shall we? It's much cozier and more comfortable."

They left the room. Emma noticed how graceful Billy-Jo's movements were. Tall and broad-hipped, she wore a loose gown of a soft dark blue material. It owed nothing to the latest fashion, but it suited her. Emma felt outclassed in her stiff brown taffeta.

Emma's son was born on January twentieth, 1918. As arranged, Charles West delivered the baby.

He invited Josh to be present, but Josh refused. "I couldn't face it," he admitted sheepishly. "Not when it's Emma." Instead he paced nervously in the waiting room assigned to expectant fathers. He knew the nurses were giggling behind their hands at this change of roles, but he pretended not to notice.

After he'd been there for six hours, a nurse came in. "Doctor Morgan, it's over. You have a fine son." Josh was sitting, and staring at the floor, his head in his hands. He looked up at the nurse as if he hadn't quite understood.

"A son, Doctor," she repeated. "And Mrs. Morgan is doing fine."

With a whoop of joy he stood up and nearly knocked her over in his race down the corridor.

Three days later, sitting with his wife late in the evening, long after visiting hours were over and when only his privileged position allowed him to be there, he told Emma about the ordeal in the waiting room, as if somehow it compared with hers. "One thing is certain, we've got to change the no-smoking rule in there. Have to offer the poor sods some consolation."

Emma looked up at him from her bed in the private room in the maternity pavilion. He was serious, he really did think the men suffered. "Yes, poor things, you should make them more comfortable during their time of trial. And while you're at it, Josh, change that wretched delivery room. That is, if you can spare a thought for the ladies."

He patted her hand. "Don't think about it, darling. It's over. And it really is the safest way."

"It's horrid. No privacy. And those awful straps and stirrups. I was miserable until the twilight sleep took effect."

"That helped, did it?"

"Of course it helped. Mind you, I didn't get it until the whole thing was almost done."

Josh frowned. "It's a mix of scopolamine and morphine. Schoener and I have reservations, because a sedated mother can't bear down. But I discussed it with Charles earlier and he wanted to use it, so I agreed."

"You didn't discuss it with me, did you, Josh?"

He looked at her in wonder. "No, why would I? I mean, you're not a doctor—" There was fire in her eyes and he broke off. Women were notoriously unstable immediately after birth. Some of them had crying jags and others had rages. He reached for her hand. "It's over," he repeated. "Let's just think about the miracle we've produced."

"Yes, where is he?" Emma glanced at her watch. "They should be bringing him now."

"That sounds like someone coming." Josh went to the door and peered down the corridor. A nurse was wheeling up a trolley load of babies, in seconds she reached Emma's room.

"Here, I'll take him." Josh reached for the infant, the nurse hesitated, but only for a moment.

"Since it's you, Doctor." She surrendered the child and Josh carried him to his mother.

Emma sat up in the bed and stretched out her arms to receive her infant son. Three days old, and so perfect. She touched the faint fuzz of dark hair on his tiny head, and kissed the minute fist he pressed against his cheek. "Look," she whispered. "Joshua Junior sleeps just like you do, with his hands close to his face."

"Do I do that?"

"You do. Oh, Josh, I can hardly believe it. It's real isn't it? Not a dream? I keep thinking that I'm going to wake up, that nobody can be this happy."

Emma recovered her strength quickly. She was home from the hospital in two weeks.

"I don't think you and the baby are ready for a trip to Gloucester," Joshua said. "So I invited your family to come see us here this Sunday."

Emma looked astonished. "My father and my brothers? Here?"

"Yes." Josh's voice betrayed his puzzlement. "I thought

you'd want them to meet little Josh. Emma, it's all right, isn't it? I just assumed . . ."

"It's fine," she said hastily. "And very thoughtful, darling. This Sunday, you said? I'll talk to the cook."

It wasn't a bit fine, but she'd never say that to Josh. The thought of her relatives in this house was too incongruous. That's why she'd never invited them to visit. In her mind she and Josh had an old life in Gloucester and a new one in Boston—two different worlds divided by a chasm never to be crossed. But maybe not, she told herself, maybe wonderful little Joshua could be a bridge.

"How many will there be?" the cook demanded when Emma announced that guests would arrive for Sunday lunch.

Emma had to say she wasn't sure. "You'd better prepare for . . ." She hesitated, if they all came, her father and her brothers and their wives and children, it could be as many as . . . "Seventeen," she said aloud.

"Seventeen! Seventeen guests for Sunday lunch and you've only given me two days to prepare? I must say, madam—"

"Eight of them are children," Emma interrupted quickly. "Only nine adults. And I don't really think they'll all come, but I can't say for sure. They don't have a telephone and there's no way to find out."

The cook harrumphed loudly and bustled out of Emma's bedroom. Emma lay back on her pillows and tried to anticipate what it would be like to have Manny and her brother Henry and the rest of them in the elegant dining room on Commonwealth Avenue. The details of the picture were beyond her ability to imagine.

In the end it was just Manny who came. Emma's father arrived shortly after noon on Sunday, clutching a suitcase and a bouquet of flowers and wearing his Sunday best suit. "The herring are running," he announced: "The lads had to go out. We're hoping to buy a second boat if the catch is good this season." He kissed Emma awkwardly and put the suitcase down beside her bed. "Bess and the gals, they sent you some stuff. Baby clothes they don't need now."

Emma made herself smile and she murmured her thanks. She knew her sisters-in-law passed their used childrens' clothing from hand to hand, but she would never let little

Josh wear things another baby had worn before. "Thanks for coming, Pa. Sit down."

Manny sat. The baby was brought in to be admired. They made conversation of a sort. Joshua returned from making rounds at the hospital, and they had a roast pork and mashed potato lunch. By three Manny left, saying he had to catch the four P.M. train to Gloucester.

"That wasn't the best idea I ever had, was it?" Joshua said after Manny was gone.

"Maybe not," Emma agreed. "But it was well-meant and very thoughtful. I know that, darling."

Joshua took her hand and kissed her and they said no more about it. The only person not so easily placated was the cook. She grumbled for a week about all the food she'd prepared and had to throw out.

Four days later, on Thursday, there was a much more successful visit. Emma invited Celia for tea. It was served in Emma's rose-and-gray bedroom, at a table by the window looking out on the distant trees of the Public Garden and the Common beyond.

"It's proving a very mild winter," Celia said. "How marvelous."

Emma rested on a chaise longue, a lacy knitted blanket over her legs. She stretched her arms above her head, luxuriating in her returning feeling of wellness. The yellow silk kimono she wore slipped back and revealed her smooth, pale flesh. "I feel indulged by the weather as well as everything else." A shaft of late afternoon sun fell over her lap, it was deliciously warm. "I feel as if the whole world is celebrating my good fortune."

"Well said." Celia studied her young friend. "You may be the luckiest woman in the world, Emma Morgan. Look at you, young and lovely, with a handsome, successful husband who adores you, a beautiful, heathy son, a lovely home—and you've been given a brain that works better than average. What are you going to do with all those blessings?"

"I don't know. Just be Josh's wife and little Josh's mother for a while, I think. We've a baby-nurse now, but as soon as I'm strong enough I mean to let her go. I want to do everything for the baby myself."

Celia grimaced. "Well, that's your business. Frankly,

I'd be revolted, then soon bored to tears. I think I was
born a perverse old maid."

"It's different for you, Celia. You're a brilliant scientist
with a real contribution to make. Which reminds me,
anything new to report about the Landry potions?"

"Not a wretched thing. I despair, my dear. I've tried
every test I can think of, but if there's a scientific explanation, an ingredient that triggers uterine contractions, it
defies isolation by any means I can apply."

"You're not giving up, are you?"

"Almost, but not quite. I'm going to rerun one series of
tests. Only because I don't trust that stupid boy who calls
himself my assistant to have recorded the results accu-
rately. I do miss you, Emma."

"And I you. But I don't believe your assistant is stupid.
You wouldn't keep him on if he were."

"No, I'm being unfair. He's all right. He just happens to
be male, and he isn't you."

Billy-Jo came to 165 Commonwealth Avenue the next
morning. She and Emma had become friends, and she
brought a gift of a hand-knitted pale yellow carriage blanket for the new baby and a potted fern for Emma. They
had coffee in the bedroom and the baby was brought in,
and Billy-Jo held him and cooed and remarked at his
beauty. Then, after the nurse had taken Joshua Junior and
they were alone, Emma broke the disappointing news of
Celia's lack of results.

"But she hasn't found anything harmful in my potions,
has she?" Billy-Jo demanded.

"Not a thing. Celia would have said right away if there
was something suspect in your remedies. She thinks they're
harmless, but she just doesn't see how they can achieve
any good."

"They do," Billy-Jo insisted. "Not always, I told you that
from the first. Only sometimes. Most times, I think. And
no terrible bleedin' nor infections afterwards. So they're
much better than anything else."

Emma cocked her head and studied her friend. What a
rare person she was, this woman from Arkansas who had
come to Boston when she was fourteen because her mother
had what Billy-Jo called, "a gentleman friend." The other
woman's world was one Emma hadn't dreamed existed,

but the very differences in their backgrounds seemed to draw them close rather than divide them. "Don't fret," Emma said softly. "Celia would be the first to tell you that just because she can't prove something doesn't make it false. It may be something science doesn't yet have the means to understand. You go on as you are, Billy-Jo. Even Josh agrees that's the best plan."

What he had said was that Billy-Jo wasn't hurting anyone, so she might as well continue dispensing her potions. "Make some women feel better, anyway. And perhaps discourage them from pursuing their murderous intentions." Emma saw no need to quote him exactly.

"You mean Doctor Josh approves of my work now?"

"No, not exactly. He just doesn't disapprove quite so strongly."

Emma knew that part of Josh's softened attitude was because he'd come to appreciate the generosity of Billy-Jo's nature. He knew now everything Emma knew. That the "gentleman friend" who brought Billy-Jo and her mother to Boston was a wealthy man. That he'd bought them a house in Scollay Square and left Mrs. Landry quite a bit of money. That after her mother died Billy-Jo had no need to do the work she did. It involved long hours of pounding and blending and bottling, trips to the Ozark mountains to collect plants that didn't grow in Massachusetts, and constant counseling of the desperate women who came to her. For Billy-Jo this was a labor of love, a kind of crusade. Both the Morgans had come to understand and respect that.

"Josh admires your dedication," Emma said. In an odd sort of way it was true.

"Morgan here." Josh pressed the receiver of the telephone to his ear and listened for a moment. "Thank you, I'll come immediately."

Emma rolled over, and forced herself to wake up so the sense of surprise and panic would go away. Having a telephone by the bed was a new experience. Josh had had it installed a couple of months before. She knew it was efficient, but it still seemed an invasion of their intimacy. She reached out to touch him. "What time is it?"

Josh took her hand and pressed her palm to his lips.

"Five A.M. Go back to sleep, darling, I have to go to the hospital."

Another birth, Emma thought as she slipped again into slumber. That was nice. She was vaguely aware of Josh dressing, and of his lips brushing her forehead before he left the room.

"It doesn't seem connected to her prenancy," the nurse in the starched uniform said. "But since Mrs. Lord is your patient I thought you'd best be called."

"Exactly right, thank you."

Josh shrugged into a white coat and followed the woman through the private medical wing. He walked along a highly waxed and polished brown linoleum corridor, on either side of which were rooms for not more than two to four patients. Small electric bulbs spaced at three foot intervals lit the pristine white walls of the passage. The smell of carbolic permeated everything here, just as it did in the charity wards, but that was the only thing the two sections of Memorial Hospital had in common.

"I've put Mrs. Lord into a private room," the nurse said quietly.

Not, as Josh first thought, because the lady was the wife of Philip Lord, an architect of renown and affluence. A single glance told Josh why his patient had merited such treatment. Her face was deep red and her breathing was shallow and rapid. Josh picked up the clipboard hanging at the foot of the metal bedstead. Temperature of 103.7 and rising. None of her other vital signs were reassuring either. He stepped to the side of the bed. "Matilda, it's Doctor Morgan, can you hear me?"

The woman made a slight motion with her head. Her usually perfect blond hair was dank. The bed linen seemed to accentuate the flush of her face and neck. Josh placed a gentle hand over the swollen mound of her stomach. Matilda Lord was seven months pregnant. "Have you felt the child move, my dear?" The woman nodded. "That's fine," Josh murmured, reaching for his stethoscope.

"Doctor Morgan . . ." A young intern stepped from the shadows of the room. "I admitted Mrs. Lord, sir. Her husband brought her in. They live just around the corner so it seemed sensible, he said. He tried to telephone you, but he couldn't get through. Will you look at her tongue, sir?"

Josh did. He had intended to anyway. But his momentary annoyance at being told his job by a boy still in medical school faded the moment he saw the reason for the young man's alarm. Mrs. Lord's tongue was red at the edges and tip, gray furred in the center. Her taste buds were swollen and prominent. It was what laymen called "strawberry tongue," a classic symptom. So, too, the enflamed throat and the distended tonsils.

Josh straightened and suppressed a sigh. He stepped away from the bed and motioned the intern and the nurse into the corridor. "Full isolation procedure at once. Get her hair cut off and burned. Sponge baths every two hours and keep her skin moistened with a mixture of mineral oil and carbolic. Scrub everything in the room with potassium permanganate. And yourselves too," he added gravely.

"Scarlatina anginosa?" the intern asked. He couldn't quite suppress the tremor of fear in his voice.

"If we're lucky," Josh said grimly. "Scarlatina maligna if we're not. Too soon to tell. I'll alert everyone in any case."

Scarlet fever had come to Boston along with the budding daffodils of spring—a gift of the exceptionally mild winter.

By noon Memorial had six more cases, four of them children under eight, which surprised no one. Calls to three other hospitals produced the unwelcome information that the city had thirteen reported incidents, and God only knew how many more not yet brought to the attention of any medical authority. Worse, it was unquestionably scarlatina maligna, the most virulent form.

It was impossible to hospitalize every victim, and in any case, most families refused even to consider it. Instead quarantine signs sprouted like new grass, and the acrid smell of carbolic mingled with the constant smoke of the burning of hair, clothes, bed linen, and anything else that might have touched the afflicted. Black hearses plied the streets like trolleys. Josh thought of them as making regular runs that began and ended in the poorer neighborhoods. They were the worst hit, but scarlet fever was no respecter of class, the only generalization possible was that children were at the greatest risk. And pregnant women.

Matilda Lord and her unborn child died four days after

she was admitted to the hospital. Josh tried a cesarian section to save the infant, but the boy was dead before he was delivered. By April tenth when the epidemic was four weeks old, it had claimed upwards of three hundred lives, seventy percent of them children under ten.

During the first month of the siege no quarantine signs appeared on the Morgans' block. In the rare hours he spent at home Josh was grateful for that, and for Emma's calm and common sense. Every precaution that could be taken was, and while Josh was half dead with fatigue, he knew that he shared his condition with every other doctor and nurse in Boston. And he was glad he had nothing more to torment him than tiredness, and a sense of futility because there was so little anyone could do.

The disease struck where it would and ran its course. Some victims lived and others died. The best that medical science could offer was advice about how to prevent the spread of the infection, and vigilance to see that the rules were followed.

"We can do so little," Josh muttered to Emma in one of their rare moments together. "So pitifully, damnably little."

"You do your best, darling. I spoke with Celia today. She and three other chemists are working on some kind of vaccine theory. She doesn't hold out much hope, though."

"No, I suppose not. Is she well?"

"Yes, thank God. Billy-Jo too. Though Celia says Billy-Jo spends every waking minute in the West End and the North End nursing the poor. I wish I could join her." Josh looked up in alarm and Emma hastened to reassure him. "Don't worry, I know that's impossible because of little Josh. You'll have to do both our shares, my love. But then, you already are."

"Little enough," he said. "But I'm glad to know about Billy-Jo. Nice to think of her trying to save life rather than take it, for a change."

Toward the middle of May there was a sudden change in the weather. It turned cold and rainy and on two consecutive nights there was a touch of frost inland. Within a week the epidemic was perceived to be on the wane. Like everyone else, the Morgans began to believe the worst was over, so it was even harder to bear when, on the twentieth of the month, Professor Schoener was admitted to the hospital.

Josh battled for six days to save the old man's life, but the professor died on a Sunday at midnight, holding Joshua's hand. "There just wasn't any fight left in him," he told Emma. "His heart gave out when he was forced out of Memorial. Scarlet fever only finished the job."

Emma knew Josh was right, but it wasn't only the hospital. "It was the women too," she said. "All the patients who used to flock to him, hang on his every word. As soon as we got into the war they . . ." She shook her head. What was the point? They had said all this to each other before. She followed Josh into the library. He picked up the telephone and began making the funeral arrangements.

Emma watched him, thinking of her husband and of the professor. Joshua was so handsome with his dark hair falling over his forehead, with his jewel-green eyes, with the deep cleft in his chin. Had it been inevitable that Schoener's patients would demand to be treated only by Joshua, just as they had these past few months? Perhaps it would have come to that even if they didn't think of the professor as one of the "hated huns."

She wondered if Josh knew there was something magnetic about him, something almost animalistic that women responded to. No. She didn't believe he did. But she did remember his saying that making love could be like a medical examination. And vice versa? Perhaps. A small chill of jealousy crept up Emma's spine, tapped a message of distrust along her vertebrae. Stop it, she told herself. She was tired and upset and had to stop making burdens for her own back.

Schoener had not been a religious man. Nonetheless, they buried him from Trinity Church in Copley Square. "He always liked the building," Josh said. "It epitomized Boston for him, and he loved Boston."

A year earlier and the pews would have been crowded with mourners. Now there was only a handful of people from the hospital, those who somehow kept sane in these lunatic days of frenzied spy hunting, and half a dozen former patients. Joshua read the eulogy, and Emma had never been more proud of him.

"A man is judged not by the prevailing mood at the moment of his death, not even by the mood of his lifetime, but by history. History will record that this man was brilliant, compassionate, wise, that he strove always to do what was right, first for his patients and second for everyone with whom he came in contact. He was also a loyal man. Loyal to his discipline, his colleagues, and his adopted land. Helmut Schoener was, in every sense of the word, a good man. I loved him."

There was a thin, cold drizzle when the coffin was lowered into the ground. Emma remembered that it was just this sort of day when they'd buried her mother. Why did it always rain at funerals, she wondered.

"I'm needed back at the hospital, darling." Josh took her arm and pressed her close as they left the cemetery. "Can you get home on your own?"

"Of course. I'll take a cab."

She was grateful that Josh would have work to occupy him immediately. That was the best antidote to grief, and she knew Josh grieved more than he'd admit even to her. Emma grieved too. The professor had become such an intimate part of their lives since they came to Boston. All the way home she thought about his not being next door anymore, not coming to Sunday lunch, not watching little Josh grow up. She felt as if part of her had been amputated.

In the front hall she removed her black-veiled hat and put it on the console table and went to find the baby-nurse. "Is little Joshua sleeping?"

"Oh yes, ma'am. I checked him just fifteen minutes ago. Sleeping sound as you please."

Emma climbed the stairs, thinking that soon she'd have to engage a nanny for her son. She wanted to do everything herself, just as she'd told Celia, but she couldn't leave an ignorant maid in charge of her child and she couldn't stay in the house night and day, so a nanny would be needed. Maybe just part-time. She wondered if there was such a thing as a part-time nanny. Probably not.

Sighing she opened the door to the nursery. Its gay buttercup-yellow decor lifted her spirits. She walked on tiptoe, but the tiny four-month-old bundle beneath the white lace coverlet didn't stir when she bent over the crib. Her stomach did silly flip-flops. She loved him so much it was almost a physical pain. Impulsively Emma reached down and gathered her son into her arms. It was nearly time for his next feeding anyway, so there was no harm in waking him now. She held him close, feeling his tiny heart beat next to hers. Then she froze and held her breath, willing herself to be wrong, willing herself to be imagining things. But she wasn't. The child was on fire with fever.

Calm, she had to be calm. Her legs were shaking, but she forced herself to walk to the window and yank back the curtains. In the sudden daylight she saw the dark red flush on his cheeks and his neck. The baby woke just then, and whimpered. It was a strange, pained cry, unlike any she'd ever heard him utter. "Oh, God, no. Please no. Not my baby, please God." The words were a moan, a prayer of anguish. Then her last shred of control slipped away. Clutching the child to her breast, Emma ran through the house screaming. "Joshua! Get Joshua! Joshua, come save my baby!"

5

*F*orty-eight hours after the onset of his fever they buried Joshua Morgan, Jr. in a tiny grave next to the professor's. Now Emma neither wept nor screamed, she was simply ice through and through. At this funeral the sun shone brilliantly and birds chirped above the throng of mourners. Emma didn't see or hear them, and she didn't reflect on the fact that she'd been wrong about it always raining at funerals.

Celia Howard came up to her as the minister's last amen died away. The older woman's cheeks were tear-stained and heedless of propriety, she wrapped her arms around her friend. "Emma darling, I'm so terribly, terribly sorry. I wish I knew something to say to you, something that would help."

Emma stood stiff and totally unresponsive and Celia dropped her arms and turned away. She looked at Joshua. He, too, was stiff with grief and hard-won control, but his reserve did not have about it the same icy air of nonbeing that marked Emma's. "Doctor Morgan," Celia said softly. "Please accept my sympathy. And if there's anything I can do, if Emma needs me, don't hesitate to call."

"Thank you."

Celia watched him lead his wife to the black carriage with its four black horses wearing tall feathered plumes and jet-trimmed harnesses. How absurd were the carefully prescribed rituals with which the affluent interred their dead. It would be much healthier to scream and wail like some bereaved fishwife. Her eyes narrowed as she saw Emma disappear behind the black curtains of the coach. Much healthier indeed.

"A damned shame," a man muttered behind her. "So fast too. Not even time to get used to the idea before you're watching them lower the coffin."

"Yes," a woman's voice answered. "Such a pity. If it was only the old who died it wouldn't be so bad. Why must children always be so susceptible?"

"The small and the weak," the man said. "Sometimes I think weakness is the only truly punishable crime in the world."

Boston passed the summer licking its wounds, and taking comfort from the war news. In July the second battle of the Marne was won by the allies, and the newspapers predicted the hun would capitulate in a matter of days. It didn't happen quite that fast, but the end was definitely in sight. Joshua read the papers dutifully, and grunted responses when his hospital colleagues discussed the hopeful signs, but his heart was in no way lifted by the possibility of victory in a conflict that seemed more remote than ever. And less important. The battles lost in his own home were too painful and too immediate.

Emma remained in a world of silence. It seemed that neither kindness nor fury could reach her. Joshua tried both tacks, but each left the chasm between them as wide as ever. He wanted desperately to share Emma's pain, to let her share his; but she was isolated in an armor of ice that he seemed unable to melt.

A few times he turned to her in the night, hungry with a need that was more than physical, though it certainly was that. Emma lay stiff and still beneath him, neither repelling nor welcoming his lovemaking. It was a response far more terrible than refusal. On each occasion Josh was left feeling guilty of rape. It made his anger grow and crowded out his anguish and his sympathy.

"Dammit, what the hell do you expect of me?" he demanded one sultry August night when she had suffered his approach in silence and turned her face to the wall when he was done.

Spoken more for herself than for him, her answer was so

low he had to strain to hear it. "Nothing. I expect nothing from you or anything else in this life."

After that he continued to sleep beside her, but he never so much as touched her hand. Her rejection opened all the ancient wounds, the insecurities planted and nurtured on Eastern Point, and they bled. Joshua coped as he'd learned to cope in boyhood, by burying his feelings, by showing nothing.

Fortunately his professional life was becoming even more demanding now that Professor Schoener was gone. Schoener's will had canceled the Morgans' mortgage and also left to Josh the old man's house, everything it contained, and full title to the practice. Josh hired two more nurses and brought in a young doctor as an assistant. To accommodate the increased staff he turned the old laboratory on the third and fourth floors into another office and more treatment rooms. The fifth floor of 163 Commonwealth Avenue he simply shut off. Time enough later to decide what to do with it.

As if all this weren't enough, Schoener's mantle, both the early good and the recent bad, seemed to have descended on him. Josh felt its weight as he never had before. It seemed as if the eyes of the entire hospital staff were always on him. He returned home each evening with a dragging step and a downcast air.

"You look terrible tired, Doctor Josh," Billy-Jo said when she met him on the steps of his house one October evening. "You aren't getting any proper rest, I warrant. And it says in the bible, 'Physician, heal thyself.'"

"So it does, Billy-Jo. But I haven't time. Have you been to see Emma?"

"I been to try. She won't see me. Just tells the maid to send me away. Like always."

Josh sighed. "Yes, I know."

"What are we going to do about her, Doctor Josh? Emma can't go on like this. She's poisonin' her soul with sorrow."

"I know," Josh repeated. "I keep hoping that time will heal. I've tried everything else I can think of."

Billy-Jo shook her head. She wasn't wearing the big straw hat today, a small one instead, with a cluster of red wooden cherries on the brim. He could see her shining chestnut hair beneath the hat, and the way her olive-toned skin glowed with life. When she spoke he found himself listening to the lilt of her voice as well as her words.

"Miss Thelma from the Planned Parenthood League is goin' to send over some articles for Emma to edit. She told me Emma always did that work better'n anyone. Will you see she looks at 'em?"

"I'll try, but I don't hold out much hope. I've been thinking of sending her up to her father's in Gloucester for a little holiday. I suggested it before, but she refused. Maybe I should insist."

"Probably do her good to get away from here for a bit," Billy-Jo agreed.

It was like living beneath the glass dome of a bell jar, like seeing life happen all around, but being unable to make contact with its participants. Emma felt as if she were one of the little animals in Celia Howard's laboratory, a caged creature unable to understand what was happening or why, or communicate the terror it felt.

She slept and she woke, and she ate enough to stay alive, but only because her body was following a long-established rhythm of its own and change required more energy than acquiescence. The phlegmatic calm she projected, the meek way in which she allowed ordinary life to continue around her—all masked something Emma would not permit to surface. Inside her was turmoil and fear and a terrible rage she fought to suppress.

Sometimes it threatened to escape, to explode and erupt. Emma would not let that happen. She could not. An atavistic instinct for survival would not permit it. Somewhere deep in her mind Emma believed that if she once let her feelings surface they would destroy everything around her. The entire world would go up in flames, her fury was such that it would call down thunderbolts from heaven, or perhaps raise them from hell.

She locked her feelings deep inside herself, so deep even she did not know they were there. On the surface there was only the frightening placidity of one who has deserted all but the semblance of life.

"I've written to your father," Josh said one day in October. "He agrees it would be good for you to go up to Gloucester and have a rest."

Emma stared at him as if he were speaking a foreign tongue.

"Look, darling," Josh said, kneeling beside the chair where she spent almost all her waking hours. "You need a change. It will be nice to see your family again, won't it? You always liked Bess, she'll take good care of you—"

"I'm not going anywhere," Emma interrupted.

"You must," Josh insisted. "You have to do something to get yourself out of this mood."

Emma shook her head and merely by looking at her he knew it was useless.

Eventually she agreed to an alternative. Josh suggested a brief holiday in a hotel in Magnolia, the little hamlet between Gloucester and Manchester. It was a fashionable place in summer, but it would be all but deserted this time of year. "You can have a proper rest," he said. "And get lots of fresh air."

"Very well, if you like," Emma said woodenly. Her lack of interest was palpable.

Over the next few weeks Josh repeatedly told himself he'd sent Emma away for her own good, so she could be soothed and healed by her proximity to the sea and the scenes of her childhood. But he knew it wasn't just that; he wanted her in Magnolia as much for his sake as for hers. Emma in her present state was a constant reproach to him, a reminder of his own failure.

Still, nothing much changed in his devastated life after Emma was gone. Josh was carrying a weight of fatigue and disappointment that seemed heavier each day, in his way withdrawing from reality as much as she had. Until the evening of November 11, 1918.

That day Joshua attended a long and difficult labor which began in early afternoon and lasted well into the evening. When it was finally over he washed and dressed in the deserted changing room and ducked out a side entrance. His ploy allowed him to avoid speaking to anyone, but it didn't shorten his route home. Josh had to pass by the front of the hospital in order to get to Commonwealth Avenue. He dragged himself wearily around the corner— and found that he'd been thrust into a carnival.

People were everywhere. They waved flags, called greetings, danced in the streets. Joshua gaped in disbelief.

"What's happened?" he demanded of the first man he could collar.

"Where you been, Mac, in a convent? War's over, that's what's happened. The goddamn huns signed the armistice in France a few hours ago. Too damn good for 'em if you ask me. Should shoot the lot. But leastwise my boy will be coming home."

Joshua watched the man disappear into the milling crowd and a knot of envy rose like bile in his gorge. Joshua Morgan, Jr. would never come back. And there was nothing his father could do about it. Marvelous Dr. Morgan, who could work miracles for strangers, could do nothing for his wife, his only child, or himself.

He let the throng jostle him forward. They were headed away from Commonwealth Avenue. No matter, he didn't feel like going home to an empty, silent house. He moved with the merrymakers, hoping their mood would change his. A few men offered him whisky from bottles clutched in brown paper bags, and he drank deep of the raw spirit, knowing that sometimes it helped.

Eventually everyone converged on the Common. A podium had been hastily erected and Andy Peters, the new mayor, was speaking. It was impossible to make out the fiery oratory over the cheering crowd. No need to anyway, tonight Peters' words were predictable. Hooray for us and our wonderful victory, never mind the millions of lives here and in Europe that have been lost or ruined forever.

Joshua stood there for a few moments trying to hear, but he couldn't, couldn't enter into the spirit of the jubilant crowd either. There was no comfort for him here. He decided to go home to bed and he'd turned away when he felt a tug at the back of his black cashmere overcoat.

"Isn't it grand, Doctor Josh? Aren't you as pleased as you can be?"

"It is indeed grand, Billy-Jo. Are you down here celebrating?"

Billy-Jo smiled at him and said something that got lost in the din. He cocked his head to hear what she was saying; once more a burst of cheers from the crowd drowned out her voice. Joshua took her arm and guided her away from the crush around the speakers' platform. "Can't hear yourself think in this mob. How are you, Billy-Jo?"

"Fine. But you look tired as ever I've seen you. When did you last eat, Doctor Josh?"

"I don't remember. And please, won't you just call me Josh, without the title?"

She smiled. He saw that she had two deep dimples on either side of her wide mouth. Funny, he'd never noticed the dimples before.

"I'll call you Josh," she said. "If you'll promise to have some supper right away. You have to take care of yourself as well as your patients."

"Very well, but you must dine with me. Please say you will. I've eaten too many lonely meals lately."

Billy-Jo's brown eyes were large with sympathy. "I expect you have. Course I'll eat with you. If we can find someplace that ain't already full of folks."

They made their way as far as the Union Oyster House near North Station, checking every restaurant they passed. Each one had a line of people waiting for tables. The Oyster House, too, was crammed with noisy celebrators.

"Tell you what," Billy-Jo said. "My place ain't too far. You come on home with me, Josh. I'll fix us both something to eat, and you can take off your collar and tie and relax. Seems to me that's exactly what you need."

Her house was one of the last private residences in Scollay Square. Less than fifty years earlier the area had been as gracious as Beacon Hill. These days Scollay Square was the haunt of seamen in port for a few hours, looking for a less than legal good time. There were plenty of sailors in evidence tonight, but Billy-Jo's home was another world.

"This here's where I do my simpling and dispensing," she murmured, leading him quickly past a closed door. "Back here is the private part."

He was in a cozy sitting room with ruffled gingham curtains and a small dining table near the fireplace. Through a half-open door he could see a spotless and welcoming kitchen.

"Come sit with me while I figure what I can fix for our supper," Billy-Jo said.

He followed her and sat in a rocking chair with flowered cushions and watched while she poked up the fire in a big coal stove, and tied a checkered apron over her long and

flowing green dress. The apron changed her appearance.
She looked more feminine to him, less alien and exotic.

"Nice fresh eggs, home-fried potatoes and bacon. That
suit you?" she asked.

"Down to the ground." Josh grinned. No reason, except
the pure pleasure of being in warm, female company
again. "Did you really mean I could take off my collar and
tie?"

"I did indeed. And if you look in that cupboard over
there, you'll find a bottle of my elderberry wine. Don't
wrinkle your nose. It's real good."

It was at least potent. After a while Josh was used to the
taste, and he felt alive and tingling. He thought idly about
the wisdom of mixing wine with the whisky he'd drunk
earlier. What the hell, it was a special evening.

The food tasted delicious, maybe the best he'd ever
eaten. They talked easily together, and laughed a lot, and
made a toast each time Billy-Jo poured more wine. "To
the boys coming home," he said as he raised his fourth
glass.

"To the boys coming home," she echoed. Her eyes met
his over the rim. Their glance held for a moment, then she
turned away and began to clear the table.

They'd eaten in the kitchen at Josh's request. Now he
watched her working at the sink and noted the way the
ties of the apron accentuated her ample buttocks and slim
waist. His mouth felt dry. Quickly he drank another glass
of wine, then rose to help with the dishes.

"Here, don't you do that. I don't hold with men doing
women's work." She took the towel from his hands and
their fingers touched. They remained so for a few seconds,
until Billy-Jo broke the contact and put the towel on the
counter. The washing up wasn't finished, but she slowly
untied her apron and put it away. Then she held out her
hand.

Wordlessly Josh took it and wordlessly they walked up
the stairs to her bedroom. Billy-Jo didn't light the lamps,
but the sheer curtains let the moonlight into the room.
When she was naked, it bathed her flesh in an almost
mystical glow. "Come and love me, Josh," she said at last.
"Just for tonight. Cause we're both alone and sometimes
even the strong ones need comforting."

She was open and generous and wholly alive and Josh

rediscovered his half-quiescent manhood in the freedom of her loins. When he buried his face in the sweet smelling flesh of her breasts, he realized that he was crying, and when he tasted her mouth he drank a tonic much needed and long overdue. Then he didn't think at all, only felt. And allowed the pent up sorrow and hunger of many months to explode into her warm and welcoming depths.

"We won't ever talk about this," Billy-Jo told him in the gray light of dawn.

"No, but I'll never forget. Thank you, Billy-Jo."

For an answer she kissed him and sent him home through deserted streets littered with the discarded remains of celebration.

Emma stared at her clenched hands and listened to the pounding surf on the granite cliffs; it almost drowned out the hurtful, hateful words.

"You're acting like a selfish bitch. What right have you to wallow in self-pity?"

"Don't shout at me, Celia, I can't bear it."

Celia pulled her tweed coat tighter against the sea chill and the biting December wind. She hesitated a moment, feeling Emma's agony as if it were transmitted through the outcropping of stone on which they sat, then steeled herself. "I'm your friend, my dear, you know that. But I didn't come all the way to Magnolia to hold your hand and weep. It's been over half a year, past time for sympathy."

"I'm not asking for sympathy. I just want to be left alone."

"You can't be. You gave up that option the day you married Joshua. 'For richer, for poorer, in sickness and in health.' Those are the words, aren't they?"

Two gulls swooped toward them, flying in tandem, wing tips almost touching. Both women noted the passage of the birds. "Hundreds of women lost their children to scarlet fever last spring," Celia said. "Thousands more lose them to some catastrophe every day. You can't be exempt from grief, Emma. Besides, you're destroying Joshua. You have no right to do that."

"Josh is strong, and he has his work. Two days after we buried little Joshua the great Doctor Morgan was seeing patients. He has no idea how I feel, and he doesn't need me."

"That's not true. Emma, your husband goes around Boston like a man without a soul. And he'll never divorce you, the scandal would be appalling. So what choice are you leaving him?"

Celia shifted her position slightly and the wind caught her words, tossing them at Emma like a challenge "He can take a mistress, of course, and live in sordid secrecy for the rest of his life. You're consigning Joshua to being half a man. You're punishing him because your son died, despite his father's famous medical skills."

Emma rose, moved almost to the edge of the cliff, and stared out to sea. She was still young, still lovely, but there was a hardness in her face now, a careworn look, a narrowing of the once-generous mouth. Anguish was painted over beauty.

She stepped closer to the precipitous drop. "I don't blame Josh for my baby's death. I don't blame anyone. I just cannot live with the pain."

For a fraction of a second Celia had the impression that Emma meant to hurl herself forward over the edge. Instinctively she half-rose and stretched out her hand. Nothing happened and she drew back. "The alternative to living with it is unthinkable," she whispered.

"Perhaps," Emma said.

They were silent for some minutes. A whistling buoy called mournfully in the distance. Emma shuddered, visibly shook off the mesmerizing grip of the vista, and faced Celia. "Shall we go back? It's getting cold."

As Josh had pointed out two months before, Magnolia was a summer resort. They were alone in the hotel. Emma ordered tea. When it came, it was an insipid brew served by a slatternly waitress who obviously resented their presence in this out-of-season time. Half an hour passed in stilted conversation. At last they could find no more trivia to discuss.

"I'll go with you to the train station, shall I?" Emma asked.

Celia nodded. "That would be nice, if you're not too tired."

There was one local taxi, a Model-T Ford driven by a man whose name Emma didn't know. He took them three miles down the coast to Manchester and parked beside the station. Emma asked him to wait, then got out and walked with Celia onto the platform. They were early. It wasn't yet five, but the evening star twinkled in the pewter sky-of winter.

Celia couldn't bear to leave with so much unsaid. "I didn't mean to be offensive," she murmured. "It's only that you have so much to give, and we all need you. Not just Joshua."

Emma felt something start to come apart inside her, the brittle veneer of control. Through stiff lips she asked, "Does Josh have a mistress? Is that what you're trying to tell me?"

"My dear, I don't know. Really. It wouldn't surprise me, that's all. Sooner or later."

"Yes, I suppose you're right." She was amazed at how much the idea hurt. The thought of Joshua in the arms of some other woman was startlingly painful. Emma had thought herself incapable of feeling any new pain.

Emma woke the next morning with a sudden sense of purpose, though she didn't know to what end. On impulse she asked the waitress who served her breakfast to send for the village taxi once more.

"Where to, ma'am?" the nameless driver asked.

"Gloucester, the bottom of Main Street will do."

Emma was almost alone after the taxi drove away, there were few people on Main Street this icy December day. Cold winds blew in from the harbor and the sullen sky threatened snow. She walked slowly, looking at the familiar shop windows. Browns Department Store had a display of layettes, little shirts and blankets and booties of lace and pink-and-blue ribbons. Emma shuddered and turned aside.

"Emma! It is you, isn't it? For heaven's sake, what are you doing here?"

Her sister-in-law's voice intruded on Emma's reverie and demanded a response. "Oh, hello, Bess. I'm just having a look around. I've been staying in Magnolia."

"Right down the road in Magnolia, and you never let a body know. So like you, Emma. Well, come along. You look perished with cold, and you're coming home with me for a bit. Don't argue because I won't listen." Bess Silva took Emma's arm while she chatted about local news, her warmth saying what her words did not, that the family knew about the death of Emma's child and sympathized.

When they reached Friend Street and started up the steep hill, Emma turned and looked out over the harbor. A few boats rode at anchor, but she did not see her father's among them.

Bess saw the direction of her glance. "They went out yesterday, headed up toward Georges Banks. Weather's not too bad yet. Bound to get worse, best they try for a catch while they can."

They reached Bess's house, the house where Emma herself had been born. When Emma stepped inside, it was as if she were a little girl again. The place looked and felt the same. She was baby Emma once more, tagging behind mama, going to the kitchen and smelling the good warm smells of childhood.

"Won't take me a moment to get the coffee going," Bess said. "Or maybe cocoa would be better for you. You're looking awfully peaky, Emma."

"Cocoa would be lovely, thank you." Sometimes when the catch had been particularly good and there had been a few pennies to spare, Jessica had bought cocoa for her daughter. Emma associated it entirely with this room.

"Kids are all at school," Bess said. "We've an hour of peace, thank God. Much as I love them, the six of them sure can wear me out."

She was a short, fat woman, with none of Jessica's faded beauty or her inbred gentility, but when Bess reached down the same mugs that Jessica had used, she reminded Emma so much of her mother it was painful.

"Here you are, drink it while it's hot. And eat your bread." Bess pushed a thick slice of fragrant yellow Portuguese sweet bread slathered with butter across the table. Emma hadn't thought she was hungry, but she ate every crumb and accepted a second slice.

"How are things with all of you?" she asked, suddenly afraid that she was taking food from the family's mouth. Bess would never accept money from her, she knew that.

"We're doing fine, Emma," Bess said softly. "Don't worry. Fishing's still a hard life, but with four of them and two boats, well, it's not like it was when you were little."

Emma was reassured. She smiled and wondered what to say next. What did she have to talk about with this kind-hearted busy woman, the shape of whose days were so different from her own.

Bess didn't wait for her to say anything. "I was real sorry to hear about your baby, Emma. We all were. Read about it in the paper here. No, don't turn away. Talk about it, sometimes that helps."

Emma blinked away the rush of tears. "I can't."

"It eases the hurt," Bess insisted. "I know. I miscarried last year. Henry didn't understand my grieving. To a man it's not real till it's born. But it ain't like that with us, it's different. Different after they're born too. Men love their children—I'm not saying they don't—but it's not the same, is it?"

"No, it's not. Joshua has his work and whatever he says, that fills up so much of him he doesn't have a lot of room left for sorrow. He's not empty like I am."

Bess nodded. "I know. Sometimes I wonder about that. What with this war and so many women going out to work. Things gotta be different, don't they. Better, maybe. Maybe it's smart for women not to let themselves get too wrapped up in always worrying about kids and men. Though Lord knows what Henry would say if he heard me talking like this."

She laughed and that set her double chin to quivering. "Only, how's it going to be now that it's over and the boys are coming home? It will go back the way it was, I expect. But the taste of freedom's bound to stay in their mouths, isn't it Emma?"

"Maybe. I had a job in Boston, before little Josh was born." Emma spoke slowly at first, then the words came faster. All at once she had a great need to confide, to talk to someone who was approachable because they sat together in this place that was so achingly familiar. "I loved working. It was, I don't know . . . I guess the word is exhilarating. I took the job because I needed something to keep me occupied and stop me from worrying about not having a baby, but in the end it was more than that."

"Took you a long time to get in a family way, didn't it?" Bess poured the last of the cocoa into Emma's mug. "Funny how it's like that for some women. Not me. All Henry's got to do is look at me and my belly's full."

They laughed together. How long had it been since she'd laughed. Emma couldn't remember. "Listen, Bess, have you ever heard of Planned Parenthood?"

Bess shook her head, then listened wide-eyed while Emma explained.

"Could you get me one of them things?" she demanded as soon as she understood. "One of them cap things? Emma, if they really work it could change my life, every woman's life." She blushed and it made her look young and vulnerable. "I mean, if you could love your man without worrying, what a difference that would make. I know you and a lot of women have the opposite problem, but it's all part of the same thing, isn't it?"

That was exactly what she'd said to Josh so long ago, about Alice Crane and Rosa Tecci. "Yes, it is. Listen, if you can get down to Boston, I can arrange for you to be fitted for a cervical cap. Some friends of mine run a little office of the Planned Parenthood League. We know a nurse who fits ladies for caps." She leaned forward and took her sister-in-law's hand. "Bess, it's illegal, you have to understand that. And the Catholic Church is bitterly opposed."

Bess snorted. "Men make the laws, don't they, Emma? In courts and in church. It seems to me this is something we women have to decide for ourselves. I'll send you a note saying when I can come. After you go home, that is. How long you gonna stay in Magnolia?"

"I'm not sure." Emma thought of Joshua and all the things Celia had said, and of Bess and the different but essentially same things they'd talked about this morning. "I'll let you know when I go back. I don't think it will be very long now. I'm feeling much better."

On Christmas Eve Joshua sat alone in his cheerless house. He'd given the servants the holiday off. And he'd not seen Billy-Jo Landry since Armistice Day. This afternoon he'd been tempted to go to Schollay Square and ask her to spend tonight with him. But he hadn't done it, he'd lost his nerve—or found it—at the last minute. Tomorrow wouldn't be so bad. He'd go to the hospital and free some other doctor to spend Christmas with his family. There were only a few more hours to get through.

When the bell rang he thought it was carolers and he was tempted not to answer. It rang again. Insistently. He went to the door.

"Merry Christmas, Josh."

"Emma. My God, I don't believe it. . . ." He stared at her as if she were a mirage.

Emma stretched out both her hands. "It's me, Josh. Don't look so startled, I'm not a ghost."

"No, of course not." Still he hesitated before taking her hands. When he did, her kid gloves felt incredibly sensuous, the warmth of her flesh seeping through them. He drew her forward, closing the door with his foot because he didn't want to release his grip on her. And all at once he felt like a gawking adolescent, shy and tongue-tied. He dropped her hands. Emma said nothing, stricken by the same awkwardness.

He studied her surreptitiously, as if she were not his wife, as if he didn't have the right. She wore the cloak he'd given her the Christmas before, navy blue with a silver fox collar that framed her face. A matching Russian style fur hat covered her red-gold hair. She was thin and pale, but also elegant and lovely. And somehow remote.

"Let's go into the library," he said. "It's warmer."

Emma nodded and led the way, and he held the door for her and waited until she'd entered. Formality was protection, it masked the drama and uncertainty of the moment. Joshua sought release in action; he poked up the fire and poured her a large brandy and insisted she drink it against the chill. "Why didn't you let me know? I'd have come to get you. You shouldn't have traveled all this way alone."

Emma warmed her hands at the fire and looked around. She didn't respond to his question, only said, "There's no Christmas tree."

"No, I'm sorry. If I'd known—"

"It's my fault. I should have been here to make all the holiday arrangements." The words dropped into the depth of silence between them. Emma looked not at him but at the flames. Her voice was very small when she asked, "Do you still love me, Josh?"

He took a deep breath and moved closer to her, at last daring to put his hands on her cheeks and turn her face to his. "I've loved you since the first day I looked into your extraordinary eyes, my darling. I always will love you." The words rose up from a place deep inside him.

"You haven't found someone else in the meantime?" Still very low, frightened, tentative.

His heart lurched. "Never anyone to take your place," Josh said. It was true, even if it was a lie of sorts.

"I'm so glad." Then, with sudden urgency and a boldness entirely new, she said, "Please, let's go upstairs."

Joshua caught his breath, a flood of desire poured through him, tightening his groin, making him light-headed. He nodded and took her hand, the flesh burning where they touched. They moved in a shared white-hot web of need and hunger.

In the big familiar bed it was different from any time before. It was affirmation and reunion, and though neither could have explained, both punishment and forgiveness. Emma felt entirely wanton, utterly naked. She wanted to suck him into her body, to possess him entirely. Her nails dug into the flesh of his shoulders and her long legs gripped his hips, and she grasped his thrusting member, rising to meet it, to take it deeper.

When it was over she lay beside him panting, and Joshua held her tenderly, gently stroking her shoulders and her back. But she didn't feel fragile, Emma felt incredibly strong.

6

"Josh, the funniest thing has happened. Billy-Jo's gone."

They were at breakfast two weeks after Emma's return. "What do you mean, gone?" Joshua didn't look up from his grapefruit.

"Just what I said. I went to her house yesterday and it was locked up tight. There was a real estate agent's sign nailed to the front door. I went to see him and he says Billy-Jo told him she was going back to Arkansas because she was tired of the Boston winters. That's crazy after all these years. Don't you think so?"

Josh watched the January snow swirling outside the windows, afraid to meet Emma's eyes. "Yes, in a way I suppose it is. But she's always been unique."

The mixture of relief and guilt he felt almost made him ill. He had wondered how it would be when he saw them together, his wife and the woman with whom he'd been unfaithful. Now that might never happen. Emma was still speaking.

"I asked if she'd left a forwarding address, but she didn't. Just sold the house and took off. Celia thinks Billy-Jo had everything planned. A week ago she gave Celia a large supply of her potions for testing. I took three little bottles home."

His head snapped up and he stared at her. "Why? Emma, surely you'd never want to terminate a pregnancy. I mean if—"

"Of course not. I simply want to keep some of her things, in case she comes back. It's silly, I suppose. But I really love Billy-Jo. I'm going to miss her."

Joshua drank his coffee and didn't reply.

The winter was long and cold and dreary, as Boston winters usually were, but the Morgans enjoyed it. Without a great deal of discussion, and certainly no objections from Joshua, Emma went back to work in Celia's laboratory. Joshua's expanded practice grew ever larger and more lucrative. Yet, despite all this activity they seemed to draw closer together, to enjoy each other more.

There was one domestic crisis. The maid decided to return to her family in South Carolina, and the cook, for some reason best known to herself, chose the same week to quit without notice. "The servant problem," Emma said with disgust. "How I hate women who are always going on about it. Now I'm doing the same thing myself."

"Don't worry about it, darling," Josh said. "Call an agency and have them send over some women for interviews."

Emma grimaced at his offhand manner, but she didn't say anything. Men always assumed that whatever else their wives did, they'd also take full responsibility for managing the household. Joshua was no exception, and ultimately neither was she. "I'd never let him do it," she told Celia. "But it annoys me when he assumes he doesn't have to."

"Perversity, Eve's legacy," Celia said tartly. "Pass me those test tubes please."

Emma handed them over, still thinking of her domestic crisis. "I'll have to take a couple of days off until I get this business sorted out." She sounded guilty and she felt it. Celia was a fool to put up with her. She'd have less to worry about with a female assistant who wasn't married, or a man with a wife to look after him.

"Of course," Celia said easily, her head bent over a microscope. "Just get back as quickly as you can. I'm lost without you, Emma."

It was a marathon; Emma interviewed six cooks and four housemaids in one day. By five in the evening she was exhausted and defeated. Not one of them had been suitable. Then the bell rang.

"I'm Tessie Marsh, ma'am. And this is me sister, Nora. The agency sent us about positions as cook and general maid." The woman handed over a letter and Emma motioned the two of them to chairs while she looked over the reference. It was good, excellent in fact. They'd been with one family the last nine years. "And before that?" she asked, looking closely at the pair.

"We was in England, ma'am. Born in London we were. I'm thirty and Nora here is twenty-seven. Never been married, neither of us. We been in service since our ma died. I was thirteen then and Nora was ten. Started as scullery maids, we did. But ten years ago we took it in our heads to come to America. A little adventure, you know. Been here ever since. We're both citizens now," she added proudly. "Went to night school so we could pass the test."

"Excellent," Emma said. "But you have to understand, this is a doctor's household, and I work as well." It came out like a set speech because she'd been saying the same thing all day. She waited for a reaction, there was none. She went on. "Sometimes meals must be delayed, or there are emergencies in the middle of the night."

"That don't bother us none, does it, Nora?" Nora shook her head and Tessie continued speaking. "And we work real hard. Nora cleans fit for Buckingham Palace. And I'm a good cook, if I do say so myself."

"Yes, I'm sure . . ." Emma liked them. They were the first applicants who hadn't raised an eyebrow when she said she worked, nor asked about children. She'd had a few today who had obviously assumed that any household where the wife worked must be preparing for the poorhouse, and others who seemed to think a childless woman was a criminal. "Let's try each other, shall we?" she said brightly.

Tessie looked at Nora, Nora looked at Tessie, then they both looked at Emma and nodded in unison. "Just one thing, ma'am." Tessie was still the spokeswoman. "Do you think we could start right away? Our lady from before died," she pointed to the reference Emma still held. "That's why that there reference came from the lawyer. Well, truth is, he's not anxious to have us stay in the house, wants to sell it you see. So we'd just as soon get out quick as we can."

"The sooner the better, as far as I'm concerned. When would suit you?"

Tessie twisted a pair of cotton gloves in her lap and spoke in a very soft voice. "Do you think it could possibly be tonight, ma'am? We could go get our things tomorrow."

Emma smiled. "I don't see why not." She stood up and led them to the kitchen.

Two hours later her judgment was confirmed. "Josh, taste this chicken fricassee, it's marvelous."

"Good biscuits too," he said, reaching for another one.

When the lightest imaginable lemon soufflé appeared for dessert, Emma was convinced she had stumbled on a pair of angels.

"Well, that's it, thank God." Celia looked out the window of the lab on the sunny morning of June fourth, 1919.

On the street below a newsboy was hawking his papers, "Votes for ladies! Women in the polling booth! Read all about it . . ." Congress had passed the nineteenth amendment, no citizen could be denied the right to vote because of sex.

Emma leaned over her shoulder. "So the suffragettes have carried the day." She moved away and poured each of them a cup of coffee from a pot brewed over a Bunsen burner. "How is it going to affect us, do you think? Will life change dramatically? Will we feel different?"

"I doubt it." Celia took a chipped mug in her square, capable hands and raised it in salute. "But let's drink to the suffragettes. A lot of women have gone through hell to make this possible."

For a time they were silent, each lost in her own thoughts of the battle waged and won. "I didn't always admire their methods," Emma said finally. "A lot of it was pretty wild and, well . . . degrading. But," she looked suddenly shy, "Celia, to tell the truth, I'm excited. I feel like a whole person. As good as any man. I can vote. The only thing is, I didn't take part in the fight and I feel guilty about that."

"Rubbish." Celia finished her coffee and set down the mug. "Nobody can fight every battle. I marched for women's suffrage in New York in 1912. Fifteen thousand of us, straight down Fifth Avenue. You were what then, sixteen?"

"Seventeen, and my head was full of nothing but Joshua Morgan. That was the year before we got engaged."

"Then you won't remember. It was quite something, all those women, a sea of women, every size and shape and age and class. And half the population of New York City jeering on the sidelines, throwing garbage and old shoes and God knows what else. Not just men, by the way. There were plenty of women who were appalled at the idea of suffrage for ladies. They felt threatened, I guess. I see that now, but at the time, they just made me furious. I got hit in the face with a rotten egg thrown by a little blond girl who looked like a fairy princess. How I hated her."

"And then?" Emma asked.

"And then I met Margaret Sanger and I knew where my deepest sympathies lay. So I chose my fight. As you've chosen yours. There's nothing to be guilty about."

"That's another thought, what about birth control? Do we have a better chance now? Are voting women going to help to make it legal?"

"That's the question, isn't it?" Celia said thoughtfully. "Wouldn't it be nice to think so, to imagine a great sister-hood rising up and demanding freedom from biological slavery." She reached for a test tube. "Frankly, I'm not going to hold my breath till it happens."

In July Emma announced that she was three months pregnant. "I didn't tell you earlier, Josh, because I wanted to be sure."

They were in bed together in the lovely rose-and-gray room. He pulled her closer, kissing the top of her head. "I understand. It's the best news in the world, darling."

"Yes, it is." Emma pulled back slightly so she could look at him. "Josh, this time I want to keep working until the last possible minute. I have to because there will be too much time to brood and worry otherwise."

He nodded agreement. "Yes, I see that. As long as your health's not in danger."

"I've already been to see Charles West, to confirm my suspicions. He'll have to see me through the whole preg-nancy this time, not just the delivery." For a moment they were both silent, thinking of Professor Schoener. "I didn't tell Charles I planned to go on working," Emma added finally. "I don't want a big fight with him over it."

"I'll speak to him," Josh promised.

The next night he came home looking preoccupied. "Emma, sit down, darling. I have to talk to you."

"About what?" She studied his face. "Josh, what's wrong?"

"Nothing's wrong . . . exactly."

"Tell me. For God's sake, Josh, tell me."

He took both her hands in his. "I spoke with Charles West today. He says you're as healthy as can be and, if you and I agree that you should go on working, it's all right with him. But . . ."

"Yes?"

"But he thinks he heard two heartbeats when he examined you. He's not absolutely sure, it's impossible to be sure. But there's a good chance you're carrying twins."

For a long moment she couldn't say anything, she opened her mouth, but no words came. Then she simply repeated the word. Twice. "Twins. Twins."

"I know, it's pretty overwhelming, isn't it?"

"Two babies."

"Yes," he said gently, a smile beginning to play around his lips. "That's what twins usually means. Two babies."

"Joshua," she said very softly. "I don't know if I can do this . . . carry two babies, give birth to two of them. And afterward, I can't even imagine what it will be like coping with two infants. But, well, to tell the truth, I think it's pretty wonderful."

He hooted with laughter and hugged her. "So do I, Mrs. Morgan, so do I. I think it's marvelous and you're an amazon." He sobered and held her yet more tightly. "I was so hoping you'd see it that way. I've delivered twins a few times. It's wonderful, Emma. The whole miracle done twice at one time."

Emma wondered if it also meant twice as much pain in labor. She decided she'd rather not know and she didn't ask.

She took to knitting baby sweaters in the evenings. "I have to start early," she explained. "Since there has to be two of everything."

"It's not certain," Josh warned her repeatedly.

"I know," Emma always said. But she went right on planning in pairs. And by late August she was past doubt.

"Look at me, Josh." She smoothed her black skirt over an already enormous belly. "I'm not five months along yet, but I'm big as a house."

They were in the library on a muggy evening. The windows were all open, no breeze cooled the night, but the lights of Boston winked prettily. "A nice house," he said, patting her belly. "Sort of a grand mansion."

Emma giggled. "That's one way to put it."

Josh looked suddenly perplexed. "Emma, how could any woman hate her own child?"

"I don't know. It seems impossible. What made you think of that?"

"Something that happened today. One of my patients asked me flat out to abort her."

"Oh, Lord, the poor thing. I take it she's not married."

"It's not that." He shook his head. "The poor thing, as you mistakenly call her, is very much married. To a wealthy banker. They have three children. The plain truth is that she's a spoiled, selfish woman who is apparently capable of hating her own child enough to want to murder it."

Emma stared at the knitting in her hands, tiny little sleeves that please God would soon be filled with chubby, tiny little arms. She pressed her hands to her stomach. "It's not that simple, Josh. It can't be. You don't understand. You've never been pregnant and you never will be. But the bond is almost instantaneous. No woman would want an abortion unless she was desperate."

"What can she be desperate about? No, the truth is she doesn't want to disturb her vacation plans. They were going to Europe for two months in the autumn."

"It has to be more than that."

"No," he insisted. "Selfish and spoiled. And I told her so."

Emma pursed her lips. He'd never understand. No man would ever understand. She went back to her knitting.

A week later, at three in the morning, their front door chimes rang incessantly. "Must be some kind of emergency," Josh muttered. "Stay here, I'll go."

Emma rolled over and drifted back into sleep. Emergencies in the middle of the night weren't that unusual in a doctor's house. Funny whoever it was didn't telephone though . . . The next thing she knew Josh was shaking her.

"Wake up, darling. Put on a robe and come to the office will you? I need help. Be as fast as you can, please," he added as he left.

She hadn't time to wonder what kind of help or why. She did as he asked and hurried next door. He'd left the street door of 163 unlocked, and when she got into the front hall she saw a thin sliver of light from one of the treatment rooms. That door was ajar too. Emma let herself in.

A woman was lying on the examining table. The white sheets beneath her were soaked in blood. Josh was bent over his patient, and he didn't lift his head when he issued instructions. "I've turned on the sterilizer. It will be ready in a few minutes. Meanwhile you'll find sutures and bandages in that cabinet on the left. First wash your hands very carefully in the sink over there. Use that brown soap. Then put on the rubber gloves and bring me the sutures. Hurry, Emma. There's no time to lose."

She took a deep breath and moved to the sink, casting sideways glances at the patient on the table. After she finished washing, she pulled on the gloves and stepped to Josh's side.

"She's unconscious," he said. "No time to deal with that now. And it's a good thing."

Emma had never seen so much blood; the woman's thighs were awash in it; a thin stream was still trickling from her vagina. The flesh all around was savaged, hacked with cuts that were also bleeding. It was horrific. Fresh blood had a smell, she'd never realized that. It was sickly sweet. She felt faint and took a deep, loud breath.

Josh glanced at her. "Steady," he muttered. "Don't quit on me."

"I won't."

"Good girl. Another suture, please."

She worked beside him for twenty minutes. Her nausea suppressed by her fascination with his competence. Josh's hands were like an artist's, they danced. And she was so incredibly awkward. The third member of the drama, the woman on the table, moaned occasionally, but she didn't come to. Once Emma raised her head and looked at her. About thirty she guessed. Not pretty, but well cared for. Her clothes and her hair and her skin all said she was fastidious, and could afford to be. But not below the waist.

"That's it," Josh said tying the last suture. "That's got it,
I think. Now we just have to pray there's no infection."

"What happened to her?"

"Nothing 'happened to her.' These are self-inflicted
wounds. The stupid, selfish little fool went to some abortion butcher in the North End. When she started to gush
blood, she came to me."

"Dear God. She's the woman you were telling me about
last week, isn't she? The one who's married to a banker."

"The same. I can't take her to the hospital. There would
be too many questions. Her husband's a prominent man,
and a big contributor to Memorial. We'll have to keep her
in our house, Emma. At least until some other arrangements can be made."

"Yes, of course. What about her husband?"

"I'm going to call him. He won't thank me for being the
bearer of evil tidings, but it will be worse if I drag him and
his wife into a court case."

They carried the patient—Josh said her name was Sara
Lewis—to one of the bedrooms next door in 165. "I thought
of the professor's old apartment, but she can't be left alone
tonight. I'm sorry about all this, darling."

"It's all right, I don't mind." Emma stroked Sara Lewis's
forehead and adjusted the pillows of the bed in the guest
room. "Poor thing," she murmured. "Poor thing."

Josh stared at her for a moment. "I think you're mad."
He left to telephone the banker, still shaking his head.

The next day they moved Mrs. Lewis to her own home.
Josh had found a competent nurse whose discretion could
be relied on. "What a mess. The man's furious, and no
wonder. But she brought it all on herself after all," he told
Emma that night.

"Not exactly."

"What do you mean?"

"We talked. This morning before you moved her. I
guess she just needed to unburden herself to someone."

"Oh, and what did she say? 'Sorry about that, I'll pick a
better abortionist next time'?"

"Josh, you are being a narrow-minded, prejudiced bigot.
A pig. It's not her fault. It's her damned husband's. That
wealthy banker you're so anxious not to offend. He has a
mistress, a bit of something on the side, as the saying
goes. And his wife adores him, though I can't think why.

Last time she was pregnant he complained constantly that she looked awful, fat, and ugly. He said he couldn't take her anywhere. That's when he took up with the other woman. Mrs. Lewis was desperate when she realized she was pregnant again. They were trying to patch things up, had planned a trip to England as a kind of second honeymoon. Then you wouldn't help her, so . . ." She shrugged.

"That's quite a story," he said softly. "Do you believe it?"

"Every word. You would, too, if you'd heard her tell it."

"I see."

She turned to him, not as swiftly as she might have a few months past before her bulk made her so ungainly. "Do you think I'm fat and ugly?"

"I think you're beautiful. Don't look like that, I mean it. I love you and I love them." He reached out to pat Emma's belly but she moved away. "I got a big contribution out of Lewis," he said.

"Wonderful. Is that supposed to soothe his conscience or yours? And what's it going to do for Sara?"

"I don't know. It's for the charity wards at Memorial. Two thousand dollars, because I told him I wouldn't take a fee."

Emma shook her head. "Josh, I know you mean well. I know you're a good man, a wonderful man. And I love you, you know that. But you're being so stiff-necked about this abortion business. It can't be as simple as you're making it, it just can't."

"It's murder. I'm a doctor and I can't sanction murder."

She took his slender, so capable hands in hers. "Listen to me, I've been thinking about it a lot. Two people make a pregnancy, but only one has to bear any visible consequences. Men take off, or deny their fatherhood, or God knows what, and there's the woman left with the whole burden."

"It's not a burden, not something impersonal, Emma. It's a child, goddammit."

"I know. But when?"

"What do you mean, when?"

"When is it a child, a human being? Celia and I talked about it this afternoon. Don't look like that, I didn't mention any names. Besides, Celia's as trustworthy as the archangel Gabriel. Anyway, she says that if abortion was

legal it could be done safely in the first month or two. Is a
fetus a child, a real child, in the first month or six weeks?
You're not even sure you're pregnant then."

Josh shook his head stubbornly. "It's going to be a child.
That's beyond doubt. I approve of Margaret Sanger, I
approve of contraception, you've heard me say so a thousand times."

"It's not the whole answer. Something has to be done,
something to give women a choice. If it isn't, Josh, I think
women may rebel in a way men will find very unpleasant."

He took his hands from hers and cupped them either
side of her face, tipping it to the light. "Do you know the
only other thing I've ever heard you speak about this
strongly? Your own need for a child. When we were first
married and you didn't get pregnant right away."

"That's true," she admitted. "It's two sides of the same
coin. I've been saying that so often, I'm beginning to bore
myself, but it's true."

"Okay, we'll leave it for the moment. Come to bed,
darling. You must be exhausted."

She was, but she couldn't sleep. She lay in the crook of
Joshua's arm and thought about Bess. Her sister-in-law
had come to Boston to be fitted for an illegal cap last
week. She hadn't told Josh about that. Everything to do
with their old life in Gloucester seemed so far behind
them now. She didn't think Josh liked to be reminded of
it. But she would never forget the way Bess had looked
when she put her on the train to go home. Triumphant,
that was the only word. She had triumphed over something, wasn't a victim anymore. But over what? Men?
God? Nature? Destiny?

Emma and Joshua spoke about it once more, the next
evening. They'd gone for a walk in the still-sultry, late
summer evening, moving slowly because of Emma's un-
gainliness. When they got to the Charles Embankment,
the air was a little cooler and fresher and they sat on a
bench and watched the boats and the people. "I've been
thinking about the two sides of your coin," Josh said.

"And?"

"And I'm sure you're right, about the basic nature of the
problem, I mean. If we understood fertility, what makes
conception happen, we'd be on our way to solving the
whole thing."

"When will we understand it?"

"God knows. There's not a lot of research being done."

"Women aren't important enough to warrant a lot of research," Emma said bitterly.

"That's silly. It's the future of the race we're talking about."

"But nothing much is happening."

"No," he agreed. "Nothing much."

"What are you going to do about that, Josh?"

He took her hand. "Listen, darling, I have you to think about, our lives, the lives of these twins we may be having. What influence I have I use to move the profession in the direction I want it to go, but I can't put our whole future at risk and start sounding like a crank with a bee in his bonnet."

But that was why they had come to Boston in the first place, Emma thought. That was what Josh used to dream about. Before he became addicted to hero worship, to being the famous Dr. Morgan whom the ladies adored. She pushed the thought aside as disloyal. Besides, she understood it. Who could resist such power? She wished they weren't in public, so she could kiss him. She took his hand instead. "Let's go home, Doctor Morgan."

"Peace?" Josh asked.

"Peace," Emma agreed.

"Pass me that stove blacking."

Nora sipped her tea and looked from Tessie, on her knees in front of the stove, to the can of polish on the kitchen table. "You just blacked that thing an hour ago."

"I see a spot I missed." Tessie got up and fetched the can herself. For a minute or two she rubbed at the offending mark as if it were a mortal enemy, then raised her head. "What time is it?"

"Fifteen minutes past the last time you asked. Nearly noon. What are we having for our lunch?"

"Lunch? Nora Marsh, I swear I don't understand you. Here we are with the best job we ever had, no butler or housekeeper to tell us what to do, just you and me on our own. And the nicest mistress, even if she does go out to work like common folks, and her in God knows what kind of agony. And you're asking about lunch."

"It ain't agony, she's having a baby, that's all. And we

have to eat. Have to keep up our strength, especially now there's going to be more work in the house."

Tessie put down the blacking cloth and wiped her eyes with a corner of her apron. "Two babies," she corrected. "Doctor says it's probably twins. And it is agony. I remember when you was born. I was only three and they kept me in the next room, but I remember how Ma screamed."

"I'm hungry," Nora said. "And it's true, you know. There's gonna be more work."

"I don't mind. Long as there's work, I don't care how much."

Nora eyed her sister. "Do you mean you think we're gonna get the sack? Why should you think that?"

"Not the sack. But what if she dies? Cor', Nora, you seed the size of her belly these last few weeks. Got to be bloody hard givin' birth to two babies that big. Dangerous even. You think we'll still have jobs here if she dies? We won't," she announced triumphantly. "Everything will change, see if it don't."

"She ain't dead yet, and I'm still hungry."

Tessie went to the wooden ice chest and removed a wedge of pork pie. "Here, eat that. Though I'm buggered if I see how you can get a morsel down."

"Ooh, ain't you the rude one! Buggered, is it? And you always tellin' me to act like a lady."

"I'm upset, that's all."

"Ah, stop your fretting, luv. Miss Emma's going to be fine. This is America, don't forget. And she's a doctor's wife."

"Childbirth is the same one side of the ocean or the other, and—" The telephone rang. Tessie looked at it, then at her sister.

"All right," Nora said. "I'm going." Tessie did the talking when people were around, but she hated the telephone. Nora had to deal with that.

"Doctor Morgan's residence," Nora shouted into the mouthpiece of the wooden instrument fixed to the wall. Nora always shouted into the telephone. How else was anyone going to hear her when they were so faraway?

"Yes, it's me, Nora, Doctor Morgan. Is madam all right?"

She listened for a moment then broke into a broad grin. "That's wonderful, sir. Very pleased to hear it, Tessie will be, too, soon as I tell her. You give madam our best congratulations. And to you, too, sir." She hung up, breathless from all the yelling.

"Well?" Tessie demanded.

"Twins. Both boys. Big 'uns, he said. And she's fine."

Tessie's smile stretched her homely face. "That's that then. We won't have to look for another job." She marched to the calendar on the wall above the zinc-set tubs where they did the laundry. Very deliberately she circled the date with a red crayon. "November twenty-third, 1919. Mark my words, Nora, from now on this is going to be a red-letter day in this house."

The older of the two, by four minutes, they named Caleb, and the younger Daniel. "How about calling one of them Helmut," Josh had suggested, "for the professor."

"No, it's hard enough being a twin. Let's not give them something else to live up to."

So it was Caleb and Daniel.

The babies didn't look alike. From the first day they seemed two entirely separate individuals who happened to have been born at the same time. Caleb was utterly bald and had a wizened face, a funny little old man; Daniel's fuzz of dark hair made him look like Joshua. Or like little Josh. Emma felt a twinge of resentment because this baby was alive and her firstborn was dead, then she rejected that feeling. It wasn't Daniel's fault that the older brother he would never know was dead. She wouldn't be as silly as that.

All the same, each time they brought her sons to her she put Caleb to the breast first.

Charles West and Joshua both agreed she must stay in the hospital a minimum of three weeks. "This was quite a feat, Emma," Charles said, patting his patient's hand. "Two 6-pound boys in one go. You're exhausted and you need to rest."

"I can rest at home," Emma protested.

"It's not the same. By the way, when you do go I've suggested a nurse to Joshua. A very competent lady I've known for years."

Emma interviewed the woman, a widow named Mrs. Standish, from her hospital room and agreed to hire her. This time she didn't say she wanted to do everything for

the babies herself. There were two of them, and that was
entirely different. Moreover, she was different.

By the end of the month, once more back at 165 Commonwealth Avenue, Emma was very uneasy about Mrs.
Standish. "She's a cold fish," she complained to Josh.
"Never cracks a smile, even with the babies. How can you
be a good baby-nurse if you never smile?"

"Beats me," he agreed. "But Charles says she's very
experienced. Don't fret, darling. You'll soon be up and
around and able to do more for them yourself."

Emma met this remark with silence.

That Christmas was the happiest the Morgans had ever
spent together. They didn't entertain—Emma wasn't well
enough for that—but the house was bedecked with greens
and baubles that the Marsh sisters put up under Emma's
directions, and Josh filled an entire room with toys for his
infant sons.

"Josh," Emma protested, laughing, "it will be years
before they can ride rocking horses or play with tin soldiers."

"I know," Josh admitted sheepishly. "But I can't resist."
He went on buying presents. On Christmas Eve there
wasn't room to put everything under the tree.

"I have something for you," Emma said when she surveyed the scene in the drawing room. "But where can I
put it?"

"Over here, next to my presents for you."

Emma eyed the packages. "Let's open our things now."

"It's not Christmas yet."

"It will be midnight in an hour. It's Christmas then."

Josh smiled indulgently. "Just one each. Until tomorrow. You're like a little girl. Let's have a little girl next,
darling. One that will grow up and be the image of her
mama."

Emma didn't look at him, she picked up a box wrapped
in silver paper inscribed, 'To Emma with all my love,
Josh.' "I'm going to open this one."

"Fine, but I have to have one to open too."

In the end they opened all the things they'd bought for
each other. Josh's gifts were a double strand of matched
pearls and a pair of sapphire and pearl earrings. "You have
to have two of everything from now on," he explained.

Her presents to him were a carved ebony pipe stand, a
silk scarf embroidered with his initials, and a very special

silver tray fitted with a well to hold the antique German ink pot the professor had given him for his thirtieth birthday, four years earlier. The tray was engraved with the words, 'Christmas 1919' and beneath that the names and birthdates of himself, Emma, and Caleb and Daniel. Listed on the very bottom was the name Joshua, Jr., the dates of his birth and death, and the letters, R.I.P.

"It's magnificent," Josh said softly. "A real family heirloom. I'll treasure it always."

Emma put on her pearls and her earrings. The blue of the sapphires heightened the color of her eyes. "They look exquisite on you," Josh said. "I knew they would."

"They're lovely, darling. I've never seen anything more beautiful." Emma admired the jewels a moment longer, then turned from the gilt-framed mirror over the fireplace to face her husband. "Do you know what I like best? We've given each other permanent things, things that will be around for a long time. So we'll never forget this wonderful Christmas."

"Never," Josh agreed.

In January Emma's health improved markedly, but she developed an infection in both nipples and had to stop nursing her sons. The pediatrician, Dr. Manners, told her there was a growing body of opinion that babies did better on formula anyway, and promptly transferred the babies from the breast to the bottle. Emma felt some sense of deprivation, but contented herself with the doctor's pronouncement, and the fact that she grew stronger once she stopped nursing.

On a snowy February evening they took their coffee to the library after dinner. The twins were asleep upstairs, the telephone had not rung for hours, and a log fire burned brightly in the grate. "We have a perfect life," Josh announced with no notion of how smug he sounded. "Absolutely perfect."

"Josh, I want to go back to work."

He stared at her, not quite sure he'd understood. "But how can you? What about the boys? Why, for God's sake?"

"I'll hire a nanny to look after Daniel and Caleb. That's how. As for why, I don't ever want to be as vulnerable as I was last year."

He could think of nothing to say. They sat in silence for

some minutes. Joshua did mental calculations and realized it was only eighteen months since Joshua, Jr. had died and Emma was cast into a world of despair that nearly overcame her. The minutes passed, marked by the hushed sound of the snow splatting on the warm window glass, and the ticking of a pendulum clock on the desk. "What finally brought you back to me?" He seemed to be changing the subject, but they both knew he wasn't.

"Something Celia said. And a conversation I had with Bess, my sister-in-law."

"Henry's wife?"

"Yes."

"I didn't think you'd seen any of the Silvas in years except Manny."

"I haven't, just Bess, once or twice."

"And she and Celia convinced you to give our marriage another chance?"

"In a manner of speaking. There's no point in going into the details, darling. It's only that in their different ways they made me realize how much I loved you. And that a man can never see things exactly the way a woman does. Right after little Josh died you seemed ready to take up our lives as usual. I wasn't. I resented you for recovering because I thought it was forgetting."

"You said loved. In the past tense. Are you telling me something by that?"

Emma sprang from her seat and rushed to kneel beside him, both hands on his knees, feeling the muscular strength of his thighs and the body warmth that came through the dark serge of his trousers. "I love you desperately, Josh. Please don't think I've ever changed about that. And I love my children and our life together. But if I allow myself to be wholly wrapped up in it, to be only Mrs. Joshua Morgan and the mother of Daniel and Caleb, then what will happen to me if . . ." She stopped speaking and let the terrible possibility of disaster hang unspoken in the air.

"Other women do it," he said stubbornly, not touching her though she was so very close. "They take the risk."

"I know. Perhaps I feel differently because I've lived through the darkness on the other side of that fine line between sanity and madness. And it is a very fine line, Josh, a short step. I know now."

He didn't answer. The clock chimed nine times, the sound of snow shovels could be heard scraping the road on Commonwealth Avenue. "They'll have it cleared by morning," Josh said.

"Yes." Emma hadn't moved, she still knelt beside him; but now her eyes were cast down, not looking trustingly up into his face.

Suddenly Josh uttered a wordless cry of something between despair and joy and pulled her convulsively into his arms. He buried his face in her sweet-smelling neck and rocked her back and forth as if she were a child. "Emma, I love you so much. I don't show it as often as I should, but you're the center of my life. You and the twins."

"Nothing will change that, Josh. I swear it. It's not as though I had a demanding career. I'm nobody important, just a clerk in Celia's laboratory. But it gets me out into the big world for a few hours each day, helps to keep my sense of proportion. And what I earn will pay for the nanny."

"I don't care about that," he protested. "You can have a nanny if you want one."

"I know, but I care about it. I don't want anyone to suffer because of my choices. But I'm sure you won't, darling. Not you and not the boys. I'm going to be a better mother if I'm not hovering over them morning, noon, and night."

Joshua sighed. "Very well. We'll try it for a while and see how it works out."

"I'm sorry, Mrs. Morgan," the woman said wearily. "I really thought the last applicant would be suitable. Perhaps I don't really know what you're looking for."

"A nanny," Emma said into the flared black mouth of the telephone. "A warm, intelligent, loving human being to look after my twins. Over the course of three weeks you've sent me eight ogres, each one more stiff and formal than the last. Don't you have anyone else?"

The woman didn't answer immediately. The silence lengthened and Emma thought perhaps the connection had been broken. She jiggled the receiver.

"I'm still here, Mrs. Morgan. I was thinking. There is someone. Frankly, I didn't intend to send her on any interviews. She registered with us last month. She has a diploma in baby-nursing from some foreign country, Poland I believe. She's never worked as a nanny here. And I must warn you, her English isn't very good. She has a thick accent. Not the best example for young children."

"Neither my husband nor I have an accent," Emma said cooly. "We'll provide the example. What is the woman's name, and what can you tell me about her background?"

"Mrs. Marya Czerniki. She's a war widow, and for the past few years she has been helping her father-in-law in his bakery."

It didn't sound very promising, but Emma was desperate. "Send her to see me this afternoon. There's nothing to be lost by one more interview."

It took only five minutes for Emma to decide to hire Marya Czerniki. When she saw the Polish woman heft a twin under each sturdy arm and coo at them in a mixture of Polish and English that the babies seemed to find delightful, she knew her search was over.

"She's exactly what I've been looking for," she told Josh that evening. "Warm and loving. She has a sense of humor, but she can be firm. She's perfect."

"How can you be sure of that after one interview?"

"I am, that's all. Just as I was sure the others were wrong. She's my age, twenty-five, but she seems a lot older. I guess because she's had a hard life. She was married only two years, to an American. Then her husband went off to war and didn't come back. No children. Which she seems to regret. So it's not surprising she wants to look after other people's children. I think we're all going to suit each other perfectly. Aren't you pleased?"

"I can't say I am, exactly. I've been hoping you'd change your mind because you couldn't find anybody suitable."

"Josh, we've been through all this."

"Yes, we have. And I'm not welshing on my bargain."

"Neither am I," Emma promised. "You and the twins will come first always, I promise."

He resented it. He couldn't help it. She was so damned preoccupied by the things she and Celia Howard did at the lab, so full of them when he came home in the evenings. He wanted domestic bliss, a woman for himself alone. Instead he had a redheaded tyro he might never tame.

He was trying to walk off his frustration in the far reaches of the Fens on a bitter cold Sunday afternoon in late March when it happened. The pond was thick with ice, skaters swooped and darted on the glittering surface. Joshua saw them only peripherally. All his vision was inward—and what he found inside himself was a seething mass of anger and dismay.

He moved away from the pond and the cutting wind, deeper into the protected walkways of the Arnold Arboretum. The trees were leafless, there was no sign of spring and flowing sap and renewal. Joshua studied the bare branches, creaking with cold. The rubbing of their frozen stems was a whining cry. He averted his eyes from a scene he suddenly found unbearably poignant. And saw Billy-Jo.

She was coming toward him along a path that intercepted his. Well wrapped against the cold, little showing but her eyes, she walked in a way that was unmistakable. Joshua swallowed a startled cry, then stood still and waited.

She had not seen him, her gaze was on the path, on the need to pick her way carefully through frozen rivers of slush and snow. "Excuse me," she murmured without looking up as she tried to go round him.

"No," he said softly. "No, I won't excuse you and just let you pass by."

Billy-Jo's eyes leapt to his face. "Joshua . . ." She lifted her gloved hands to clutch at the knitted shawl wrapped round her head and shoulders. "How did you find me?"

"I didn't, not the way you mean. I was walking here, that's all."

Her sigh was a long expulsion of pent-up sound, a breath she'd been holding for some eighteen months. "I guess I always figured it would happen like this," she said. "Sooner or later."

"And that's why you're here? Not in Arkansas, as everyone thinks. So we'd meet someday by accident?"

Perhaps it was the almost unreal cold, or the suddenness of the confrontation. Whatever the reason, in that moment there were no pretenses between them. Emotions were naked and shivering, open to pain and probing and discovery. "Yes. That's why I'm here," she said.

It was not so much an admission as an affirmation. He was too vulnerable to resist, indeed he had no desire to do so. Joshua was aggrieved, and once more Emma was the cause, and Billy-Jo Landry the cure at hand.

She took him to a small flat in Jamaica Plain, carved out of former servants' quarters on the fifth floor of a grand mansion. In mood and feeling it was a replica of her Scollay Square house. Cheerful, unpretentious, it spoke to Joshua of tradition, of women who supported their men rather than opposing them.

They were hardly in the door when she turned to him and opened her arms. Joshua grabbed her ample body and pressed it to him. One kiss was the only prelude. Within seconds he was on her like a rutting bull, in the grip of some need he made no attempt to understand or control. Billy-Jo didn't resist when Joshua forced her to the floor. She seemed in no way offended by his assumption of right, or the harshness of his assault.

He thrust himself into her while they were both still almost entirely clothed. She thrashed her legs free from her entangling skirts and raised her buttocks. Finally she gripped his hips with her thighs. Matching his grunts and groans with her own, Billy-Jo accepted his swift plunge into her body and turned rape into union.

It was over in seconds. Joshua rolled away and didn't meet her eyes. "Forgive me," he murmured. "That was unspeakable behavior. I don't know what . . ."

She took his face in her hands, turning him to her. "Ssh, it's all right, Josh honey. I don't mind. I understand, really."

He kissed her again, in thanksgiving and apology this time. For some seconds they lay together, then he helped her to her feet and politely turned away while she readjusted her dress. It was his first opportunity to really look around. The furniture was worn and faded, the carpet on which they had lain was threadbare. "Billy-Jo, I didn't know. It looks like things have been hard for you."

"Not really. Not like you think. I still got the investments my mama left me. It's just that under the circumstances, well, they've got to go a bit farther."

"Under what circumstances?" Joshua stared at her and guessed the truth, but he willed her to deny it.

"I've a child, Josh. A little girl."

He sat down heavily in a chair covered in faded homespun. "My child," he whispered.

Billy-Jo made no direct reply. "She's with the neighbor downstairs. Wait here, I'll get her."

When she returned, he had not moved. He sat exactly as she'd left him. White-faced and frozen. Billy-Jo came nearer. The baby was sleeping in her arms, swaddled in layers of pink flannel and handmade lace. She held her out. "Take her, Josh."

He did, moving the coverlet a bit so he could look into the tiny face. It was surrounded by a halo of chestnut hair, just like her mother's. Joshua stroked the silken cheek with one finger and the baby woke. He noticed the dimples first. She had two, just like Billy-Jo again. Then he saw her eyes, they were vivid, vibrant green. Exactly the eyes he saw in the mirror every morning when he shaved.

"Her name's Morgan." Billy-Jo said. "I put it on her birth certificate. All proper and as it should be."

Involuntarily his head jerked up and he stared at her, almost gave in to the urge to protest. A birth certificate was a public record. Unbidden, the scope and shape of the scandal came to him. It pressed on his chest like a weight.

Billy-Jo laughed softly. "Don't look like that, Josh. Morgan's her first name. Morgan Landry. That's what the birth certificate says. Course I never wrote nothing down about her father."

She took the child from his leaden arms and moved toward the kitchen. "I keep a little crib in here. So's me and Morgan can be together when I'm cooking or simpling. Take off your coat, Josh. I'll brew some tea."

7

*L*iving a double life, that's what they called it in books. Joshua found it remarkably easy to do in the next few weeks. Perhaps because the circumstances were so extraordinary, and because Billy-Jo was unique. Besides, she was removed from his ordinary world, had taken herself out of it. He never thought about her or the child unless he was with them. That was seldom; he went to Jamaica Plain twice more in March and once the first week in April. The rest of the time he was Dr. Morgan, Emma's husband, the father of Caleb and Daniel.

The days lengthened perceptibly, the air warmed a bit, the spring social season began. "Did I tell you I've accepted an invitation to dinner at the Wests' on Saturday?" Joshua asked Emma one night when they were getting ready for bed.

She made a face of distaste. "No. I'm not sure I want to go. I'll feel peculiar sitting across the table from my obstetrician. I'll keep thinking about how I looked on that wretched table."

Josh laughed. "Forget it. Doctors separate patients from women in their minds. All Charles will see is the beautiful wife of lucky Josh Morgan."

"Does that mean your patients are seen just as bodies?" Josh merely laughed again.

Emma dressed with great care the night of the Wests' party. Her long black evening dress was formfitting in front, and gathered into graceful folds in the back. It had wrist-length sleeves and a remarkably deep square neckline. Too low? No, she decided, she could get away with it. Her shoulders and her neck were still her best features, they were like alabaster, with none of the freckles that plagued so many redheads. And the sapphire and pearl earrings Josh gave her at Christmas looked wonderful below her upswept hair.

"A prize for anyone who guesses I'm a fisherman's daughter," she whispered to Josh in the back of the taxi taking them to Brookline.

"No one can possibly win it." He patted her hand reassuringly.

Emma knew he was right. She settled back contentedly and gazed out the window at the starry April night.

The conversation at the Wests' dinner table was lively and gay. Emma sat at the left of Charles's wife Maude, separated from her hostess only by a taciturn little doctor from Vienna who kept his eyes on his plate and didn't enter into the proceedings. The talk was of debutante balls and theaters, a new exhibition at the Museum of Fine Arts, a traveling dance troupe. Later the men might get together and discuss medicine, now the conversation was about what Emma thought of as Culture, with a capital C.

Suddenly Maude West's clear, well-modulated voice rose above the chatter. "Emma dear, you really must join the Chilton Club. A group of us have lunch there every Friday before going on to symphony. We'd be delighted to include you. I'll put your name up, shall I?"

Emma's fork was halfway to her mouth. She finished the motion, gaining time to think. That's the way Boston people always referred to their famous orchestra, just symphony, never the symphony. And the Chilton Club was the most exclusive women's club in town. The meaning of the invitation was obvious. Joshua Morgan's wife had been found worthy. She sensed that everyone at the table was waiting for her response. They wanted to see her thankful pleasure, her gratitude at being handed the prize.

"Thank you so much." Emma spoke with all the sincerity she could muster. "It's very sweet of you, Maude, really. But I have to refuse. I've gone back to work for Celia Howard, the chemist. I'm not free on Friday afternoons."

God, how perverse of her, why had she done it? She could have said something noncommittal and explained to Maude later in private, but she did so hate their pretensions and assumptions. Now the room was blanketed in heavy, embarrassed silence. It seemed to Emma to go on forever, but it was only a few seconds before everyone began chattering again. She glanced down the length of the table at Josh. His face was flushed and he was staring at her, but when her eyes met his, he turned away.

Josh couldn't bear to look at her. Damn her, why did Emma have to be such an original? Why couldn't she do anything the way other women did? There was a soft touch on his arm and he turned gratefully to his left.

"Have I told you about my new poodle, Doctor? He's named Joshua, but you mustn't be angry with me. He'd been christened before I got him."

Josh smiled at a tiny wisp of a woman, a pretty brunette whose curls fluttered around a winsome, heart-shaped face and framed large, dark eyes. Elizabeth Bradley was Betty to everyone who mattered in Boston. She was a famous hostess and an active participant in every worthy cause. She didn't look her thirty-plus years, and she seemed altogether too fragile to have buried two millionaire husbands. "Is it a very clever poodle?" Josh asked.

"Oh yes, the breed's known for cleverness. So I think he's well named."

"You flatter me, Mrs. Bradley."

"Of course, any man who looks like you and is a genius besides is surely accustomed to flattery."

The brown eyes smiled at him and a carefully manicured hand rested on his arm. Joshua felt comforted, and knew himself to be a fool. Betty Bradley was a notorious flirt, even if she was too rich and too wellborn ever to be taken to task for it. "What about you?" he asked. "Are you so accustomed to flattery that it will mean nothing if I say you're looking particularly lovely this evening?" He let his glance travel over her pretty curls and settle somewhere around her bodice of artfully draped pink chiffon.

"No woman alive is as jaded as that, Doctor. Least of all me."

Marya Czerniki fitted into 165 Commonwealth Avenue as if she'd been born there. Not the least of her charms was the delicious Polish rye bread she introduced to the household. Once a week Tessie Marsh happily relinquished her kitchen to Marya, and by evening six loaves of black bread redolent with the earthy smell of grain and malt were wrapped in clean towels and sitting on the pantry shelves.

Tessie wasn't jealous. "Saves me a parcel of work, does Marya," she pronounced. "Thank heaven madam hired her and not one of them snooty nannies like they have back in England."

Even Josh couldn't help but adore her. Like Emma he chuckled at her funny accent and was soothed by her unfailing good humor. Besides, he loved the bread.

"If I were a praying woman," Emma told Celia, "I'd be on my knees in church giving thanks for the perfect harmony at home."

"Maybe you should anyway. It's a miracle of sorts. And I'll join you." Celia smiled her broadest smile. "I'm so thrilled to have you working beside me, my dear. If you leave again I think I'll simply shut up shop."

"I don't intend to stop working ever again. Not until I'm old and doddering and they carry me out of the lab."

Celia cocked head and eyed her. "No more babies?"

"Well, maybe one more eventually. But that will only mean a temporary absence while I have it. I'm cut out to be a working lady, Celia. I realize that now."

"And Josh, does he realize it?"

"Of course," Emma said airily. "Josh always says he's not some nineteenth century tyrant. He knows I'm happiest when I'm working, and that suits him."

Celia found it all a little hard to believe, but that was Emma's business, not hers.

"Good morning, Mrs. Bradley." Josh moved the telephone on his desk into a slightly more comfortable position. "Of course you're not disturbing me. I'm delighted to hear from you. How can I help you?"

Her laugh tinkled across the wires, like her voice it was soft and whispery. "It's I who can help you, I believe. But first, didn't we progress to Christian names last week at the Wests'?"

"Yes, of course we did. Sorry, Betty, I'm distracted."

"Naturally, poor man. I know how hard you work and I

shan't keep you. But you must stop by for tea very soon. I have a brilliant plan to raise some money for the charity wing at Memorial. You are chairman of the hospital charity committee, aren't you, Joshua?"

"As a matter of fact I am. And the coffers are all but bare, as usual. The endowment is generous, but there are always so many places for the money to go. I hope your plan works."

"It will. But I need your approval of the details before I can go ahead. Shall we say tomorrow at four?"

It wasn't an invitation, it was a royal summons. Josh flipped the page of his desktop calendar. He saw the initials B.J. penciled in for the following afternoon. "I've surgery scheduled after lunch, would five be too late?" He lied so easily these days. The right words came to his lips automatically.

"Five will be fine, Joshua. See you then."

She fed him perfect little cucumber sandwiches and exquisitely fragrant tea. "It's called Earl Grey. Flavored with a touch of bergamot oil. I have it specially sent from London." The drawing room of the Bradley house on Beacon Hill had a marble floor spread with pale Chinese silk carpets, and walls of some golden wood polished to a satin glow. He sat on a sofa of ivory brocade scattered with cushions of creamy rose and softest green, the same colors as the rugs. Betty perched opposite him on the edge of a dainty slipper chair upholstered in an ivory-colored fabric, and managed to convey the impression that she was sitting at his feet.

"You see," she said, dark eyes dancing with enthusiasm, "no one has ever shaken up staid old Boston like Mrs. Jack."

"I'm afraid I don't know who Mrs. Jack is, or was."

"Was. The fabulous Isabella Stewart of New York. She married John Lowell Gardener of Boston in 1860. The town was never the same after that. More tea, Joshua?"

He nodded and she poured it gracefully from a pretty china pot. Her hands were soft and elegant, like everything about her. They didn't look like Emma's hands. Or like Billy-Jo's. "What did this Mrs. Jack do to disturb Boston's calm?"

"Everything. Kept a lion on a leash, never went into the

stores, just had her carriage brought to the door and waited for the clerks to bring things out to her. Of course her greatest extravagance was the house."

"You mean the Gardner house, Fenway Court? The one that's a museum now?"

"Yes. It was originally a European palace and she had it brought over and rebuilt here, stone by stone. Then she filled it up with all that art."

"I went there once when I was a student. I couldn't see what was so wonderful." Josh smiled ruefully. "I'm afraid I know nothing about art. One pretty picture looks much like another to me. And some of them weren't even pretty."

Betty's laugh twittered in the exquisite drawing room. She bent forward and covered his hand with her own. "How refreshingly honest you are, Joshua. Everyone usually makes ponderous comments when the Gardner collection is mentioned, but not you."

"I've never had time to learn to make ponderous comments."

He was suddenly conscious of her scent. It was floral, but with a musky, sensual undertone that slightly unnerved him. He wanted the conversation to return to mundane things he understood. "Are you thinking of holding some kind of event at the Gardner place?"

"How clever you are, Joshua. You've guessed my secret." She rose and her pale yellow tea gown swirled appealingly around her perfectly proportioned form. There were folders on a table on the other side of the room, and she collected them and brought them to where he sat.

"I've started making a few notes. My idea is for a Midsummer Day ladies' luncheon, to be held at Fenway Court. By invitation only, but requiring a subscription fee of ten dollars per guest."

"That's pretty steep, isn't it?"

"Of course it is. But it's for charity. I'll absorb the costs of the affair, Joshua. All the proceeds will go to the hospital."

"That's extraordinarily generous of you, Betty. Thank you."

"It's my pleasure. Now we must have a teensy glass of sherry to celebrate my plan." She poured while she spoke, giving him no opportunity to refuse. "You don't mind that it's illegal now, do you?"

Prohibition had become law the previous January. Josh thought it absurd. "I don't mind."

Betty smiled as she handed him the glass. Her eyes sparkled as if the fact that the drink was illegal made it something intimate. "I'd like Mrs. Morgan to take charge of one of the luncheon committees, perhaps the table decorations. Shall I ask her, or will you?"

"I'm afraid that's not possible." Josh felt his mouth go dry. "Emma's working with Celia Howard, as you know. And there's the house and the twins. She hasn't time for charity committees."

"Oh, of course, I'd forgotten. Poor Joshua, it must be quite a challenge having a wife who's brilliant and ambitious as well as beautiful."

He saw Betty Bradley frequently after that first tea. She was scrupulously careful to get his approval of every detail of the fund-raising luncheon. "I do rely on your opinion, Joshua," she said repeatedly. Since it was his first term as chairman of the Doctors' Committee on Charity, he didn't know if things were usually done this way. On occasion he chafed at the time it took, more often he enjoyed spending the odd half hour with Betty.

Once she arrived at his tiny office at Memorial and put her papers down and gazed at him and shook her head. "You look exhausted, Joshua. You mustn't let them work you so hard."

He'd just had a vitriolic exchange with Frank Rhineman, and he wasn't so much tired as tense with anger. He understood what was behind the other man's increased hostility: There was talk of Joshua being appointed head of the gynecological service, the Board of Governors was expected to announce a decision soon. Rhineman was using his considerable influence to see that they chose anyone but Dr. Morgan. Frank would never muster enough votes to get the job himself, but he could be a spoiler. That's what was causing the blinding pain now throbbing behind Joshua's sinuses. "It's nothing, only a headache."

"Let me help you. I'm very good at it. My late husband taught me."

Betty stripped off her gloves and stepped behind him. He felt her fingers gently massaging the skin of his temples while her thumbs kneaded the base of his neck. He thought he should say something, pull away perhaps. But it felt wonderful.

"You're a miracle worker," he said at last. "It's all better. We should make you an honorary doctor."

She laughed. "You should not. I have no aspirations for a career, my dear Joshua. I'm simply a woman who cannot bear to see a man in discomfort. Now, can I ask you just one teeny question about the accounting procedures of the ticket sale? Then I'll be off."

They bent their heads together over her lists of figures, and the problem was easily solved. "Thank you," she murmured as she straightened. Her perky little flowered hat bobbed gaily above her curls. "I always feel so much better after you put things right, Joshua."

"Glad to be of help." He walked with her to the office door, but before he had an opportunity to open it she put her hand over his, then she stood on tiptoe and kissed his cheek. It was merely a friendly gesture, devoid of passion, but the spot her lips had touched tingled for the remainder of the day.

"You'll be going to the luncheon, won't you?" Josh asked Emma in early June.

She looked at him across the breakfast table, her eyes blank. "What luncheon?"

"The charity affair for the hospital. The one Betty Bradley is sponsoring on Wednesday."

"Oh, the do at Fenway Court." Emma didn't glance up from the newspaper she was reading. "I can't attend, darling. I'm a working lady, and Celia expects me to show up at my job. Did you see this story about President Wilson? He says forbidding alcoholic drink is a noble experiment. Can you imagine such rubbish? They can't really expect to enforce this Volstead Act, can they?"

"I don't know. Prohibition's not just a law in the ordinary sense. It's a constitutional amendment. Hard to overturn, enforceable or not. I thought we were discussing the luncheon."

Something in his tone alerted her. Emma glanced up and saw the white line of anger around his mouth, and the twin furrows of tension between his brows. "Joshua, we agreed. You said I could go back to work. It isn't fair to be

angry with me when I can't go to some silly ladies luncheon in the middle of the week."

"I hardly think something expected to raise hundreds of
dollars for Memorial's charity wing can be called silly.
Besides, I'm chairman of the charity committee. How will
it look if you're not there?"

Emma narrowed her eyes and gazed speculatively at
him. "Josh, are you actively going after the appointment as
head of gynecology?"

He flushed. It hadn't occurred to him that she'd disapprove. "What's that got to do with this discussion? But
since you ask, yes, I am. It's a chance to direct policy,
encourage the kind of research I believe should be done.
Why shouldn't I go after it?"

Emma's face split into a broad grin. "Why indeed?
Good for you, darling. I was afraid you'd let Frank Rhineman
intimidate you, or decide it would take too much time
from your rich lady patients. Very well, Josh, if it's important to you, of course I'll go to the luncheon. Celia will
give me a few hours off, I'm sure."

Oddly, that didn't please him. The more he thought of
it, the angrier he became. Emma awarded him her com-
pliance like a prize, like something he had to earn by
doing things of which she approved. He seethed about it
all week, and when he came home the night of the luncheon, he didn't ask if she'd had a nice time, or if it had
gone well. All men were excluded, even he, but he'd
already had an exciting report from Betty.

"Two hundred and twenty guests, Joshua," Betty said.
"That's two thousand two hundred dollars for your charity
wards. Now tell me what a good girl I've been."

"You're fantastic, but you know that."

"Yes, but I do enjoy hearing you say so, Joshua. Please
say you'll come and collect the check yourself. I want to
put it straight into your hands."

"I'd be delighted."

"Wonderful, then I'll expect you Sunday at four."

Sundays he and Emma usually spent together with the
twins, they gave Marya the day off and enjoyed their
fast-growing sons. But this was special. "I'll be there."

On Sunday Josh didn't say anything until nearly four.
He was watching Caleb's attempt to stand up and Daniel's
to crawl. Dan was always first in everything; he'd already

mastered standing, he was ready for the next exploration of the universe. Joshua gathered up his son and kissed him, then set him back on the floor. "I have to go out for a bit, I'm afraid. Only an hour or two."

Emma was bouncing Cal on her lap, her reply seemed perfunctory. "We'll miss you, darling. Hurry back."

Joshua didn't feel it at all likely he'd be missed. He walked to Betty's house with a pleasant tingle of anticipation.

She wore a tea gown of raspberry taffeta and she swirled into his arms. She smelled of gardenias and she melted against him in a way that made her fragility seem a trust. "Isn't it marvelous, Joshua? Over two thousand dollars. I'm so pleased."

"It is marvelous, and so are you." He held her lightly, half-afraid of her delicacy, conscious of her small pointed breasts pressed against his chest. Long seconds passed and neither of them broke the embrace.

Finally Betty tipped her head back and looked up into his face. "Dearest Joshua, you're always so wise. Tell me what I'm to do now that I've fallen in love with you?"

For answer he kissed her. The kiss lasted a long time and when it ended she lay her head against his chest. His chin rested on her soft black curls. She was trembling and he stroked her back, making wordless noises of comfort and reassurance into her sweet-smelling hair.

"Joshua, what's to become of us?"

"I don't know." He heard his own voice as from a far distance. It sounded strangled, not like his voice at all. "There's Emma, the children, my work. And—" He broke off. The rest he would never tell her. Never. "I don't know," he repeated. "But I'm in love with you too."

Betty drew back and took both his hands in hers, tugging him gently toward the stairs and the bedroom above. "We will take what joy we can from life," she whispered. "Tomorrow be damned, Joshua. We have today."

On a stifling hot day at the end of July, the Board of Governors of Boston Memorial Hospital made the official announcement of Joshua Morgan's appointment as head of the Department of Gynecology and Obstetrics.

The chairman of the board was a wizened old man of eighty, with a thin, reedy voice. His grandfather had held the post before him, and his father after that. The office was passed from generation to generation, like the family bank. It was coveted for moments like this, when the chairman held center stage and displayed his power.

"Not only is Doctor Morgan a fine physician and a worthy successor to his distinguished predecessors, he is a scholar who will carry on the tradition of active application of the latest benefits which science can afford our patients. Moreover, he has shown himself a man conscious of the practical as well as the theoretical needs of our great hospital. May we have a few words from you, Doctor Morgan."

Joshua rose, surveying the faces of his overseers, those laymen for whom this hospital was both a treasured trust and a mark of their wealth and influence, and his peers, the doctors who would serve with him. He spotted Frank Rhineman in the rear. He wished Betty were here. In a sense this was her triumph. It was the fact that she'd presented him, and he the hospital, with the largest single check ever to be garnered by a fund-raising event that had clinched the appointment for him. But it was men only today.

Joshua cleared his throat and said all the right things.

At that moment Betty Bradley was buying gloves in Stearns, but she was conscious of the time. In the midst of deciding between navy kid with or without a button at the wrist, she paused and flipped open the etched gold cover of her watch. She wore it suspended from a pearl pin which Joshua had given her the week before. It was just two-thirty; he'd be making his acceptance speech now.

She smiled. There would be many such triumphs, she'd see to it, and when she was Joshua's wife she'd mark each one with a gala dinner party. There would be no such celebration tonight because Emma hadn't thought of it. Betty felt a glow of satisfaction when she considered Emma Morgan's many sins of omission. Emma was almost making it too easy. But she had to be clever. It wouldn't do to rush Joshua into a scandalous divorce. She must be very patient—and she was prepared to be.

Betty returned her attention to the salesclerk. "I think I'll take both pairs. Now, what do you have in black?"

It took Emma a very long time to realize things were

different between her and Josh. When she did, during the summer of '22, her perception was of a slackening. It was as if the taut springs that had pulled them together when they first saw each other had let go. Not all at once and not painfully, it had been just a slow, continuing relaxation. Emma told herself this probably happened to every marriage. Maybe it was to be expected after seven years.

Sometimes Josh still turned to her in the night and they shared the sweet passion of the early days, as if their bodies hadn't forgotten how it used to be, but it didn't happen often. By the twins' *third* birthday in November Emma had convinced herself that her marriage was perfectly normal. She wasn't a girl anymore, she had to realize that romantic love didn't go on forever.

Betty Bradley also knew she was no longer a girl. "I'm not getting any younger, Joshua. I shan't wait forever. An hour at teatime isn't a life." She looked distastefully at her cup, as if to emphasize her rejection of these afternoon assignations. "You said you wanted to wait until after the twins' birthday. That was three weeks ago. Have you told Emma you're leaving?"

Joshua walked to the window. Usually the golden dome of the State House was visible from Beacon Hill, today it was obscured by falling snow. The cobbled street below was deserted. "This could turn into the season's first real blizzard," he murmured.

"That's not an answer to my question, dear."

"No. And no."

"I take it you mean you haven't told her."

"Betty, I can't." He turned to her, his expression ravaged by guilt and grief. "I love you, you know that. But . . ." *But I love Emma too*, that's what he wanted to say. *Exasperating as she is, I love her. And there's Billy-Jo.* He looked out the window again and wondered if the snow was as heavy in Jamaica Plain near the Arnold Arboretum. Probably it was. The poorest neighborhoods always seemed to get the worst of it.

Betty's voice brought him back to Beacon Hill. "Josh, what you're saying is that you haven't the courage of your convictions." She rose and went to him, tracing the care lines of his face with cool fingers. "Don't anguish so, Joshua. I'll wait a bit longer . . . until you realize what an injustice you're doing us both."

Later, after he was gone, she studied her own face in
the mirror above her dressing table. The lines were faint,
but permanent, and not appealing the way Joshua's were.
Men had everything their way, even aging. "Thirty-nine,"
she told her reflection. "And forty in two months. There
will never be another opportunity like Joshua Morgan."
Shuddering slightly, she applied cream with a lavish hand
and told herself to be patient. Like a spider. And like a
spider she must spin a web almost invisible, but strong as
iron.

"I heard rumor of some new cream, supposedly miracu-
lous," Joshua said. He looked at Emma across the dining
room table. The candlelight flattered her. Not that she
needed it; Emma was as lovely as ever, a flamboyant
beauty, not sweet and soft like Betty, but lovely.
"What kind of cream?"
"Something a woman can use to prevent pregnancy.
They say Margaret Sanger brought it back from Holland.
So you must have known about it. Why didn't you tell
me?"
"Oh," she said softly. "The jelly. Yes, I know about it.
Celia's done the analysis. It's very simple to produce and
reasonably effective. As to why I didn't tell you, you can
no more legally dispense it than you can fit women for a
cervical cap. Where did you hear about it?"
"From Charles, one of his patients mentioned it. She
keeps having spontaneous abortions. They're ruining her
health, and the poor woman's desperate. She told Charles
she'd heard about this miracle jelly that might keep her
from getting pregnant. I still think it's odd you didn't
mention it."
"I haven't had much opportunity to talk to you lately,
Josh." Only Emma's long fingers nervously crumbling a
piece of bread belied her calm. *Don't tell me why*, she
pleaded silently. *I don't want to hear you say you don't
love me anymore*. Aloud she asked, "Is Charles going to
say damn the law and prescribe the cream for his patient?
Celia can get him some."
"Too risky. We talked about it today. He's going to do a
hysterectomy instead. It's justified, if her reproductive
organs were healthy she wouldn't keep aborting."
"Is she a young woman?"

"Twenty-four."

Emma shook her head. "Very young. And it's so permanent, Josh. So drastic."

"I know." He frowned. "Emma, are you ladies distributing this cream at Milk Street?"

"Don't ask me, Josh. It's better if you don't."

He grunted and abruptly left the table. Not in anger, though Emma didn't know that. He was thinking of her spunk, and the fact that there were things he could discuss with her that he'd never mention in Betty's rarified drawing room. Not in her bedroom either, for that matter. She'd told him early on that she was barren. He'd tried to talk to her about it, express sympathy, concern. She'd closed off the topic. "It's too scientific for me, my dear. I only mentioned it so you wouldn't worry."

"I can't see the point," Frank Rhineman said. He wore one of the new Valentino-inspired suits, a double-breasted, muted tweed with flared lapels, and he looked as dapper and immaculate as always. Even after a day's surgery, Rhineman seemed to have stepped from the society pages of the *Herald*.

Joshua had a sudden mental image of his own rumpled appearance. He knew he looked like a backwoodsman compared to the other man; he knew too that most women considered that part of his charm, but it made him uncomfortable. He tugged at his vest, wishing it fit more comfortably over his broad chest. "The point," he said, "is that the doctor is in charge, not a victim of circumstances."

"But you can endanger the rectum. Surely it's far better to allow a natural tear," Rhineman said.

"What you're calling natural isn't, by definition," Joshua protested. "Women's bodies shouldn't tear open. That's not natural, Frank."

Charles West reached across the table and pulled Joshua's large sketch closer. It was an anatomical drawing on which Joshua had penciled a number of new lines. "You're suggesting a mediolateral cut to enlarge the vaginal orifice. Is that it, Josh?"

"Yes, but only at the last stage of delivery. And only if it's obvious that the child's head is too large to emerge without damage."

"So we have the Morgan episiotomy to accompany the

Morgan cesarian," Rhineman said softly. "You do get your name about, don't you, Joshua?"

"My name's not the issue. Don't be an ass, Frank."

"Time gentlemen," West said quietly. Often he seemed to usurp Joshua's role as head of the service, usually it was an attempt at peacemaking. "I suggest we adjourn," he added. "Thanks for sharing your idea, Josh. I'm going to try it next time it seems to be called for."

A number of men tried it, just as they had tried Joshua Morgan's suggestion that while high forceps should never be used, there could be some value in assisting birth in its very last stages with low forceps. It was a simple concept, but like most of Joshua's ideas, it caught on. He'd never admit as much to anyone, but he quite enjoyed the stir his innovations caused. They kept him buoyed up and able to ignore the shambles he'd made of his personal life.

On one point he remained adamant, Joshua allowed a bare minimum of sedation during labor. "A drowsy woman can't bear down, and a prolonged exit is dangerous to the child." It didn't stop patients from flocking to him. He was now, beyond question, the most popular obstetrician in Boston.

It was Betty who summed it up. "Perhaps women like a touch of pain, it makes it all so primitive and basic. No wonder they adore you, Joshua. You're having sex of a sort with each of them."

The painful weeks lengthened into months, and Josh and Emma drifted farther and farther apart. They were a pair of strangers living together in the same house—except for one thing, they both adored their sons.

Daniel was the opposite of his brother, as dark as Cal was fair. He was a scamp who raced through life trailing mayhem in his wake. Caleb was a sweet and placid child, old beyond his three years, with an intuitive sensitivity to those around him.

One evening Josh went up to the nursery to kiss the boys good night. Emma was already there; he could hear her voice, and he heard Caleb ask, "Are you sad, Mommy?"

The question stopped Joshua in the hall; it took his breath away. It was astonishing that a lisping toddler could sense something like that. She was sad. It had been more and more obvious of late. So he should probably put them both out of their misery, leave her and have done with it. But . . .

The sound of Emma's voice drifted into the hall. He did not want to hear whatever she was going to say to her son. He turned and fled back down the stairs.

His young son's perceptions continued to trouble him. Not just because of Emma, but because no tiny boy should be thinking about such things. In the end he decided that it was to be expected, Caleb and Emma were remarkably close. He'd always suspected that she favored him. But he couldn't criticize because he knew he favored Daniel.

Daniel had an irrepressible zest, a hint of deviltry in his smile which fascinated his father. Daniel was the twin who most delighted in the swing Joshua had erected in the backyard, the one for whom the rubber tire never went high enough. Caleb disliked riding through the air. It was Daniel who first learned the way to Tessie Marsh's pantry and climbed up on a chair to raid the cookie jar; Daniel who rocked so hard and fast on his carved wooden horse that the runners had to be replaced before his fourth birthday; Daniel who wore out even the tireless Marya. And Daniel who allowed his father to satisfy the craving for the ideal childhood he'd never had. Joshua loved Caleb with his blond curls and his gentle, affectionate ways, but he doted on Daniel.

Prohibition did not make dramatic changes in Boston society. The balls and teas and dinner parties of the Morgans' world went on, merely substituting fruit punch for wine, and only a few dirges were sung for the loss of champagne. So Emma was entirely clearheaded the autumn night in 1923 when she danced with Frank Rhineman at a party in a lovely old house in Louisbourg Square.

"I just got back from New York," Rhineman told her. "Did you know that Margaret Sanger has finally convinced the state legislature there that she should be allowed to open a birth control clinic in Manhattan?"

Emma stopped dancing. The Strauss music swirled about her head and the other couples on the floor had to circle them to avoid collision. "Are you sure?"

"Positive." Rhineman smiled. "So it's true, you have been involved with the Sanger movement. I'd heard about it, but I wasn't sure."

Emma shook her head impatiently. "Every woman's involved in her heart of hearts. What did they say in New York? What's the law to be?"

"We'd best keep moving, hadn't we?" Rhineman tightened his arm around her waist and moved her back into the patterns of the dance. "Come, my dear, one two three, one two three. Just the way you learned it in dancing school. There that's better."

"I never went to dancing school," Emma murmured. "We couldn't afford it. My mother taught me to waltz. She had gone to dancing school."

"Ah, a drama. Lady marries beneath her station, brings up her daughter to appreciate the nice things she's forfeited."

"Something very much like that. Frank, don't tease. Tell me about the New York law."

The music stopped just then, there was a flurry of applause. Emma joined in dutifully. Rhineman took her arm and led her off the floor before the orchestra began playing again. There was a room across from the ballroom that had been arranged for conversation, lots of small tables with flowers and candles and waiters serving punch. They found a corner out of the crush. "Tell me," Emma repeated.

"Simple, really. She can open her clinic, as I said. She's to dispense information about hygiene and child care, and under its auspices doctors may fit married ladies for diaphragms. If, in their judgment, such a device is needed for the 'cure and prevention of disease.' "

Emma jumped up. "Thank you, it's wonderful news. I have to tell Josh."

She found him at the center of a crowd of men and women. Josh was holding forth on some theory and everyone was paying rapt attention. Emma touched his arm. "Darling, excuse me, but may I speak with you for a moment?"

Apologies were made, and Joshua slipped into a corner with Emma. She told him what Rhineman had said. " 'Cure and prevention of disease,' it's a euphemism, nothing more. They're going to let her dispense birth control information, Josh, and where it's most needed—among the poor."

"How did Rhineman find out about it?"

"He came back from New York this afternoon. Apparently it's the main topic of conversation for all the city's medical men. Isn't it marvelous?"

She was flushed with elation and excitement. It occurred to him that she'd never looked more beautiful. Josh saw Betty out of the corner of his eye, she was talking to a man he didn't know, but he felt that she was looking at him, and at Emma. "I didn't think you liked Rhineman," he said.

"What? Of course I don't like Frank Rhineman. He's too pretty to be real. Why are we talking about him? It's wonderful news, Josh, aren't you thrilled?"

"Sure, congratulations. You can count yourself part of a successful pioneering movement."

Emma avoided his eyes, she looked down at the white silk roses nestling in the cleavage of her ice-blue satin gown. "I'd like to go tell Celia right now, she only lives two blocks away on Mount Vernon Street."

It occurred to Joshua that in all these years he'd never known where Celia Howard lived. He thought of her as being forever in her laboratory, imprisoning Emma there. "We can't leave now," he said. "They haven't served supper yet. And I haven't talked to that French doctor I wanted to meet."

"We're having dinner with him next week at the Wests'. You can meet him then. This is such a special piece of news, Josh. I can't bear to go on as if nothing has happened."

"Do as you wish, Emma. I'm not going anywhere."

Her gaze flew to his face, the tone of his voice was like a physical assault. "Josh, please . . ."

Her plea was lost in the music and the crowd, and wasted on Joshua's retreating back. God, he was so handsome in his black dinner jacket. Not another man in the room was even in the race. And the way he walked, there was so much authority in just the way Josh moved across the floor.

She saw him step into a group that included the flirtatious Betty Bradley and a few seconds later he danced her out onto the floor. Was there something intimate in the way the little brunette looked up at Josh? Emma felt her heart stop for a moment, then she told herself it was ridiculous. The Bradley woman was notorious. If Josh was going to cheat, he wouldn't do it with someone so flagrantly obvious.

Anger came then, bitter and intense and composed of
old wounds as well as the new. How dare he act as if this
silly party and some foreign doctor were more important
than a goal she'd pursued for six years? Emma slipped
away from the ballroom.

"You're sure he was telling the truth?" Celia asked.
"Positive. Why should he lie about such a thing, why
would anyone?"
"I don't know. It just sounds too good to be true. Oh,
Emma, what a breakthrough! What a fantastic, unbelievable breakthrough!"
Celia had been sleeping when Emma arrived. Now she
was wrapped in a plaid flannel dressing gown and her
short gray hair was in its usual tangle, also as usual, she
was unconcerned about her appearance. "I'll probably have
a letter from Margaret in a day or two, but we can't wait to
celebrate until then. We'll do it right now."
Celia strode to a cabinet in her old-fashioned sitting
room. "I was born in this house in 1863, and damned little
has changed since. There was always an old bottle in the
back of this cupboard . . . Ah, here it is. Portuguese
Madeira, from 1850. Bought by my grandfather so the
story goes. I don't know if he'd think this a proper occasion to open it, but I do."

It was more than an hour before Josh realized that
Emma had left without him. When the buffet supper was
served at eleven, he looked for her red head and didn't
find it. A discreet inquiry of the maid in charge of the
ladies' cloakroom produced the information that Mrs. Morgan had claimed her wrap before ten. Grim-faced, Morgan
returned to the party and ate lobster mousse and grapefruit salad with Betty. The import of that was not lost on
her.
"You usually avoid being with me at affairs such as this,
Joshua. Why so attentive this evening?" She stretched her
neck and looked around. "Am I mistaken, or is the lovely
Emma not here? Deserted you, my dear? A tiff perhaps?
Another man?"
"Please spare me any bitchiness," Joshua muttered. "I've
had all I can handle tonight."
"Poor Joshua. But not from me, my dear. I am always

sweetly reasonable and patient, am I not? The ideal other woman."

"Betty, please."

"Yes, dear. Now do smile, our hostess is coming this way."

The Boston matron whose home this was arrived at their table and chatted for a few moments. Her final words were open to a number of interpretations. "Wasn't I clever to think of turning the dining room into a French café for the evening? It honors our guest, and lets people who want to be alone together manage it. *Au revoir, mes petites,* do enjoy yourselves."

"My, my," Betty murmured. "Such unsheathed claws, and right here in Louisbourg Square. What are we coming to?"

Josh had risen when the hostess departed, he didn't sit down again. "I'll have to move on, Betty. It won't do to be talked about. Perhaps I'll see you later. Frankly, I'm not sure I intend to return home this evening."

Betty stared up at him and her dark eyes narrowed. "You may spend the night where you wish, Joshua. But not in my home. I believe I'm suddenly developing a headache."

"Oh, look, I'm sorry, I didn't mean to sound as if I were taking you for granted. You understand, Betty."

"I do, Joshua dear. Very well. It's you who must learn where the lines are drawn. Good evening."

Josh spun on his heel and left, his fury propelling him out the front door and into the street. The night was crisp and lit by stars. He began walking west, unsure whether he was going to let himself into his office or his home when he arrived on Commonwealth Avenue. Damn all women anyway. There was no pleasing the creatures. No, that wasn't fair. Anger didn't alter facts. He was a married man and he was having a prolonged affair with another woman. Whatever complications that produced in his life, he ought to have expected them.

He understood very well how he'd come to be involved with Billy-Jo, but how in hell had he gotten into this present situation? He loved his wife; she was beautiful and charming and talented. They had two wonderful sons. What in God's name was he doing putting all that and his career at risk? But it wasn't entirely his fault, Emma had a hand in making things as they were. If she could only see that, things might be different. Like tonight for instance. Walking out like that. Everyone must have noticed and speculated on the cause. No, they wouldn't have to speculate. Rhineman was sure to say something. She was just giving more ammunition to the gossips who already disapproved of her radical ideas.

He was seething by the time he reached his block. He paused for a moment and looked at his two front doors, 163 and 165. He could go into his office and spend the night on the couch. No, dammit, she wasn't going to drive him out of his own house, and not out of his own bed either.

He didn't put on any lights, just climbed the stairs to the bedroom. Emma wasn't sleeping; she was pretending, he could tell. Faking it to avoid a scene. Well, there wasn't going to be any scene. For once he was going to assert his rights.

Josh stripped off his clothes, letting them drop to the floor. He strode to the bed and yanked back the covers.

"Josh—"

"I think it's better if we don't talk."

There was no foreplay, no courtship, he simply took her. The word rape even crossed his mind, but that was ridiculous, she was his wife. All the same a small voice in his head told him his behavior was appalling, beyond forgiveness. He was acting like an animal, like a caveman.

But Emma didn't reject him or struggle beneath the extraordinary frenzy of his approach. She opened herself to him with abandon, and writhed beneath him with urgency. Joshua heard her gasps of hunger turn to moans of fulfillment. He emptied himself into her with a gutwrenching totality that carried them both to the heights, and made an anguish of the plummeting return to their painful reality.

"What's happened to us, Josh?" Emma whispered when the tumult was past.

He had no answer, so he pretended to have fallen quickly to sleep.

Two months later, on a January morning in 1924, Emma said, "I've something to tell you, Josh."

He paused in his dressing, alerted by her tone. She was

going to say she was leaving him, that she knew about Betty and would tolerate no more of his infidelity. He felt sick with apprehension. "Yes, what is it? I'm running a bit late this morning."

"This won't take long. I'm pregnant. Just two months, but I'm quite sure."

Relief flooded him, made him weak-kneed and started him shivering. He didn't want her to go, he told himself. He didn't want to leave her. He didn't want to be without Emma.

"I'm sorry," she whispered, obviously choking back tears. "I didn't think it would upset you so much. I didn't know you were so set against having more children."

"But that's not true. I'm not, Emma, I swear it. I was just startled." He moved toward her and took her hand. "I think it's marvelous. You must see Charles right away."

"I've made an appointment for Saturday morning. I didn't plan this, you know that, Josh. It just happened that night when—"

He pressed a finger over her lips. "I know you didn't plan it, and I know when it happened. Don't talk about it anymore. It's our baby, Emma. Conceived in love, at least for me."

She nodded. "For me too. Whatever else."

For the first time in months he kissed her before he left the house and that night she fell asleep in the circle of his arms. That hadn't happened in nearly three years.

Next morning he sat across from her in the breakfast room, watching the winter sun make a red-gold delight of her hair. "Listen, darling, I've been thinking. How about that honeymoon we never had? What would you say to a couple of weeks at Niagara Falls? Just the two of us."

"Josh, do you mean it?"

"Of course I mean it." He leaned over and covered her hand with his own. "I mean a great many things, my love." He saw tears in her eyes and felt his own grow dangerously moist. "I can get away the first two weeks in February, can you manage that?"

"I'll manage it."

"Wonderful. I'll make the reservations today."

He walked to the hospital with a spring in his step. No turning back now, he'd made his choice. Josh went into his office and locked the door behind him, then picked up the telephone.

Betty had been sleeping, he could tell by her voice. "Sorry to wake you so early, but I have to speak with you. I'll come this afternoon at four."

He didn't lead up to it, just blurted it out over the Earl Grey tea. "Emma's pregnant. I'm sorry, but you must see that I have no choice now. We'll have to stop seeing each other. I feel I have to be honest with her, under the circumstances."

She stared at him and didn't say anything.

"Thank you for the good years," Josh went on. He reached for her hand, then thought better of it and drew back. "I'll never forget you, Betty. I owe you so much. I only pray we can go on being friends."

She took a deep breath while he watched all the color drain from her face, then flood back in. "Get out of my house, Joshua."

"Betty, please. We're two adults—"

"Shut up. And get out."

He went, aching with sorrow and regret for both of them, but glad, so very glad, that it was finally ended.

The next day he went to Jamaica Plain. That was much easier. They weren't really lovers, never had been to tell the truth. Just united by an accident of fate. They spoke for an hour, then he said good-bye to Billy-Jo and the child he'd always thought of as hers, not his.

They were scheduled to leave for Canada the first Sunday in February. The days flew by and finally it was time. The entire household assembled in the front hall to say good-bye amid a flurry of suitcases and lists and last minute instructions.

Emma looked wonderful. Josh couldn't take his eyes off her. The pregnancy had flushed her cheeks and begun to fill out her thin form, though it couldn't yet be said to show. He liked the new blue wool dress she was wearing. The skirt ended halfway down her legs and showed off her slender ankles. He held her coat and slipped it over her shoulders, lingering over the pleasure of touching her. The coat was blue wool, too, with a black seal lining. Her face was framed by a blue cloche hat with a dashing black feather. Beautiful Emma. Beautiful wife.

She scooped up Cal for a final hug and he tried to grab the feather in one pudgy hand. "No you don't, you rascal." Emma passed him to his father in a swinging arc and bent over Dan, hugging him to her. "You be a good boy, darling. For once try to be a good boy for Mommy's sake."

Marya snorted. "Is not possible. If he's good boy, he's not Daniel."

Everyone laughed. Then the doorbell rang.

Josh stood nearest the door so he opened it. It took him a moment to recognize Betty, her appearance was so unexpected it served as a disguise. Then he knew it was she, and why she had come to his home. Cold washed over him, an arctic chill that froze him where he stood. He opened his mouth, but no words came. His anguish was a silent scream of protest.

"Such a pretty domestic scene of farewell," Betty said. "I realize I'm interrupting, but I'll only stay a moment." She pulled her full-length sable coat closer around her tiny, curvaceous body and the diamond brooch she wore sparkled against the dark, sumptuous fur. Her scent was cloying and sweet; it overwhelmed every other scent, somehow confirming her dominance in this situation.

In that single moment Emma knew everything. She stared at the other woman and she knew. She wanted to hurl herself at the intruder, to scratch out her eyes and tear off her clothes. She wanted to physically protect what was hers—her husband, her children, her home. But it was too late. The expression on Joshua's face told her it was too late. Everything had been stolen long before. This was merely her punishment for so long closing her eyes to the theft.

"I only came to give you a message, Emma dear," Betty said sweetly. "I'm told you're expecting another child, so I thought under the circumstances you'd want to know that Joshua has been my lover for nearly three years. You did say you wanted to be honest with her now, didn't you, Joshua darling?"

He didn't even glance at his wife. The hall had grown so still, Joshua thought he could hear everyone breathing, while he fought for air. He couldn't avoid looking at Betty, she was standing right in front of him, smiling with satisfaction. "Why?" he murmured. It was all he could manage. "Why?"

"To inflict pain on you, darling," Betty said softly. "To make you suffer. Why else?"

Only when the door had closed behind her was the silence in the hall broken. The twins began to howl, sensing the vibrations of fear and rage and dismay that charged the atmosphere. Joshua continued to stare after Betty, as if he saw her ghost. Then he heard a dull thud and knew without turning round that it was the sound of his wife's body hitting the floor.

It was impossible to say with certainty that Emma's spontaneous abortion was caused by shock, Josh knew that. Still he believed it was, not because of any medical knowledge, just a visceral certitude. The same instinct told him that now Emma would withdraw from him again, as she had when little Josh died, and that this time she would not return. The conviction grew in him while he waited for Charles West to come out of her room.

The other man appeared about ten minutes later. "Could have been a lot worse," he said reassuringly. "She's a good, strong girl, your Emma. She's going to be fine. Not too much bleeding and no uterine damage. No reason she shouldn't conceive again. Go on in, she's asking for you."

Joshua walked hesitantly down the corridor of the obstetric pavilion. Nurses accustomed to seeing him stride its length with a covey of interns hanging on his white coattails looked away, as if his so apparent grief demanded privacy. When he reached the door of Emma's private room, he paused for some seconds before opening it.

She lay very still. Her eyes were closed and her long lashes made dark shadows on pale cheeks. At first he thought she was sleeping, then she reached up one hand. Joshua realized that she wanted him to take it. He did, and sank slowly into the chair beside the bed. Emma's hand rested lightly in his, but she didn't open her eyes. They remained so for some moments. "Emma," he whispered finally. "Emma."

"Don't speak," she murmured. "I'm so tired, Josh. Don't speak, just stay by me."

When a nurse came in half an hour later, the couple was still in the same position. "She's sleeping, Doctor Morgan," the nurse said softly. "Don't you think you should go and get some rest, sir?"

Josh gently disengaged his hand. "Yes, I guess I'll go do that. I'll get some rest."

"I've never been able to talk about it before," Joshua said two days later. "Not even to you. That time before we came to Boston, when we drove out to the Point, I came close. But I've never really let myself remember how I felt about Captain Sweet. When he died, I closed the door on all that."

"Perhaps it's better if such doors remain closed." Emma lay with her face turned to the window, not daring to look at her husband, not sure how to deal with the assortment of feelings that accosted her now that her strength was slowly beginning to return.

"No," Joshua said. "That's something I see now. Burying feelings doesn't get rid of them, it just lets them fester. A lot of what I've done is because of my anger at that old bastard. Somehow it got turned on you."

"I'm angry, too, Josh. I'm furious and hurt and frightened, and I don't know what to say or what to think. I don't even know if I want to continue this conversation."

Joshua remembered her reaching out to him in the first pain and sadness of the loss of the child. He made himself respond not to the way she sounded at the moment, but to that memory. "Darling, I've no right to ask anything of you, but hear me out before you make any decisions. All the time Sweet was rubbing my nose in it, showing me over and over again that he couldn't stand the sight of me, I told myself it didn't really matter. But of course it did, I desperately wanted some sign of acceptance from him and it never came. So I built up defenses for myself. They all had to do with never letting myself be rejected; I'd reject someone else before they had a chance to reject me. Do you see?"

"In a way," Emma said. "But I never rejected you, Josh. I pursued you for three years and talked you into asking me to marry you. Because I loved you and believed you loved me. And I married you and bore you three sons. Why did you repay me by turning to that . . . that bitch!" She spat out the unaccustomed curse as if it were capable of expelling all the anger in her soul.

Josh took a deep breath. This was the hardest part. He had to make Emma recognize a truth which had only become clear to him in the past forty-eight hours. If he didn't, their life together was finished. "Because I did believe you were rejecting me. No, wait before you say anything, please. That's how I saw it, because of everything that went before. When you went out to work, something inside me interpreted that as a signal I wasn't enough for you. I took up with Betty because I had to prove to myself that I didn't need you, and didn't care."

He knew how lame the argument sounded. And he was still unsure about the rest of it, the decision not to make a clean breast of the whole thing and tell her about Billy-Jo. It would hurt Emma so much more than the affair with Betty. If he told her about that they had no future. There was only one other thing he could say. "I never stopped loving you, Emma. I never will."

Outside snow was falling in big, sticky flakes that attached themselves to the window pane; fragile splendors which lasted a few seconds, then melted into oblivion. Emma finally spoke, but she said only his name. "Joshua."

"Yes?" He bent forward, wanting to hear his sentence and have done with it.

"Oh, Joshua, what perverse, foolish creatures we are. I love you; nothing either of us does can change that. We won't change either, I suppose. But let's try. We have come too far not to try."

BOOK TWO
1944 — 1947

RUTH

8

*T*he jeep bounced over the track, raising a cloud of red dust. It mingled with the sweat of the two men in the vehicle, forming tiny rivulets of mud that coursed down their necks. Midmorning and already stifling.

"Hard to imagine it's Christmas next week, ain't it, Cap'n?"

"That it is, Schultz." Captain Daniel Morgan hummed a few bars of "White Christmas."

His driver turned and grinned. "I guess Crosby ain't never been in Africa."

"Wrong as usual, Schultz. You are a congenital idiot. The song is about dreaming of a white Christmas, not having one."

"Yeah, I never thought of that."

Schultz drove on in silence. Daniel stared at the back of his head. Was it depressing, he wondered, to be constantly reminded that some guys were born with looks, money, charm, and brains? It must be, he decided. Nonetheless, being his driver was good duty, and Schultz must know he was lucky to have the job. Like most of the doctors, Daniel ignored differences of rank when they were alone, and he had cut Schultz in on a number of sweet little deals.

Daniel dismissed the other man from his thoughts. He leaned back in his seat and watched the dun-colored landscape. From the military hospital in the minuscule watering hole of El Tofā—only God and the Allied Command knew what kind of monumental fuck-up caused it to be built there—to Casablanca on the coast, it was all like this. The low foothills of the Riff flattened gradually to a broad, undulating plain of ocher dust. Dan's eyes watered, irritated by grit and confused by emptiness. He swiped at them with the back of his hand, then reached into the pocket of his khaki battle fatigue jacket and withdrew the only solace near at hand, the week's mail.

As usual, he read Jessica's letter first. He and his kid sister had formed a mutual admiration society eleven years before when she was born. The letter was a detailed account of her fifth grade school days, followed by a hilarious tale about a white mouse that escaped in Celia Howard's laboratory and came home in Mama's handbag. Daniel chuckled softly.

Schultz caught his eye in the rearview mirror, clearly about to say something. Daniel hastily looked away and began on his second letter. It was from his father, a long report of Caleb's progress as a gynecology resident at Memorial Hospital. That his father was Dr. Joshua Morgan, head of the gynecology service, obviously hadn't hurt.

He read quickly, not lingering over the words, not enjoying them. His twin was usurping his traditional role as favorite son. Worse, Caleb had it all—professional progress and a free hand with the man-starved girls in Boston. Daniel's mouth tasted sour. But he couldn't suppress a wry grin.

The only reason Cal was exempt from military service was his damaged arm, hurt when they were kids. In a fight started by Dan. So he was reaping what he'd sowed, just as Marya always promised. The grin faded, replaced by a quick, twisted grimace of homesickness. Like Jessie, Marya was someone he truly missed.

Marya was his childhood; she represented home and warmth and love, because she had been there when they were sick, bandaged their scrapes, encouraged their explorations, settled their arguments—Marya, not his mother. What a crazy thing for a wealthy woman to do in 1920, work outside the home. But Mom was an original, one of a kind, and Dad accepted her behavior, because of something to do with the baby who'd died before he and Caleb were born. Daniel was never quite sure of the meaning of all the undercurrents between his parents. He heard Schultz speaking and jerked himself back to the present. "What?"

"I asked if you wanna stop here, or go to the old quarter?"

They were in Casablanca now, rolling along broad boulevards of disintegrating nineteenth century colonial grandeur. The ostentatious European facades of residences and government buildings looked down on streets littered with uncollected garbage. Camel dung steamed in fly-specked heaps. Donkeys and bicycles were more in evidence than the oversize limousines for which the road had been designed.

All the signs were printed in French, but mostly the noisy crowd spoke guttural Moroccan Arabic. Since the fall of France her colony was in limbo, cut off from its head. But those who might have used the opportunity to claim independence were inhibited by the allied presence in this so-called international zone. Daniel surveyed the scene with distaste. He disliked the sight of foundering, useless power, it did not agree with his notions of the ordering of the universe. "The old quarter," he snapped.

"As far as you're concerned, all Africa is one glorious whorehouse, isn't it, Schultz?" Daniel asked as they drove on. "You can have your choice of how to get laid any hour of the day or night. Goddamn marvelous. Right?"

"Well, it ain't bad, Cap'n."

"Except for one thing," Daniel said. "Casablanca's a whorehouse without a madam. There's no one to keep order and the place is full of sluts."

Schultz probably didn't understand, but he nodded his head in agreement and turned east into a rabbit warren of crooked alleys and narrow lanes. Here, Daniel knew, nothing had changed for centuries. Squat white buildings with flat roofs and small square windows baked in the endless sun, some were hidden by angled walls that hinted at seductive mysteries behind their featureless expanse.

The jeep roared through a huge puddle of stinking camel urine and splashed a throng of pedestrians. They waved their arms and called down curses on the driver, his passenger, and all their misbegotten forbears.

"Up yours too," Schultz shouted back. He turned a corner and left the piss-soaked antagonists behind, then braked beside a tiny, nondescript café. "This do, Cap'n?"

"Yeah, this is fine." Daniel waited for Schultz to jump out and open the door, an observance of form to impress the natives. He even returned the other man's salute. "Pick me up here in two hours, Sergeant." He dropped his voice, "And in the meantime try to avoid getting another dose of clap."

The café was cool and dim; the deeply recessed windows with their wide-spaced wooden bars kept out the blazing sun, but not the flies. There were hundreds of them and their buzzing made an audible hum. In one corner a limp coil of sticky paper was black with the dead of this endless war between man and insects. The flies were winning. That's what all the buzzing was about, their "Hallelujah Chorus." Daniel stared malevolently at the flies.

"Good morning, captain sahib." A slight man in a filthy jellaba appeared. Once it had been striped black and white, now the robe was a uniform-gray. It flapped above the Arab's sinewed ankles and bare brown feet.

"Mustapha, if I brought you some screens for the doors and windows, would you put them up?"

The man looked puzzled. His mahogany face twisted as he struggled to understand. "What for are screens, captain sahib?"

"To keep out the flies. They're disease carriers, Mustapha. They make you sick."

"I am very well, thank you, captain sahib. And flies too are creatures of Allah. Will the Captain take tea?"

Daniel sighed. "Yes. Is Abdul here?"

"I regret, not yet. But if the Captain will only wait a few moments . . ." Mustapha made elaborate bows in the direction of one of the low, backless stools that were scattered about. Daniel sat down, folding his long legs in something like the fashion of the supple natives, trying to make his face as blank and noncommittal as theirs.

Mustapha brought the tea; hot and sweet, and pungent with crushed mint. Daniel sipped it gratefully. His throat was parched with dust; it seemed to him it had been so during the entire three years he'd been in Morocco. After a few seconds he glanced at his watch.

Perhaps in response to the impatient gesture, the man Daniel knew only as Abdul appeared. "Salaam aleikim."

"Aleikim salaam." Daniel nodded to the stool opposite.

The man sank down gracefully. He wore a tasseled red fez and a black western style suit. According to rumor, he was an Egyptian. Daniel didn't know if it was true, and

didn't care. Mustapha came with two more steaming serv-
ings of tea and whisked away the American's empty glass.
"I trust you are well, Captain," Abdul said. He spoke
excellent English with a pleasant British accent.

"Not bad, considering this disease-ridden hellhole."

Abdul shrugged delicately. "The fortunes of war, Captain."

"Yeah, something like that. And are you well?" Cut the
crap, he wanted to say. Get to business. But he'd learned
better.

"Allah is good to me, praised be his holy name. And to
you, too, I may add." He pushed a scrap of paper across
the low table. "This will interest you, I think."

Daniel squinted at the terse notations. They consisted of
an address and the words, "whisky, twenty-six cases." He
memorized the address and produced his Zippo lighter.
The paper burned to ash in seconds. "Guards?"

"At midnight this Tuesday they will all be occupied for
half an hour. No more, no less."

"Fine." Daniel reached into his pocket again. This time
he withdrew an envelope. Inside were three hundred
crisp new American dollar bills, carefully counted out
beforehand, unmarked. "Same time next week," he said,
rising.

"If Allah permits," Abdul said, fading into the no-man's-
land behind the beaded curtain.

Mustapha reappeared. Daniel pressed a twenty-dollar
bill into his outstretched hand. The Moroccan smiled,
displaying three yellow teeth in an otherwise empty mouth.
"Captain sahib will honor us with his presence again?"

"If Allah permits," Daniel said. He managed to keep a
straight face.

"Alors! He comes again, your American."

"He said he would be back today for the cloth, why act
surprised?" Ruth Morhaim looked scornfully at her younger sister, but nonetheless raised a quick hand to her black
chignon.

The little girl pulled back from the narrow door of the
shop in the Jewish section of the old quarter. "He comes
to see you. He will take us to America if you are clever."

"You are a wicked child. Go in the back. *Vite!*"

A few seconds later Daniel stepped inside, ducking his
head to negotiate the low doorway. When he straightened,

he seemed to fill all the available space. He was six feet
two inches tall, with broad shoulders, black curly hair,
startling aquamarine eyes with pale irises, and a slow,
sweet, devastating smile. Ruth Morhaim allowed herself
three unguarded seconds in which to drink in his smile.
She often dreamed of it. Then she spoke in the same
formal manner she always used with the American. "Good
morning, Captain Morgan. I have everything ready for
you."

"Good girl. I've located a pilot to take the stuff home, if
I get it to the airfield by noon."

It was hard for Ruth to imagine that an airplane could
actually take off from Morocco and land in America. That
cloth from her little shop should be in that fabled place in
two or three days seemed a miracle. But Captain Morgan
said it would, so it must be true. She reached behind her
for the three dress lengths he had ordered.

"This one is for your mother," she said, adding with
pride, "from my cousin's shop in Marrakesh. No one here
has seen such silk since before the war." The fabric she
spread across the narrow table was pale blue, shot with
gold thread and bordered with a design of interwoven
leaves, also in gold. "If, as you say, Madame Emma has
the same color eyes as yours, it will be perfect."

"The very same." Daniel grinned. Madame Emma. The
title would suit his mother. Beautiful, regal, remarkably
intelligent . . . Madame Emma, very apt. "You know," he
said, "no one in my family has black eyes. What do you
think a child of ours would look like, Ruth?"

He reached across the counter and took her chin in his
hand, turning her face to the light slanting in the door.
She had delicate features dominated by the dark, almond-
shaped eyes and a broad brow, accentuated by the severe
way she swept back her hair. Ruth did not struggle in his
grip, but Daniel finally let her go. "Too bad you're a good
girl and we can't find out." She blushed furiously. He
liked that, these days it seemed a forgotten art.

"You must not say such things," she admonished softly.
"Someone may hear." Ruth put her hand to her cheek; it
was tingling. She turned away and reached for a second
piece of cloth. "This one is for your little sister. She is
called Jessica, no?"

"Yes." He fingered the dark rose velvet approvingly. "I can see this on Jessie. What about Marya?"

"For your old nurse I thought this one." Ruth showed him a length of dark brown satin.

Daniel shook his head. "No, too much like the kind of thing she always buys for herself. Marya isn't really old, she's the same age as my mother. We just call her old Marya."

Because she is a servant, Ruth thought. Aloud she said, "Very well, perhaps you would prefer this."

Daniel shook his head again, frowning at the bright yellow cotton. "Still too ordinary. Marya' s special."

Ruth was pensive for a moment, then she clapped her hands together in a gesture of delight. "I have something very special. Wait. Shama, come here!"

The little girl appeared instantly, obviously having been lurking nearby. The sisters spoke in rapid French, Shama seemed to be protesting something. Finally she disappeared again. When she returned, she had a bolt of pale ivory lace clutched in her scrawny arms. She lay it down with evident reluctance, stared hard at her sister for a moment, then turned and ran.

Daniel wondered at the private drama. Maybe the kid had been promised a dress of this lace. He thought of asking, but there wasn't a minute to waste if he wanted to get his presents to the airfield on time. Besides, the lace was lovely.

"Will this do?" Ruth asked.

"Perfectly. Now if you'll wrap all this I can—Wait a minute, I forgot Tessie and Nora. The cook and the maid," he added.

Somehow he'd formed the habit of discussing the people at home with Ruth Morhaim, as if she were likely to meet them one day. She never would, of course. He just enjoyed talking about them. And Ruth had a serenity that refreshed him and invited confidences. She was a pleasant change from the brash, modern nurses at the hospital. And she was delightful to look at. Particularly when she was preoccupied as she was now, considering the problem of providing two more suitable pieces of cloth from her war-depleted stocks.

A few minutes later they had decided on dark blue satin for the Marsh sisters, and the package was neatly tied and ready. Daniel paid in U.S. dollars, adding ten more to the twenty-six she had asked for. He saw her tuck the bills into her bodice with a look of relief. Casablanca had escaped the fighting which drove Rommel and the Germans from North Africa, but the war had taken its toll, even here. The Morhaim sisters had lost both parents to a bomb dropped not in a raid, but by some allied pilot needing to lighten his load in order to get safely back to base. Life for Ruth and Shama had been very hard. Daniel knew how much his thirty-six dollars represented.

"Look," he said by way of farewell, "I'll be in town again in a few days, and I'll bring you some stuff from the PX."

"Some sugar would be very welcome, if you can spare it. I will pay of course," Ruth added gravely.

Daniel thought of the mountains of bags of sugar on the base. "Sugar it is. See you soon."

Shama waited until he was gone, then confronted her sister across the narrow counter. She was white-faced, her cheeks streaked with tears. "That was your wedding lace. *Maman* always said so."

Ruth sighed. "I know, *ma petite*, but times are hard and *Maman* would understand if she were here." She reached out to touch the little girl, but Shama bolted into the back.

Daniel walked quickly through the alleys of the old quarter, ignoring the jostling crowd. He was already a few minutes late for the rendezvous with Schultz. And someone was trying to make him later. A hand clutched at his arm. He didn't turn, just tried to shake it off.

"Give a girl a hand, will you, Captain?"

The words were in English and the voice was familiar. Startled, Daniel glanced over his shoulder. The woman so fiercely hanging on to him was a tiny redhead with a scattering of freckles on her turned up nose. At the moment they stood out unpleasantly, dark specks on ghostly white skin. "Kitty Donnely . . . Hey, what's the matter? You look like death."

"Death, I'm afraid, is about to be the operative word." She managed to get the sentence out before sagging against him in a faint.

Daniel gripped her wrist with practiced fingers; the pulse was very rapid, but strong. Swiftly he picked her up and shoved through the crowd to where Schultz was waiting.

"What's the trouble, Cap'n? Say, that's Lieutenant Donnely, ain't it? What's she doin' here?"

"You ask too damn many questions, Schultz, and the only one I can answer is that yes, this inert bundle is Nurse Donnely. So kindly get your ass in gear and help me get her in the back."

Daniel kept his fingers on her pulse. Still strong, still much too rapid. He'd been a twenty-one-year-old intern right out of Harvard Medical School when he joined the army, but in the speeded up world of wartime, the military had finished his medical training in a baptism of fire taking half the usual time. He'd been a qualified doctor for over two years now, so an unconscious woman was all in a day's work. "Pass me that bottle of booze you keep under the seat, Sergeant. Then get us the hell out of here and back to the hospital."

"What about the stop at the airfield?"

Daniel looked at the package he'd carried from Ruth Morhaim's shop, then at Kitty sprawled on the seat beside him. She was beginning to come round and she was moaning. "Skip the airfield," he said ruefully. "And make time." Schultz roared into the traffic of donkey carts and camels and bicycles, scattering all in his path. A cloud of dust and curses trailed in the jeep's wake.

As they cleared the town Kitty Donnely's eyes fluttered open. "Have a heart, Captain," she murmured. "Don't throw me to the wolves back at the base."

"Who knocked you up?"

"Haven't a clue." Kitty drew deep on her cigarette. "Anyway, I don't want anything from any of the half dozen bastards it might have been. I paid for my own abortion, thank you."

"You could have died. And if I'm found out I could be court-martialed for keeping you in here."

They were in an unused storeroom behind the morgue. Schultz had suggested it. Sometimes they stashed goods there for a day or two, while they waited for a buyer or more permanent storage space. To date no one had wandered in uninvited. The morgue wasn't a popular place.

Daniel watched the nurse and waited for the explanation and the remorse he expected. Kitty was eyeing him speculatively through a blue haze of cigarette smoke. It struck him that she was not in the least remorseful.

"Danny boy, you have everything so well greased around here that the chance of a court-martial for any of your offenses is remote. It was my guardian angel's big day today. I could have run into one of the real pricks on this base, but I didn't, I ran into you. Praised be the blessed Virgin and all the saints."

"Okay. But how come you didn't try me or one of the other doctors first? Dammit, Kitty, you should know better than to mess around with some filthy native woman in the old quarter. Haven't you seen enough infection these past few years?"

"Would you have done a D and C, lover? All nice and sterile and no questions asked?" He looked away and she grimaced. "See, even you get squeamish about abortion. All you goddamn doctors get your trousers in a twist when the subject comes up. Besides, the old lady wasn't filthy. She was very clean and she boiled everything before she started. I watched her. And I'm not in bad shape, am I? I just passed out from the pain."

It was true. Daniel had examined her as soon as he got her into the room. She was still bleeding a little, that's how he'd known where to look, but there was no evidence she'd been mauled. With luck she'd be on duty tomorrow as scheduled. "Tell me again how she did it," he demanded.

"With a catheter, a long curved cannula, and a rubber bulb. Abortion by injection, washing out the uterus. Apparently it's been going on here for years. Very effective and fairly safe. I may go into business when I get home."

"Jesus! She could have pierced the uterus, Kitty. You know she could have."

"But she didn't, did she? You had a look with the speculum."

"No. Everything seems okay. All the same, you're damn lucky."

"And not pregnant. Now go away, guardian angel, and let me sleep."

Daniel was on duty that afternoon and until he was relieved he thought no more of Kitty Donnely. Then he checked the room behind the morgue and found it empty. Apparently she'd felt well enough to return to her own bed. He thought of going down to the canteen, but decided against it. He had a bottle of scotch in his quarters and wanted to drink alone.

There was a note propped on the table in his room. Not from Kitty as it turned out. He was still waiting for gushing gratitude, but it seemed less and less likely. The note was from Schultz. He'd located another pilot willing to carry Captain Morgan's Christmas presents home. The package was already on its way. The captain owed him a hundred bucks because the fly-boy insisted on being paid in advance. Daniel grunted and pulled a C-note from his pocket, so he wouldn't forget to give it to the sergeant in the morning.

Time was, just a few years ago, when he'd have thought a hundred bucks a fortune. Not anymore. He had squirreled away quite a bundle in this war. Hell, he'd be going home a rich man. And what would the folks say to that? Nothing good probably. So he wouldn't tell them.

Dad was the most prominent gynecologist in Boston; Mother had started as Celia's assistant, but now she was a chemist in her own right. Upstanding pillars of the community were Joshua and Emma Morgan. Respected people. No, more than that, in some circles his father was worshiped. The doctor who'd changed the face of his specialty.

Daniel grinned and poured himself another whisky. Not the face exactly. Dear old Dad put the final seal of glory on his reputation when he got the notion of shaving women's cunts before delivery. Of such extraordinary innovations had he fashioned a revolution in obstetrics. Well, Joshua's son was an innovator too. Only Joshua wouldn't understand, so he'd never hear the gory details. Daniel was already laying the groundwork; he kept writing home that he was winning lots of money at poker.

Caleb Morgan was as tall as his twin, but that was the only physical resemblance between them. Caleb was spare and compact; he had Emma's litheness, not Joshua's brawn. He had Emma's red hair, too, thick and straight and worn short so it wouldn't fall in his eyes when he was bending over a patient. Caleb's eyes were green, like Joshua's, but he didn't have the electric smile shared by Joshua and Daniel. Caleb's smile was reserved and shy. Women reacted to it differently, but not without enthusiasm, particularly now that there were so few young men in Boston.

Dr. Caleb Morgan had his pick of female companions and until recently he'd been exercising that freedom of

choice. But lately things had changed. He believed the
change was of his making, which was a mark of his
innocence.

Susan Davenport first saw Caleb Morgan in the autumn
of 1944, when she went to Memorial Hospital with a
committee of the Junior League to roll bandages for the
war effort. The committee worked in the doctors' lounge
in the obstetrics unit, deemed suitable because maternity
wasn't a disease, and the young ladies wouldn't be exposed
to unpleasant smells or sights or sounds.

In only one afternoon Susan decided to snare Caleb.
Initially she noted his good looks, but alone that would not
have interested her. Susan's plans involved more than a
handsome husband. What attracted her to the tall, spare,
redheaded doctor was his air of quiet authority. It was
confirmed by the expressions of the two nurses to whom
he was speaking. They treated him with a mixture of awe
and adoration, and hastened to do his bidding.

"Who is that man?" Susan demanded of the other members of the committee.

Alicia Williams glanced through the half-open door
toward the nurses' station. "You mean the carrot top who
just left?"

"I do. Do you know him?"

"Of course, he's Caleb Morgan, Doctor Joshua Morgan's
son. He's a gynecologist too."

Susan felt a small, inexplicable thrill. All doctoring conveyed a sense of power, but gynecology with its aura of
sexuality added something extra. "How come he's not in
the service?"

"Too old," one of the others teased. "He's really fifty,
Sue, just well preserved."

"Don't be an idiot." Alicia closed the lid of a carton full
of neatly rolled bandages and replaced it with an empty
one. "Caleb's twenty-four, same as my brother Jim. They
were at Harvard together. He has a bad arm as a result of
an accident when he was a kid. That's why he's four-F."

"Do you know him?" Susan demanded. "To speak to, I
mean."

"Sure. He's been at our house lots of times. He and
Daniel, his twin. Daniel's in the army now, and since Jim
is, too, I haven't actually seen Cal in ages."

"Unless I miss my guess," a third girl commented tartly,

"Sue plans for you to see him again soon. With her in tow. But be on guard, Susie. He must be one of the few eligible males in captivity, and the competition will be fierce."

Susan Davenport smiled.

It was two weeks before Alicia and Susan managed to bump into Caleb in the hospital cafeteria. When it happened, Susan watched Caleb's reactions carefully. They were satisfactory.

She could practically see Dr. Morgan catalogue her vivacious charm, her large and luminous pearl-gray eyes, and her long blond hair. She wore a white cashmere twin sweater set and a flared blue tweed skirt. The sweaters showed off her perfect little breasts and a wide leather belt enhanced her twenty-inch waist. Susan rose so that Caleb could get the full effect of the outfit, as well as her excellent legs, exhibited to advantage by the sheer silk stockings she managed to buy on the black market, and the high-heeled navy pumps she wore.

"We're having a small gathering at our house next Sunday afternoon, Doctor Morgan. Will you join us?" Susan tossed her pale corn silk hair in a gesture that always served her well.

"I'd be delighted, Miss Davenport. I don't have to be on duty until six P.M. on Sunday. Will that fit in?"

"Perfectly. It's just sherry and coffee and cake at four. Mostly Daddy's cronies from the university. Number ten Marlborough Street. I'll look forward to it."

"So will I." Caleb watched her depart and was unaware of the smitten look on his face.

The Davenport home was old Boston of the best sort. Mrs. Davenport had been a Cabot; the fine furnishings and paintings—many of them valuable originals—reflected that, not her husband's meager earnings as a professor. Caleb didn't notice any details, just the general impression of subdued wealth. He was thinking about Susan, not her home. He'd spent every day since he met her wondering if she was really as enchantingly pretty as he'd first thought.

She was, and the gracious setting enhanced her charms. Susan's hair was piled on top of her head and caught with a blue satin band. The style showed off perfect little ears and large, long-lashed eyes. She wore a blouse of pale blue crushed velvet and a skirt of swirling rainbow-colored silk. To Caleb she seemed to move in a pastel symphony of soft, sighing sounds. He held her hand a few seconds longer than necessary when they said good-bye, and two days later he called to arrange a date to go ice-skating the following weekend.

From then on everything went exactly as Susan planned.

"Mom, you're a surprise. What are you doing here?" Caleb jumped up from the small marble-topped table and got his mother a chair.

"I left the lab early, thought I'd see if it was true that Stearns had some silk stockings. It wasn't, so I came in for coffee. Caleb, aren't you going to introduce me to this beautiful young lady?"

"Of course. Sorry. Mom, this is Susan Davenport."

"Hello, my dear. How nice to meet you at last. Caleb's spoken of you so often."

"And of you, Mrs. Morgan. What a shame about the stockings."

Emma sighed. "Yes, but I didn't really think it would be true. Feminine vanity leads to wishful thinking." She smiled at the girl, examining her all the while.

"What can I order for you, Mom?"

They were in Bailey's Ice Cream Parlor on Tremont Street. The young were indulging in two of the famous hot fudge sundaes. "Just black coffee," Emma said. "At my age I can get fat looking at ice cream."

Should she have said that? Would they then wonder why she'd come into Bailey's? No, probably not. They were too wrapped up in each other to imagine that Emma had overheard her son make the date and had arranged this "accidental" meeting. With a sudden sense of shock Emma realized Susan was waging a campaign to get Cal. But she'd never be able to make him see it. If she even tried he would resent it. Oh, God, he was besotted by her. But this girl was wrong for him. Emma had seen her for only ten minutes and knew she was wrong. One word of criticism to Cal though and she might alienate him for life. She couldn't bear that, not with Cal.

She'd taken up crewel work lately. In the evenings when she and Josh sat in the library, he read while Emma stitched. Such a cozy domestic scene, so hard to equate it with all the drama of their lives. Now she was going to disturb the surface calm, make more drama. Josh was going to say she was imagining things, that she was not quite balanced where Caleb was concerned. But she had to try. For Caleb's sake she would try anything.

"I think Cal is becoming serious about the Davenport girl," Emma said. "I don't approve."

"Why not? Her father's a professor of some sort, isn't he?" Josh didn't lift his eyes from his medical journal.

"Her father is a professor of law at Suffolk University. I don't disapprove of her family."

"What then?" Still turning pages. "She seems nice enough. Pretty too."

Emma was startled. "You've met her?"

"Yes, as a matter of fact. They were going someplace and she came to the hospital to meet Cal. I happened to run into them."

The same way she had "happened" to run into them at Bailey's, Emma thought. She knew it wasn't Josh who had engineered his meeting with Susan Davenport; it had to have been the girl herself. Susan must want whatever allies she could get in her campaign to win Caleb. And no doubt she knew that a man was more susceptible to her charms than a woman would be. So she had concentrated on Cal's father rather than his mother.

Emma guessed that it was pointless to voice such thoughts. Josh would never believe them. "Yes, the girl's pretty," she said instead. "If you like the blond, baby-doll type. It's not her looks that bother me."

Josh sighed and put down the magazine. He could tell from Emma's tone that she meant to continue the conversation. "You've got to let him live his own life, my dear," he said gently.

"I've never been a hovering mother, you know that. So don't take that tone. Besides, it's easy for you to talk. Caleb's following right in your footsteps. And you're with him all day at the hospital."

"We don't live in each other's pockets at Memorial, Emma. Hospitals simply don't operate that way. Caleb had to prove himself, like any other young resident."

"And he has, hasn't he?"

"Yes, as a matter of fact. I admit being surprised. I didn't think Cal had so much originality in him. And it's shown up at just the right time. When this damned war is over, medicine is going to change dramatically. Some of the things being discussed now have been simmering on a back burner for decades."

Joshua warmed to his subject, waving his magazine for emphasis. "My God, Emma, think about how it was when I started. Think about how slowly things changed back then. In '26 we found out that the pituitary gland governs the production of reproductive hormones. In '29 we knew about estrogen, in '34 progesterone. But nothing much was done with any of that, because birth was something sacred, not to be meddled with. Well, it's not sacred anymore."

Emma glanced up from her sewing. "Isn't it, Josh? I think it is. It's still illegal to buy a condom or be fitted for a diaphragm in Massachusetts."

"I know," Josh agreed. "But the whole climate is changing as a result of this miserable war. All of a sudden things are heating up, there's money for research." He waved the magazine yet again. "Do you know what I'm reading in here? An article by John Rock, he's been experimenting with refrigerating human sperm. Think of it, Emma . . . the possibilities boggle the mind. Caleb is going to profit from all that."

She wondered how he could be so enthusiastic, so completely without bitterness. "Josh, do you ever regret not doing more research?"

He looked at her a moment before answering. "No." There was just a slight coolness in his tone. "I had my family to take care of, I don't regret any of you."

"No," she said placatingly, "of course no. But are you satisfied for Caleb to be the one to take it up, not Daniel as you planned? A switch, isn't it, Josh?"

"There will be room for Daniel, too, once he gets home."

Emma threaded a needle with pale pink yarn. It gave her a reason not to look at her husband. How had this happened? In some subtle way they'd become divided into two camps; she on Caleb's side, Josh on Daniel's. She loved both her sons, she knew Josh did too. And yet . . .

Emma pulled the yarn through the needle and knotted one end. Back to her role as peacemaker, keeper of the family hearth, guardian of unity. "Yes, I know there'll be room for Daniel. Of course both boys have a wonderful future. Darling, that's exactly why I'm unhappy about the

Davenport girl. She's not right for Caleb, not for a lifetime. But that's Cal's style, he won't think of her in terms of a fling."

Josh looked startled. "Has he asked her to—" He broke off because there was a light tap on the library door.

Marya let herself in, she looked worried. "Can you come to Jessica, Doctor Josh? I think she has temperature."

Joshua rose quickly. Jessica's fevers were frequent and occurred whenever she was the slightest bit sick, a legacy from the rheumatic fever she'd had at age six. And the fevers could never be ignored. "Right away, Marya." He turned to his wife. "Will you come too?"

Emma didn't lift her head from her needlework. "There's no need of that. You're the one Jessie always wants if she's ill." She took another stitch. Joshua stared at his wife, opened his mouth, then didn't say anything. For a moment tension was palpable in the library. Then he turned on his heel and followed Marya.

Jessica's room was on the third floor. It was graphic evidence of a pampered childhood. The place was a kaleidoscope of color. Every inch was filled with stuffed animals, miniature dolls dressed in costumes of all nations, an elaborate dollhouse, and an enchanting decor of pink-and-white ruffled chintz. Emma had outdone herself in here. Perhaps because—Josh shook his head to drive the notion away.

Everything in the room was very neat, Jessica was that kind of child. The only exception was the letter she held in her hand. It was smudged and dog-eared from numerous readings and the fact that she'd carried it with her for three days, slept with it under her pillow for two nights. She was reading the letter when Joshua came in.

"More news from Daniel?" he asked. He knew it must be that. Nothing and no one meant as much to Jessie as her big brother Daniel.

"Not more news. The letter I got Monday. I haven't had another since."

"Well, Daniel does have some things to do over there besides write letters. Now, let's have a look at you. Marya thinks you've got a bit of a fever."

"Daniel says he's sending some super Christmas presents. They come from Ruth's shop." She allowed her father to turn back the lacy quilt while she spoke. Doctor's ministrations—her father's and at least three others—were

an ongoing part of her life. Jessica ignored them unless
they hurt. Usually they didn't.

"Who is Ruth?" Joshua asked while he prodded her
stomach.

The child sighed with resignation. "I told you lots of
times, Daddy. Ruth is the Moroccan Jewess who runs the
fabric shop on the Rue des Juifs in the old quarter."

"Sounds as if you've actually met her."

"Of course I haven't. But Daniel writes me everything
that happens, just like he promised before he went away.
He says Ruth is very pretty, and she and her little sister,
Shama, are orphans. Shama's two years older than me.
Their parents were killed in the war."

"Lots of that these days, I'm afraid," Joshua said sadly.
"Now, miss, stick out your tongue and say ah."

Marya watched anxiously and was relieved when Joshua
turned to her with a smile. "Nothing serious. We'll give
her two aspirins tonight and a day in bed tomorrow."

Jessica didn't flinch at the prescription. She liked staying
in bed with her books and her dolls and Daniel's letters. But
she had one worry. "I don't need Doctor Manners, do I?"

"No. But don't you like Doctor Manners?" The pediatrician had been caring for Jessica since she was born, six
weeks premature, and this was the first time Joshua suspected that his daughter didn't like Manners.

"Oh, he's all right. Except he always tells me to get up and
do things. How can I do things when I'm sick all the time?"

Joshua had no answer for that. He merely chuckled and
patted the child's hand. It was a small and dainty hand,
like everything about her. And her hair was neither his
black nor Emma's red. Jessie had a curly, dark chestnut
mane with auburn highlights. And golden skin tones. A
throwback to her Portuguese maternal grandfather perhaps. Her eyes were like his, too, brown flecked with
gold. Too bad Jessie had never known Captain Manny
Silva, she might have profited by contact with a less rar-
efied soul.

"What are you thinking, Daddy?"

"I'm thinking how pretty you are."

Jessica laughed and her fever-flushed cheeks turned
deeper pink. "I'm not. You are though. I like all the silver
in your hair. Mommy showed me a picture of you when it
was plain black. I like it better this way."

"Beauty is only from the skin deep," Marya interrupted. She had a fund of such expressions, sometimes mauled in English, but she had wisdom as well. The Morgans fussed over Jessica too much. Marya wanted to make the child more independent. But only she and Dr. Manners shared that goal. Dr. Josh just wanted to protect her, and Mrs. Emma mostly ignored her. Guilt, of course. No one knew that better than Marya. But the past couldn't be changed. Only the future. "Time for bed," she said firmly, shooing her employer from the room.

Emma was still sewing in the library. Joshua paused a moment before speaking, watching her. Jessie had a point. Emma had pronounced silver wings at her temples now, but they only added to her beauty. At forty-nine Emma remained startlingly lovely. She seemed unbothered by his scrutiny and she didn't look up. "How is she?"

"All right. Her heart's fine. Just a slight cold. I've said she's to stay in bed tomorrow."

"She won't mind that. More time to moon over Daniel's letters."

"I know. She's practically gone through the war with him. Though I doubt he tells her everything, as she imagines. Have you heard about a Jewess named Ruth?"

"Yes, but only from Jessie. Daniel's letters to me are invariably brief. Mostly they're about card games."

Josh walked to the sideboard and poured himself a cognac. "Care for a nightcap?" Emma nodded. He brought her a sherry and they sat in silence for a few moments. The clock chimed ten and Emma folded her sewing and put it away, murmuring something about needing to be at the lab early in the morning.

"Wait a minute, before Marya came in, were you trying to tell me that Cal's asked this Davenport girl to marry him?"

"No. I don't think he has, yet."

"But you think he will?"

"I'm afraid he will."

Josh sighed. "There's nothing we can do about it, is there?"

"I hoped you could do something. Get him transferred to some other hospital for a while perhaps."

"It wouldn't work, Emma. Even if I could do it, which I probably couldn't."

She sat very still for a moment. "No," she said finally. "I suppose it wouldn't work. If only Daniel were here, maybe he could talk sense to Cal."

"You may be wrong you know," Josh said softly. "Maybe she'll make a wonderful wife and they'll be happy ever after."

Emma smiled. "Still believe in fairy tales, do you, Josh?"

"Just that good can come out of everything, even this rotten war." She looked at him oddly. "I'm thinking of what we were saying about the giant steps in medical research. A lot of it's due to the necessities of war, but look what it's going to mean in peacetime."

"God grant that peacetime comes," Emma said fervently. "We're running tests on the effect of starvation on pregnant rats at the moment. The government ordered them because of concern about Hitler's slave labor camps. I fail to see any good in that."

"I know. But you and Celia have three times as much space and four assistants now. When the slave labor is ended you'll be able to put that to other use."

Emma smiled. "Joshua, you are an eternal optimist." She rose and went to him and leaned over and kissed the top of his head.

Together they put out the lights and climbed the stairs. Once he turned to her and smiled a special smile and Emma recognized one of those private signals that meant tonight he would want to make love. They had been together nearly thirty years; she was seldom mistaken.

And despite those many years of marriage, Emma felt excitement and pleasure at the prospect of being in his arms, of feeling his mouth pressed to hers. Whatever else Joshua might be, he was still her only love.

9

*T*he officers' canteen at the military hospital in Casablanca was decorated for Christmas. A local tree, an acacia, had been cut down and pressed into service, but it was quickly losing its leaves in the hot desert air. Tinsel garlands drifted overhead, the ever-present fans moving them in a surrealistic dance.

On Christmas day some wag had produced a four-foot snowman made of cotton swabs and gauze pads. Now, two days later, it was covered in a thin sifting of the reddish-brown Sahara dust that filtered through the doors and windows. And surgery was screaming that they were short of cotton swabs and gauze pads. The joys of the season, Morocco style. Daniel sipped warm beer and thought about home.

He was still thinking of Boston when a tall, white-haired man with a gold eagle on his shoulder approached. "Captain Morgan, not interrupting am I?"

Daniel jumped to his feet. "No, sir. Of course not."

Colonel Warren James casually returned the younger man's salute. He was carrying a beer and he set it on the table next to Daniel's. "Let's sit down, shall we? Too damned hot to stand."

Daniel waited. The hospital wasn't a formal place in the military sense, but a bird colonel who happened also to be chief of staff didn't usually drink beer and shoot bull with a lowly captain.

"I want you to take a look at a patient of mine," James said without preamble.

"Me, sir?"

The colonel smiled. "You." He took a sip of his beer and grimaced. "Poisonous stuff. About my patient, he's in medical seven. Major Henry White, a fly-boy. At least he was. About two months ago he started losing weight, seeing double. He's gone downhill ever since. None of the tests prove anything. I want to know what you think."

Jesus. A few lucky diagnoses made when some of his idiot colleagues couldn't tell their asses from a hole in the ground and all of a sudden he was a shaman. The goddamn hospital was a rumor factory. Daniel swallowed hard. "I'm sure you've considered that it may be psychological, sir. Just plain fear and exhaustion."

"Yes, but it's not. I've known Henry White since he was born. Son of an old friend. He's not lacking in courage or fortitude. It's medical, I'm sure."

"I'm not particularly experienced, sir," Daniel said. He sure as shit did not relish getting landed with something nobody else could solve, which just happened to involve a personal friend of the chief's.

"Experience helps," the colonel admitted. "But it's an odd thing about good diagnosticians, they seem to be born, not made. Stop worrying, son," he added quietly. "I won't put you in the stockade if you get it wrong. But I've been meaning to talk to you about your special talent for some time. Henry's problem galvanized me into action."

Daniel swallowed hard again. His special talents were not, he hoped, known to the colonel. "I'm not sure I follow, sir."

James chuckled. "Oh, I expect you do, but you're driving up the wrong road. Your extracurricular activities are your own affair." He took another swallow of the awful beer and let the younger man think about that. "Listen," he said when he lowered the glass. "I put on this uniform a while back, but I've been a doctor much longer. Long enough to know that some men have a sixth sense in the matter of diagnosis. I've watched you and I think you've got it."

Daniel was startled. He considered the statement for a few seconds. "I've made some lucky guesses, that's all."

"No, not luck." James shook his head and stood up. "See Major White as soon as you can, then tell me what you think. And spend some time considering what I've said. I've never met your father, but I know his reputation. I imagine he wants you in ob-gyn, but I think internal medicine's where you belong."

Daniel stared after the colonel's retreating back. He was still staring when a young dermatologist posted to the area three weeks earlier ran in, waving a piece of yellow paper he'd torn from the bulletin board. "Hey you guys, listen to this!"

It took a few moments for the dermatologist to get the attention of the men and women in the canteen. He didn't start reading until he had it. Then he jumped up on a table and megaphoned his voice above the droning sound of the fans. "Word has just arrived that allied forces are now in complete control of the Ardennes. The so-called Battle of the Bulge is over and we have achieved victory." He stopped reading. The room stayed silent. "Whatsa matter with you creeps? Can't you hear? That's it. That's the end of the war, or near enough that it doesn't make any difference."

Daniel dismissed the dermatologist's information as one more rumor, finished his beer and headed for medical seven and the mysterious illness of Major Henry White.

Within forty-eight hours he'd told Colonel James he thought White had incipient sickle-cell anemia and yes he knew it was very rare among Caucasians, but nonetheless, that was his diagnosis and he was practically certain of it.

"An old southern family," James said pensively.

With maybe a black bed warmer or two somewhere in the past. Both men thought of it, neither was prepared to voice the suggestion. But James pumped the younger man's hand and thanked him and said again that Daniel should specialize in internal medicine. "When this war is over, come see me in Los Angeles," he added.

"Yes, sir, perhaps I will," Daniel said. "When the war is over."

And amazingly, unbelievably, that looked like it might be fairly soon. The cognoscenti were suddenly echoing the judgment of the dermatologist. The Battle of the Bulge had been a turning point. A mopping up operation, that's all that was left. Daniel looked for his favorite sergeant. "Schultz, what's our position?"

"Well, Cap'n, we got a gross of butter to unload, and those twenty-six cases of booze we liberated last week."

"What about the hashish?"

"Nothing left. It ain't the right season to get more."

"Excellent. No more contact with the suppliers. It's time to liquidate our assets and call in all debts. Word is we're going home, son."

"Yeah, I heard. You think it's true, Cap'n Morgan?"

"Likely, Schultz, likely. So get rid of the butter and the booze and sit tight. No side action either. This is not the moment to take any risks."

Daniel took his own advice. The new year of 1945 saw him quit each of the operations in which he'd been involved. The only thing that stuck to him was the thirty thousand dollars he'd earned during the past twenty-four months. Being free of the demands of business allowed Daniel to think about other things. He remembered that he'd promised to bring some food from the PX to Ruth Morhaim.

Both sisters greeted him with delight when he arrived at the little shop on the Rue des Juifs. "We thought you had forgotten us, Captain Morgan." But there was only pleasure and no reproach in Ruth's smile.

"*Regardez!*" Shama snatched up an oval can from among the pile of wonders Daniel had deposited on the counter. "*C'est jambon.*"

Ruth pressed her fingers to her cheeks and murmured something in French which Daniel didn't understand. He looked from her to the apparently inoffensive can, then he realized what he'd done. "Damn! I put my foot in it, didn't I? I forgot that Jews don't eat ham or pork. It's not . . . what do you call it?"

"Kosher," Ruth supplied. She had regained her poise and she looked at him gravely. "But that is not important, we are no longer kosher. Since my parents are gone, Shama and I eat what we can get. The old ways are not appropriate any longer. Please, Captain, come and share a meal with us. You will show us how to cook this ham and we will have it together."

Daniel noted the seriousness of her black eyes and the creamy quality of her olive skin. She reached barely to the middle of his chest, and when she tipped her head back to look into his face there was something irresistible about her. He'd planned to visit a skilled Egyptian whore this evening, one of the many such women tossed into his path in Casablanca, but he found himself accepting Ruth's invitation instead.

They ate delicate steamed grains of wheat called couscous, topped by a rich stew of ham and fresh vegetables and seasoned with a fiery sauce that brought tears to Daniel's eyes. When he saw that Ruth, too, was crying, he imagined it was because of the sauce. It never occurred to him that she was weeping in acknowledgment of the funeral of those old ways she had so firmly pronounced dead.

The evening was memorable for one other thing. He finally convinced both Ruth and Shama to drop the formality and call him Daniel.

Caleb found his brother's letters from Morocco as basically uninformative as Emma did, but Daniel's letters to Caleb hinted at the erotic delights of his posting, something Daniel certainly didn't mention when writing to his parents. Caleb was envious, but not surprised. During their college and medical school days Dan was always able to score. Caleb had been jealous then and he was jealous now. Not just for the obvious reasons, Caleb had a secret cross to bear. He was a virgin.

When he was ten, Caleb sneaked a copy of one of his father's medical books and read it under the covers with a flashlight. Daniel always slept as soundly as the dead; it was Caleb alone who read about impotence and syphilis and gonorrhea. In his mind they became linked with the diagrams of coitus also in the book.

Even after he was old enough to know better and his medical education had corrected all the misinterpretations, Caleb couldn't shake his emotional reactions. He wasn't saving himself for marriage and he wasn't practicing some high-flown morality. He was a virgin because he was scared.

Twice, necking with some girl in the backseat of a car, he'd come close to achieving intercourse. Both times he'd been incapable of sustaining an erection. Now he was the joke of the century, a highly trained gynecologist with a brilliant future in reproductive medicine, who had never had a woman. It was damned funny, but Caleb wasn't laughing.

Particularly not now. He intended to marry Susan Davenport and he couldn't imagine foisting a bungling, inexperienced husband on her. Susan was so delicate and vulnerable, it was unthinkable. Besides, unless he could prove to himself that the erections he sustained and orgasms he had alone worked with a woman, he wouldn't dare marry Susan or anyone else.

He considered going to a whorehouse. Was there such a place in Boston? Caleb didn't know, but he was sure that if such a place did exist it would be in Scollay Square. He wandered around that area for an hour or so; a few women offered themselves to him, but they looked like diseased hags. Caleb was repelled.

Maybe a private arrangement? Some willing and charming older woman, a libertine rather than a whore. He didn't know any of those either. There was Alicia Williams, of course. Word was that Alicia was fast and available, but she was nonetheless part of Susan's set and any encounter with her would be reported back to his love. Unthinkable. Caleb could find no way out of his dilemma until a fortuitous evening in late February of '45.

That Sunday night Caleb and Susan went to the RKO Theater on Washington Street to see Fred MacMurray and Joan Crawford in *Above Suspicion*. They emerged from the movie, arms linked, smiling, chatting about the story in which a young married couple outwitted a handful of incompetent Nazi spies. Outside they were greeted by a new white world. Snow fell, silent and gentle; the roofs of parked cars already had a two-inch frosting. "Looks like this is going to shape up into a biggie," Cal said.

"Mmm, yes." Susan pulled his arm closer to her body and his heavy tweed overcoat rubbed against hers of mouton lamb. "I hope Mom and Dad get back from New Hampshire."

The Davenports had gone with friends to the country for the weekend. Caleb looked at the steadily falling snow and thought of the professor's erratic driving. "Maybe they'll wait it out up north."

"Maybe. Anyway, it's beautiful to be out in." Susan smiled at him. "Let's walk home, Cal. We probably can't get a taxi anyway."

They cut through the Common and the Public Garden and crossed Commonwealth Avenue and Beacon Street, walking in a world that caressed them with soft white hands. The air was cold, but not icy, and the silence induced by the cushions of snow made Caleb feel that he'd wandered into some earlier time, before the advent of automobiles and streetcars. Nothing moved, no one spoke; they were abroad in a land of enchantment.

And waiting for them, the warm and welcoming house.

Caleb made a fire in the sitting room, Susan produced mugs of hot cocoa. Best and worst of all, they were alone. Caleb found that very exciting, but he'd have to leave soon. There was Susan's reputation to consider, her parents trust of him. But there was also Susan. So lovely, so sweet. Just looking at her made him dizzy with longing.

"Stay for a while," she said when they finished the cocoa and were stretched out on the rug in front of the fire. "My folks should be back any minute."

"I have to be on duty at six A.M." Cal glanced at his watch. It was ten o'clock. "Maybe just another fifteen minutes."

"You mean you'll leave me all alone, an orphan of the storm?"

"Susan, I'm sorry. It didn't occur to me you'd be frightened."

She laughed softly, a gay little sound that warmed him almost as much as the trusting look in her dove-gray eyes. "I'm teasing, silly. Of course I'm not afraid. But I love to be with you, Caleb. And I hate to see you go."

Caleb's breath caught in his throat. The declaration was the most direct she'd ever made. That a creature as exquisite as Susan truly cared for him filled him with wonder. Caleb distrusted the sincerity of most young women, they were so flip, so casual. Susan was different. He reached out and took her hand. "I'd rather be with you than any girl alive."

"I'm not a girl, Caleb," she whispered. "I'm a woman of twenty-two. Sometimes I don't think you realize that."

"I do. That's one of the things I find so special about you."

"Then kiss me. Not one of your brotherly pecks, kiss me for real, Caleb."

Trembling he leaned over and placed his mouth on hers.

Susan parted her lips and her little tongue flicked into his mouth. Caleb gasped with surprise and hunger. The kiss lasted a long time. When it ended, they were lying pressed together and he could feel her breasts against his chest, the strength of his erection next to her thigh. "Susan, this is dangerous."

"I don't care. Do you love me, Caleb?"

"Oh yes, you've known that all along, haven't you? I'm crazy in love with you, Susan."

"Then touch me." He tightened his grip on her slender waist. "No, not like that. Touch my breasts."

Caleb was first startled, then wildly excited by her saying it flat out like that. He moved his hand to cup her breast and she fumbled with the buttons of her blouse and guided his fingers inside the silky fabric. Her bra was of silk, too, and he was astonished when she released it with one quick snapping movement. He'd never known about women's bras that unhooked in the front. The details concerned him only momentarily, because when the bra and the blouse had been pushed aside he could see her small, firm breasts in the firelight. The aureoles were dusty rose-pink and the nipples were erect. Instinctively he bent his head to kiss them.

Susan moaned and pressed his head closer to her flesh. "Oh, Caleb, I love you so. I want to belong to you."

They remained that way for some minutes. One part of Caleb's mind told him that her parents might come in any second and that would be awful. But such thoughts were overcome by the insistent sound of her sighs and the throbbing, demanding claims of his body. When she touched the zipper of his trousers, he knew a moment's shock, then only his wanting—and hers.

Susan's skirt was pushed up around her waist and the tops of her stockings made a dark border against the incredible whiteness of her thighs. Little silver clips held the stockings in place and beneath her lace-trimmed panties Caleb saw the faint outline of her garter belt across the taut flatness of her stomach, and the darker shadows of blond hair which curled at the edge of the delicate lingerie.

Hundreds of naked women had marched before his eyes for three years, and he had touched them and probed them and diagnosed them endlessly, but that was in no way comparable to this. Gently he let one finger trail along the line of the garter belt. Then no power on earth could prevent him from taking hold of the waistband of her panties and drawing them slowly down her rounded hips to her knees.

Somehow his trousers were open and he was lying over her, feeling his tumescence pulse and throb on the soft flesh of her belly. And then he was inside her, a passage effected without pain or protest. Seconds later Caleb shivered and shook in that coupled climax he had waited so long to achieve.

Afterward he held her in his arms and kissed her corn silk hair and her cheeks and her tiny, perfect nose and murmured, "I didn't hurt you, did I?"

"No. Caleb," she added shyly, "why do they say it always hurts the first time? It didn't."

He chuckled softly, elated at the opportunity to parade his knowledge, floating on the euphoria of having proved to himself that he could do it, and winning Susan in the process. "The hymen isn't all it's cracked up to be. In modern young women it often breaks of its own accord when they swim or ride horseback or something like that. Probably that's what happened in your case."

"I'm so glad to have you to explain things, Caleb."

"There's something else too," he added. "Since we're being technical for a minute. It will get better for you, you'll enjoy it more when we're married and you're relaxed. Don't believe that women simply endure sex, Susan darling, it isn't true." Textbook stuff, but he'd read it, not she. And he was charged by virtue of maleness and training with the education of this precious girl. He kissed her again, all the protectiveness he felt was in the caress.

Susan felt a thrill of triumph more intense than any orgasm she had achieved with the two more experienced men she had known. "Caleb, are you asking me to marry you?"

"You silly child. Of course I am. After tonight how could you doubt it?"

"You're supposed to wait for my answer, you know. Not just assume everything."

Caleb knew a pang of intense fear. He pulled back so he could look into her eyes. "You aren't saying no, are you?"

She let him wait for a moment, then her delightful little laugh pealed forth once more. "I'll marry you, Caleb darling. After all, you have to make an honest woman of me."

He chuckled and hugged her and was very happy. "Thank God your folks got stuck in the storm."

"Mmm," Susan said. There was no way Caleb would ever know that they weren't due back until tomorrow.

Six weeks later she told him the wedding would have to be sooner than they planned, because she was expecting. So he wouldn't be able to wait for his twin to come home from the war and be best man.

"That's pretty quick, honey," Caleb said. "Maybe you're only late."

"I'm very regular, Cal," she insisted. And got a tight look around her mouth which he'd learned to fear. "Do you want to examine me to be sure?"

The thought of being clinical with Susan was abhorrent. "Of course not. Anyway, it doesn't matter. As long as your mother doesn't mind pushing the wedding forward, I'm sure Daniel will understand."

In April the Russian and Western allies linked forces at Torgau in Saxony and the German army collapsed. On May first Hitler committed suicide in his Berlin bunker . . . and Susan and Cal were married in Trinity Church in Copley Square. A reception at the Davenport home followed the ceremony. If Susan was pregnant it certainly didn't show. She looked exquisite in her gown of white organdy trimmed with a piece of Aléncon lace that had graced Cabot brides for generations.

Emma Morgan could find no fault with her new daughter-in-law's appearance, nor the beautiful wedding arranged by Mrs. Davenport. She knew that she herself looked lovely in turquoise chiffon, that Jessica made a charming junior bridesmaid in pale yellow organdy, and that Joshua and Caleb were both stunningly handsome in their tailcoats and striped morning trousers. Everything and everyone seemed to have been specially arranged for the society photographers busy taking pictures for newspapers and magazines. Still Emma wept. But then, mothers always wept at weddings.

A week later, on May 7, 1945, V-E Day was announced amid pealing bells and general rejoicing. The war in Europe was over and at least some of the boys would be coming home.

The APO military mails were always erratic, especially so in that chaotic spring of 1945. Living through such cataclysmic events and the rumors they spawned, the servicemen complained less bitterly about the unreliability of letters from home. Daniel Morgan found himself going for days at a time unaware that Boston and his family existed.

It was during those weeks that he developed the habit of visiting Ruth and Shama Morhaim every two or three days, but not simply because he enjoyed their company. Ruth listened to radio broadcasts in French and Spanish and Arabic, as well as English. Her linguistic talents sometimes allowed her to confirm or kill one of the endless, conflicting rumors that swept through the military hospital.

"This place called Dachau, near Munich," Daniel asked, "have you heard anything about it?"

Ruth nodded and turned away. A chill crept up Daniel's spine and lodged in the back of his neck. They'd been hearing horrible stories at the hospital. The troops marching through Germany were liberating places whose existence nobody had really believed in. "Jesus," he breathed softly. "Jesus Christ . . . the bastards . . ."

Ruth's fists were clenched, her dark eyes wet with tears. Shama was standing in the door, staring at them both, a look of pure terror on her small, pinched face.

"Hey," Daniel mustered as much bravura as he could manage, "don't worry, kid. It's all over now, and none of those guys are anywhere near here." He ruffled the little girl's hair. She always seemed so young to him, probably because she was small and undernourished. Shama was thirteen, but he could never quite believe it. "C'mon, let's you and me and your big sister go out and have dinner somewhere."

Shama turned a questioning face to Ruth and the older girl translated into rapid French. Daniel was always forgetting that Shama understood very little English. Ruth turned back to him. "We would like to go out with you, Daniel, if you have time."

"All the time in the world, Ruthie. I'll wait while you close up."

He watched the two of them, taking pleasure in the routine of securing the small, unpretentious shop, in the way Shama looked with her face scrubbed and her hair brushed back. In Ruth's competent hands adjusting her simple black dress. And all the while his gut was tight with rage. The brutalized, emaciated ghosts of millions of their fellow Jews seemed to march across the rough white walls of the little shop. "C'mon," he said again when they were ready. "We'll find someplace with lights and music. Thank God for Casablanca."

After that night he began to worry constantly about
Ruth and Shama. The stories of Dachau and Auschwitz
and Mauthausen poured in, got worse as each day brought
new revelations. They obsessed him. His dreams were
haunted by visions of the Morhaim sisters at the mercy of
insane doctors performing mutilating surgery without an-
esthetics, and laughing hysterically while their victims
screamed.

When he woke from these nightmares, Daniel told himself he was an idiot. The war in Europe was over. Ruth
and Shama had survived the war in North Africa. He'd
give Ruth some money before he shipped out, see that she
was started on the road to a new and better life. What else
could he do? Nothing. He was being morbid because he'd
lived too long performing the same dreary tasks in the
same dusty setting. He needed to go home as much as any
battle-shocked infantryman. At least he needed to hear
about home. Not a single letter had arrived since early
March. It was the same for the whole post, as if the allied
command had forgotten its existence.

One early June morning he made the fruitless trip to
the mail room more disheartened than ever. It began to
seem that news from home would never get in and they
would never get out. Kitty Donnely was there before him.
She was taking her frustration out on the young soldier
who faced her with empty hands.

"When are you slobs going to get your asses in gear?"

"Tain't my fault, Lieutenant." The boy couldn't be more
than twenty. He had a strong Tennessean accent and a
woebegone expression. "Sometimes ah think them big
shots don't 'member Casablanca is heah. Not us neither."

"He's probably right." Daniel took Kitty's arm. "Thirty
years from now they'll remember us and come see if we've
been buried under the shifting sands. Let's get out of this
den of desperation. I'll buy you a beer."

They went to the officers' canteen and drank insipid
beer that turned warm as soon as it was poured, and
chatted about nothing in particular. Kitty seemed unaffected by her abortion six months before. She looked
healthier and tougher than ever. "What are you going to
do when you get home?" Daniel asked.

"Make a fortune. I told you my plans. A little private
clinic where ladies can get a very special kind of douche.

Want to join me? It will take capital, and word is you've got plenty of that. We'd make a good team, Danny-boy."

"You're nuts. We opportunists better resolve to go straight once we're stateside, Kitty. The days of wine and roses and heisted booze are coming to an end. Honest work and loud proclamations that we're for motherhood and against sin. That's the only way."

"Bullshit. And I'm definitely antimotherhood. Listen, I'm more than a little serious. Why don't you come in with me? The technique is terrific. You'd be a whiz in no time. I'd offer to introduce you to the old broad who did me, but after last night it's not in the cards."

Daniel had a sudden memory of meeting her in the Jewish quarter the day of the abortion. "What about last night?"

"There was a fire in the Rue des Juifs. The wind spread it and almost the whole quarter burned. It's chaos down there. They're bringing in the burn cases now. Where the hell have you been, Danny-boy?"

He'd been sleeping, nothing more extraordinary than that, but he didn't wait to explain to Kitty. He threw a dollar bill on the table to pay for the beers and ran to the medical wing. The first person he cornered was an orderly.

"Not too bad considering, sir. That's why there wasn't a call for all hands. Mostly property loss and not too much personal injury. You don't have to stick around if you're not on duty."

Daniel wasn't, but he remained long enough to check the new admissions. Neither Ruth nor Shama was among them. That settled, he went looking for Schultz. It didn't take long because his sometime driver and business associate was also looking for him. "Hey, Cap'n, where you been? They just got a load of mail and you got four letters." Schultz thrust the envelopes in Daniel's hands.

"Never mind that. Get a jeep and meet me at the gate in five minutes, no, make it three."

"Where's the fire?"

"In town, in the Jewish quarter. Now get a move on!"

Daniel read the letters while they drove, just to occupy his mind so he'd stop worrying about the Morhaim sisters. The news of his brother's engagement and subsequent marriage came to him in ten telescoped minutes; conveyed in a speeded up blur like a movie gone mad.

He tried to digest the idea of Caleb having a wife and couldn't. No picture of the pretty Boston socialite who was now his sister-in-law came to mind, except for Jessie's comment, ". . . she's okay, but she kind of simpers when she talks." He did consider the effect on Caleb's career of marrying someone related to the imperial Cabots, but the idea came and went quickly.

"Look at that," Schultz murmured. They were approaching the town. A pall of black smoke hung over the Jewish quarter. Boston seemed a world apart and not entirely real.

It took him twenty minutes to discover that where Ruth's shop had been there was now only a charred and smoking ruin, two hours more to locate the sisters. He finally found them among a group of the homeless being sheltered in a tiny Lutheran church. By then he was long overdue at the hospital, but he didn't care. He was too overcome by relief at the sight of the two girls.

They were frightened and shocked, but unhurt. Ruth flung herself into his arms with totally uncharacteristic abandon. "Oh, Daniel, I'm so happy to see you. It's all so terrible and so hard to believe."

"You're both okay. Nothing matters but that." He held her tight, feeling a number of things to which he could put no name. He stretched out one arm and drew Shama into their embrace. "How did it get started? Does anybody know?"

Ruth merely buried her face in his chest but Shama's halting English was edged with rage. "They say it was on purpose started. By someone who does not like the Jews. A Nazi."

"There are no Nazis around here," Daniel said automatically, but a knot of icy hatred was forming in his stomach.

"Daniel," Ruth whispered. "What am I to do now? Shama and I, we have no home." She looked away as soon as she spoke, embarrassed that her plight had caused her to complain. Ruth Morhaim never complained.

Daniel put two fingers under her chin and turned her tear-stained face to his. "Everything is going to be fine, you mustn't worry. You and Shama are coming to America with me."

He hadn't known he was going to speak the words until they were out of his mouth. Once they were, he realized that he'd been wanting to say them for a long time. They were his personal apology, Daniel Morgan's single-handed effort to right an enormous, unthinkable wrong.

"It will not be permitted," Ruth said softly. "But thank you anyway. It is a very sweet thing for you to think of, Daniel."

"It most certainly will be permitted," Daniel said. "You don't understand, Ruthie. You're coming home as my wife. I'm asking you to marry me."

In Boston the June day that witnessed the aftermath of ruin on the Rue des Juifs in faraway Casablanca was a spring symphony of buttercup-yellow and piercing blue. Jessica Morgan was convinced she could smell apple blossoms, though there were no apple trees on Commonwealth Avenue.

Last year she'd gone to a farm in New Hampshire for two weeks. She'd smelled the apple blossoms there. She hadn't been sick one day on the farm. And only Marya was with her. Marya let her do all kinds of things that were forbidden in Boston. Jessica stared at the sunshine gilding the street outside her bedroom window and remembered last summer. Impulsively she ran down the steps and out the door.

Tessie and Nora were downstairs in the kitchen, Marya was resting, no one else was home. No one noticed when Jessica decided to go for a walk. An hour later she was on Charles Street.

The narrow road in the West End was a melange of small, poor shops selling things Jessica had never seen, filled with people speaking languages she didn't understand. It was exotic and foreign and exciting. She'd never realized such a place existed so close to home. Jessica walked idly, thinking of how changed everything was since Caleb married Susan and moved into the unused apartment above Daddy's office next door. She didn't like the changes. Maybe she'd run away and come live here on Charles Street, and wear a shawl and a kerchief around her head and sell apples from a pushcart.

Except that she'd have to wait until Daniel came home. Maybe Daniel would come with her. They could live together and she'd keep house for him. He liked sausages and pancakes. That's what she'd make for his dinner every night. And she'd make their house so pretty, she'd fill it with flowers and plants, like the ones in the window into which she was staring.

It wasn't like any of the other shop windows on the street. It was beautifully kept and carefully arranged. And the flowers were very unusual, not fresh as she'd thought at first. But not artificial either. Dried flowers, she finally realized. All gray and green and yellow. In the corner was a hand-lettered sign that read, "Herbs for Health."

Next to the sign was a tiny pillow covered in mauve silk and trimmed with white lace. Jessica coveted that pillow the moment she saw it. She fingered the coins in her pocket. She had an allowance of fifty cents a week; she hadn't spent all of last week's, so she had seventy-five cents today. Perhaps it would be enough.

"Hello." The young woman behind the counter was tall and built in a manner Jessica had heard her mother refer to as 'stately.' She had dark brown hair tied back with a green ribbon and green eyes. "Can I do something for you?"

Jessica noted that the other girl had an odd accent.

"How much is that little pillow in the window, please? The purple one."

The older girl got the pillow out of the window and handed it to Jessica before she answered. "Here, smell. Isn't it wonderful?"

Jessica pressed the pillow to her nose, then looked up in surprise. It had never occurred to her that the thing might have a scent. "It's a sachet, isn't it?"

"Not exactly. It's a hop pillow. It helps you sleep when you need something to calm your nerves. I don't think that's likely to be your problem. How about this?" She held out another, smaller pillow, covered in red-and-white gingham. "This one really is a sachet. It's filled with lavender to make your undies smell sweet."

Jessica shook her head. "No thank you. I like the color of this one best. Can you please tell me how much it is?"

"One dollar."

"Oh. I only have seventy-five cents. I can have a dollar next week though. Could you save it until then?"

"Well sure, why not? But I still don't think you really need a pillow for insomnia, a little thing like you." The girl smiled and Jessica noted that she had two big dimples either side of her wide mouth. "But folks allow as how the customer's always right," she added. "So if you want the pillow you can have it for seventy-five cents. It's the last one anyway. That's the kind of thing most folks want up here in the north. They don't care 'bout serious herbalism."

Jessica was enchanted by the woman's accent, and the fact that she was getting the pillow at cut price, but she hated it when adults used words she couldn't understand. She always made them explain. "What's herbalism?"

"The study and use of plants for health. It's been 'round a lot longer than these modern, artificial drugs and things. But most northern folks have forgotten all about herbs, if they ever knew."

"You aren't from Boston, are you? I can tell because of the way you speak."

"I'm from Arkansas, and every time I open my mouth somebody stares. Only been here six months, and I've never been stared at so much in all my born days."

"Do you mind? Doesn't it make you feel odd?"

The older girl laughed. "I gave up feeling odd a long time ago. Nothing to be gained by it, as my mama used to say."

"Is your mother from Arkansas too?"

"Well, yes and no. She was born there, but she came to Boston when she was fourteen and didn't go back home for years n' years."

"Is that why you came, because your mother used to live here?"

"You know, for a little girl, you ask a powerful lot of questions."

Jessica sighed. "I know. Everyone tells me that. I don't mean to be rude. I just like to know things."

"It's okay," the girl with the dimples said. "I don't mind. I like to know things too. How old are you and what's your name, for instance?"

"I'll be twelve come September. And my name's Jessica Morgan."

The green eyes narrowed, the girl stared hard at her. "Really, you ain't teasing me?"

"Of course not." Jessica was startled. Something had changed. "I'm Jessica Morgan and I live at 165 Commonwealth Avenue."

"What's your pa's name?" The demand was issued in a harsh whisper.

"He's Doctor Joshua Morgan," Jessica said. She wanted to get out of the shop, she felt chilled and frightened, but the other girl was still holding the wondrous little pillow.

Suddenly Jessica's inquisitor smiled. She reached out and lay a cool, soft hand against Jessica's cheek. "Well fancy that, I been wonderin' and tryin' to decide, and you wander in here all on your own. . . . Don't look so scared, honey, you startled me that's all. My name is Morgan too."

Everything changed again. Jessica forgot her momentary fear, she was back in the midst of a marvelous adventure, finding a new friend all on her own. Perhaps more than a friend. "Hey, that's terrific! Maybe we're cousins." Jessica always mourned the fact that she didn't have her big family of aunts and uncles and cousins around her.

"No, I don't think so. Morgan's my first name. My last is Landry."

Jessica looked puzzled. "I never heard of anyone having Morgan for a first name."

"It's an old Celtic name. And before you ask, Celtic means Irish, sort of. And Morgan means fairy."

"Did your mother pick it because she liked Irish fairies?"

Morgan Landry laughed again. Her laugh was very gay and alive and made Jessica want to laugh, too, though she didn't know what was funny. "No," Morgan said. "That's not the reason."

"What then?"

"It's a secret. Maybe I'll tell you someday if we get to be real good friends."

10

*T*he windows of the breakfast room were open, Emma could hear Marya urging Jessica to stop dawdling. In between those admonitions were others about not leaving the house without telling someone where she was going.

Emma was amused, Marya was always saying they must make Jessie more independent, but when it came down to it the nurse was as protective of the child as either she or Josh. And all for their own separate reasons—few having anything to do with what Jessica really needed. Emma sighed and promised herself she'd try harder to build a bridge to her daughter.

She set down her coffee cup and glanced at the morning's mail. It might help. Three letters from Daniel. One addressed jointly to her and Josh. That was a little strange since he usually wrote to them separately. One was addressed to Dr. & Mrs. Caleb Morgan—so Daniel had gotten their letters about Cal's marriage. And there was a letter for Jessica. Each one should have word of the same glad tidings: Daniel was coming home. The radio and the newspapers were full of such announcements, and Daniel had been overseas for three and a half years.

Impulsively Emma put the letters in the pocket of the gray linen redingote she wore over a red-and-gray silk dress. She'd give Jessie hers right away. It would be something for them to celebrate together.

"Good morning, Mama."

"Good morning, Jessie dear. How do you feel?"

"Fine. I'm not sick, Mama, nothing happened to me." The child slid into her seat and helped herself to one of Tessie Marsh's fresh biscuits. She spread butter and honey liberally while she spoke. "I don't know why there was such a fuss. I didn't do anything, I just went for a walk."

"I know." Emma reached over and pushed the recalcitrant curls from her daughter's forehead. The child seemed startled at the gesture.

I almost never touch her, Emma thought. *My own daughter, and she's astonished by my touch.* She left her hand next to Jessie's cheek for a moment. When she spoke her voice was gentle. "I don't think you did anything wrong by taking a walk, darling. But next time leave Marya a note to say where you're going and when you'll be back. That's all. You don't have to sneak out like a criminal, as long as we know not to worry about you."

Jessie's smile was sunshine. "I will, I promise." Daddy and Marya had been furious; her mother's attitude was a wonderful surprise. She looked at her mother and wished for the thousandth time that she, too, was tall and redheaded and smart. "Mama, do you think stately women are the only kind men like?"

"Stately! Jessie, where do you get such words? And what do you know about men and women?"

"You say it, I've heard you. You're stately, aren't you?"

Emma chuckled. "No, I don't think I qualify. Tall and a bit scrawny. As for what gentlemen like, sometimes they much prefer tiny ladies with brown curly hair and big brown eyes."

"Do you think so?"

"I am absolutely certain of it."

Jessie grinned. "That's good. But I do think stately ladies are nice. I met a super one on my walk." She clamped her lips together after that. Stupid to bring up the awful walk again.

"Oh, did you? Where? Tell me about her."

"On Charles Street." Jessie stared at her glass of orange juice and didn't meet Emma's gaze.

"Charles Street. So you went all the way to the West End, did you? Didn't stop on the Common as you said."

"I didn't mean to lie. It's just that everybody was asking

questions at the same time. I got confused." Her voice was a shy whisper.

"Very well, we won't mention it. But what about the stately lady?"

"She's super," Jessie repeated. "She has the nicest shop on the street. It's full of herbs. There's a sign in the window, Herbs for Health. And she's from Arkansas and her name is Morgan. Not her last name, her first."

Emma felt the blood drain from her cheeks. She raised the coffee cup to her lips with trembling fingers. Silly, she was being silly. It couldn't be her. Women from Arkansas interested in herbs must be as common as sparrows. Even women who could be described as stately. Besides, people didn't suddenly reappear after almost thirty years. And this woman was named Morgan, not Billy-Jo.

Jessica was saying something about a pillow. "I didn't show anyone last night because of the fuss, can I get it and show you now? Will you wait, Mama? It will only take a minute."

Emma glanced at her lapel watch. "Very well, but hurry, Jessie, I'm a bit late as it is."

She watched the small figure dash out of the room. The thought of how anxious Jessica was to please her, to talk to her, brought tears to her eyes. I must try, oh God, I must try. It's not Jessie's fault. . . .

Emma rose and walked to the French doors overlooking the tiny garden. Not Billy-Jo Landry's fault either. Why did the thought that her one-time friend might have returned to Boston disturb her so? All of it was her own doing. Why take it out on Jessica, or on a woman she hadn't seen since long before the child was born?

"Here it is, Mama. See. Didn't I tell you it was the prettiest pillow ever? And smell it. It's stuffed with hops to make you sleep. Morgan told me all about it. Her last name's Landry. Do you think I have to call her Miss Landry, or can I say Morgan? She's not very old."

The room was swaying. Emma reached out and grabbed the doorknob to keep herself upright.

"Mama, are you sick? What's the matter?"

Emma regained her composure by sheer force of will. "Nothing's the matter, Jessica. I just had a moment's dizziness. And I am late for work. Behave yourself today, please. Don't go getting Marya all upset again." She snatched her handbag from the sideboard and started for the front hall.

Jessie stood where she was, trying to understand the abrupt change in her mother. "You didn't look at the pillow," she whispered to Emma's departing back. "You didn't even smell it."

It was evening before Emma remembered Daniel's letters. As soon as she got to the lab she removed the redingote and slipped a white cotton smock over her dress. Not till she changed again, preparatory to going home, did she see the corners of the envelopes peeking out of the pocket. Something else to berate herself for. Not bad enough that she'd been so beastly to Jessica, now she could reproach herself with having forgotten the one thing that might have made the child happy. Not to mention forgetting Daniel.

Celia Howard watched from across the room. "What is it, Emma? You look terrible. Have all day. Tell me to mind my own business if you like. Or tell me what's bothering you. Take your choice."

Emma leaned her forehead against the wall. Her voice was low, and as weary as she felt. "I am a terrible mother, absolutely unnatural."

"Well, that's today's quota of nonsense. Now how about the real story?"

Emma straightened and shook her head. "No, talking about it will just make it worse." She reached up and took her wide-brimmed straw hat from the shelf. "I'd better go home and see if I can repair the damage."

Celia shrugged and delved into the pocket of her crumpled white coat for a Lucky Strike. She lit it with deft, nicotine-stained fingers. Since the war more and more women were smoking, perhaps to ease the worries about their men overseas, but Celia had taken up the habit years before. In this as in so much else, she was ahead of her time.

It was thanks to Celia that Emma wasn't just a clerk in the lab any longer. Celia had trained her to use the equipment, to run experiments, to be—in all but the matter of a degree—a chemist. Technically she wasn't qualified, but practically she was, and within these walls she was so treated. But even more valuable than Celia's respect and confidence was her friendship. "Would you like tomorrow off?" she asked. "You could spent it with Jessie. She's what's worrying you, isn't she?"

Emma smiled. "You and I have been together too long, my dear. We can read each other's minds. But no, I'll be in tomorrow. Thanks anyway." She started to leave, then turned back. "Celia, do you remember Billy-Jo Landry?"

"My God! Of course I do. Who could forget Billy-Jo and her 'simples and potions'? What made you think of her now? You haven't heard from her, have you?"

"No, not the way you mean. I'm late, tell you about it tomorrow."

"He's done what?" Joshua stared at his wife, the drink in his hand forgotten.

"Married," Emma repeated tonelessly. "Here, you can read the letter for yourself."

Joshua carefully placed his drink on the side table, took the envelope, but didn't open it. "Are you sure? You could be misunderstanding one of Daniel's jokes."

"Yes, I'm sure, and it isn't a joke. Daniel thinks he will be home by the end of August. He is bringing with him his new wife and her sister who is thirteen years old."

"I can't believe it. . . ." Joshua took a long swallow of his whisky and set the glass down. Still he held the letter in his hands, unopened. "Well, I suppose it's not so remarkable. Lots of the boys are bringing back brides, one hears. I just never thought of Daniel wanting to settle down so young."

Emma sat by the window, looking not at him but the street. He couldn't believe that the mere fact of Daniel's unexpected marriage would make her look so defeated. "There's more, isn't there?" Josh asked softly. "You'd better tell me, Emma."

Typical, he wanted his bad news filtered through her, not raw off the page. "Yes, there's more. Daniel's wife is a Moroccan Jewess."

Joshua groaned. "Oh, Lord. The one with the shop where he bought the cloth. A Jewish peddler." He dropped the envelope on the couch and went to refill his glass. "How in the name of all that's holy could he be so stupid? What's going to happen to her when he brings her to Boston, of all places?"

"I'm sure I don't know." Emma turned from the window at last. "Josh, I would like a large sherry. It has been an appalling day."

They drank in silence for a few seconds. Finally Joshua asked the question in both their minds. "Do you think she's white?"

"I've been puzzling about that. Yes, I do. I've never heard of a Negro Jewess. But then, I know nothing of Morocco."

"Neither do I. Well, we'd better do a bit of preparatory study, hadn't we?"

Emma started to tremble. "Don't! Don't make light of this disaster and cover up for Daniel the way you always do. He has been awful. As thoughtless and egoistic and ungrateful as ever—"

He stopped the tirade by putting his hands on her shoulders, shaking her gently. "Emma, Emma, you're getting yourself in a state over split milk. As always. Please, darling, don't make yourself ill. It will all work out. We'll make it work out, I promise."

She buried her face in his broad chest, relaxed in the protective circle of his arms. This sense of peace, of security Joshua could always give her and always had. The bigness of him, the very solid feel of his strength. It had sustained her many times, even when Joshua himself was the cause of her anguish. It did not fail her now. "Why did he do it? Can you imagine any reason?"

"Maybe he loves her?"

Emma laughed wryly and moved out of his embrace to pick up the letter and put it neatly on the mantel. "Perhaps, but I rather think it's more likely to be his white knight complex. The most exasperating thing about Daniel is that he always wants to be either a devil or a saint. There is nothing in between."

"Yes. There's a lot of truth in that. Have you told Caleb?"

Emma stood rigid where she was, staring at her husband with a look of horror. "Oh, my God . . . Daniel wrote to Caleb and to Jessica. I gave them each their letters when I came in. Before I read ours. I felt so guilty you see, because I'd forgotten this morning."

Joshua took a deep breath and let it out slowly. "So Jessie probably knows. She won't take it well. Not coming so soon after Cal's marrying and moving out."

"She'll be destroyed, Josh. She worships Daniel. He's her idol. Oh, how could he do it like this, so suddenly, with no warning?"

"Where is she?"

"I don't know. In her room I would think. I'll send for her."

"No, don't do that. Let's go up. Come, the two of us together. Jessie needs to feel part of a united front at the moment."

They found Jessica sitting on her bed. She was surrounded by her dolls, her books, the vivid, vibrant decor of the picture perfect world they'd created for her. They did not need to ask if she knew. In the midst of the gaiety Jessica was a black-and-white wraith, even her plaid cotton sundress seemed devoid of color. Joshua knelt in front of her while Emma stood at the door.

"Don't fret, Jessie," he said softly. "It's wonderful news actually. You told me you felt as if you knew Ruth from Daniel's letters. And we're getting to be a big family pretty quickly. Think what a Christmas we're going to have."

Jessica didn't answer her father, didn't even look at him.

It was on the tip of Emma's tongue to say that Jews didn't celebrate Christmas. Stupid. Like everything she'd done today. And done before. So many mistakes. Emma's eyes filled with tears of impotent rage. Through them she could see the little mauve satin pillow filled with hops. It lay at the foot of Jessica's bed. Such an innocent thing to remind her of so much painful history.

In the late winter of 1933, while newly elected Franklin Delano Roosevelt endeavored to give depression-racked America a "new deal," Emma Morgan lay awake night after night. Tense, frightened, angry with Josh for sleeping so peacefully beside her, Emma tried to deal with the unthinkable.

Her problem had nothing to do with money; it wasn't about the depression. Joshua's patients were the very wealthy, those for whom economic ups and downs were mere annoyances. Emma was in torment because she was sure she was pregnant.

Each morning she'd dash to the bathroom, praying as she went. Please, God, let my period have come. But it never did. The morning she vomited before breakfast she knew beyond doubt that her diaphragm must have failed her. Nobody ever said it was foolproof. Tell Josh, she said over and over to herself. But she kept putting it off. Because telling him would make a reality of what was assuming the proportions of a nightmare.

How could she have another child now? It was ludicrous, worse, it was obscene. She was thirty-eight years old, a wife of eighteen years, the mother of teenaged twins as tall as she was. She had a full-time professional career she adored and a marriage that was settled and secure. Emma imagined her body growing heavy and ungainly, and she shuddered with horror. No woman her age could look graceful while pregnant. All that should be behind her. It wasn't, it was here and now.

A week after the morning sickness began Joshua was asked to address the American Medical Association in New York. He passed the letter of invitation to her across the breakfast table. "Why don't you come along? It's only three days, but the change will do you good. You're looking a bit pale lately, darling."

"No, Josh, I can't. We're very busy at the lab just now."

Her tone was sharper than it had any right to be, and he looked at her quickly, then went back to his paper. "Suit yourself, but I still don't like the look of you."

He'd like it less when she was fat and swollen and embarrassing.

Joshua went to New York and Emma spent three more sleepless nights imagining what her husband would say when she told him, what their friends would say. Then she remembered Billy-Jo.

She switched on her bedside lamp. It had a glass Tiffany shade of vivid purple and green and made a puddle of vibrant light in the dark room. Slowly she got up and padded across the gray carpet to her dressing table. She didn't open the drawer right away. Instead she stood staring at her backlit image in the gilt-framed mirror. It was like seeing herself in silhouette, a picture from a magazine. Portrait of the elegant, successful, cherished Mrs. Joshua Morgan.

"I've earned my peace," she whispered to her reflection. "I've earned the things I have."

Emma yanked open the drawer and fished in the back.

They were still there, still in the silk handkerchief she'd wrapped round them fifteen years before. Three small vials that offered a way out.

She'd almost forgotten what Billy-Jo Landry looked like, but now it was as if the woman from the Ozarks stood beside her. "They don't always work, my potions. But often they do. And then it's much better'n some of the terrible things women do to themselves trying to stop being pregnant."

Yes, indeed. Not that she'd ever use a knitting needle or a knife or visit some squalid abortionist. She'd be too frightened. But what about Joshua? He could end her torment simply and safely in his office or right here in the bedroom. But he wouldn't do it. Joshua's opposition to abortion as violent and total. She'd never ask him because she knew he couldn't do it—and she couldn't bear to hear him refuse.

The little glass bottles weighed down her hand. Outside the March sky glittered with the cold blue starlight of incipient spring. Around her the house slept. Probably Joshua slept, too, but he was two hundred miles away and she faced her terror alone.

"Oh, God, what should I do?" She spoke aloud, but no voice answered her in the silent bedroom. Emma wrapped her arms around her torso and rocked back and forth. Silent tears streamed down her cheeks; anguish was a physical pain, twisting her insides in an agony akin to labor itself. "Oh, God," she murmured again.

Each small bottle was stoppered with a tiny cork, each appeared to contain about a tablespoon of whatever Billy-Jo had put in them so long ago. "Harmless." She remembered Celia saying. "If they work I don't know why. But in any event, there's nothing in here that could hurt anybody."

Emma hesitated only a few seconds, then broke the wax seals and pried out all three corks. The liquid was dark green, viscous, with a pleasantly astringent smell that hinted of alcohol. She stood the tiny bottles on the dressing table and stared at them.

Downstairs the clock chimed the half hour. "Yes," Emma said aloud. The sound of the affirmation startled her, she hadn't realized that she'd made up her mind. "Yes," she said again, more firmly. She drank down the contents of each vial, one after the other. Afterward she couldn't remember if they had any taste at all.

When she had drained the last drop of Billy-Jo's potion, she carried the empty containers into the bathroom and deliberately smashed them to smithereens on the hard surface of the porcelain tub. Which was how she cut herself.

It was a bad cut, deep. Blood streamed from her palm and stained the white bathtub a brilliant red. She watched it. Dead. If she didn't staunch the flow, and if for some reason the normal healing process didn't take place, she would die. Her life would pour out and eventually the thing she thought of as herself would cease to exist.

For some seconds Emma contemplated the notion of nonexistence, the snuffing out of personhood in favor of some heaven beyond human understanding. If there really were such a place. In one moment of total clarity she knew she could not go through with it. She didn't want to die, and she could not deliberately deny life to the child starting to form in her body. Maybe it was right for some women to do so in some circumstances. Nor for her, not now—and not for the simple reason that pregnancy was inconvenient.

She wrapped her bleeding hand in a towel and knelt by the toilet, shoving her finger down her throat repeatedly, until she gagged and wretched and vomited everything in her stomach. Finally she dragged herself back to the bedroom and fell asleep in the big, half empty bed.

The next morning she was violently ill. Marya found her shaking and retching in the bathroom, attracted by Emma's weak cries for help. "Mrs. Emma! What is it? You have eaten something, maybe. Come, I put you to bed." And with her strong arms she'd lifted her employer and carried her to the bedroom as if she were an infant. "Now I call the doctor," she had said when Emma was settled.

"Yes," Emma agreed weakly. "But it may as well be Doctor West, my obstetrician. I'm pregnant, Marya."

The Polish nurse had gazed at her silently for a few seconds, and finally nodded. She was not such a fool as to offer congratulations. Not in view of the expression on her employer's face.

When Marya left the room, Emma dissolved into sobs, but they lasted only moments. She could not endure this, too, not a total loss of self-esteem. However she felt, it was entirely her affair. By the time the doctor arrived she was composed and outwardly calm. And she had found a manner of dealing with the situation, prideful dignity.

It was a ghastly time, a terrible pregnancy. Emma fought through every hour of every day, seething within while she maintained the facade of calm that was her most important defense. She dragged herself to the laboratory, refusing to take any time off. When her condition showed, she imagined people were staring at her and she had to resist the urge to closet herself in her bedroom and hide until it was over. Joshua's surprised pleasure, the twins' curiosity and excitement, that all made it worse.

The most terrible thing of all was how she felt about the child. In the dead of night she'd wake in a cold sweat, thinking, *I hate you;* then shoving her fist into her mouth to prevent the words from being shouted. And all this fury, this rage, this anguish, Emma hid. No one suspected. Except perhaps Marya who had seen her in that first unguarded moment. But wisely, Marya remained silent.

Jessica Morgan was born six weeks premature in September of 1933. The labor was as harrowing as the pregnancy had been. For the first time Josh joined Charles West in the delivery room, and it took every bit of medical skill the two men possessed to save the lives of Emma and her child. Because of this it was some days before Emma actually saw her daughter. She had hours alone in her hospital bed to think through the past months, and these endless musings were punctuated by reports on the baby's struggle to survive. There was a parallel there which was not lost on Emma.

She blamed herself for her daughter's ill health. She was absolutely certain that her attempted abortion and subsequent unhappiness had marked Jessica. But she had perhaps passed on something else as well, a certain fighting spirit, a will to win.

By the time they brought the baby to her mother, Emma no longer hated her. She had instead developed a grudging admiration for this mite who was so determined to live. It wasn't love, not the sort she had felt for her other children, but it was something. "We'll survive, you and I," she whispered against Jessica's fragrant, soft cheek.

"We may never be a model mother and child, but we will learn to tolerate each other."

Jessica's struggle didn't end when she came home from the hospital. She was always a sickly child. When she contracted rheumatic fever at six, they almost lost her again. But Jessica tenaciously clung to life, always fighting back from the brink.

Despite the truce she had secretly proclaimed between them, Emma watched her daughter's attempts to survive with a secret and terrible guilt.

She felt that same guilt with greater-than-ever poignancy the night Jessie learned of Daniel's hasty marriage. It almost overwhelmed her while she watched Josh try and console Jessie for a wound which Emma knew would never be healed. Her daughter had sustained the first real loss of her life, the first assault on her innocence. Like the rest of humankind, Jessie would survive. But she would never be the same.

The General George O. Squire was a ship some five hundred feet long. Most of her vast interior was an enormous hold suitable for transporting the bulky, varied material of combat. Now her cargo was men. The ship could carry five thousand of them per crossing in a cavernous hole below the decks. She had brought them to the fight, now she was taking them home. Neither journey was likely to be made in comfort.

Daniel Morgan shared the general sense of euphoria when his unit boarded at Marseilles, but it didn't blind him to the primitive accommodations, or dull his considerable maneuvering abilities.

The navy wanted as little as possible to do with the army personnel aboard. The man in charge of assigning quarters was a harried major, clutching plans of the Squire's layout, and shouting orders in a hoarse voice that squeaked with tension. Daniel watched from the sidelines for a few minutes, then approached the officer. "How long have you had that sore throat, Major?"

The man was about Daniel's age, a little shorter, very dark. Brown eyes flicked quickly to the identifying bars on his inquisitor's sleeve. "I'm a bit busy just now. Move along please, Captain."

"Sorry, sir." Daniel pointed to the caduceus on his

collar. "Medical Corps, sir. I'm a doctor, and the sound of your voice worries me."

The major folded his arms around the clipboard containing his much marked and dog-eared ship's plans and stared. "What's your name, Captain?"

Daniel told him. He also added a bit more information, "There's been an epidemic of a rare throat infection, Major. Started in Africa. These troops are all fresh from Africa, sir. We're keeping a careful watch. May I know your name, sir."

"Major DiCello, Anthony DiCello. What are you watching for? Why wasn't I informed?"

"We don't want any panic, sir."

The major's eyes narrowed. "What kind of panic? What the hell kind of infection is this anyway?" His voice grew even more hoarse.

Daniel looked around. Hundreds of bodies were crammed into every inch of space. "Begging your pardon, sir, but I don't think this is the place."

"Jesus! Come with me, Captain."

In the tiny cubicle that functioned as Major DiCello's office, Daniel produced a throat stick. The other man dutifully said "Ah." Daniel made vague noises, then asked, "Mind dropping your trousers, sir?"

"My trousers? Captain, you said a throat infection."

"Yes, sir. But that's the problem. It goes to the testicles pretty quickly. Sorry, but you'd better know. Sterility, sir. That's the best of the results once the infection takes hold. Impotence can follow within twenty-four hours."

DiCello was white, the hands that loosed his belt buckle shook. The penis presented for Daniel's inspection was shriveled and flaccid with terror. Daniel said, "Mmm . . ." a few times.

"Well," DiCello demanded, "have I got it or not?"

Daniel straightened up and motioned his superior officer to pull up his pants. "It looks like you've been lucky so far, Major," he said finally. "We won't know for sure for a few days."

"A few days! And what happens in the meantime? I just sweat it out? Can't you do something?"

"That's the trouble, sir. It's why we're being so quiet about this. There is a successful treatment, but we have only a minute supply of the serum. Nothing like enough to treat all the men on board."

DiCello eyed him warily, flicked his tongue across parched lips, finally sat down and indicated that Daniel should do likewise. "I'm a democratic man, Captain. I've tried to be a good officer and a fair one, but . . ."

"But what, sir?" Daniel was the picture of innocence.

"But rank has its privileges, Captain. I want some of that damn medicine. The U.S. government spends a fortune training an officer. He isn't any use to the army dead, is he?"

"It isn't fatal, sir. I didn't mean to imply—"

"Sterility and impotence, that's what you said, right?"

"Right, sir."

"In my terms that's fatal, Captain. I got married my last leave. I've had one night with my wife. One lousy, stinking night."

"I know how you feel, sir. I just got married myself."

"Really? Where's your wife? Stateside?"

"No, sir. She's aboard this ship. A Moroccan girl. A refugee. And her kid sister's with us."

DiCello sat back and studied Daniel's face for a few seconds, then he looked at the clipboard with the ship's plans. "Pretty uneven accommodation aboard the Squire, some's not too bad, even okay. Most of it's a dungeon. Of course, I'm in charge of assigning quarters, and officers— and their families—are supposed to get some consideration. Now, Captain, about this medicine . . ."

"But, Daniel, Shama and I do not need such luxury." Ruth surveyed the cabin she and her sister were to share with a Wac colonel and a diplomat's wife. "There are others perhaps who need it more."

Daniel chucked her under the chin. "With me it's first class all the way, Ruthie. Relax and enjoy it. It's small compared to what you're going to have once we're stateside."

They were alone, neither the Wac nor the wife were present and Shama was off exploring. Ruth leaned her head on Daniel's chest. "You are very good to me and . . . and I love you, Daniel."

She spoke the words softly, shyly. She'd said them first a month ago on their wedding night, when so much previously unknown to her about herself had been revealed.

Since then she repeated the words at least once a day, needing to reaffirm the extraordinary truth, shy because Daniel always said what he did now, "I know, Ruthie. You're a great girl."

It did not seem to her enough, but she told herself she mustn't be greedy. Daniel was an American. What did she know of Americans and their ways? Still, some worries she could not hide. "What you told the major, about the throat infection, it isn't true, is it?"

He hooted with laughter. "Of course it isn't true. My God, Ruthie, do you think I'd really barter medicine for fancy quarters? Medicine that a lot of people might need?"

Ruth pulled back, staring at him, trying to fathom the twists and turns of his personality. "I do not understand you, Daniel. You are both—what is the English word? —moral and not moral."

"Immoral. That's the antonym. And maybe you're right. I have my own kind of crazy code, Ruthie. You'll get used to it. Meanwhile, just settle in here and relax."

"I wish we could have a cabin together. How long is the crossing?"

"Five days. And one minute you're complaining that I'm a cheat, the next that I don't cheat well enough."

He said it with a grin, but Ruth turned pale. "Oh no, I am not complaining. You mustn't think that, Daniel."

"I don't. And I'd like a cabin for two as much as you would. We'll just have to live on dreams for a few days." He put his hands on either side of her oval face and studied her dark, serious eyes. "Can you do that, Ruthie?"

Ruth put her hands over his, pressing his palms closer, reveling in the touch. "I can do anything for you, my husband."

He was just bending his head to kiss her when Shama burst in. *"C'est fantastique, le navire—O, pardon."*

"It's okay, kid." Daniel let go of Ruth. "You like this old tub, huh?"

"What means tub?"

He walked to the door. "I'll let Ruthie explain. See you both later."

For long moments Ruth stared at the spot where he'd stood, ignoring Shama's demand for a lesson in American slang.

Daniel, too, had a cabin above deck. He shared his with

two bird colonels. It was on a corner and had the incredible luxury of two portholes. On balance he'd gotten himself a better deal than he'd arranged for Ruth and Shama.

Emma had imagined they would meet a ship somewhere near the Charlestown Navy Yard. All during the war she'd seen the ominous gray hulks slip in and out of those docks, their silhouettes were threatening behemoths looming over her life. But Daniel was discharged in New Jersey. He called his family the day he was released and announced that he and his wife and sister-in-law were coming to Boston by train from New York; they'd be on the Yankee Clipper the next afternoon, arriving in South Station at five-thirty. "Will you reserve us a couple of hotel rooms, Mother?"

Emma swallowed hard. "Don't be ridiculous, Daniel. You and your . . . wife can have your old room. We'll put the little girl in the guest room."

"If you're sure it's okay," Daniel said quietly.

"Of course."

But, God, she was anything but sure; Emma was terrified. Fortunately this was one time Joshua took over the domestic arrangements. Daniel, his fair-haired boy, was coming home. Never mind who or what he was bringing with him. "We'll all go to the station to meet Daniel," Joshua decreed. "Caleb, I'll arrange that neither you nor I are on duty tomorrow afternoon."

"I don't want to go," Jessica muttered. Joshua silenced her with a look.

The family mustered on the platform in the hot summer afternoon. South Station was a sea of uniformed men and joyful civilians come to greet them. Emma noted the numbers of crutches and casts and slings and canes. The flotsam tossed back after the war was damaged merchandise, no amount of rejoicing could change that.

She was lucky, she thought. No matter what, she mustn't forget it. Daniel was alive and whole. Compared to the possibility of missing arms and legs and eyes, to death itself, what weight a disastrous marriage? Almost none. Not even a Jewish daughter-in-law could spoil the sense of having won an enormous gamble. Emma squared her shoulders and watched the Yankee Clipper steam into the station.

Daniel descended first, still wearing his uniform, a little

thinner than she remembered, older looking, more mature. And painfully handsome. Emma eyed him in wonder, then turned to Joshua. They grinned at each other, shared pleasure in the knowledge that they'd produced this marvelous-looking young man and fate had chosen to spare him.

"Well, there she is," Joshua murmured.

Daniel was handing Ruth down from the train to the platform. She wore a starkly tailored navy linen dress, a small navy straw hat with a white ribbon, and white gloves. The dress she'd made herself; the hat and the gloves she'd bought the day before in New York. Also the dark green cotton dress that Shama wore, it had a high neck and long sleeves. Warm for August, but it didn't look foreign or exotic. Emma sighed.

"Thank God," Joshua whispered in her ear. "You were right, they are white."

It was Caleb who broke ranks first. He left Susan standing with the others and pushed through the crowd to Daniel's side. Daniel didn't see him immediately. "Ah declare, suh, you is needin' a bit of help with yore bags, ain't you, suh?" Caleb said in a broad Negro drawl.

"Yes, here are the tickets." Daniel turned to hand over the baggage checks and saw his twin. "Hey, you old bastard! You've become an actor while I was gone." They clasped hands first, then Daniel wrapped his brother in a bear hug. Ruth and Shama stood still and waited, ignoring the crowd jostling around them. A few seconds passed before Daniel remembered them, and when he faced Ruth she noted that his eyes were suspiciously damp. "Ruthie, this is my twin brother, Caleb."

Ruth put out her hand. Caleb took it, then impulsively leaned forward to kiss her cheek. Of them all, he was the one least disturbed by Daniel's news. "You're just as pretty as I knew you'd be. Daniel always picked winners. Welcome to America and to the family."

Ruth felt a lump in her throat. "Thank you. And this is my sister, Shama."

Caleb turned to the little girl. She was smaller than Jessie, though he knew she was a little older. Her face was pinched and very pale. Her hair, not quite as dark as her sister's, was pulled back with equal severity and almost hidden by a wide-brimmed straw hat with a long ribbon.

Caleb gave her his full attention and the benefit of all his green-eyed charm. She curtseyed and he grinned, then took both her hands in his. "Hi, kid. Glad you made it."

"Her English isn't much yet," Daniel said. Ruth translated rapidly.

But Shama was smiling at Caleb, and it was obvious she didn't need her sister's French to understand the warmth of Caleb's greeting. When he leaned down and kissed her, she turned bright pink and the flush of color was a hint of how pretty she might be one day.

"C'mon," Caleb said. "The rest of the clan is waiting over there out of the jam." He kept hold of Shama's hand while he led them through the crowd.

Emma clung to her son for a measurable amount of seconds, overwhelmed and surprised by the fierceness of her joy. Joshua shook Daniel's hand formally at first, then grabbed him in a hug. Susan presented a cool cheek for a dutiful kiss when Caleb introduced them. Daniel decided instantly that he didn't like her, then told himself he was an idiot to make such a snap judgment. "Where's Jess?" he demanded. Louder than necessary, unnaturally hearty, a device to cover the confusion of his reaction to Caleb's wife.

Emma turned to look for her daughter. "She was here a second ago."

Jessica was standing against the wall, about six feet from them, leaning on the brick, pushing her fingers against it, as if she wanted to force her way through to the other side and away from all of them. She wasn't looking at Daniel but at Shama. And the other girl was aware of that consuming stare.

"Jessica," Emma called. "Come say hello to Daniel. Whatever's got into you?" It was mother-talk in a faintly scolding tone. And it was wholly inappropriate, because she knew what her child was feeling; but it was the only defense she could find against the dark hatred in Jessica's eyes. "Jessie, please . . ."

Daniel understood everything immediately. He didn't wait for his sister to come to him. He crossed to her and swept her up into his arms, whirling her around the platform as if they were alone. "How's my girl?" He repeated the question a number of times. "How's my all-time favorite, number one sister?"

"I'm fine, Daniel. Put me down, please."

He set her feet on the concrete floor, but didn't loose his grip on her. "You too big for games now? No kiss for a brother home from the war?"

She raised her head and turned her cheek to him. He kissed it, waited, then let her go. It was going to take time, he could see that. Daniel left her where she was and returned to his parents.

"Mother, Dad, this is Ruth."

She'd been standing quietly, waiting, while the Morgans greeted Daniel. Now she took a step forward and shyly extended her hand. "I am delighted to meet you *Monsieur le docteur et Madame Emma*. This is my sister, Shama."

Shama obeyed Ruth's tug and stepped up to Emma and Josh. She dropped two separate curtseys, one to each of them. *"Enchant, Monsieur, Madame."*

"How charming," Emma said. She looked carefully at the family her son had brought home and she felt the beginnings of relief. White, both of them. And with beautiful manners. Dressed rather dowdily, but at least not in exotic foreign robes as she'd imagined. It just might be all right. She smiled as brightly as she could. "Come along, everyone. There's a celebration dinner waiting at home."

Before the dinner there were the servants to greet. The three of them were lined up in the front hall. It occurred to Emma that they were like characters out of some mannered English novel. But there was nothing mannered about the way they hugged Daniel, nor in his genuine delight at seeing them again.

Tessie and Nora were first, then Marya. She wrapped him in her arms and held him against her bosom, as she had so many times. For a second he was a little boy again. Daniel closed his eyes and let the feeling of warmth and safety and security overwhelm him. When they parted, a few of the tears that had been in his eyes all day rolled down his cheeks. He fought visibly for control, and won. "Marya, Tessie, Nora, this is my wife, Ruth, and that shrimp is Shama." There was only a trace of hoarseness in his voice.

Ruth stepped forward. She looked at each of the three women, her eyes grave, her manner both dignified and warm. "I am so pleased to meet you. Daniel has told me much and I have looked forward." Ruth shook hands with each in turn, then signaled Shama. The younger girl dropped three careful curtseys.

"Will you look at that." Nora sighed. "Just like in London when we was young." Her tone was full of wonder. Marya, too, was enchanted. She bent over and kissed Shama. Tessie said nothing, merely blew her nose loudly, then announced she had her dinner to see to. In the kitchen she began peeling more potatoes.

"You already got a mountain of spuds," Nora said.

"Didn't you see how thin that poor child is. I gotta fatten her up, don't I?" She went on wielding her knife, cursing Nazis and Japs and all war as she did so.

The family went into the library for sherry. Marya watched them go, then escaped to her room. It was small and cramped, located under the eaves of the attic, but it faced Commonwealth Avenue. The larger room across the narrow hall belonged to Tessie and Nora, and its windows overlooked the tiny yard and the roofs. Marya preferred her room. She liked to see people coming and going, to watch the world pass below. But now she saw nothing. Her eyes were squeezed shut and she shook with sobs.

She hadn't cried once in nearly four years—not when Daniel went off to war, not during the agonizing months when every day that didn't bring a dreaded telegram from the war office was another reprieve. She didn't even cry when it was over and they knew Daniel would come home safe and whole. Only now, when at last she'd seen him and touched him, and knew finally that the thing she'd most dreaded would not happen. There really would be no repeat of an earlier, terrible tragedy. This time the war hadn't cheated her. She pushed away the memory of the other war and went to the sink in the corner and bathed her face.

It was after seven. The family would be at dinner. Marya descended the stairs slowly, feeling somehow not herself. She walked to the door of the dining room, needing to hear them, to convince herself that it was really as she hoped. They were together, here in this house, hers in the way they'd always been hers.

Joshua's voice, saying something to Susan, the two of

them laughing loudly, the others joining in, but with less
enthusiasm. Marya pictured Daniel's wife. It was the first
time she'd really thought about her since the meeting.
Nice, a nice girl. Even if she was a Jew. A contrast to
Caleb's choice. She shook her head and turned away.
Always Daniel got the best. Caleb settled for what was
left. Nothing she'd ever managed to do had changed that.
Even now, when Daniel had gone to war and Caleb had
remained safe at home, Daniel had turned out the winner.

Marya hesitated, not ready to stop eavesdropping. She
heard Emma address a question to Jessica, but if there was
a reply it was too soft to catch. There would be trouble
with Jessie. She was full of pain. And the other child,
Shama. Everyone was making a fuss over her. That would
make it worse for Jessica.

Marya smoothed her dark dress over her full hips. The
Morgan family still needed her. It was as it should be.

11

"*T*his was your room, with Caleb when you were little?"
Ruth looked around at the large, high-ceilinged bedroom,
the red plaid curtains and matching bedspreads on the
twin maple beds.

"Yup. Until I went into the army. This is a new touch
though." He pointed to a bunch of bright red anemones in
a white vase. It stood on the bureau with a card bearing
the word "Welcome" in gold-embossed letters. "In your
honor. Cal and I never had flowers."

"Everyone in your family is being so good to me. This is
from your mother?"

"No, I don't think so. That card's not mother's style.
More likely Marya."

Ruth nodded and smelled the bouquet. Then she turned
and looked at the twin beds. "In my house when I was
little, a bed as big as that would be for three people. You
and Caleb had one each."

Daniel wore a robe over pajama bottoms. Now he untied the robe and shrugged it off. His broad back was still
tanned from the African sun. He tossed the robe on a chair
and sat on the edge of the bed nearest the window, the
one that had always been his. "Ruthie, in some ways you
foreigners are a lot smarter." He grinned and held out his
arms. "Come here."

She crossed to him, standing between his splayed legs.
Daniel took both her hands and spread them wide, behind

her a lamp cast a revealing shadow through the thin, high-necked cotton nightdress. "Take off that thing," he murmured huskily. "Let me look at you."

She'd never have believed she could be so forward, so entirely without shyness. But she was. She pulled the nightdress over her head and dropped it on the floor. Her dark hair hung loose to her shoulders, and she lifted it in her hands and pushed it to the top of her head. Posing for him, conscious of her heavy breasts, her narrow waist, her rounded hips.

Daniel put his arms around her, pressing his palms against the smooth flesh of her buttocks, her face to the taut golden skin of her belly. He kissed her, drawing his tongue round her navel, lowering his mouth slowly, but with a purpose and destination they both knew. Ruth shivered, and one tiny moan escaped into the silence of the room and the sleeping house. Finally he drew her down beside him in the single bed, then he was atop her and inside her and she quivered with the rage of passion he'd unloosed so unexpectedly a few short weeks that were a lifetime ago.

"I don't want to rush you, Daniel, but what are your thoughts about the future?"

Daniel surveyed his father's office in 163 Commonwealth Avenue. It was large and handsome, just as he remembered it. The big mahogany desk was elegantly bare except for pictures of his mother and himself and Cal and Jess. There were a few pictures on the walls and dark blue wall-to-wall carpet covered the floor. "This is okay," he said. "I'll take over next week."

Josh grinned. "Not quite that fast." He grew serious. "It will be yours someday, though. If you want it. Is it to be ob-gyn, son?"

"You and me and Cal, we're all in this together, right?"

Joshua leaned back and studied him. "Is that a joke or, what's the modern phrase—a put-down? I'm not quite sure."

"Not a put-down, maybe a joke. Dad, there was a guy at the hospital in Morocco. A bird colonel named Warren James, an internist, chief of staff." Daniel stopped speaking.

"Yes," Josh said. "What about him? Does internal medi-

cine tempt you, Daniel? There's no law that says you have
to specialize in gynecology."

Daniel stretched. "I don't know what tempts me, that's
the problem. James says I have a gift for diagnosis. He
claims good diagnosticians are born not made."

"He's right about that. Medicine's an inexact science at
best. And some men do have a sixth sense about diagnosis.
As to whether you have it, your Colonel James would
know better than I. I've yet to work with you." There was
a hint of longing in Josh's voice.

"I don't know either," Daniel said. "James is out of the
army now. Gone back to private practice in L.A. I could—"
He didn't finish the sentence.

"He's offered you a place in his practice, is that it,
Daniel?"

"That's it."

"You should be flattered. Are you going to take it?"

"At the risk of repeating myself, I don't know. There's
Ruthie and Shama to think about."

"Yes, indeed. You brought quite a load of responsibility
home with you, son. Are you feeling the weight?"

Daniel waved his hand. "Hell, no. They're no trouble.
Terrific girls, both of them. I just meant that maybe they'd
do better here in Boston with the whole family to sort of
look after them."

It occurred to Joshua that it was a most extraordinary
way for a young man to speak about his bride of less than
two months. He could think of no way to say that to
Daniel. "We will, of course. Ruth is charming. Your mother
is quite taken with her. We have wondered a bit about
what it means, their being Jews. Is there something special we should know?"

"Beats me," Daniel said easily. "You'll have to ask Ruthie
herself. Near as I can figure out they'd rather not eat pork
or bacon, and that's about it."

Josh felt more discomfort, more unease. Daniel spoke of
them as if they were souvenirs he'd brought home from
the war, pets that needed tender looking after. He'd have
to discuss it with Emma, maybe she could probe that
swamp. For himself he needed a safer topic of conversation. "Don't feel you have to rush into anything in terms of
your career, Daniel." Joshua reached into the drawer of
his desk and withdrew a checkbook. "How about my put-

ting a thousand into your account? Walking-around money until you get settled and decide what comes next."

Daniel cleared his throat. "Thanks, Dad, that's really good of you. But I don't need it."

"Don't be bashful, Daniel." Josh reached for a pen. "What were they paying you, some six hundred a month as I recall. I suppose you saved much of it, nothing to spend it on, but still—"

"Dad, I mean it. I don't need money." He'd known this had to come. Nothing to do now but plough straight in. "I've got quite a bit put by."

Josh looked up. "How much is quite a bit?"

He'd stashed forty thousand dollars the day after he arrived home, carried it into First Federal Savings in a wad and tucked it all away with his friendly neighborhood banker. "A good few thousand. I got to be quite a poker player. I wrote you about that."

"So you did." Joshua lay down his pen and closed the checkbook. "Nonetheless, if you run out before you've made up your mind about the future, don't be shy about asking."

"I won't be. Thanks, Dad."

Daniel escaped the office with a sense of relief, but it wasn't finished yet. Emma tackled him a few days later, over a midmorning cup of coffee in the breakfast room on a day when a cold had kept her home from the lab.

"Daniel, I want to take Ruth and Shama shopping for some clothes. I thought I'd best check with you first."

"That's great, Mom. No problem, I really appreciate it."

"It's not you I'm worried about," Emma said tartly. "Ruth doesn't think she can go. I believe she said, 'permitted to go.'"

Daniel grinned. "She's got a lot of old-world notions about a wife's proper place. Walks three steps behind me, that kind of thing."

"Well, we must make her understand that things are not done that way in America." Emma eyed her son. "You young rascal, you really enjoy it, don't you?"

"Sometimes. A little bit."

"You have to stop it, Daniel. You're just amusing yourself, but Ruth has a difficult adjustment to make and you have to help, not hinder."

"I know. I'll tell her to go shopping with you. Tell her she can spend whatever she wants."

Emma thought about what Josh had reported of his conversation with Daniel. "I planned the new clothes to be my wedding present."

"We're not short, Mom. I told Dad that."

"So he said. It's still my right and my pleasure to buy presents for my new daughter-in-law and her sister." Emma frowned. "In a way it's Shama that worries me."

"Why? She's a great kid, bright as they come. Wait until her English gets better, then you'll see."

"I know she's bright. And she's as charming as Ruth. It's the problem of her and Jessie."

Daniel sighed. "Yes, that's not a terrific situation. Instant mutual hate. Mom, I was thinking of sending her to Jessie's school in the fall. But I'd better come up with another plan, hadn't I?"

"Perhaps it would be best." Emma poured another cup of coffee and stirred in a dollop of cream. "A private school is quite expensive, darling. Are you sure you can manage? We'll be glad to help, of course."

"No problem." He leaned forward and covered her hand with his. "Mom, can't you and Dad just accept that I've got enough money? We don't have to talk about it a lot. But I've got enough."

"Very well. Does that mean you're planning early retirement? Starting this afternoon, perhaps."

He laughed. "Is that what Dad thinks?"

"No, I'm the one who sees you choosing a life of leisure. Your father believes you simply haven't decided on a specialty."

"Well, this time he's right." He finished his coffee and rose. "I'll go find Ruthie and tell her she's to go shopping with you whenever you say."

On a Saturday morning two weeks after Daniel's return home, Emma took Ruth on what she meant to be a spree. Shama was at an English lesson with the tutor Daniel had hired. Emma was glad of a chance to have Ruth on her own. She quite liked Shama, but it was distracting always having to wait while Ruth translated what was said. This way she had the older girl to herself for a time. "I want us to be friends, Ruth," Emma said. "Please believe me."

"I do, Madame Emma." Ruth's eyes grew very big. "I must not ever make you think I do not believe what you say. It's only that my English is not good."

They were walking across the Common on their way to Tremont Street, and Emma took Ruth's hand and drew her to a bench under the silvery shade of a birch tree. "My dear, your English is fine. Look, you and I come from different worlds, we seem different. But I grew up very poor and when I first married Josh he didn't have much money. Besides, we both love Daniel, we have that in common. And we're women, perhaps that's the strongest bond of all. Am I being clear?"

Ruth nodded. "I love your Daniel very much, Madame Emma," she said shyly. "I want to be a good wife."

"I know. And I'm sure you will be. Now, let's go see what they have that suits you in Chandlers."

As shopping trips went, it was not one of the most successful. Ruth inevitably chose the most conservative, the dullest things. A few times Emma tried to influence her selection, one fall dress in heather-colored wool she thought particularly lovely on the dark girl, but Ruth was so obviously unhappy about it that Emma didn't insist. "Maybe it's something to do with her religion," she told Josh later. "Maybe Jews aren't permitted to wear bright colors."

"God knows, the only Jews I've ever seen have been in the charity wards at the hospital. Those women couldn't afford bright anything."

"Daniel, is it permitted to have a synagogue in America?"

They were sharing one of the twin beds in Daniel's old room—they never used both of them. A tiny night-light made a soft pink glow. Daniel enjoyed having the night-light on when they made love, he delighted in watching her. But now their passion was spent for a while and he was almost asleep. Ruth's head was on his shoulder, he stroked her long dark hair. "A synagogue's a Jewish church, isn't it? Of course, it's permitted. We have freedom of religion here, honey. It's in the constitution."

"I am glad. I want to go to a synagogue, Daniel. If you don't mind."

"Of course I don't mind. I just don't know where one is."

I'll check. It didn't occur to me before because I didn't think you were religious."

"I didn't think so either. But I have a special favor to ask."

He yawned. It was after midnight, he was sleepy. "What special favor?"

"We are married three months and I am not yet starting a baby."

Daniel sat up in the bed. "Oh, Jesus. I thought you understood. Ruthie, I guess I'd better explain."

"What? What's the matter, Daniel? You are angry with me? I'm sorry—"

"No, I'm not in the least angry. Don't look like that, honey. It's not a problem, I just forget how innocent you are. To me you're foreign and exotic and I think that means you're sophisticated, which, of course, it doesn't."

"Daniel, you're speaking too fast. And I don't understand all the words. I'm sorry my English isn't better, but—"

He put a finger over her lips. "Ssh, stop apologizing, you've nothing to be sorry for. It's my fault for not explaining. Listen, Ruthie, we can't have a baby just yet. It's too soon. I want to decide about my future."

She looked at him, her lovely face showing her perplexity. "Because you don't want a baby yet it doesn't happen? How can that be?"

"It's not because of what I want, not the way you think." Daniel reached over to the night table and opened the drawer and took out the white package marked Trojan with the stylized black horse's head on the front. "Look, you've seen me use these things." He pulled a rolled condom out of the box and held it in the palm of his hand.

Ruth blushed. "I did not wish to ask you why. I mean I did wish, but it seemed I should not ask. I thought all American men are maybe happier if they use such a thing with a woman."

"Not happier, honey. But it's a necessity if the girl's not going to get pregnant." He gave a brief lesson in biology and contraception, speaking as slowly and clearly as he could. "Got it?" he asked finally.

Ruth nodded, her eyes were solemn. "I got it."

"Have it," he automatically corrected himself and her.

"I have it," she repeated. "Daniel, I still want to find a

synagogue. And I want to go to school. I am told there are
free schools in America."

"Sure there are. What kind of a school?"

"One that will teach me to speak better English. And to
know all the things your wife must know. It will use up my
time until you are ready for us to have a baby."

He patted her cheek. "You know enough to suit me,
Ruthie."

"I want to go to school," she insisted.

"Okay. I'll look into it. I promise."

Two weeks later Daniel announced that he'd bought a
house in Brookline.

Ruth's face turned ashen when he told her. "Your parents will not accept me?"

"My parents? What have they got to do with it?"

"The mother-in-law is the mistress, I know that. I and
your brother's wife, we are to work under her. But Madame Emma never gives me any work to do, Daniel. I
keep asking, but she says there is no need. And the
Susan doesn't speak to me and I don't see her. So it isn't
that I'm lazy or a bad daughter-in-law, but—"

"Slow down, Ruthie. You're jumping all over the lot and
I don't know what this is all about."

They were in the bedroom, the only place they had any
real privacy, and he drew her to sit beside him on the
bed. "Now try again, slowly. Why are you upset about my
buying us a home of our own?"

"This is your home, Daniel. Your father's house. Your
brother and you, this is your home. Susan is acceptable,
but I do not know the ways, so you have to leave in
shame." She was sobbing now, her shoulders heaving.

"Ruthie, ah, sweetheart, stop crying. I think I understand and you've got it all wrong." He fished out his
handkerchief and wiped her eyes and held her close.
"Stop crying," he repeated. "And I'll explain."

The sobs ended and gradually she quieted in his arms.
"I am not crying now, Daniel."

"No, so listen good. You've got to get this right, Ruthie,
or you're going to make a lot of unnecessary trouble for
yourself. I forgot how things were in Morocco, with the
Arabs anyway. Everybody living together. We don't do
that here, honey. In America it's normal for a man's sons

to take their wives and set up a new house. All I'm doing
is what every guy in the country does. It's got nothing to
do with whether or not you're an acceptable daughter-in-
law. Besides, you are. Mom's crazy about you."

Ruth drew back and looked at him. "I don't think you
should say your mother is crazy, Daniel. That's not showing respect. And if what you say is true, why does Caleb
keep his wife here?"

"They're not here. They live in the apartment next
door, over the office."

"Who owns the building in which Doctor Joshua has his
office and Caleb and Susan live?" she demanded.

"Dad does, but—"

"Hah!" she interrupted triumphantly. "So they are living under your father's roof. But you are being turned out,
because of me. Don't lie to me, Daniel. Just tell me what
to do so your parents will be pleased with me."

Daniel pushed her away and stood up, running his
fingers through his dark hair. "You are acceptable, I keep
telling you that. The only reason Cal and Sue live next
door is that Cal can't afford a place of his own. He's
earning slave wages as a resident."

"Caleb is a slave? Daniel, I don't understand . . ."

"Oh, Jesus . . . Ruthie, just take my word for it, will
you? There's no problem. I can afford to put you in a
house of your own and I'm doing it. That's the way we
operate here. No, don't start weeping again. I did it for
you, damn it. And Shama. So she can go to a different
school than Jess and not feel she has to compete." And for
himself, so he wouldn't feel so much his father's son, so
much required to measure up to Joshua's standards. But
he couldn't explain that.

Ruth stared at him. The beloved, handsome face was
flushed with anger. She lowered her eyes and prayed for
wisdom and understanding. It was all so strange, but if
Daniel was displeased with her, if he divorced her and
turned her out, she would die. She needed no help understanding that, she knew it with her whole heart and soul.

Joshua tipped back his head and studied the large house
separated from the road by a broad sweep of green lawn.
It was red brick with white wooden trim. Two white
pillars supported a shallow portico over the imposing front

door and a dozen elm trees lined the long drive that led to it. "Just a little nest of your own for you and Ruth," he said, quoting his son's earlier explanation. "Sweet God, Daniel, what did you pay for this place? How much of a mortgage are you saddled with?"

"Got it cheap. Guy who built it dropped dead, and his widow wanted out quick." Daniel mumbled the words and didn't look at his father. Emma was standing a few feet away, looking at the house and not saying anything. "It's furnished, Mom. I bought it lock, stock, and barrel, as they say. But it needs some homey touches, so I hope you'll help Ruthie—"

"How much is the mortgage?" Joshua demanded again. "Don't tell me that's not my business, son. I know you're a grown man and married, but I can't stand by and let you assume burdens that will cripple your career."

Daniel turned to him. It was time. He couldn't put it off any longer. Maybe a public street in broad daylight wasn't the place he'd have chosen, but it was where it was happening and it was time. "There's no mortgage, Dad. I paid cash. Twenty-two thousand, if you must know. And it didn't break me. I've got enough left to support myself and Ruthie and Shama for a few years if necessary."

Joshua took a few seconds to absorb the immensity of that. "I see," he said slowly. "You mean you have enough to buy this house and live without working if you choose, don't you?"

"Yeah, that's what I mean."

Emma had moved closer. Obviously she'd heard every word. "Is that the kind of life you want, Daniel? Doesn't it strike you as rather . . . well, decadent?"

"Jesus!" he exploded. "Sorry, Mom. I don't mean to— Look, I'm not saying I don't want to practice medicine, of course I do. I'm just trying to tell you two that finances aren't a problem. So you won't worry. I need help getting Ruthie and Shama settled into an American way of life and I want you to concentrate on that, not on where the money came from."

"I don't think I want to know where the money came from," Joshua murmured.

"Okay, so let's leave it that way, shall we?"

Daniel waited, neither of his parents said anything for a

few seconds. They heard a car approaching. "That will be
Cal and Sue and Ruthie and Shama. Can we please go in?"

Emma took a deep breath. "Yes, let's do that." She led
the way up the drive and Joshua and Daniel followed.

The front hall was spacious and flooded with sunlight
that entered through long windows either side of the front
door. The floor was polished parquet and there was an
elegant central staircase leading to the floors above. Joshua
and Emma were relieved of the need to comment because
Cal and the women came in just then.

Caleb whistled softly. "Wow, look what I missed by not
fighting for my country. Pay was pretty good in the army,
apparently. Maybe I could move in as your butler. Sue
can be the parlor maid."

Daniel ignored him and turned to Ruth. "Welcome to
your new home, honey." He took her hand. "Come see it
all. Ignore my brother the clod, he's just jealous."

Ruth followed him, but before they moved out of the
hall she caught a glimpse of her sister-in-law's face. In
French it was called *la envie*. No, that wasn't strong enough.
In Susan's eyes she read *la convoitise*, she didn't know the
English word for that.

Emma did. She didn't know what Ruth was thinking,
but she knew very well that the emotion momentarily
distorting Susan's pretty face was lust, not for the man
perhaps, but for the things his money could buy. Emma
felt a wave of despair, what was being sown here in this
elegant foyer? What had Daniel unloosed with his mysterious wealth? She turned to Joshua for some sign of understanding and reassurance. He was studying a detail of the
carved mahogany banister and he seemed unaware of the
entire drama.

Disturbed as she was by the mystery of the money to
support the lifestyle Daniel had adopted, Emma felt somewhat relieved after he and Ruth and Shama moved out of
165 Commonwealth Avenue. Jessie was less of a problem,
and that left Emma a bit more time to pick up the threads
of her life. She resumed her volunteer work at the Planned
Parenthood office for a start.

The office was still on Milk Street, still staffed by Thelma
Willard with Emma helping out whenever she could.
Celia, now in her early 80s, but spry as ever, was active,

too. These days their efforts were aimed largely at the state legislature. Most women knew about birth control now, what it was and how it worked, but in Massachusetts the sale of condoms and diaphragms was still illegal. Everyone who wanted them could get them, because of a general conspiracy to ignore the law, but neither Emma nor her co-workers would consider the battle won until it was changed.

They kept up a steady barrage of letters and leaflets, fairly buried the State House in them. On a September Saturday afternoon two weeks after Daniel moved his family to Brookline, Emma went to Milk Street intending to stuff a few hundred envelopes with yet another report of the statistics equating unlimited childbearing with poverty and disease.

She was surprised to find two strange women sitting with Thelma. Very few people came in off the streets now, the campaign had moved beyond direct service before the war.

"Emma, this is Miss Becky Johnson." Thelma indicated the older of the callers. She was a small, skinny woman with a disconcerting cross-eyed stare and a pinched expression. She wore rusty black, none too clean.

"How do you do?" Emma extended her hand and the other woman took it in a limp, fleeting grip. The second visitor hadn't looked up.

Emma turned a questioning glance to Thelma. It was met by one of something like desperation. "And this is Miss Johnson's younger sister, Kate," Thelma said.

Kate turned vacant gray eyes toward Emma and ignored her outstretched hand. "She ain't rude," the first woman said. "Just backward. That's why it happened."

Apparently the blond girl was the focus of the visit. She wore black, like her sister, but her dress seemed two sizes too small for her. Voluptuous breasts strained the bodice and wide hips pulled the skirt tight over the curved thighs which made up her lap. No girdle, Emma realized. And probably no bra. Extraordinary. With a little animation and some soap and water the child might be pretty, but as she was at present Emma felt vaguely repelled—and she was instantly guilty about it. Poverty wasn't a crime. She turned to Thelma again. "What seems to be the difficulty?"

"Miss Johnson came to me three days ago, Emma. She

believes her sister is pregnant." Thelma's words were as
clipped and matter-of-fact as always, but there was still
something haunted in her expression. "I told her we had
no means of helping with such a situation, and no advice
to give, but—"

"It ain't like she knows any better," Becky Johnson
interrupted. Her voice rose and grew shrill. "I told you,
she's backward. Ain't never had no sense since she was
born. I look after her as best I can, but I got to go out and
work don't I? How else are we gonna eat?"

Emma put a hand on the woman's bony shoulder. "Please
calm yourself, Miss Johnson. Just try and answer a few
questions so we can see if there's some way to help you.
What kind of work do you do?"

"I clean some shops. Every day, regular like."

"And where do you and your sister live?"

"With my aunt. But it ain't charity, mind. We pays for
our bed and board. Five dollars a week for me and Kate
and Pa."

"Oh, your father lives with you, is that it?"

Becky Johnson dropped her glance and murmured as-
sent in a barely audible voice. Emma looked from her to
the vacant-eyed blonde and drew a deep breath. "And
does your father work too?"

"No." A shamed whisper.

"So he's home all day looking after Kate, is that correct?"

The woman nodded. Emma glanced at Thelma. She
understood her desperation now. They had heard about
such things. There was no byway of sexuality they hadn't
heard about in this office, but this was the first time either
of them were face-to-face with such horror. Emma took a
deep breath. Thelma obviously couldn't cope, it was up to
her. "How many months pregnant do you believe Kate to
be?"

"Three nearly. I check each month to be sure she gets
the curse. I has to, don't I? Her being backward and all.
But this here's September and she ain't had it since early
May."

"I see. Miss Johnson, will you and your sister please
wait outside. If Miss Willard and I can talk for a few
minutes, perhaps we can think of some way to help you."

Thelma waited until the door closed behind them. Then
she buried her face in her hands. "Dear God, Emma, I'm

right, aren't I? The father has impregnated his own mentally retarded daughter."

"I think it's a fairly safe assumption," Emma said quietly. "Obviously the older sister thinks so too."

"I've read about it," Thelma whispered. "But I never thought . . ." She began shivering violently.

They kept a bottle of brandy for medicinal purposes in one of the file drawers. Emma got it and poured a small amount into a glass. "Here, drink this. I know how you feel, but we have to try and figure out some way to help. The man's probably not entirely sane either, and between them they've doubtless bred another mentally deficient child."

"When she came in the other day, I suggested I'd call the Sisters of Charity, see if they'd take Kate into their home for unwed mothers. Becky wouldn't hear of it. She's the sort who thinks nuns have horns and a tail. Anyway, I don't think the nuns would take someone who wasn't a Catholic. The only other alternative is the insane asylum. But in all conscience, Emma, I can't actually suggest to someone that they go there."

Thelma pulled a handkerchief from her sleeve and dabbed at her eyes. Emma had never seen her cry before. She patted her shoulder. "I know, neither can I." There was nothing Emma could think of worse than the insane asylum, except Hitler's concentration camps. Poor retarded Kate deserved neither. "Becky will have to cope with her sister, Thelma. There's nothing else to be done."

"She should have an abortion."

"Of course she should. But how, Thelma? Who?"

Thelma turned her wet brown eyes to Emma. "I suppose it's out of the question that Doctor Morgan might—"

"You're right," Emma interrupted brusquely. "It's out of the question." She started for the door. It was time to invite the Johnson sisters back in and tell them there was absolutely nothing that either Thelma or Emma could do.

Two days later Emma returned to the office to find Becky and Kate there again. Kate sat in a corner, as mute as before, the same vacant expression on her face. Becky was more animated. "I got the name of somebody," she whispered. "But I'm dead scared of goin' alone. I was

hopin' you could take us." Her hands shook when she held
out a piece of paper with a pencil-scrawled address.

"Miss Johnson," Emma said haltingly, "I know how
desperate you are. We both know. But people like that"
—she indicated the offending slip of paper—"can't be
trusted. They don't know what they're doing half the time.
Anything could happen."

"Auntie knows," the woman said dully. "She says she'll
throw us out if somethin' ain't done and Kate starts showin'.
She says she's respectable and we ain't." Her eyes raked
over Emma's smart linen dress, her little straw hat, her
carefully manicured nails. "It's all right for some, but if
we're throwed out there ain't no place for us to go."

Thelma grabbed the paper. "It's in the North End," she
said. "Not very far." She rose and took her hat off a peg on
the wall of the small office. "Come, Miss Johnson. I shall
go with you."

Emma gasped. "Thelma, you can't."

Thelma turned to her. "What else can I do?"

There was nothing else. Emma nodded and moved to
the chair behind the desk. "I'll stay here until you get
back."

It was ten days later, shortly before nine p.m., when
Thelma telephoned. Josh was at the hospital working late,
Emma took the call alone in her bedroom. She listened a
moment, spoke quickly, then replaced the receiver.

Daniel was downstairs, packing some children's books
that had belonged to him and Caleb. He thought they
might help Shama with her English. Emma went to the
library and paused at the door, staring at her son for a
moment before she spoke his name. "Daniel . . ."

"Hi, I thought you were having an early night." He
turned and looked at her. "What's the matter, Mom? You
look awful."

"Daniel, I need your help. There's no time to explain.
Your father keeps an emergency medical bag in the cupboard under the stairs. Would you get it please. I've
phoned for a taxi. It should be here any second."

She wouldn't explain on the brief journey. Daniel saw
her grim expression and stopped asking questions. The
cab let them off at the corner of Milk and Tremont Streets.

"This way," Emma said. "We'll go in the back door. Though at this hour no one's likely to see you."

Daniel put a hand on her shoulder. "Just a second, Mom. Whatever this is, it's illegal, isn't it?"

"Yes. Does that mean you don't want to come?"

"No, but I don't want you to. Tell me where to go and I'll go and do whatever I can. But if we're breaking some law then I don't want you involved."

"It's too late for that, I'm already involved. Please, Daniel, just come with me. I'll explain later."

He hesitated only a moment longer, then shrugged and followed her.

Kate Johnson was lying on the couch in Thelma's tiny office. She was in a pool of blood and writhing in agony. Daniel took one look at her and began rolling up his sleeves.

"That's all I can do here," he said twenty minutes later. "We have to get her to a hospital. She needs blood, fluids."

He glanced at the faces of his mother and her friend Thelma Willard. They were implicated in an abortion, it was a criminal charge. "It better be Memorial, Mom," he said quietly. "We're going to need all Dad's clout for this one."

Kate Johnson died at three A.M. the following morning. Joshua Morgan signed the death certificate which stated the cause of death as severe hemorrhaging caused by a perforated ulcer.

Two days later Daniel met his mother in a coffee shop near her lab. Emma had summoned him, but she was late. He took a Coke to a table in the rear and settled down to wait. She arrived ten minutes later and kissed his cheek and hugged him hard for a brief moment. "Thank you for coming, darling. And for the other night."

"Nothing to thank me for on either count. You okay now?"

"Fine. But I'd like a cup of coffee."

He went to get it for her, then watched while she stirred in cream and sugar. "Is Dad ever going to speak to me again?" Joshua's rage following the event had been apoplectic.

Emma looked up, startled. "Of course. He wasn't angry with you, just me."

Daniel shrugged. "These days I think he's always angry with me."

"That's not true, Daniel. He's worried about you, that's all." So was she, but this wasn't the moment to go into it. "And he's over his anger with me. At least mostly."

Daniel smiled. "He never stays angry with you for very long."

Emma permitted herself a small, rueful grin. How little children ever knew about their parents' lives. "Darling, I think you're due an explanation. That's why I wanted you to meet me here."

"I'm curious, but only if you want to tell me about it. You don't owe me anything, Mom. I'm a doctor. I find somebody bleeding to death, I do what I can. That's the drill, it's not a big deal."

"This is," Emma insisted. "A very big deal, as you would put it. She'd been to an abortionist, as you and Josh both guessed, but that wasn't what caused the mess you saw. He wouldn't touch her."

This time Daniel was genuinely startled. "He must have. I saw the wounds."

"No, the girl's older sister aborted her with a kitchen knife." Emma took a long swallow of coffee. It was hot and it burned her throat, but not as much as the words. "There's more," she said. "You can't understand unless you know the whole story."

She spared him none of the details of incest or retardation or desperation. Not even of the useless visit to the North End abortionist. "He wouldn't touch her. Thelma came back and told me the whole thing. The man said Kate was too far along."

Four months rather than three he'd insisted. And Thelma had described the room where he made his examination. "It was filthy, crawling with cockroaches. And the smell, Emma, it was unbelievable. I stayed with her. He didn't want me to, but I insisted. Becky waited downstairs. Emma, that man, he made Kate take off all her clothes; he touched her everywhere. He was enjoying it, I could tell from the look on his face. If I hadn't been there—"

"I know," Emma told Daniel she had said. "But you were there. Where are they now?"

"Becky and Kate? Gone home I guess, I had no other place to take them."

There had been no further word for ten days, not until the evening when Kate came alone. "She was hysterical when she got to the office," Emma explained to her son. "Screaming about a knife and how she'd run away from Becky. Thelma didn't know what to do, so she called me. I would have gotten your father, but you were right downstairs, and . . ." She shrugged helplessly. "It was terribly unfair, Daniel. I could have gotten you in awful trouble."

"No problem," he repeated. "And nobody's in trouble. Not even the lady with the kitchen knife. Only problem is that the kid is dead."

"I know," Emma whispered. "I suppose I should report the other sister to the police. Joshua thinks I should. But I can't."

"Neither would I," Dan said quickly. "From what you say, she's as much a victim as her dim-witted sister." He reached for his mother's hand. "We'll just forget about it, Mom. Dad's covered it up and that's that. Personally, I think you and Thelma Willard are real heroines. If anybody should go to jail, it's those jackasses who make the laws that let things like this happen and nothing to be done about them."

12

*D*aniel pressed the phone to his ear and stared out the window at the stark outline of bare elms against a gray November sky. Those trees had been a damned nuisance last month when they shed their leaves, and he'd had to hire a full-time gardener. "Yes, Dad, I know," he murmured into the mouthpiece, then went back to studying the trees and listening with only a quarter of his mind.

Joshua sensed his son's distancing. Not hard to do, there'd been so much of that lately. "Daniel, you cannot just let this slip. The board is very well disposed to you, but you have missed three of their monthly meetings. With less than believable excuses. You have to appear for an interview if you want the residency. Next week or never."

"It's on my calendar, Dad. I'll be there. I promise."

"Good. How's Ruth?"

"Fine. She's taking night courses at the high school. Shakespeare and citizenship. And Shama seems to be settling in."

Josh said something approving and mentioned the fact that Emma was expecting them for a birthday dinner on Friday evening. Daniel again promised to be there, and at the meeting of the board of governors.

He hung up and stared at the calendar on his desk. He'd already noted the meeting of Memorial's board the following Wednesday. In pencil. He picked up a red pen to underline it, his hand hesitated over the page. Eventually he put down the pen.

It was after the Kate Johnson affair that he'd decided to take the gynecology residency. Maybe he could be like his father, lead the profession into new areas. Maybe he could take up his mother's fight for legalized birth control and safe medical abortions for women who had no other choice. It had seemed a fine idea when he thought about it like that. It seemed less fine now. The proposed residency carried the handsome stipend of one hundred and seventy-five dollars a month.

Daniel lit a cigarette, leaned back, and put his feet on the big teak desk. Like the rest of the furniture in the eleven-room house, it had been included in the purchase price of twenty-two thousand dollars. A bargain. Real estate was beginning a spectacular post-war boom. He could sell the house tomorrow for close to forty. Which was a nice paper asset, but he didn't want to sell.

He'd told his father he could support his family for a couple of years if necessary. That was bragging. It had been very expensive getting them set up in their new lives, as of yesterday he had ten thousand in the bank. Not enough. And not very much aided by the prospect of a monthly stipend of less than two hundred bucks. The gardener, the cook, and the maid cost that much.

He heard the front door slam. It would have to be Shama. She still darted in and out like a street urchin. They hadn't done much about that at Chestnut Hill Girls Academy.

"Shama," he called. "C'mon in the study and say hello."

Daniel caught his breath when she appeared. He still couldn't get used to Shama these days. Gone the pinched face, the wide, frightened eyes. Three months of decent food had filled out her cheeks and put color in them. The dark eyes sparkled with merriment now, and proper nutrition had catapulted her into puberty. There were little breasts beneath the navy jumper and white blouse of her school uniform.

"Hi. How is you?" She flopped into the chair across from his, letting her armload of books fall to the floor.

"How are you," he corrected. "And I'm fine. *Et tu, ma petite?*"

"I am very well, thank you. See? I can talk the perfect English. And you must not speak to me in French."

"Ruth doesn't want you to forget your own language. Not that my dozen-word French vocabulary is likely to help much."

"English is my language now. I am American," Shama said firmly. "Like you. Like everyone at the school." She leaned forward and her eyes were earnest. "You are understanding me, Daniel?"

"Do you understand me? And yes, I do. All the same, it will be very useful for you to retain your French and Arabic. How was school?"

"Okay. Only I cannot learn the science. We are going to cut up a frog. I tell the teacher I don't cut up anything unless I will eat it."

"Oh, you did, did you? What did she say?"

Shama made a face. "Never mind. I think about Mrs. Emma. For why does she like the science, Daniel?"

"Ask her. We're going to her house for dinner Friday night."

"I don't go. I stay home."

"Good Lord, why?"

"Because Jessica will look at me the knives. See! That is good American talk, no?"

"Look daggers at me. And Jessie never did it in her whole life."

"Oh yes. At me she does it all the time. Now I go to eat something. But not a frog, I hope. Where is Ruthie?"

"Shopping. I have to go out for a couple of hours, kid. You going to be okay?"

"I'm all right, Jack," she announced as she left the room.

Daniel's grin wasn't just amusement, it was satisfaction. Screw you, Mr. Hitler. You're dead and Shama Morhaim is alive and well and living in Brookline. Ruthie too. Though maybe that wasn't quite as successful a transition. He pushed the thought away and got ready to leave the house.

Susan Davenport Morgan's dressmaker was located in Coolidge Corner, a stone's throw from her brother-in-law's home. But she'd been going to the dressmaker for ten years, Daniel had bought his house two months ago. It didn't occur to Susan to visit Daniel and Ruth the many times she went to see Mrs. Turnovski.

It was Susan's mother who had discovered a decade before that the Polish woman could take a picture out of *Vogue* or *Harper's Bazaar* and produce a copy at a fraction of the dress's original price. That eased somewhat the dilemma of having superb taste and being the wife of a professor. Susan had thought herself free of such considerations when she married into the Morgan family. Instead they were all the more pressing.

"The new look takes a lot of material, Mrs. Morgan. I can't make the dress with less than eight yards of silk."

Susan pursed her lips and calculated. The silk was eight dollars a yard. Too much, Cal would be furious. "Couldn't you give me a discount, Mrs. Turnovski? I really can't spend more than six dollars a yard for this. It's just a little something to wear around."

The woman shrugged. "If you don't want the dress for special occasions, I make it for you in rayon. Only four dollars a yard."

Rayon. The whole damn war it had been rayon and skimpy dresses without ruffles. Now there was Dior and the new look and billowing skirts that skimmed the ankles. "I'll have the silk," she said firmly. "In lavender." Caleb be damned.

She left the dressmaker's, buoyed up by her choice, and decided she'd have a cup of cocoa at Brigham's before she went home. She was turning into the ice cream parlor when she spotted Ruth across the street. Her sister-in-law was carrying an armload of groceries. God, didn't she realize Daniel could afford to pay for deliveries? How else the big house and the servants? And he must be able to buy his wife better looking clothes than what Ruth was wearing.

She had on a dark tweed coat that wasn't becoming and a woolen hat pulled over her ears. The word kike flitted through Susan's mind. It wasn't the thing to say anymore, not since everybody was feeling so sorry for Jews because of the concentration camps. And not since her in-laws had gotten over the shock of Daniel's war bride. Emma was positively devoted to Ruth. Susan grimaced and hurried into Brighams before she was spotted by the other woman.

*   *   *

Daniel had his name on the list for a new Buick, but it hadn't come through yet. Post-war production was still behind demand. Just as well, he'd have to pay twelve hundreds dollars when it arrived. Now was not the best moment for that. He took a streetcar to Park Street and the subway to Maverick. After that it should have been another streetcar. But he was bored by the whole, tiresome journey, and anxious. He stepped out onto the East Boston street and found a cab. "Revere Beach."

The driver looked startled. "You sure, bud? This time of year? Ain't nothin' open down there."

"I'm sure," Daniel said.

The driver shrugged and headed for the Sumner Tunnel. Twenty minutes later he deposited Daniel on the Boulevard in Revere. As he'd predicted, everything was boarded up for the winter. There was only the bitter wind, the sullen gray sea, and the weather-beaten remains of summer's pleasures. Faded, barely readable signs advertised fried clams at forty cents a quart and frozen custard cones for twenty. Daniel turned up the collar of his overcoat and began walking.

Abdul was waiting by the bathhouse. He'd given up the fez, now his thinning black hair was parted in the middle and slicked down. His double-breasted suit had a nipped waist. Modern European, but over here it made him look like a fugitive from the twenties. "This is one hell of a place to meet." The words were Daniel's only greeting. "Not one of your better ideas, my friend."

"Oh yes, I think it is. Come, I've found a bar that's open. Not very hospitable, but it will suit us."

They didn't speak while they cut through an alley to the road behind the Boulevard. Predictably the bar was called Kelly's. It smelled of stale cigarettes and sour beer, but it was warm, deserted, and obscure. They ordered drinks and found a booth at the rear.

"You are well, Captain? Yes, I can see you are. And prosperous. Perhaps my little proposal will not be of interest to you."

Games again. Like in the old days in Morocco. Why the hell was he here if Abdul's telephone call hadn't provoked his interest? The Egyptian knew that. All this was the customary preamble, the only thing missing was the mint tea. "I'm okay. But I don't know whether or not your proposal is interesting until I hear it. First, how did you get to the U.S.? How long have you been here?"

Abdul made a deprecatory gesture. "My small talents, Captain. And a few influential friends. The war was not all bad, as you and I know. I arrived in July. A month before you did."

"You seem to know a hell of a lot about my movements, Abdul. Like where to find me. Your talents again?"

The Egyptian laughed softly. "That required hardly any talent at all. You are the son of a celebrated man, my friend. The Morgan family is well-known in Boston."

"For a start, I think it's best we leave my family out of the discussion."

"Of course. I was only answering your question. And I admire your style. You have an impressive home, Captain. And how good you have been to your wife and young sister-in-law. They blossom under your beneficence."

Daniel sat back and sipped his beer. It gave him a few seconds to think. Blackmail. A generous helping of *baksheesh* so Abdul wouldn't tell his mother and father where he really got the money he brought home from the war. And the F.B.I. might be interested too. He could see it coming. His stomach felt queasy. All the way from Casablanca. Who in hell would have expected the little bastard to turn up here? He waited. The next move was the Egyptian's.

"I do not wish to cause you problems, Captain."

"Glad to hear it, Abdul. Suppose you tell me what you do wish."

"To convey the greetings of a mutual friend. A lady."

Daniel's eyes narrowed. "What lady?"

"A member of your esteemed profession. But first, may I ask why you aren't practicing that profession? Do you not wish to take up your interrupted career now that the war is over?"

"You can ask." Daniel added nothing.

Abdul smiled. "What you Americans call a 'put-down.' Very well, I'm down. We will return to your question about our mutual friend. She sends you greetings, as I said."

"What you haven't said is who she is."

The Egyptian put his hands to his head in mock chagrin. "I'm getting old and forgetful, Captain. The lady is Miss Donnely, Miss Kitty Donnely. You remember her, I trust?"

Daniel felt his stomach sink to somewhere around his ankles. Everything about this conversation boded ill. "Oh yeah, I remember Kitty. Is she in Boston too?"

"In New York. And she wishes to see you, Captain. We both will be honored if you come to see us in New York the day after tomorrow."

"Such a gracious invitation, Abdul. Your legendary Arab hospitality. I didn't realize Kitty had picked up the habit."

The other man smiled and waited and said nothing. Daniel took another swallow of his beer. "Very well, let's say I'd be delighted to see Kitty Donnely, but not the day after tomorrow. It's my birthday. A detail you overlooked, Abdul. You must be slipping. Family party, it wouldn't do for me to miss it."

"I shall try to be more thorough in the future," the Egyptian said quietly. "Shall we expect you on Saturday then?"

"Sunday. And where do I find my two old friends?"

Abdul slid a piece of paper across the scarred and stained table of the booth. Daniel looked at it, memorized the address, and automatically used his Zippo to reduce it to ashes.

Caleb was late getting home from the hospital Friday evening. Susan was clearly impatient and annoyed. "You did promise to be on time tonight, Cal."

"Sorry, darling. An emergency toxemia. We had to do a cesarian. Anyway, Dad was the surgeon, so he's late too, and Mom will understand. She's used to it." He kissed her. "You look lovely and you smell delicious." Caleb tightened his grip on her waist, but Susan pulled back.

"Not now, darling. You'll ruin my makeup. I've brushed your dinner jacket. It's in the bedroom. Do hurry."

"Okay. But I want a rain check. We don't have to stay too late at this brawl, do we?"

"I don't think your mother would appreciate having her birthday dinner called a brawl. And how late we stay is up to you."

"Then we'll leave right after the dessert and presents so I can spirit you up here and ravish you posthaste." He headed for the bedroom and didn't see Susan's grimace.

It wasn't the sex she objected to. Caleb was sweet and tender in bed, and she could always think about something else. It was this damned flat. Up here. That's how they always referred to their home. An apartment above Joshua Morgan's office was like living over the store. Susan sighed. She thought about Daniel's Brookline mansion. She told herself to be patient. After all, Caleb was through his residency in six months. Then he'd go into private practice with his ever so celebrated father. The money would roll in. She picked up the latest issue of *House and Garden* and thumbed through the pages dreamily.

The Marsh sisters had outdone themselves. Emma viewed the dining room with satisfaction. The damask cloth was pale ivory, the centerpiece irises and stephanotis. The blue of the irises was repeated in the glowing azure rim of Rosenthal china. The plates had a thick edging of silver as well; it complimented the candlesticks and the heavy English cutlery.

She had acquired all this finery after she found out about Betty Bradley and lost the baby, after she and Josh were reconciled. It was a way of convincing herself that the past was indeed past, that her home and her family and her life were stable and permanent.

She stared for a moment at the lovely crystal and china and silver. God, the memory of all that had happened could still make her shiver. For years after the terrible scene she would sometimes wake in the night and hear the Bradley woman's voice. But she had conquered the bitterness left after she and Josh reconciled, and she certainly wasn't going to allow it to surface now. Her husband was as he was; she'd made herself accept that truth, made herself live with the knowledge of the streak of weakness that flawed Joshua's apparent strength. There were worse sins, she knew.

Emma paused, thinking of years gone by despite her good resolutions. Her hand hovered over the slightly skewed handle of one exquisite silver knife while Betty Bradley's face seemed to swim toward her out of a mist. There were other ghosts in the fog as well: Billy-Jo Landry and a young woman Emma had never seen named Morgan. No! She wouldn't, she mustn't— Why was she thinking of all this tonight when she had so much to be thankful for?

Emma straightened the knife with a decisive gesture

and adjusted the position of a goblet. "Forget all that," she
mumured under her breath.

"Were you speaking to me, ma'am?" Nora asked. "Is
everything the way you want it?"

"Oh yes, Nora. It's perfect. I do appreciate all the
trouble you've taken."

"As it should be, I daresay," Nora added with the familiarity of long service. "First birthday we've had both Master Cal and Master Daniel home in four years."

"Yes, it is. Now I'll go up and dress and leave everything to you and Tessie."

She'd bought a new gown for the evening, and told
everyone the dinner was to be formal and gala. It was
different from the many meals they'd had together in the
past few months. It was a celebration. There really was a
lot to celebrate, not least that her initial judgment about
Ruth was confirmed. Daniel's wife was a delightful young
woman. Which proved that life was not predictable. Caleb
married a girl who should have fulfilled all her expecta-
tions but didn't, and Daniel brought home an exotic war
bride who won her over in a matter of hours.

Emma thought about that while she twisted her long
red hair into a coronet on top of her head. Her hands
moved automatically, her mind was free to wander. Ruth
was charming, but everything on that front was not perfect. Jessie still wasn't resigned to Daniel's marriage and
the fact of Shama made it worse. Jessie could accept Ruth,
she liked her in spite of herself. But she viewed Shama as
a rival for the special affection between Daniel and herself.
And to add to Emma's concerns there was Susan. She
frowned again.

It was dark and cold by the time the Morgan family
gathered for the birthday party. The woman standing across
the street from the house was hidden from view. She
peered intently through the bare branches of the trees
that marched down the center island bisecting the road.
She could see lights in the dining room. The drawn drapes
glowed from behind, and every few minutes the shadowy
form of one of the Morgans moved across them. They
seemed larger than life, as they'd always been for her. A
legend, a fairy story she'd imbibed with mother's milk.

Morgan Landry was well wrapped against the cold. In

the damp, raw night she stood and watched a long, silent, thoughtful time.

"Birthday cake for dessert," Joshua announced after Caleb and Daniel had opened their presents. "I told your mother it was the only acceptable choice. None of your fancy puddings on a night like this." He uncorked another bottle of champagne. "Bring on the cake, Nora. We're still hungry."

They couldn't possibly be. There had been turtle soup and poached salmon and roast beef with half a dozen different vegetables. Nonetheless, they greeted the cake with delight. Tessie brought it in herself while Nora, who always served at table, stood by and beamed. "Chocolate," Tessie said. "Some folks say a birthday cake gotta be white. But my boys like chocolate best."

Caleb rose and kissed her loudly. Daniel insisted that she and Nora join them for a glass of champagne and a piece of cake.

"Absolutely not downstairs," Daniel said over their protests. "It's my birthday and I say you have it in here, with us. Where's Marya?"

Nora went to find the nurse, and the three servants joined in the toasts and the applause when Caleb and Daniel blew out the twenty-six candles. "I never am sure whether to double the candles," Tessie said. "All these years and I ask myself the same thing each time. Do they get a whole set apiece or share 'em?"

"Always I teach them to share," Marya said firmly.

"Yes," Tessie agreed. "And otherwise it's just too many candles."

It was a decidedly festive evening.

"Coffee in the drawing room," Emma said when the last crumb of cake was gone.

"What means drawing room?" Shama was avid to increase her vocabulary. She never missed an opportunity.

"Same as living room," Caleb supplied. "Mother's being fancy and old-fashioned." He rose and pulled out Shama's chair. "Will you allow me to escort you, madam?" He offered his arm and she giggled and took it. Daniel was wonderful, but Caleb was special. Shama adored Caleb.

"May I be excused?" Jessica asked.

Emma looked pained. Jessie had hardly said a word all

evening. But it was Daniel who stepped into the breach. "No, you may not be excused. I've hardly had a chance to talk to you. C'mon, Jessie, let's you and I have a chat."

Later, sipping her coffee, Emma watched them. Daniel was doing all the talking, Jessica listened in silence. Typical. But, Emma reflected sadly, it used to be only with her that Jessica was so closemouthed. Now it was with everyone, including Daniel. She wondered if she dared tell Daniel about a girl named Morgan Landry. Could she get him to try and find out if Jessie had seen her after she'd forbidden it? No. Sleeping dogs, better to let them lie. Emma glanced at her husband, in animated conversation with Susan, and sighed.

"You are tired, Madame Emma," Ruth said. "All this has been a great deal of trouble for you."

"No trouble, my dear, a real pleasure. And won't you please stop calling me Madame? Just Emma will do fine."

"I don't wish to sound disrespectful," Ruth said. Her dark eyes were earnest. The gray dress she wore didn't suit her, it made her skin looked washed out.

"I don't feel at all disrespected," Emma said smiling. "And why don't you come shopping with me again, my dear. Maybe this Saturday."

"I take courses so I will be a good American wife for Daniel, and I must study. And already Daniel has spent so much money on Shama and me."

Emma's glance flicked again to Susan. She was exquisite in a Grecian-draped gown of off-white silk jersey with a broad gold belt. God only knew what it cost. She turned back to her other daughter-in-law. "Listen, Ruth, you must encourage Daniel to do the gynecology residency at Memorial. He's well suited to the specialty. Ladies adore him, as you and I know."

Ruth looked solemn. "Yes. But I do not think Daniel is sure about spending the rest of his life as a doctor."

"What an extraordinary idea! He's already a doctor, Ruth. What else could he be?"

The girl shrugged. "It's only my idea . . . Emma." She grinned. "See, I always do what I am told. But you must not worry. Daniel is just becoming adjusted to the end of the war. And I will encourage him, as you say."

Caleb and Susan were the first to leave. The others had another brandy, then said they too must go. "Thanks for an extraordinary evening," Daniel said as he kissed his mother good-bye.

"You're more than welcome, darling." Then, very quietly, "Daniel, did you get anywhere with Jessie?"

"Break her out of her shell, you mean? No. And Shama didn't want to come because she says Jessie 'looks at her the knives.' I can't seem to win, can I?"

Emma cocked her head and looked at her handsome son. "Knowing you, Daniel, I expect you will win. Sooner or later."

Caleb rolled off his wife with a sustained groan of pleasure. "Thank you, Mrs. Morgan." He pulled her head onto his chest, running his fingers through her soft, silken hair. "Susie, can I ask you something?"

"Yes, as long as you don't call me Susie."

"Sorry. Listen, do you . . . I mean when we . . . Hell, I'm trying to find out if you're satisfied by my lovemaking."

Susan giggled. "Are you going to offer me a substitute if I'm not?"

"Be serious. Are you?"

"Of course, Cal darling. Don't I please you?"

He groaned again. "Please me. You besot me, my adorable Susan. It's just that I worry about you. I know I'm supposed to be an expert in these matters, but I don't have a lot of experience." He'd never told her how little, and he probably never would, but he did worry about his prowess as a lover.

"I'm a very contented wife," she whispered. "Except . . ."

"Except what?"

"Well, I do look forward to your going into private practice, so we can have our own home." She felt him stiffen. "What's wrong, Caleb? Your father is looking forward to it too. He told me so just tonight."

"I know, that's part of the problem."

Susan reached for a cigarette. "What problem?"

"I wish you wouldn't smoke, it's not feminine. And there isn't really a problem. Only an offer."

"From another gynecologist? You mean you'd go into practice with someone other than your father?"

"Not exactly. Do you remember my mentioning Dr. John Rock?"

"He was one of your professors at Harvard, wasn't he?"

"Yes, brilliant research. Gregory Pincus—we called him Goody—taught at Harvard when I was there. He's an egg man." She giggled. "Not those kind of eggs," Cal said. "Ova. The kind that make babies. Now he's teamed up with a guy named Chang, he's an expert in sperm. They do a lot of commercial stuff to stay afloat, but the thrust of their work in Worcester is human fertility and infertility."

Susan untangled herself from his embrace, sat up and drew deep on the cigarette, expelling a blue cloud into the moonlit bedroom. "And what does it all have to do with you, Caleb?"

"I've been approached by a mutual friend. Very obliquely you understand, there's nothing definite. But Goody Pincus wants to see me. I think he's going to offer me a job."

"In Worcester? My God, Caleb, it's at least fifty miles from here. Think of the travel time."

"We could live there."

Susan took a deep breath. What hit her first was the thought of leaving Boston, but there were other implications of such a choice. "What does a job like that pay?"

"I don't know. I'm not even sure I'll get an offer. It wouldn't be as lucrative as private practice, of course. But it's fascinating, Susan. John Rock has been doing pioneer stuff with barren women, and he has a hell of a success rate. If you put his stuff together with what they're doing in Worcester, the possibilities are terrific."

Susan was very cold, she was shivering. Tears of frustration clogged her throat, but she didn't allow them to fall. Not yet. And she mustn't say too much, too soon. "We'll talk about it tomorrow, Cal, okay? I'm rather tired now."

"Of course, darling."

He fell asleep with his head on her breast.

Susan didn't sleep for a long time. She was convinced that she could feel the presence of her diaphragm. It was Emma who, soon after the wedding, took Susan to be fitted for the device. "I don't imagine you and Caleb will want a child right away," she'd said. Susan had heartily agreed.

Predictably, Emma had known a doctor who would ignore Massachusetts law and fit a diaphragm. "Joshua does too now," she'd explained. "But I'm sure you'll be more comfortable with a stranger." Susan had nodded and turned away, afraid her mother-in-law might read in her face the sudden vision the words conjured. Joshua Morgan with his fingers deep in her vagina.

"It's quite impersonal," Emma promised. She arranged everything. Susan found herself in the hands of an elderly man whose examination was quick and disinterested but competent. He barely looked at her when he issued instructions on inserting the diaphragm and the accompanying contraceptive jelly. "Never take it out until the next morning." Those were his final words. Susan always followed the instructions religiously. She didn't want to get pregnant, did she? And Caleb wasn't in any hurry either.

Caleb had been quite relieved when she told him the pregnancy that precipitated their wedding was a false alarm and that she'd been fitted for a diaphragm. A resident didn't earn enough to support a wife, let alone a child, and Cal hated taking anything from his parents. So if she did get pregnant he might have to decide against the lower income of a researcher, mightn't he? The thought gave her some comfort and finally she slept.

13

*E*ast Eighty-sixth Street was the main artery of a section called Yorkville. German immigrants had settled there at the turn of the century, because it was cheap. Now it cut through the golden ribbon that unwound along the midsection of the island of Manhattan, from the upper Eighties to Grand Central Station. Fifth, Madison, and Park Avenues, and most of the streets between them, were bastions of fabulous wealth; Yorkville was a wrinkle in the fabric of luxury.

Daniel walked east, crossing each of the famous avenues where they bisected Eighty-sixth Street. He covered every inch from Central Park to the East River. Surveying the territory. Reconnoitering. The address Abdul gave him turned out to be a brownstone between First and Second Avenues. Nothing glamorous about it or the neighborhood. There was some kind of storefront church across the street, and a bakery next door. He stood in front of the church for a while, watching the pedestrians. Finally he looked at his watch. Two P.M. He crossed the road and started up the stairs of the brownstone.

Kitty looked fabulous. Angry and unnerved by all this as he was, Daniel couldn't help but notice. She wore a green dress of the sheerest wool, and pearls, and her hair was cut in a short bob that suited her gamin looks. "Much nicer than a uniform," he told her.

"You can bet on it, Danny-boy. And look at you. Quite

the gentleman about town. Well, come in and have a drink."

The apartment was simple, almost austere. If Kitty's outfit shouted money, her home didn't—presuming this was her home. "Where's Abdul?" he asked. "I thought both of you wanted to see me."

"Abdul did his bit. He got you here. Now, Captain Morgan, what will you drink? I can give you anything as long as it's scotch and water."

"That'll do fine."

She chatted about inconsequentials while she got the drinks. Only when they were seated on the cheap tweed chairs that were her living room furniture, did she become serious. "I hear you have a fabulous home in Brookline."

"That's putting it too strongly. It's a nice, comfortable old place."

"Just like this, huh?" She watched him through narrowed eyes.

"I didn't say that."

"No, I did. This is a shitty place to live, Danny. I don't intend to remain long."

"Okay. Is that what you brought me here to discuss?"

Kitty giggled. "In a way. Danny-boy, I will get to the point. I'm getting ready to open that abortion clinic I told you about. There, it's straight out now. Cards on the table, right?"

"No, I don't think so. Not all the cards." He took a sip of the scotch. "What does it have to do with me, Kitty?"

"You're going in with me," she said softly. "I told you you'd be terrific at it."

"You also told me it would take capital. I haven't any at the moment. In fact, as they say in the world of high finance, I'm a bit overextended."

"Yes. Abdul is very thorough, he found that out. But it's your lucky day, Captain. We've got the capital. What we don't have, and need, if we're to attract the kind of clients who can pay big bucks, is a real live doctor. One with bona fides, who isn't squeamish. Women are going to feel a whole lot better if the procedure is done by a genuine doctor."

"You've got it all figured out, haven't you? And it's not illogical. But what makes you think I want to play? Seems to me I told you back in Morocco what I thought of your idea."

"So you did. That was before I met Abdul."

He put down his glass and stared at his hands. "There's a word for this, isn't there?"

"Blackmail," she said cooly. "Yes. Sweet and simple, Danny-boy. And don't look at me like that. I'm doing you a favor. Forty percent of the net to you, forty to me, and twenty to Abdul. What could be fairer? Besides, you haven't done anything else since you've been back. And I know why, because you don't want to slave away for a pittance in some stinking hospital, or work eighteen hours a day in private practice. It's not your style. I'm throwing a heaven-sent opportunity in your lap. Christ, smile, Danny boy."

For a few seconds he stared at her. He thought about his mother and his father, and about Kate Johnson. Then he did smile.

"Why New York?" Joshua asked. "What can you possibly find in New York that isn't here in Boston, Daniel?"

"Maybe just freedom from Joshua Morgan's shadow," Daniel said softly.

Joshua was silent for some moments, then he said, "Warren James called me a few weeks ago. From the west coast."

Daniel shifted in his chair. "Did he? Then it's a good thing I told you about him, isn't it?"

"Yes, that prepared me. It's not ordinary for a chief of staff to notice a young doctor, Daniel. Not so thoroughly that he calls his father when that young doctor doesn't answer his letters."

"What else did he tell you?"

Joshua toyed with a gold pen on his desk. They were in the consulting room again, in the elegant environment where Joshua counseled and comforted his patients. "James thinks you have a brilliant future in internal medicine. He spoke about your gift for diagnosis."

"Yeah, well, he's a generous guy." Daniel lit a cigarette and didn't meet his father's eyes.

"Not generous to a fault I expect. His judgment confirms what I've suspected all along. You have a brilliant future in medicine. Of course, I always presumed you'd specialize in ob-gyn, but as I said before, if you prefer internal medicine that's fine with me. And if he's right about your skill as a diagnostician, you have something that can't be taught in any medical school. Diagnosis is a combination of observation and deduction and inspired hunches."

Daniel leaned forward. His mouth was dry and the cigarette tasted foul. He stubbed it out in a heavy crystal ashtray. "Look, I made some lucky guesses in Morocco, that's all. The conditions out there weren't exactly on a par with Memorial, you know. And any creep with a medical degree was okay for the army. Didn't matter if he came from Podunk U. In a setting like that you only needed half a brain to look like a genius."

"Why are you denigrating yourself?" Joshua sighed. "I just don't understand you lately, Daniel. You seem determined to be your own worst enemy. If you don't want the residency here, go out to James. He has an excellent reputation, an important practice. You'll work with the best men in fine facilities. Why join some inconsequential practice in New York and become the partner of a man who's never made any mark?"

That's what he'd told his father, that he was joining a general practice, going into partnership with an old man who might leave it all to him someday. Daniel stood up. "Sorry, Dad. This isn't advice-giving time. I merely came to let you know my decision."

"I see. What about Ruth, does she approve of this plan?"

"Ruth's not going to oppose me. She's an old-world type. You know that."

"But to uproot her like this, after she and Shama are just getting settled. . . ,"

"You've just been suggesting I take them three thousand miles away. Anyway, it's all settled. Sorry if you're disappointed, but I've made up my mind. And I'm not uprooting Ruth and Shama, for the reasons you point out. I'm going to be in New York Monday to Friday and home weekends."

"Sounds like a strange kind of practice. What happens if your patients get sick on Saturday or Sunday?"

"You're forgetting my partner."

Joshua rose and went to the window. Commonwealth Avenue was locked in winter's grip. Snow was piled high either side of the wide road, the weak sunshine glittered on patches of ice. "Have you told your mother?"

"Not yet. I wanted to talk to you first. And I want to ask your opinion of another idea."

"I thought I was being told things this afternoon, not invited to offer an opinion."

"Not in this case. What would you think of my suggesting that Jessie move in with Ruth and Shama for a while? She can go to the Chestnut Hill Girls Academy during the week. Come home Saturdays and Sundays if you and Mother wish."

"What would come of it, Daniel? Shama and Jessica don't get along at all well."

"Only because Jessie's jealous. Asking her to live with us should put an end to that. And what it's going to help along is getting Jess to come out of her shell. I'm worried about her. I think it would be good for her to have more companionship."

"Yes," Joshua agreed. "That would be good. But would Jessie do it? Even if your mother and I agreed?"

"If you agree, you can leave Jessie to me."

At first Emma was appalled. "Why should Jessica leave her home, Josh? What an extraordinary idea."

"At first blush, I admit that. But not when you think about it. She's so withdrawn lately, my dear. Jessie's never been an easy child. Right now she's terribly difficult and very unhappy. Daniel thinks that she'll feel special again, in his good graces, so to speak. It could work."

"But she doesn't get along with Shama."

"I said the same thing. Daniel thinks they'll get to be friends once Jessie doesn't feel jealous."

Emma put down her hairbrush and stared into the mirror. "Joshua, I'm getting old."

He chuckled. "You're like fine wine, Emma. You get better. Now don't change the subject. What do you say we have a try? For six months perhaps."

"I don't suppose you can argue Daniel out of this idea of joining a practice in New York."

"No. I tried. He said he wants out from my shadow. And Caleb's, I imagine." Joshua slipped out of his dressing gown and into the bed. "It may not be such a bad idea at that, Emma. Maybe three Morgans at Memorial would be just too much." He hadn't told her about the call from Warren James. Emma would be even more upset at the thought of Daniel moving so far away.

She shook her head. "You're incorrigible, Josh. No matter what Daniel does or says, you end up supporting him."

"I thought you liked Ruth."

"I do. Very much. And what's that got to do with it?"

"I'm not sure."

She got in beside him, lay her head on his chest. "Neither am I, not of anything. The world seems to be changing at breakneck speed. It's all I can do to keep up. Very well, let's see if Jessie wants to go. If she does, I'll agree to a six-month trial." The rest of the night Emma lay awake wondering how she'd console Marya.

"Was it Mama's idea or yours?"

"Hey, that's hitting below the belt," Daniel said. "Are you implying you've been fobbed off on me?"

"They don't really want me around, you know that." Jessica continued walking, kicking at the soft snow with the tips of her boots.

It was a bitter cold day, Franklin Park was almost deserted. Daniel reached down and picked up a handful of snow, made a snowball and tossed it overhand. They both watched it sail above the trees and listened for the sound of a landing. They heard someone shout and giggled. "You hit somebody," Jessica said.

"An accident. And what you said before, about them not wanting you around. It's not true."

"Yes it is. I was an afterthought. I heard Mama tell someone that once. She was thirty-eight when I was born. Do you know that?"

"Yup. I was there, remember? And we all thought you were the greatest thing that ever happened to the family. Cal and I never expected to have a baby sister. You were a bonus."

Jessica sighed. "You're humoring me, Daniel."

"Where the devil do you learn words like that?"

"Doesn't matter. It's true."

He stopped, and put out his hand to stop her too. "Listen, Jessie, I'm getting tired of this conversation. You want to feel sorry for yourself, you go right ahead, but don't do it on my time. I've asked you to move in with us for a while. Because I have to be away in New York five days a week, and Ruthie and Shama need somebody who's a native-born American, someone who can show them the ropes. Do you want to come or not?"

Jessica turned her face away from his. "Shama hates me."

"Wrong again. She's scared stiff of you. She says you 'look knives at her.'"

"Look daggers. That's what you're supposed to say. She's awful dumb sometimes."

"Yes. Because she's trying to learn everything all at once. And she'd be very happy if you'd be her friend." He put his gloved hands on either side of her red stocking cap and made her look at him. "So would I. What do you say, Jessie?"

"You're sure you want me?" she asked in a voice so small and frightened that it broke his heart.

"Absolutely sure," he said solemnly,

"Well, okay then."

Daniel whooped with pleasure and picked her up and swung her round. In the end they were both tumbling in the snow and laughing. When he brought her home, she was soaked and he was worried sick. But Jessica had absolutely no ill effects from the outing.

"Marya, where are you going?"

"I have much to pack. Better I get started."

Emma stretched out both her hands in a pleading gesture. "Marya, please. I don't want you to leave. Doctor Josh doesn't want you to leave. Why must you be so stubborn?"

"If there are no children in this house, why do you need a nurse? I don't take charity, Mrs. Emma. Not even from you."

"Charity is an absurd word in this context. Marya, you have been with us for twenty-six years. This house wouldn't be a home without you. Besides, the arrangement with Jessie is only temporary. It's just a six-month trial and I don't think it's likely to work. And when she moves back home, what then? How will Jessica manage without you? How will any of us, for that matter?"

Marya didn't say anything for a few seconds, Emma held her breath. Astounding how important to her it had become, holding on to Marya Czerniki. A link with something, her own youth perhaps.

"If Jessie doesn't come back," Marya said finally. "Then I go."

"Very well, unless of course there's another reason to remain."

"What reason?" A puzzled look on the broad, Slavic face, a trace of longing in the voice.

"I'm thinking of grandchildren, Marya," Emma said softly. "After all, both Caleb and Daniel are married. . . ."

Marya smiled.

Joshua looked up from his desk when his nurse ushered in the next patient. "Susan, this is a surprise, my dear."

"Yes, Josh, I know. But I wanted to talk to you in absolute privacy. This seemed the best place to do it."

Joshua looked at his nurse, she withdrew immediately. "Sit down, Susan. Now, first thing, are you well?"

She was wearing an ice-blue wool suit with a full skirt that fell gracefully when she crossed her legs. Joshua found his eyes drawn to those legs. They were remarkable. He looked up quickly to find her smiling at him. "I'm perfectly well. It's not me I want to talk about, it's Caleb."

"I see. Go ahead, Susan, I'm listening."

"He's thinking of taking a research job in Worcester, with Doctor Rock."

"Yes, he's mentioned it to me."

"And do you approve?"

Joshua shrugged. "I'm disappointed, of course. But I won't oppose him if that's what he wants. Once upon a time I wanted the same thing."

She leaned forward and took a cigarette from the box on his desk. Joshua lit it for her. "What changed your mind?" she asked after she exhaled. "About doing research?"

"I had Emma, the children, the house, a lot of responsibilities. Researchers were even more poorly paid in those days. It wasn't practical."

"That's what I think, Joshua. It isn't practical for Caleb either. He owes you so much, for one thing."

Josh leaned back and folded his arms behind his head. "I already told you, I do understand and I won't oppose him."

"Yes. But there's something else. I'm going to have a baby, Joshua."

He sat forward quickly. "That's wonderful! Does Cal know?"

"Not yet. I wanted to talk to you first. You see, I'm really quite upset at the thought of moving to Worcester, leaving the family. Particularly at a time like this."

"Surely, Susan, this is something you should discuss with Caleb, not with me."

"I feel safe with you, Joshua. I adore Caleb, you know I do. But he is young. We both are. And Caleb can be headstrong, unwilling to take advice. So I just want to know if you really want him to join your practice."

"More than anything in the world, if the truth's to be told," he said softly. "I'm not getting any younger, neither is Emma. It would be nice to think that everything we've built was going to be carried on. And nice to have you all nearby. That's selfish, I imagine. I'm only telling you because you asked."

Susan stubbed out her cigarette and put her hand over her father-in-law's. "Thank you for trusting me with the truth, Joshua. I'll talk to Caleb, tell him about the baby and how I feel. I'm sure he'll agree to join the practice. Until I do, can we keep this meeting our secret?"

"Of course."

Upstairs Susan went into the bathroom and opened the drawer of the small, chintz-covered chest where she kept personal things. The diaphragm was in its own little taffeta case with a zipper fastening. She'd made the case herself, the clandestine sale of condoms and diaphragms didn't encourage frills. Hers had come in a plain cardboard box. She'd hated that. Now she took it from its silken coverlet and dropped it in the toilet. Then she pulled the chain. She put away the little case. Eventually she'd need it again.

Susan looked at her reflection in the full-length mirror on the bathroom door. Awful to imagine herself fat and ungainly. But only for a while, and only to achieve a greater good.

It was the end of March when the fact that Susan was pregnant became common knowledge. Emma was the only one who wasn't enthusiastic. Despite what she'd said to Marya, the thought of a grandchild—Susan's child—disconcerted her. Susan seemed less than thrilled for one thing, and for another, Emma sensed a web drawing ever tighter around Caleb. Webs of deceit and pain were things Emma recognized. She had a sixth sense about them.

In April the days lengthened. It didn't get dark until nearly seven. It was usually long after that when Morgan Landry took up her vigil. Tonight it was nearly midnight, and cold. An icy wind chafed the branches of the trees and ruffled the incipient green of the first buds. Spring was always so late here in the north. It had not yet come to Boston, whatever the calendar said.

Morgan wore a black knit muffler wrapped around her head and neck. It shadowed her face, and the ends hung down her back and blended with the black wool coat. From behind this dark camouflage her green eyes watched the house. Its windows were dark, so too, those of the office next door, but in the apartment above the office a light shone dimly. That was where Caleb lived, with Susan, his pregnant wife.

Morgan knew everything about the family, knowledge accrued in the nearly twelve months of her long watch; she'd added it to what she already knew, the story of a tragic romance. Morgan didn't believe in the tragedy, at least not in the way Billy-Jo detailed it. Her mother had insisted the tale was without villains, a drama peopled with star-crossed, fallible human beings. But Morgan knew better now. Everything she had observed had strengthened her preconceptions, her idea of the real shape of the wrong done to her. Soon she would decide how to right that wrong.

She stared unblinkingly at the two buildings. She did not know that from behind sheer curtains another pair of eyes looked into the night.

As he had for so many nights past, Joshua remained at the window for many minutes; motionless, he was as conscious of the watcher in the dark, as he was of Emma in the bed a few feet away. Emma's breathing was deep and even, she always slept soundly. Eventually he must return to his place beside her. But sleep would not come easily to him. Joshua knew he would lie awake for hours, thinking of the woman on the opposite side of the street. Tonight he must do something, take some action. Yes, tonight. Still he didn't move.

It was as if there were a current between them; the woman in the shadows and himself behind the curtain were linked and held in place by blood and fear and accusation. At last Joshua wrenched himself round, severing for the moment that connection, and crept into the alcove that served as a dressing room. From there he could go directly into the hall.

She was still there. He saw her as soon as he came through the front door; not her exactly, but a thickening of the shadows, a distortion of the light, the only things he ever saw. He paused, acutely aware that her eyes followed his every move, then started across the wide road.

Morgan was fascinated by this sudden, late-night appearance of her father. A medical emergency perhaps. But he wasn't hurrying. It was something else that brought him out, something clandestine perhaps and in some way usable for her own ends. She shrank further back into the shadows. When he passed her, she'd follow him. But he didn't pass her.

The body of Morgan Landry was discovered forty-eight hours later, when the earth and the moon juxtaposed themselves into the position that made revelation possible. In the half-light before dawn an old man searched the rubbish around Pier One. He shuffled along the dock kicking at piles of debris, staring down because that was the only way he would find whatever he sought. Of necessity he must peer through gaps in wood silvered and splintered by time. Normally he saw only the oil-slicked gray sea lapping the rocks below the jetty. This morning the tide was dead low. It exposed a heap of tangled anchor chains and discarded oil drums. And from amid them the bloated face of a woman, her body shrouded by pitted, rusted tin, caught and held by the detritus of progress.

The story broke too late for the morning papers, the *Globe* and the *Herald*, but the evening tabloids both carried it. "Mystery Woman dies in Boston Harbor" blared the *American* on page two; the *Record* reported the drowning on page seven, immediately before the racing results. But neither paper could say much, such facts as there were the police kept to themselves.

Tessie Marsh always read the *Record*. That's how she kept track of the twenty-five-cent bets she placed on the illegal numbers' pool. The winning combinations were selected from an arcane and sub-rosa system known only to initiates, based on the first digit of a series of parimutuel results. Tessie barely skimmed the story of the drowning, which did not report the victim's name. Naturally, a paper with the reputation of Hearst's *Record* never found its way upstairs.

William Francis Xavier Flynn was the name on the identification cards. Nora Marsh stared at it, then at the man standing in the door. Behind him sunrise gilded the avenue and the line of trees. It shone on his dark brown tweed trousers and a darker overcoat. How come he wasn't wearing a uniform if he was really a policeman, like the card said?

He read the distrust in her eyes. "I'm with the plain-clothes division, ma'am. Detective Lieutenant Flynn. Now if you'll just tell Doctor Morgan I'm here. . . ."

"Ain't even seven yet. Family haven't had their breakfast."

"That's too bad," he said, but didn't budge.

Nora hesitated, then finally motioned him into the hall. "You wait here. I'll see if the doctor can come."

He acted as if it were a medical emergency. "If you wait a moment, we can go over to my office."

"That's not necessary, sir. I just want to ask a few questions." Joshua looked blank. "It's official business, Doctor Morgan."

Those words were still hanging in the air between the two men when Emma came into the hall. "What is it, Josh? Nora said something about a policeman."

"Nothing, my dear. I'll handle it."

The detective put up a hand to prevent Emma from leaving. "Mrs. Morgan, isn't it? Long as you're here, ma'am, perhaps you wouldn't mind staying a moment. Might be easier to talk to you both together."

Emma looked questioningly at Joshua, then quickly looked away. "Very well, let's go in here, shall we?" She led them into the living room.

The room's formal decor was an uncomfortable contrast to Joshua's lack of a tie and jacket, and to Emma's navy dressing gown. Flynn seemed to be the only one at ease.

He took a notebook from his pocket. "Now, let's see, woman that let me in, she's Nora Marsh, right? And the cook is her sister, Tessie. Only other servant is the nurse Marya Czerniki?" He looked up for confirmation.

Joshua nodded. And felt a chill at the base of his spine. The police were surprisingly well-informed.

"Of course there's also your daughter, sir." Lieutenant Flynn was unfailingly polite, but there was nothing in his tone to reassure Joshua. "Miss Jessica, I believe." He consulted some further notes. "Just twelve years old."

"Jessica is staying with her brother and his family at the moment. In Brookline."

The policeman frowned. "Nothing here about Brookline. According to my information your son is Doctor Caleb Morgan, lives next door with his wife."

Joshua was pleased. The error made him feel in charge again. "That's right as far as it goes, but my other son is Doctor Daniel Morgan. Recently discharged from the army. He has just started a practice in New York. Jessica is staying with Daniel's wife and her sister."

Flynn shrugged. "Well, it had to be fairly quick work, they couldn't get it perfect, could they? Happened less than thirty-six hours ago."

Emma had not spoken. Now her voice was as clear and without tremor as if she met with policemen in her living room every morning before breakfast. "What happened thirty-six hours ago, Lieutenant?"

"No more than thirty-six hours, ma'am. Maybe less, according to the medical examiner. Young lady was drowned in the harbor. Maybe you read about it?" He paused and looked at them.

"A tragedy, I'm sure," Emma said. "But what has it to do with us?" Unconsciously perhaps she addressed the question to Joshua. He didn't meet her eyes. The detective didn't appear to take any notice of that.

"We found some stuff in her pockets," Flynn said. "Fortunately she hadn't been in the water long enough for it to be completely destroyed. The lab was able to make out her address from a letter she had in her pocket."

Joshua felt tension constricting his throat, he tried not to allow it to distort his voice. "I can't see what you're getting at, Lieutenant. Why have you come here?"

"It's what we found in the apartment, sir." Flynn was

still carefully respectful. "All over the place. Written on scraps of paper she left in the bedroom and the kitchen, even chalked up on the walls."

"And that was?" Emma found herself involuntarily making her hands into fists.

"The doctor's name, ma'am. Joshua Morgan, M.D." Flynn folded his notebook and pushed it into the pocket of his suit coat. The pocket sagged, as if it had been long abused.

Joshua found his voice. "I see. Well, it accounts for your presence here. But there must be some ordinary explanation, Lieutenant. Perhaps she'd been a patient of mine, someone I saw in the clinic. Women do get odd ideas about doctors."

"Yes, sir. Something like that probably. That's what I came to ask you. Any ex-patients been bothering you lately? Threats or anything like that?"

Joshua spoke slowly and deliberately. "No, nothing of the sort."

The policeman turned to Emma. "And you, ma'am? You have any idea about all this?"

"Now see here!" Josh stepped close to Emma, as if to protect her physically from the other man. "This has gone far enough. There's no need to bother my wife."

"Don't fuss, Josh. He's just doing his job. There's no reason we shouldn't cooperate." Emma turned to face the Irishman. "There's something you haven't told us, Lieutenant. Who was this young lady? Do you know her name?"

Flynn reached for his notebook again, but Emma had the distinct impression he was indulging himself in a dramatic pause. He flipped back the soiled cover of the small diary. It was cheap and common, the kind of thing sold by the thousands in every Woolworth's. Flynn wet his thumb with his tongue and turned the pages, coming at last to the one he wanted. But he didn't glance down, instead he stared straight at Emma. "A Miss Landry. Morgan Landry. That's all we know so far. Name mean anything to you?"

Emma did not go pale or tremble. She stared back at him while a deep red flush rose from her neck into her face. Her body was visibly rigid, fists clenched by her sides. For seemingly endless seconds she said nothing. When she spoke, her voice was a whisper. "I know of someone by that name, yes."

Joshua reached out to support her with his arm, then dropped it, sensing the barrier she had erected against him as well as the policeman. His heart beat in his chest in a suddenly erratic rhythm and tears rose in his throat and stung his eyes. Emma knows, he thought. She's known all along. He could see it, could almost smell the knowing in her. So, it had all been in vain after all.

"Josh, you'd better see a lawyer."

"Emma, listen to me, it's not what you think." He put up a hand to touch her, but she moved out of his reach, pretending to do something with the curtains of the long drawing room windows facing the street.

"I don't think anything," she said dully. "Just that it's better to have legal advice immediately."

The slightly sour smell of the police lieutenant still lingered in the room. Emma opened one of the casement windows and the cold, early spring air rushed in. "Emma," he said. "Look at me, please."

She turned, they faced each other over a distance of some four or five feet. It was a chasm that could not be crossed. "I did not murder that girl." Joshua spoke very slowly, very distinctly, as if afraid that the space between them might distort his words. "I did not kill her."

Emma drew a short, sharp breath, it sounded like a knife rasping on iron. "I never thought you did, Josh. Not for a moment."

"Then why are you looking at me like that?"

Emma sank to a chair, her robe pooled around her legs, a small wave of navy blue against the wine-colored carpet. "She was your daughter, wasn't she?"

He didn't answer, just gave one quick nod, then added, "In a manner of speaking."

"A manner . . . Josh, if you fathered her she was your child. And Billy-Jo's, I presume."

"Yes." He crossed to her now, bridging the gap with two quick strides, and knelt beside the chair. Her hands were very cold when he took them in his. "Emma, it wasn't planned. It was a one-time thing. You were in Magnolia, I was very lonely and depressed. It was 1918, Armistice night. We ran into each other in the crowd, we both had a bit to drink. That was all," he finished lamely.

"Not all. Billy-Jo had a little girl. Did you know?"

"Not until a long time later, and then—" He broke off. "Look, there's not much point to this, is there? God help them, they're both dead now. Billy-Jo died in Arkansas some years ago. It has nothing to do with us, with the reality of our lives together here and now, our children. Please, don't let it poison everything."

Emma was silent for a long few seconds. She was thinking of the things she'd suspected for years, but refused to face. She was thinking of how she had hated Betty Bradley, and of how destroyed she'd been when she first heard the name Morgan Landry. But she could never have hated Billy-Jo. Not then, not now. There were many more questions she could ask Joshua, but she didn't want to. After all this time she was inured to his fatal flaw. And he was in terrible pain, she could see it on his face.

She took a deep breath, then leaned forward and kissed his forehead. "It's all right, Josh. As you say, it's in the past, let's leave it there. But you must see a lawyer, just to protect yourself."

"I will," he promised. He let go of her hands and put his arms around her, pressing his head against her breast. "I love you, Emma. I love you so damned much. Always have, always will."

"I know," she whispered, stroking his hair. "I know."

"I've seen an attorney," he told her two days later. "I went to the fellow who did our wills, and he sent me to a Mr. Thompkin. Apparently a specialist in these matters."

"And?"

"And he says sit tight and do nothing. The police are fishing, that's all. The next move is up to them, and Thompkin thinks it's unlikely they'll make any, at least in my direction."

"Very well," Emma said. "That's an end to it then." She managed to smile at him.

Joshua smiled, too, but it wasn't really over for him, it couldn't be. In the next few weeks he became a creature of the small morning hours, a man possessed by the dark. Usually he would sleep for a few hours, then something would wake him, the grandfather clock downstairs, perhaps, or some movement on the street outside. He'd lie still for a few moments, listening to Emma's breathing, to the sounds of night, and wait for sleep to return. Frequently it did not, that's when he would rise and dress and slip silently from the house.

The spot across the street beckoned him, an evil talisman he could not ignore. Little Morgan, child of chestnut curls and dimples, lisping her first baby words in Billy-Jo's Ozark twang, climbing on his knee and mirroring his eyes with hers. Little Morgan waving good-bye when he put them on the train that spring of 1924, when Billy-Jo held her and smiled at him and said, "Don't fret, Josh honey, it's better like this. Makes more sense for all of us. I should of gone long time back, before she was born, like I meant to."

Standing beneath the trees where the grown-up Morgan had mounted her long vigil, where he'd confronted her, he could smell South Station, the acrid smoke of the steam engine, the lavender scent Billy-Jo always wore. Did Morgan wear lavender? He'd never know now. She was dead. So was Billy-Jo. Morgan had told him her mother died in her beloved Ozarks a couple of years before. She'd hurled the words at him in a whisper that sounded like a scream. Billy-Jo died slowly and painfully, short of money as she'd been for years, unwilling and unable to do what Morgan wanted, come east and see if the doctors in Boston could make her well.

"I don't want a monthly check, Josh," Billy-Jo had insisted twenty-two years ago when he made the offer. "It'll be like opening a wound twelve times a year." So, he'd given her a lump sum instead. Five thousand, as generous as he could manage in those days. "I'll save it for Morgan when she grows up," she'd promised.

Standing where Morgan had stood, he could hear Billy-Jo's words, and her daughter's. They were a chorus of lament that gave him no peace. The night would shroud Joshua, black like his thoughts, and he'd walk on.

They walked with him, the women in his life. Emma and Billy-Jo and Morgan, even Betty Bradley. God, he hadn't thought of her for years, hard to imagine that once he'd fancied himself in love with her. And for some crazy reason he could not fathom, Susan, too, was part of the malaise that gripped him. Young, beautiful, sweet, innocent, Caleb's wife was all those things. She was like a daughter to him, but very different from Jessica. Susan and Morgan were both entirely different from Jessie. The two older girls blended in his mind, peopled his fantasies, gave terrible shape to his guilt.

Sometimes when Emma slept she dreamed that she was alone, that Joshua was not beside her in the bed they had shared for thirty-one years. The sensation would come in the dead of night, at the time of deepest sleep, and she would turn restlessly and struggle to free herself from the odd sensation of some connection being severed. In the morning he was always there, lying beside her or sometimes coming up from downstairs, carrying two cups of steaming coffee for them to share before facing the world. She would look at the leonine bulk of him, at his silver-haired handsomeness, the brilliance of his smile, and reality would supercede dreams.

Ruth sat on the edge of the sofa, staring at her husband, trying to understand. "But just because this poor girl who was drowned had your papa's name written in her house . . ."

"It's not just that. Not now. The police started from there because it was obvious. Then my mother reacted to the name of the victim, said she'd known her. So naturally enough, the cops have come around a few times."

Ruth's body was rigid, her hands clasped in her lap. "We must do something, Daniel. Now, before anything terrible happens. I know! We will send your parents to Morocco, to my cousin in Marrakesh. Never will the police find them there."

"Hey, baby, wait a minute. What's got into you?" He crossed the room and sat down beside her, taking both tightly clenched fists into his hands. "Calm down, Ruthie. There's no danger. Neither Mom nor Dad had anything to do with this Landry dame's death. It's some cop's screwy idea, that's all. They've gone to a lawyer because it's the prudent thing to do, but nobody's brought any charges, and if you ask me, nobody's going to."

Ruth yanked her hands away. "Oh, you are stupid sometimes, Daniel. Sometimes in America everyone is very naive. The police— "

"—are different here," he interrupted. "Ruthie, haven't you been learning anything in those citizenship classes?

The cops have to prove somebody's guilty. It's damn hard to prove if it's not true."

Her tensed frame relaxed slightly and her dark eyes studied his face. "You are sure, Daniel?"

"One hundred percent certain, Ruthie. It's in the Constitution."

"Yes," she nodded her head. "Last week we read the Constitution. I remember."

"Okay. So you're going to stop worrying about this, right? And I can go to New York without feeling that I'm leaving you a nervous wreck."

"Okay," she echoed. Her gentle smile softened all the worry lines that had furrowed her brow. Daniel leaned over and kissed her lightly. Swiftly Ruth reached up her arms and twined them around his neck.

"Hey," he murmured against her neck. "I've got a train to catch, remember?"

Ruth twisted her head to look at her watch. "You have forty minutes before you must leave."

He laughed softly. "And my wife has no objections to a quickie, right?" Her answering smile managed to be both wanton and shy.

They climbed the stairs to their bedroom with as much nonchalance and dignity as they could muster, just in case Shama or Jessie saw them. But when the door closed behind them, there was no reticence, no courtship dance. Ruth stripped off her clothes and fell on the bed, legs splayed, arms outstretched to receive him. Daniel hesitated only a moment, turning slightly while he fitted a condom over his pulsing erection.

"Don't," Ruth whispered.

"Don't what?" Coming toward her, his voice husky with passion.

"Don't wear that thing. Take it off, Daniel. Let's make a baby."

"Forget that," he said firmly. Then he was above her, bending his head to lick her breasts and her belly, playing artfully with the curled black hair between her silken thighs, his fingers making her moan and gasp and causing her nails to dig into his shoulders as she pulled him closer.

When it was over and she lay languid and content, watching him dress, Ruth found her courage again. "I don't want to be a pest to you, Daniel."

"A pest! What a nutty thing to say. I really don't object to performing my marital duty, sweetheart. I find the exercise quite tolerable, as a matter of fact."

She did not return his grin or his bantering tone. "I mean about a baby. When can we have a child, Daniel?"

Daniel turned to the mirror to knot his tie, avoiding her eyes in the reflection. "I don't know, kid. We'll see, huh? Maybe when I don't have to be in New York so much. . . . Anyway, you've got Shama and Jessie to keep you busy."

14

"*M*arya, what do you know about all this? Who was that girl, what did she have to do with Mom and Dad?" Caleb's voice was edged with concern, his eyes shadowed.

"What are you worrying about, *notchnik*?" She hadn't called him that in years, not since he went off to Harvard. Marya saw the beginnings of Caleb's slow, sweet smile, and her heart lurched. Sometimes she thought he was her favorite, other times she was sure it was Daniel. The truth was she loved them both with the same absolute passion. And she ached to see either of them unhappy about anything. "The police can't say your mother or father had anything to do with that poor girl getting drowned. It's crazy."

"I agree. So why do Mom and Dad look like the walking wounded? And I know for a fact Dad's seen a lawyer. He let it slip, by accident I think. But why run off to a lawyer unless there's some connection? I want to help, Marya, but I don't know how."

They were alone in the kitchen because it was Tuesday. On Tuesdays Marya baked the black Polish bread the family loved. On Tuesdays Caleb knew where to find her for a private chat.

Marya dug her fists into the mound of dark, yeasty dough. There was no break in the rhythm of her kneading. "Listen, I'm an old lady. I seen plenty of life, sometimes it ain't so simple. And better you should let alone the sleeping dogs. Anyway, that Flynn guy hasn't come back for three weeks."

Caleb pinched off a small piece of dough and rolled it in his fingers. "It's not the police I'm worried about. There's a connection," he repeated. "Mom said she knew the girl."

"No," Marya shook her head vehemently. "That means nothing. Always I tell you, Caleb. Don't jump right away and think you know everything."

"But how did my mother know somebody who ran a store in the West End? Why had that somebody written my father's name all over her walls?"

Marya didn't answer right away. "Maybe better if you ask your mama. I don't talk about the family, you know that."

"C'mon, Marya. This is me, Cal, remember? I'm not looking for idle gossip. I want to know what's going on and what I can do to help. And my mother isn't likely to tell me. Which you also know."

Expertly she divided the mound of dough into six equal portions; each became a tapered oval loaf with a few deft movements of her capable hands. "I think once I hear your mama say years ago she had a friend whose last name was Landry. A lady who moved from here before you were born. That's all I know. Now get out of the kitchen and let me work."

Caleb kissed her cheek before he left. Marya watched his departing back. She knew him, this wasn't the end of his curiosity, he was simply being patient. That's how he was. Caleb quietly waited, but he never forgot. Daniel screamed and yelled and made a fuss, and whatever he thought he wanted he forgot ten minutes later. Always, since they were babies. Sighing, she returned her attention to the bread.

Night and day, you are the one. Only you beneath the moon and under the sun . . . Caleb was deafened by the new Cole Porter tune as soon as he opened the door. The front hall of Daniel's house reverberated with Sinatra's dulcet tones. No wonder the maid hadn't answered the bell, she probably couldn't hear it.

He followed the sound to the den. Jessica and Shama were sitting on the floor in front of the latest model

Victrola, a stack of records to one side. Neither girl saw him, both had their eyes closed. Both small, young bodies swayed to the rhythm of the music. "Hey, you two, how about a hello? You don't really like that skinny guy's wailing, do you?"

"Ssh. . . ." Jessica didn't open her eyes, much less greet her brother. But Shama jumped up and threw her arms around his neck.

"Caleb! You are big surprise." And when Jessie hushed her, "Don't tell me be quiet. The Voice you can hear any time. Caleb is more important."

Disgustedly Jessica rose and turned off the phonograph. "You are a nuisance, Cal. And a bad influence on Shama. She'll think real Americans are like you, with a tin ear." Jessie flounced from the room.

Shama pulled Caleb toward the sofa. "She will come back later. We're going to the movies. *The Best Years of Our Lives*, a jerktear, you want to come?"

"A tearjerker, little one, and sorry, I can't come. But I'm glad to see you and Jessie getting along so well. You are, aren't you?"

Shama smiled. "We are best friends. Now we don't know why we hated each other at first."

Her hair was very long and tied back with a red ribbon. Caleb tugged on one curl. "Doesn't matter, does it? As long as you're happy."

"No, it doesn't matter."

"Good. Where's Daniel and your sister?"

"You didn't come to see me?" Shama's dark eyes were full of pain.

"I'm afraid not this time. I need to talk to my brother, he's not still in New York, is he?" It was Saturday. Daniel was usually in Brookline from Saturday morning to Sunday night.

"No, he came home this morning. But he and Ruthie went shopping. They come back soon."

Caleb glanced at his watch. He had half an hour at best. He had just made up his mind to leave and come back later when he heard the front door open.

"For God's sake, Ruth, will you stop moaning about the money. It's a great dress, it looks terrific on you. It's not going to put us in the poorhouse."

"I don't want you to spend so much for me, Daniel. I want to save so—"

Cal stepped quickly into the front hall. They saw him and the argument stopped instantly, but not before he was aware that behind him Shama had frozen with embarrassment, as if she were accustomed to such exchanges, and dreaded them.

There was an awkward pause and Daniel hastened to fill it. "Hi, didn't realize you were here. Shama, take some of these bundles and help your sister put things away. C'mon in here, Cal. I can use a drink."

Caleb followed his twin into the large, well-furnished living room. Nothing had been changed since Daniel bought the house, but the previous owners had pleasant taste. It was a comfortable, quietly pretty room. He watched Daniel pour a large scotch and shook his head when it was offered to him. "No thanks. It's only four, too early for me. Besides, I'm on duty in an hour."

Daniel shrugged and drank a long swallow, then topped up the glass. "Stop looking like I'm an incipient alcoholic. It's been a tough day. All women are a little nuts; Moroccan women take the prize. I just spent two hours arguing Ruthie into buying some decent clothes. I want her to come to New York for a few days next week. All she can think about is what things cost."

"Maybe she remembers being poor and hungry," Cal said softly. "Probably finds it hard to realize she's now a rich American wife. Things are going well in New York, huh?"

Daniel turned away. "Yeah, sure. You know, the big city, lots of cash hanging around waiting to be picked up."

"And lots of sick people, apparently. What shape is the practice taking, Daniel? You've never said much about it."

"Not much to say. Ordinary stuff, your regular quota of chicken pox and cardiac arrests." He turned his back and poured another dose of scotch into his glass. "What brings you here? Not curiosity about the nature of disease in the far country, I presume."

"No. I want to talk about Mom and Dad."

Daniel frowned, then crossed the room and shut the door to the hall. "Ruthie heard about it from Tessie and Nora. She thinks the police are after the folks. She gets hysterical whenever it's mentioned, wants me to send

them to Morocco to hide. Her experience of the police is
something different from yours or mine. So, I don't want
her to overhear." He paused and waited. Cal was obviously searching for words. Daniel plunged. "Cal, is Ruthie
right? Are the police after them?"

"No. Dad finally had word from his lawyer. I pried it
out of him that Boston's finest have decided the Landry
woman's death was an accident. But it stirred up something for the folks. Mom looks bad and Dad worse. And
neither of them will explain about any of it. Who was this
dame? What did she have to do with them?"

Daniel shrugged. "Who knows? Seems to me there have
always been things between them we don't know anything
about. And it's probably none of our business."

"If it wasn't that I think they're both miserable and
worried as hell, I'd agree. As it is, I can't. I talked to
Marya, she says Mom knew somebody named Landry
years ago, before we were born."

"Okay, maybe she did. That's no big deal." He paused
and studied his twin through narrowed eyes. "Cal, why
are you getting so worked up about this?"

"I'm not worked up. I keep telling you, they have some
kind of problem. My guess is it's serious, I'd like to help."

"Seems to me you're giving the maximum help possible." Daniel's voice gentled. "Dad tells me you turned
down Rock and you're joining the practice."

Caleb turned away. "Yeah." He walked to the decanter
on the side table and fingered the crystal stopper, but he
didn't pour himself a drink.

"Your enthusiasm overwhelms me," Daniel said. "For
Chrissake, Cal, you wanted to go with Rock, why didn't
you? The old man would have gotten over it."

"I know, it wasn't that. I was all set to go into research
and start working on my Nobel prize. Then Susan got
pregnant. If we'd waited a couple of years, maybe . . ."

Daniel shook his head ruefully. "Somebody forget to tell
you there's a drugstore on every corner in the U.S.?"

"No, I know that and so does Susie. It was an accident."
A little too heartily, not showing any hint of the crazy
doubt that had been plaguing him. His wife had been
shocked by the notion of his going into research and
moving her to Worcester. Had her diaphragm been flawed
or did she deliberately—? He carried the thought in

another, less threatening direction. "By the way, Rock's got a handle on something foolproof. He's working on absolute control of both fertility and infertility." Cal spoke with a rising note of enthusiasm, heard himself, and realized the implications. "But research is always a crapshoot. Probably better to treat patients with problems soluble in the here and now."

"Yeah, probably." Daniel avoided Caleb's eyes. "Anyway, Dad's pleased as hell." He wanted to offer Caleb money, enough so his twin could follow his dream, but he didn't dare. For one thing Cal would resent it, for another Daniel couldn't explain a new practice so lucrative it allowed him to make substantial loans.

Caleb rose. "How about coming round to see the folks tomorrow? Cheer them up. And maybe they'll talk to you."

"I doubt if they'll talk. But I'll come, Jessie's due for a visit anyway."

Daniel stood at the window and watched Caleb disappear down the driveway. A misty haze of palest April-green clothed the elms. The cycle of life as the poets were always pointing out. But life wasn't poetry. It had a nasty habit of demanding choices, and none of them were perfect. They had effects, endless ripples. Morgan Landry. A nice name, a dead girl. Maybe Cal was right and she was part of something in the family's past, but God alone knew what. Probably better if the whole thing was buried with the unfortunate Miss Landry.

The address was on Thirty-first Street between Park Avenue South and Lexington. The block was quiet this hot August morning, the building innocuous. Typical of the district, known as Murray Hill, it was a brownstone, two-rooms wide, four-stories high. Apparently converted from residential to business use, a discreet brass plaque said Nile Import & Export. The door from the street opened into a small office.

There were two desks. One was for a secretary, a young foreign-looking woman. A man sat behind the other; he was of indeterminate age, looked American. The only other things in the room were a bank of files and a door marked Ladies.

The caller glanced hastily at the setting, not really seeing it, only wondering if, perhaps, she'd made a mistake. She clutched her navy handbag over her stomach, a protection of sorts. "I want to see Doctor Smith. Is this the right address?"

The foreign-looking woman examined her with dark, oval eyes, the shape accentuated by a black line drawn across the lids and extending up in the corners. "Doctor Smith? This is an importing company, madam. Are you quite sure you're in the right office?"

"I'm not sure, but I think so." Alicia Williams dug in her handbag and studied the note again. "This is 254 East Thirty-first Street, isn't it?"

"Yes, but as I said . . ."

Alicia remembered the other part of the instructions, the thing she'd been forbidden to write down. "Doctor Smith has an office nearby. And he's there only part-time."

"Oh yes, that Doctor Smith. We do sometimes take his messages." The secretary smiled, but Alicia thought there was something decidedly nasty about it. "If you'll just go through there, madam." She nodded her head in the direction of the bathroom.

Alicia walked toward it slowly, felt the man's eyes studying her. What did he see? A pretty blonde in her midtwenties wearing an expensive navy linen suit, real pearls, navy-and-white spectator pumps, spotless white gloves—and hanging on to a good leather handbag, in which she had fifteen hundred dollars in small bills. The money that would pay for her abortion.

She closed the bathroom door behind her quickly, leaning against it. There was no lock, but nothing else was unusual. The space was furnished with a toilet and a sink. What happened now, did she simply wait here? Was some man going to come and abort her while she straddled the hopper? She began to feel sick. The room seemed to swim. When the apparently solid far wall opened inward, she thought it was her imagination.

But it wasn't. A nurse stood in the doorway, a redhead wearing a starched white uniform, even a cap. And behind her was a steep flight of narrow steps. "Good morning, will you follow me, please."

She was a little calmer after that, but her legs still trembled. The nurse led her upstairs and into a small room. There was a white-sheeted bed, a utilitarian chair, a night table and the inevitable folding screen. She could be in any good hospital. There was even a grace note, a bunch of late summer asters in a vase. "If you'll just get undressed and put this on," the redhead indicated a white hospital nightgown, the kind called a johnny, "I'll get you ready for the doctor."

"Thank you," Alicia mumbled. For what? For getting her out of the stupid, dangerous hole she had gotten herself into, that's what. "Will this take long?" She unbuttoned her jacket as she spoke, the ordinary actions making her feel more in control.

"Not long at all." The nurse glanced at her watch. "It's ten A.M. You should be out of here by two. The operation only takes a few minutes, you understand, but we'll keep you here resting for a while after that. Just to make sure everything is okay." Her tone softened. "Don't look so scared. It's going to be fine. This is a first-class setup. I'm a real nurse and Doctor Smith is a real doctor. That's what you're paying for."

Having said that, she held out her hand. Alicia Williams opened her bag and removed the envelope containing the money. The redhead counted it, then smiled. "Okay, I'm going to give you an injection to relax you and make you sleepy. Take a deep breath, it will all be over in a little while."

"What's the matter, Danny-boy? You look like you've seen a ghost. Complications?"

"Not the sort you mean." Daniel dropped into the chair in the small room they used as a staff lounge. He'd removed his surgical gear and he wore an open-necked sport shirt and slacks. There was a bottle of scotch on the table. He poured himself a drink, gulped it, and poured another.

Kitty Donnely watched him. "She wasn't more than three months gone, was she?"

"Nope. She's a smart girl. If she said three months, that was it."

Her eyes narrowed. "How the hell do you know if she's smart or stupid? She was groggy as a prizefighter by the time you got to her."

"Yup, so she was. But I've known the lady since she was sixteen, name's Alicia Williams. Her brother was a pal of mine at Harvard. Used to go to his house all the time.

Alicia was the kid sister who was always hanging around. A real cute little thing."

Kitty whistled softly. "So that's why you look like you do." She stubbed out her cigarette and crossed to him, smoothing the dark hair back from his brow. "Feeling squeamish, Danny? Your half-assed morals again? Just because she's somebody you knew once upon a time?"

"Yeah, I guess so."

"Listen, ten will get you a thousand she isn't married. So it would be better for her to have an illegitimate kid, right? You could have done your old friend a big favor, sent her home to Boston to face the music. Then maybe she could have found some filthy butcher in a slum somewhere to get rid of it for her. Lots better, of course. Danny Morgan would be pure and uninvolved. Or how about another scenario? You refuse to fix her up, so she has the kid and it gets put in an orphanage. You like that version better, Danny?"

"Jesus! Will you shut up, Kitty. Your wit is tolerable only in small doses."

"It's not wit, sweetie. It's logic. And you'd better lay off the scotch. You've got another patient in half an hour, and a third after that. They don't pay fifteen hundred a crack for a surgeon with shaky hands."

She bent over him, allowed her small, hard breasts to brush his arm. Her mouth was on his for only a moment, a gesture brief but ripe with promise. Daniel reached for her, Kitty ducked out of his grasp. "Later, lover boy." Chuckling softly, she left the room to see to her patient, the sleeping and now unpregnant Alicia Williams.

Daniel watched her go, admiring the swing of the tight, round buttocks. Kitty made sense, if Alicia wanted an abortion she might as well get it done right. That wasn't all of what was bothering him. There was something more, the tone and the texture of Alicia's skin, the dull look of her eyes. It could just be the circumstances, but that sixth sense old man James had spotted in him was active again, he had an uncomfortable feeling that Alicia was ill. But he wasn't a genuine doctor these days, not a real healer, so it wasn't any of his damned business.

He looked ruefully at his whisky, then put it down, Kitty was also right about that. He was hitting the bottle too hard lately. Not smart. What the hell was he worrying about? Alicia had plenty of money, a fine family. If she was sick, she'd go to some first-class Boston doctor and be made well. It was only the small inconvenience he'd taken care of this morning that she couldn't deal with at home. And if by some chance she wasn't as groggy as she'd seemed and recognized him, Alicia sure as hell wouldn't pull the plug. None of the women who came here would ever report the place to the cops. They were too damned grateful at having it all done so smoothly with such professional expertise, Kitty even provided flowers and soft music.

They averaged three a day. Monday to Friday. Which was twenty-two thousand five hundred smackers per week. He was netting close to forty thousand a month out of what they called Nile Import & Export.

The building was owned in that name and Abdul had at least three layers of corporate veil between himself and the clinic. Now they were talking about the possibility of branch operations. And maybe Daniel would open a real practice here in New York. Get some hungry medical students to do the abortions. That way he'd just be the medical supervisor. He'd have a laundry through which to pass money he told his two partners. What he didn't mention was that he'd also have something to show Joshua if his father ever took it in his head to come see Daniel in New York. That was one of his recurrent nightmares. So far it hadn't happened, but he lived in terror that it would. So, he argued vehemently for a real front for himself when the three of them discussed ways to capitalize on their success; at business meetings chaired by Kitty in her stunning Park Avenue penthouse.

Daniel's mouth tasted sour. He had a small suite in a residential hotel, but he spent most of his time in that penthouse. He'd been sleeping with Kitty for the last four months. Ever since April, after Ruth came to New York for a three-day stay. That had been his idea, not his wife's. A last-ditch attempt to avoid the relationship with Kitty he'd suspected as being in the cards.

There was a certain amount of danger in bringing Ruth to the city with no office to show her, no way to support the fiction that he was a general practitioner. But there was Ruth's innocence, her old-world belief in a wife's submission. She would accept whatever he said, and ask no difficult questions. Which she didn't. The trip was a disaster nonetheless.

Ruth was overwhelmed by New York, frightened at being left alone in the hotel for eight hours a day while he went to work. Eventually they'd both realized that Ruth only felt safe in the Brookline house, with the girls and her endless classes. Good-bye scheme to keep him on the straight and narrow, hello Kitty. Swearing softly, he gulped the last of his drink.

Alicia Williams allowed the nurse to help her dress, then followed her down the back stairs and waited while a cab was found. All during the ride to the Waldorf, Alicia thought about Daniel Morgan. She'd recognized him instantly, despite the drugs and the fact that he was swathed in surgical whites with a mask covering half his face. But those aquamarine eyes were unique. She'd never known another man with eyes like that.

She wondered if Daniel had recognized her. And if he knew that Susan Davenport Morgan was Alicia's best friend, that in fact it had been she who introduced Caleb and Susan? Alicia pondered the possibilities of those links, but she couldn't concentrate. There was too much pain.

The nurse had warned her to expect it. "You're going to be pretty uncomfortable for a couple of days. The doctor prescribed these." She had produced a vial of small red capsules. "Take one every four hours until the pain stops." Now Alicia fumbled the cap off and swallowed one eagerly. It was difficult to get down without water, but she managed. Alicia Williams' life had not prepared her to endure discomfort.

"So the founding fathers were men of remarkable foresight." The teacher of the citizenship class, whose name was Ben Porter, drew a large chalk circle around the twenty amendments to the Constitution which he'd listed on the blackboard. "They created a document which could change, but stay the same in essence. And always remember that change only comes after a lot of thought, and when the majority of the country has indicated that it wants the change."

Ruth scribbled busily in her notebook. Ben Porter glanced up at the clock on the wall. The hands pointed to eight

P.M. "Right, that's it for the evening. See you all on Tuesday."

The class of assorted foreigners who wished to become Americans rose, and there was the sound of rustling papers and shuffling feet as they collected their things and left the classroom. Porter looked up. One student remained. He remembered her name, Ruth Morgan. "Do you have a question, Mrs. Morgan?"

Ruth nodded shyly.

"Great, I love questions, makes me know a student's really thinking about the course. What is it?" He grinned at her. "It's okay, really. Ask away."

He had a blond crew cut and freckles and he wore glasses with brown horn rims. Ruth didn't think he was really handsome, but he was nice looking and more important he was kind and unthreatening. She moved a little closer to his desk. "You must not think I am being a smart Alex."

Porter choked back a chuckle. "A what?"

"A smart Alex. It's a good American expression, isn't it? My husband always says don't be a smart Alex."

"Oh, I get it. A smart alec. Not Alex, that's a man's name."

Ruth frowned. "What is an alec?"

"I've no idea, it probably was Alex originally. You need an English expert. My field's history."

Ruth opened her notebook and jotted down the unexplained word. "I will ask my English teacher."

"What about the question you had for me?" Porter asked. "And I won't think you're a smart alec, promise."

"You said that an amendment can only be put in the Constitution when most of the people in America want it."

"Yes, I did."

"But it's the congress who makes the amendment, so it's not everybody who has said yes or no, is it?"

"Ah, but you're forgetting something I explained earlier. After the congress adopts an amendment it must be ratified, that means agreed to, by a vote in each state. Unless three quarters of them approve, the amendment can't be made part of the Constitution."

"When did you say that?" Ruth demanded. "I didn't hear it."

"Last Tuesday night."

"Oh," she said in a small voice. "I wasn't here. Shama had a fever."

"Is Shama your daughter?"

Ruth shook her head. "My sister. I do not have any children yet."

"Neither do I." Ben Porter gathered his papers from the desk and walked to the door with her. "I'll copy my notes from Tuesday's class and give them to you next week. But don't worry, you're bound to pass your citizenship exam. When do you take it?"

"I am here only thirteen months," Ruth said shyly. "They say I must wait five years. But I study now because I want very much to be an American."

Ben Porter smiled. "I think we'll be lucky to get you. Good night, Mrs. Morgan."

The following week he asked her to wait when the class ended. "I have those notes for you. Do you want to read them over and make sure you understand everything?"

"You are very kind, Mr. Porter. I do not think I should take so much of your time."

"No problem," he said easily. "I don't have to be home for a while yet. There's a drugstore across the street. Let's go have a cup of coffee and you can look those notes over."

At the soda fountain she took the pages he handed her and bent her head over them in concentration. Porter watched her. A very pretty lady, though the way she dressed usually hid that fact. "Is your husband an immigrant as well?" he asked.

Ruth looked up. "Oh no, Daniel is an American. We met in Morocco during the war."

"I see, you're a war bride then."

She frowned. "I don't like that expression. I am married to Daniel, not the war."

Ben Porter chuckled. "You have an interesting mind, Mrs. Morgan. I think you should take some regular courses, your English is good enough, really it is. Ever thought of studying history?" He was embarrassed as soon as he'd asked the question. Night school for foreigners was free at Brookline High School, advanced education in some college was not. "I mean I know schools cost money, but . . ."

"It is not a problem to pay for school," Ruth said. "But

maybe I will have a baby next year, then I'll be too busy to study."

"I see." He looked away.

"You are married, Mr. Porter?"

"Yes. For six years."

"But you do not have any children? You said so last week."

"I remember. No, no kids. My wife and I wanted them, but she's ill."

"I am sorry," Ruth said gravely.

"So am I." He'd ordered a Coke rather than coffee, now he drew the last drops through the straw and got up off the stool. "Do you get a trolley from here?"

"No, I only must walk a little way. To Carrington Avenue."

"Oh, I see." Carrington Avenue boasted some of the most beautiful houses in Brookline. So this lady's American husband was not a poor man. He was glad, she was delightful. "See you Friday," he said, hoisting his briefcase.

Ruth watched him go as far as the door, then she clapped her hand over her mouth and ran after him. "Mr. Porter, I forgot. A smart alec, I found out about the word."

"Did you? Where does it come from?"

"A name, just like you said. Alec was somebody. But in the last century, now no one knows who."

"Glad to have that cleared up," Ben Porter said as he waved good night. "And you really should think about going to college. You have the makings of a scholar, Mrs. Morgan."

Susan gave birth to her son on September tenth at noon. It was the day and the hour she had chosen. Such precision was possible because she had a cesarian delivery. She had insisted on it. Charles West was her obstetrician and he was opposed. Like Joshua, West was appalled by the number of young women demanding cesarians now. Faced with his reluctance, Susan had involved her father-in-law.

"My dear," Joshua had said when she came to his office with her plan, "I simply do not approve. It's dangerous and very unwise."

"In what way dangerous, Josh? The procedure has been

perfected for some years now. I've heard Caleb say so.
And you were the one who refined it, according to him.
Why should I be denied the benefits?"

"Because they're intended for emergency use. Or for
women who cannot undergo a normal delivery. Childbirth
is essentially a natural function, Susan. What you're asking
for is a surgical intervention, with all the inevitable risks."

She had reached across the desk and taken his hand.
"Josh, you're more than just my father-in-law, we both
know that. You're my friend. I often think you're the only
one in the family who really understands me."

Her gray eyes were pleading, looking deep into his.
Joshua took a deep breath and came round the desk to
where she sat. Even seven months pregnant she was adorable. He noted how full her breasts were now, the way
they pushed at the fine cotton of her rich plum-colored
maternity dress. It had a ruffled neckline that framed her
piquant face. Her pale blond hair was up, but a tendril
had escaped to curl along her neck. Joshua twined it in his
finger, enjoying the silken feel. "Susan, I still don't understand. Why do you want a cesarian?"

She lowered her gaze and pressed her hand over his,
holding his palm against her neck. "Because I'm frightened, Joshua. I can't admit it to Caleb. He'd never understand. But you will. You must. I cannot endure pain." Her
voice became a faint whisper. "I'm a coward. You've got to
help me, Josh. Caleb wants more children, not just one. If
I have to go through a normal delivery and it's bad, I'll
never be able to face another pregnancy. And that will be
terrible for Caleb, and for our marriage."

He remained silent for some seconds. Finally he'd sighed.
"Very well, my dear. I'll call Charles this afternoon. And
we'll tell Caleb there are indications warranting a cesarian."

Susan had rewarded him with a smile that was pure
sunshine.

They named the baby Joshua Davenport Morgan. "We'll
call him Dav, so there won't be any mix-ups in the family," Caleb told his parents. He thought the birth of their
first grandson would cheer Joshua and Emma, and certainly they seemed delighted, but to Caleb they still acted
like people under a terrible strain.

Six months after it happened, the shadow cast when

Morgan Landry drowned continued to darken their lives. At least Caleb thought so. Daniel didn't see enough of them to notice, Marya refused to discuss it, and Susan said he was being silly. In fact, she insisted, it was time she and Cal bought a home of their own and moved out of the apartment above Joshua's office.

"I don't think I ought to rock the boat just now, honey," he said. "The folks enjoy having the baby close by. They need cheering up."

"They don't, it's your imagination. But I need cheering up, darling. It's awfully hard living in so small a space now that we have Dav."

Caleb admitted it was crowded with three of them and a baby-nurse, but he thought they could hang on a little while longer. "We'll get something bigger soon," he promised. "Just not right away."

Susan smiled at him, the special smile that always melted his heart, that assured him his suspicions when she conceived were disloyal and unwarranted. That smile was his reward for foregoing the romanticism of being an underpaid, overworked researcher. "We'll find something," he repeated before he kissed her.

"I've found it, Cal," she announced one evening in mid-November. "The perfect house!"

He hadn't known she was actively looking at property. "Hey, hold on, honey. I've just started earning a decent living. We should get some money saved, maybe even take a vacation before we saddle ourselves with a mortgage." He put his fingers under her chin and tilted her face toward his. "How about that? A real vacation, just you and me. Someplace romantic. Bermuda maybe."

"Please, Caleb," she pleaded. "A vacation would be lovely, of course." She moved closer, lay her cheek against his chest. "But we need a home of our own. Besides, when a holiday is over it's gone. Property is an investment."

"They're not strictly quid pro quo, Sue. A house costs a damned sight more."

Susan swallowed her anger. She knew it was never the most effective tool. When she tilted her head to look into his face, her eyes were full of unshed tears. "Caleb, you haven't even asked about the house I found. Won't you look at it? Just to please me?"

"I—oh, God, honey, don't cry. Of course I'll look at it. Whenever you say."

Eleven Dartmouth Street was very much like the Morgan family home on Commonwealth Avenue. It, too, dated from the late nineteenth century. It was five-stories tall, two-rooms wide, built of mellow brick with a mansard roof, and still possessed of the elegant touches which had been the norm of an earlier time. Susan led her husband through it as if it were already theirs and she was mistress of all she surveyed. "Isn't it grand, darling?"

"Grand's the word all right. Susan, this isn't a house, it's a mansion."

"Oh, Caleb, don't be so shortsighted. It's exactly right for us. You're a doctor. Soon you'll be a very important doctor. This is the right house for a man of your standing. Besides, I haven't told you the best part. The owners died in a car crash and left a lot of debts, the estate is anxious to sell quickly. We can have it for thirty-one thousand."

He whistled softly through his teeth. "It's cheap for what the place is, I'll grant you that. But it's more than we can swing, Susie. Please, darling, try and understand."

There was a window seat built below the casements of what had been the library. Susan perched on it, pressing her cheek to the glass. A linden tree grew on the street beyond the window and a trick of the early winter sunlight made it seem that the branches were a crown on her head. She was so lovely, Caleb had to catch his breath.

"Please," he said again. "Try and understand. I want you to have whatever you want, you know that. But it's not just that we can't afford to buy this place. We can't afford to keep it up. A house like this needs a full staff of live-in help. And it would all have to be done over, paint, wallpaper, furniture, everything. . . ."

"It's close to your parents' house," she reminded him. "You want to be near them. And your father would help with the expenses, you know he would."

"Yes. But I hate asking him for money. I want to be my own man, Susan. I want to take care of my wife and son myself." She didn't answer and he crossed to stand beside her, laying his hand gently on her shoulder. "Listen, I'm not saying, no house. Just not this one. Not yet. Maybe we can find something a little way out of town. Newton perhaps, or Natick. Something smaller."

Some tacky, middle-class, suburban ranch house, that's what he had in mind. He wanted to put her in one of those horrors being built at breakneck speed to shelter all the ex-servicemen and their newly fecund wives. Susan shuddered with revulsion. But she was careful not to let Caleb see.

The Beth Israel Synagogue was on Market Street in the oldest part of Brookline. It was a conservative shul; the congregation sought the middle ground between the strident Americanization which to them marked reform Judaism, and the clinging to old-world ways which they saw as orthodoxy. Ruth hadn't known about the three branches of Judaism in America. She chose Beth Israel because it was a short, streetcar journey from her house. She went to services most Saturday mornings, but she found the place bewildering.

Its sanctuary was a large, brightly lit auditorium. Gone were the stained glass windows, the candles, and the elaborate carvings which had marked the synagogue where she worshiped as a child. At Beth Israel the only decoration was an American flag beside the ark containing the torah scrolls. Here there was no balcony where the women hid themselves behind filigreed wooden screens; everyone sat together in seats that folded down like they did at the movies. But the prayers were offered in Hebrew and the men wore skullcaps and prayer shawls, so she knew she was in the right place.

Ruth left the synagogue on a Saturday morning in December thinking about the differences and the similarities, unaware that anyone had noticed her until she felt a tap on her shoulder.

"Mrs. Morgan, good morning. I didn't know you were Jewish."

"Oh, Mr. Porter. I didn't know you were Jewish either."

Ben Porter chuckled. "We sound like a bad, slightly anti-Semitic joke." Ruth looked blank. "Forget it," he hastened to say, "too complicated to explain. Is your husband with you? I'd love to meet him."

"No, Daniel is in New York. Besides, he isn't Jewish."

"I see." They were outside and down the steps by now. "Can I give you a lift home?" he asked. "My car's just around the block. It's a prewar jalopy, but it runs."

"Thank you, but I don't want to be any trouble. There's a streetcar."

"That's silly, it's no trouble. Carrington Avenue's on my way."

He took her arm and led her to a battered black Oldsmobile parked nearby. "Looks like snow," he commented as he helped her step onto the running board and into the passenger seat. "I don't imagine you saw much snow in Morocco."

"Never," Ruth confirmed. "I think it's marvelous."

Porter started the car and grimaced. "Personally I loathe it. But that's probably because I grew up in Maine and I've had a bellyful of the stuff."

"Sometimes we miss the things from our childhood," Ruth said wistfully. "I have never before seen you at the synagogue."

He shrugged. "No, I don't come often, not since I was a kid in fact. But Bertie is worse." He hesitated. "I guess I just felt the need of a little outside help."

"Is Bertie your wife?"

"Yes. It's a nickname for Roberta. She has multiple sclerosis. It's a crippling disease and there's a lot of pain."

"I am so sorry. But here in America the doctors do wonderful things."

"Not for M.S., I'm afraid. There's no known cure. She got it the same year we were married. We have to have a nurse around the clock now. I couldn't afford that on a teacher's pay, but fortunately Bertie's family was well-off. They left her some money—not that they ever thought it would all go to medical care." He paused. "Sorry, I don't know why I'm pouring all this out to you."

"I am glad to be poured out to," Ruth said softly. "And that's my house across the street."

Porter pulled up in front of the red brick mansion. "Very nice. What does your husband do, Mrs. Morgan?"

"Daniel is a doctor. His practice is in New York. Usually he comes home for Saturday and Sunday. This week he couldn't leave. Will you come in, Mr. Porter? I would like you to meet my little sister, and my sister-in-law. She lives with us."

"I really shouldn't."

"Why not?"

"You're right," he said, turning off the ignition and

pocketing the key. "Why not? Bertie will be sleeping anyway."

Shama and Jessie were playing Monopoly in the den, they looked up just long enough to be introduced. "Now, you must entertain Mr. Porter while I make some lunch."

"No, please, Mrs. Morgan. You mustn't go to any trouble."

"It's not trouble. I got it ready yesterday. I'm old-fashioned," she admitted with a shy smile. "I don't cook on shabbat. But not kosher. Daniel wouldn't understand kosher. We have tomato soup and chicken salad, do you like those things?"

"You'll like Ruthie's," Jessie said before he could answer. "She makes everything with all these crazy Moroccan spices. Her food's terrific."

"After that kind of endorsement how can I refuse?" Ben settled down to watch the Monopoly game until Ruth summoned them all to lunch in the big, cheerful kitchen.

It was an easy, friendly meal. Ben Porter decided he liked both girls—he already knew he liked Ruth Morgan. "Let me help with the dishes," he said when they had finished the last crumb of a Moroccan pastry made with ground almonds and honey.

"Shama and Jessie do the dishes," Ruth said firmly.

She led him back to the den and they sat on opposite sides of the couch. Suddenly she didn't know what to say to him. She fastened on their meeting place of the morning because it was the first thing that came to her mind. "Are you going to go again to the synagogue, Mr. Porter?"

"Please call me Ben. As for going to shul, I don't know. It seems a little like cheating. Here I am Lord, remember me? I haven't been around much, but I've got this problem. . . ."

"I think that is not very unusual," she said. "For me everything at the synagogue is strange, not like in Morocco. But to pray when you have trouble, that I think is the same everywhere."

He frowned. "Maybe it is. And I never thought of it, but obviously Moroccan Jews must have very different customs. Judaism in America is pretty much a central European import. I suppose everything in this country is strange for you."

"A little," Ruth admitted. "You have been here a long time?"

"My family came to America from Holland before the Revolution. That's not the norm, most Jews are more recent immigrants. But there were a few who came earlier. Porter's not a Dutch name, but what it was before or when it got changed I don't know."

Shama and Jessica appeared. "I am already finished beating Jessie at the Monopoly," Shama announced. "I have seven hotels and twenty houses and all her money. We can play again with four and I am beating all of you."

"I will beat all of you," Ruth corrected automatically. "It's the future tense. That's right, isn't it, Mr. Porter?"

"That's right. And you were going to call me Ben."

Shama was dealing out four piles of Monopoly money. He stood up. "I'm afraid I'll have to take a rain check on the game."

Shama turned to the window. "It's not raining. It is going to snow I think."

"Rain check's just an expression," Jessica said. "It means you get to come back another time."

"Exactly," Ben said, wrapping his scarf around his neck and pulling on his coat. "I would definitely like a rain check to come back and play Monopoly with this budding tycoon here. May I, Ruth?"

"Yes, please come again. I would like that very much. Maybe next time you can meet Daniel."

Susan decided against going down to Joshua's office, this time she phoned and asked him to come upstairs. It was late afternoon on a Wednesday; she knew Cal's schedule, he'd be at the hospital seeing patients. "Josh, can you get away for a few moments and come upstairs?"

"Are you ill, Susan?"

"No, I'm fine. It's Dav, I think he has a slight fever and I don't want to bother the pediatrician if it isn't necessary."

Joshua asked her about the child's nurse. Susan explained that the woman was off for the day. "Very well," Josh said. "I have a free half hour after my next patient. I'll come up then."

He did and Susan took him immediately to the tiny room they'd turned into a nursery. Joshua examined the baby, then kissed him tenderly and put him back in his crib. He turned to Susan with a smile. "He's healthy as a little horse. You're acting like every new mother, seeing a problem every time the baby gets the hiccups."

Susan nodded. "Yes, I thought I might be. But I wanted to hear you say it. You know me, Joshua, I'm never content about anything unless it has your seal of approval. He'll sleep for a bit now. Come and have a cup of tea with me before you go back to the office."

Joshua followed her into the small living room. Always cramped, it was now almost impassable; toys, a small bassinet, a folded playpen waiting until Dav would be big enough to use it—the accessories of life with a child filled every space. "Looks like you two plus Dav are outgrowing your nest," he said. Outside, the first snow of December fell in large flakes that melted as soon as they touched the window. "You'll hardly have room for a Christmas tree," he added.

"Indeed we won't, but . . ."

"But what?"

"But Caleb doesn't think we can afford a home of our own."

He looked at her in surprise. "Susan, that's absurd, of course you can. I'll help you at first, Caleb knows that."

"He doesn't want to take anything from you, Joshua." She poured a cup of the fragrant jasmine tea she had waiting and handed it to him. "Caleb is very proud."

"And damned inconsiderate, if you ask me. Imagine him keeping you squeezed in up here. It was all right while he was a resident and before the baby, but now—"

"Ssh, don't excite yourself, Josh dear. Drink your tea. It's all right, really. I don't mind."

"Then you're a very foolish young woman. You should mind, Susan. You've got to insist that Caleb provide a proper home for you. The hell with his silly pride."

She sat down on the one corner of the sofa not filled with folded diapers, and crossed her legs. As always she noted Joshua's quick, appreciative appraisal of her best feature. "Since you mention it, Josh, I did try. I found the perfect place. Just three blocks away on Dartmouth Street. It's being sold by the estate." She told him the price.

"Sounds like a bargain to me. You two ought to snap it up."

"That's what I said. Caleb said we couldn't afford it."

Joshua looked around, but there wasn't another available sitting space in the room. He perched on the arm of the sofa and it brought his chest within a few inches of her head. "Let me think a minute, my dear," he said softly. Almost unconsciously he stroked her hair while he did so. Susan didn't move.

"Tell you what seems best to me," he said at last. "I think I'd better just buy the place and give it to you two. If I argue with Caleb and make him do what he doesn't want to do, it will only cause hard feelings. A gift is something else again. And if he protests too much I'll say he can treat it as a loan. Pay me back. What do you think?"

The face she lifted to his was milky pale, with just a faint flush of delicate color in the cheeks. Susan's eyes were two bright jewels, moist and sparkling. "Joshua," she whispered, "would you do that for me?"

"I'd do anything for you, my dear . . . and for Caleb and Dav, of course."

Without another word she reached up and pulled his head down to meet hers. They had kissed before, father-daughter pecks, and this started the same way. But Susan allowed her mouth to linger on his for a fraction of a second longer than usual. And ever so slightly she parted her lips. Then she pulled away and Joshua was sure he had imagined the sexual quality of the caress, though he knew he was not imagining the extent of his response. He said good-bye hastily and fled down the stairs to his office.

Susan remained where she was for some moments after he left. Eyes closed, lost in a dream that was half-filled with handsome, powerful Joshua Morgan, half with the lovely new home that would soon be hers. Eventually she sighed and rose and began putting away all the baby paraphernalia she'd strewn about the room.

15

*U*sually Caleb bounded up the steps to their front door, no matter how long and tiring his day had been. Tonight Susan thought a stranger was coming. She did not recognize the slow, plodding tread, or the moment's hesitation before the key turned in the lock. "Caleb, what's wrong? You look frightful."

He didn't answer immediately, just stared at her, then let his eyes travel the length and breadth of the small but tidy living room. "It's not a mess, nothing like Dad said," he murmured, speaking to himself, not to her. "You must have arranged it for him, the whole horror show he described."

"Cal, what are you talking about?" Susan's fists were clenched, her back rigid. Almost involuntarily she was girded for battle, but it didn't show in her voice. "Darling, you must have had a dreadful day. Come sit down, I'll make you a nice big rye and ginger, shall I?" She gestured to his comfortable chair in the corner by the tiny fireplace, but Cal ignored her and remained standing.

Susan left him and went into the kitchen. She fixed the drink quickly, not allowing herself to think about anything. One step at a time, that was the way to deal with this. She could handle Caleb, just as she always did. Dav's nurse, Miss White, was waiting for her when she came out. "Our little man is sound asleep, Mrs. Morgan. I'll be going now, if that's all right."

"Yes, of course. Thank you." The nurse didn't live in, that wasn't possible in the apartment. From seven in the evening until seven in the morning, Dav was her responsibility. It was her sleep which would be interrupted if he woke. Susan hated the injustice of that. She was frowning when she rejoined Caleb.

He took the drink from her hands and finished it in three long swallows, then held out the glass. "I'll have another if you don't mind." She had to fix him two more before he was willing to eat dinner.

The whisky changed his mood, no longer somber and withdrawn, Caleb seemed unnaturally gay. Susan responded in kind, but the knot of fear in her stomach didn't go away. He was like a banked fire, smoldering beneath cold ashes, preparing to burst into flames. She decided it would be best to divert some of his energy. "Darling," leaning over, stroking his cheek with one finger, her voice husky and low, she asked, "how about early to bed?"

He looked at her quizzically, his green eyes dark. "To bed, yes, that's one answer." The liquor had slurred his speech slightly.

Susan cleared the table quickly, then disappeared into the bathroom. When she came out he was waiting for her in the bedroom. He was standing by the window, staring out into the night, wearing only his trousers. His bare torso was lean and hard in the lamplight.

Susan turned down the spread and removed her negligee. Her nightgown was white satin, edged in tiny pink silk rosebuds. When she sat on the edge of the bed, one strap fell from her shoulder and partially exposed a breast. She allowed it to remain so. "Caleb . . ."

He turned and his face was a rigid mask. "I forgot to tell you the big news."

"Oh, what is that?" Her heart was hammering in her chest and she buried her hands beneath the covers so he wouldn't see them tremble.

"Dad gave me our Christmas present this afternoon. It's over there on the dresser."

She looked. A sheaf of folded documents had been placed atop the lace runner. "What is it?"

"The deed to number eleven Dartmouth Street. Your house, Susan. The one I told you we couldn't afford. Dad's bought it for us."

"But, Caleb, that's wonderful! And so generous of Joshua, don't you think so? Really, darling, you mustn't be so silly."

He was beside her before she'd finished speaking, both hands gripping her bare shoulders. "No, I don't think it's wonderful. I think it stinks. I listened to my father explain about his goddamn present and I realized my wife is a scheming little bitch who connived to get what she wanted after I made it clear how I felt." His eyes burned into hers. They were wild, half crazy eyes. "No research job, it doesn't pay enough. Not if your wife is pregnant. So, I went into the practice. But that wasn't the end of it. Oh no, Susan can't wait. Susan wants what she wants. Never mind how much manipulating or lying is involved."

"Caleb, you're hurting me."

"Am I?" He took one hand away and in a moment's insight she knew he was preparing to hit her. But the gesture never materialized, the impulse was born and died in seconds. It was too foreign to his nature, his upbringing, his view of the world. Caleb Morgan did not strike a woman, not his wife or anyone else. Instead he kissed her. Forcing his tongue into her mouth, kneeling over her and pinning her to the bed with his weight.

Susan remained docile and pliant beneath his assault. A diversion for his anger and his energy, that's what Caleb needed. Sex was useful at a time like this. Afterward he'd be apologetic and she would be forgiving.

He pushed the nightgown off her shoulders and down over her waist and hips. His mouth sought her breasts while his fingers kneaded her belly. One hand went lower still, massaging the flesh of her thighs, forcing them apart. Then, with one extraordinary and unprecedented gesture, his fingers were inside her. Expert and practiced they slid past the slithery contraceptive jelly and found the thin rubber rim of her diaphragm. A moment later he'd yanked it out and thrown it across the room.

"Caleb, what are you doing? No! Not like this, I'll get pregnant again—"

But he was inside her before she could squirm away, in seconds he was spurting hot seminal fluid into her depths. In the lamplight she could see his face, screwed into a mask of passion and anger. And when he withdrew there was no tenderness. "Quid pro quo, Susan. I want another

child, right away. You wanted your fancy Boston house
and you've got it. But I'm going to have what I want too."

She thought about it long after he'd fallen asleep. He
hadn't said anything about a second baby. Not until tonight. They'd talked about having more children while she
was carrying Dav, but in a vague sort of way. Something
for the future. And she had not indicated by word or deed
that she had no intention of going through the horror of
pregnancy a second time. So why had he chosen this
means of punishing her? Because he knew. He'd seen
through her facade of happy mother-to-be, doting parent.
He knew she hated everything about children.

Susan clasped her hands over her stomach. Was she
conceiving at this moment? Was Caleb's seed becoming
another baby to swell her body and distort the shape of
her life? She couldn't know, but it made little difference; if
not tonight, some other night. Susan did not mistake the
determination in her husband. Hot, silent tears slid down
her cheeks and wet the pillow.

It was like living with a stone. Caleb almost never spoke
to her. He came home, played with Dav for a little while,
ate a silent dinner, then took her to bed. Each time he'd
force his fingers into her first, to see if she was using her
diaphragm. If she was, and a few times she did try putting
it in, he would remove it. Then he'd insert himself into
her body like a surgeon performing an operation, with
deliberation and skill. There was no foreplay, no afterglow
tenderness. He intended to impregnate her, and Susan
knew there would be no truce between them until she
told him he had.

It went on this way for a month. Christmas came and
went followed by the cold, gray days of January and she
didn't have her period, but she said nothing to Caleb.
Moreover she allowed no one in the family to see that
there was anything wrong between them, and she con-
soled herself by beginning the redecoration of the new
house.

Caleb never came near Dartmouth Street. He took no
part in the choice of paper and paint and furnishings. And
she didn't attempt to involve him. Once, seeing a stack of
fabric swatches on the side table in the hall, he picked
them up casually, thumbing through the heavy velvets and

satins. "Have you considered how we're going to pay for all this?"

Susan smiled sweetly. "Oh, that's no problem, Cal. I'm sure your father will help."

He stared at her for a moment and the pain on his face was a living thing, a separate entity come to dwell between them. Then he turned and went into Dav's room.

It was while she stood there, listening to him talking and laughing with his son, that Susan realized how close at hand was the weapon of her revenge. She trembled with excitement.

Daniel said it again, as he'd said it so many times. "Not yet, Ruthie. We can't start a family until things are more settled in New York."

Ruth bit her lip and turned away, but this time she didn't drop the subject. "When will that be, Daniel?"

He ran his fingers through his hair. "Jesus, let it alone, will you? I can't say exactly. I'm thinking of moving to a new office. Maybe after that." It wasn't exactly a lie. He really was on the verge of opening a small, legitimate office of his own. He'd finally convinced Kitty and Abdul that such a move would give all three of them protection on numerous fronts. "Six months," he told his wife. "Maybe a year, we'll see."

It was a Saturday afternoon, they were in the Brookline kitchen, the girls were out. Ruth was watching snow fall softly beyond the window. She was still the young woman from Morocco with so much new to see and wonder at, but she was not quite so buffered by innocence. "What you are saying really is no—for a long time, maybe forever." One tear escaped and rolled down her cheek.

"Oh, shit. Don't cry, goddamn it. I hate it when women cry. I don't know, Ruthie. I just don't feel ready."

She turned her face to him. Her eyes were as dark and deep as ponds. "I am ready, Daniel," she whispered. "I need . . . I need some part of you that is truly mine."

He stared at her and didn't answer. Instead he walked out of the kitchen, paused in the hall to grab a thick sheepskin jacket, and left the house.

He didn't have a plan; he just wanted to get away. And so it was habit that took him to Franklin Park. He'd always loved the place. This afternoon it was as he liked it best—

silent, almost empty, seeming vast and primeval and apart
from the real world. The snow had petered out. Beneath
his feet a light dusting of new powder covered the frozen
residue of previous storms. He moved with his head down,
lost not so much in thought as in feeling.

Once he kicked at a mound of melting slush and it
splintered into fragments. He walked on, aching with the
knowledge that whatever had been between Ruthie and
himself was disintegrating like the snow, and that she
knew it. It was some minutes more before he realized that
someone had fallen into step beside him.

"Hello, Daniel."

He turned his head and stopped walking. She was
swathed in fur from head to toe and only her face showed.
It was white and pinched and the eyes were dull, but he
had no difficulty recognizing it. Still countable seconds
passed before he replied. "Hello, Alicia."

"Aren't you going to say something about my being all
grown-up?"

"No, I don't think I am."

She smiled but it didn't reach her eyes. "Not even
considering how long it's been since we've seen each
other?"

Daniel shook his head. "Not so long." He'd read knowledge in her eyes and her voice the first instant, so there
wasn't any point in playing games. "How did you find me
here of all places?"

She gave up the pretense of the smile. "I followed you.
I'd been waiting outside your house, hoping you'd come
out alone. It didn't seem wise to barge in."

"No, it wouldn't have been. Okay, let's go someplace
and talk about whatever you want to talk about. You look
frozen despite the Eskimo getup."

They made their way to Bluehill Avenue and found a
place called Moe's Delicatessen, open even though it was
the Jewish section of Dorchester and this was the Jewish
Sabbath and the other stores on the block were closed.
"Moe gets a medal for not being God-fearing," Daniel
said.

He ordered coffee and jelly doughnuts and watched
Alicia shrug off her fur coat and fumble a cigarette out of
her purse with shaking fingers. He leaned forward to light

it, and their eyes met and held for a moment, then Alicia broke the contact.

Daniel leaned back in his seat, still watching her. "Are you about to try a little blackmail, doll?" he asked finally.

She shook her head. "Don't be ridiculous. I couldn't very well, could I? Not without admitting how I knew. Besides, why should I?"

"That's what I'm trying to figure out. I hadn't thought about it before now because I didn't think you recognized me."

"Your eyes," she said with the first genuine smile. "No one who's ever met you would forget your eyes, Doctor Morgan. Better take to wearing dark glasses at work."

He grinned. "I'll think about it. What do you want, Alicia?" She didn't answer, just took a few nervous puffs of her cigarette, and he pushed harder. "If it was something simple, you'd have rung the bell on Carrington Avenue, or telephoned. Spill it."

She gulped her hot coffee then set the half empty cup down and ignored the doughnut. "Ever since you . . . shall we say helped me out, I've been a nervous wreck, depressed."

"Seen a doctor?"

"Yes. He says there's nothing wrong."

Daniel studied her, he put his hand over hers in what looked like a friendly gesture but allowed him to take her pulse. "Maybe. But could be he's wrong. Go to somebody else." He'd suspected she was ill five months ago when he'd performed the abortion on her. To him the symptoms were now even more apparent.

She shook her head. "No. I don't want any more poking and probing and tests. It's a waste of time. I just need something to get me through this bad patch. The man . . . the one who—" She broke off and took another gulp of coffee. "He's married. And he's decided he prefers his wife to me. And don't tell me I brought it on myself, I know that."

Daniel motioned to the pimply-faced boy behind the counter to bring them more coffee. He didn't speak until after it came. "Sorry things have been so rough," he said softly. "But I still think you should see another doctor."

"Damn you!" She didn't raise her voice but her red-tipped fingers were clasped so tight, the knuckles were white. "You've got to help me, Daniel. I don't know any other person I can turn to."

"I would if I could. But I can't. I'm not exactly in practice, remember? I have no hospital affiliation, Alicia. No testing facilities. You've got to see that."

She looked at him for some seconds, realization dawning behind her eyes. "You think I want you to be my doctor, don't you? You don't understand?"

The aquamarine eyes narrowed. "No, apparently not. Exactly what do you want?"

"The little red capsules," she whispered through stiff lips. "The nice happy pills that make me sleep. I used all you prescribed, then I got some more from my own doctor. But he's cut off the supply."

"I see. Sorry to have been so obtuse." He lit a cigarette to stall for time. "I can't write prescriptions, doll. I remind you again that I'm not in private practice."

"You get the pills though. Your nurse gave them to me."

"Yes, I get them." Abdul was in charge of that too. Whatever drugs Daniel asked for were supplied without question. "I don't have any here," he added. It was the truth.

"I'll come to New York. Give me a couple of months' supply and I won't bother you again. I'll be over this whole thing in another couple of months."

He didn't answer right away. When he did all he said was, "Yeah, sure. Why not? A couple of months and everything will be fine."

They made arrangements to meet in New York Monday evening at the classic venue, under the clock at the Biltmore. Daniel paid the bill and left. Alicia remained where she was.

He walked along the cold and deserted street, past shuttered stores displaying cheap, foreign-looking merchandise under signs he couldn't read because they were written in Yiddish. At first he felt lousy, then his mood lightened. Alicia was seriously ill, but she didn't want to face it. Okay, that was her choice. Daniel Morgan was not the conscience of the western world. So why not give her what she did want, the way to ignore her symptoms? He couldn't bring himself to say yes to Ruth because if he did an abyss would open and swallow him. Alicia was digging her own grave, but whatever happened he wouldn't have to climb in after her. Might as well say yes to Alicia, if he didn't somebody else was bound to. And that was exactly the way he felt about the abortions. Daniel had learned to be comfortable with that kind of reasoning.

On that same Saturday, the nineteenth of January in this year of 1947, Caleb and Susan were lunching with the senior Morgans. There was a moment when both Cal and Emma were out of the room and Joshua and Susan were alone. "Come to the new house tomorrow around two," she whispered. "I want to show you a surprise." They exchanged conspiratorial smiles.

Joshua met her the next day. The surprise was the draperies she'd chosen for Caleb's study. They were rich wine-colored tweed, a stunning contrast to a pale gray rug. Susan displayed them with pride. "I'm thinking of a light oak desk," she said. "Something big and square and terribly modern. What do you think, Josh? Will Caleb like it?"

"If he doesn't, he's a bigger fool than I imagine him to be. You're marvelous, Susan. Not only lovely, but a wonderful decorator. I can't believe Cal is so disinterested in all this. Has he really not seen his study?"

"He hasn't come to the house since you gave it to us." Her words caught on a sob in her throat, and Joshua reached out a hand in comfort. Susan took hold of it and smiled at him. "It's all right, I'm not worried. He'll come around in a little while. It's just his silly pride."

"I could murder the wretch," Joshua said through clenched teeth. "Look what he's putting you through. And for no damn good reason."

"Don't be angry with him. That's only going to make things worse. Come see the rest of the house, Josh dear. Might as well, now that you're here." She whispered the next words. "It's so nice to have someone to share it all with."

None of the rooms was finished, but the shape of elegance and high style was already apparent. The years of study and planning had paid off. Susan knew exactly what she wanted and she was creating the home of her dreams.

Joshua murmured appreciatively at the choice of colors, the selection of fabrics, the exact rightness of each piece of furniture.

"Now," Susan paused before a closed door. "The pièce
de résistance." With a flourish she opened the door. They
were in the master bedroom. And unlike the rest of the
house, it was complete in every detail. The rug was white
shag, the walls papered in a dark blue-and-gold print of
stylized feathers; there was a long row of mahogany chests
either side of a mirrored door which led to the bathroom,
and the wide bed had a draped canopy of ice-blue silk and
a matching spread. "Like it?"

He whistled softly. "It's spectacular. And it suits you.
You look completely at home in this room, my dear. I'm
more delighted than I can tell you."

"It's all thanks to you, Joshua. I don't know the words to
tell you how grateful I am."

"I'm the one who is grateful. You give an old man a
great deal of pleasure. There's no point in having come to
my time in life, except to see one's children happy."

The face she turned to him was suddenly tear streaked.
"Don't say that, Joshua. I can't bear to hear you refer to
yourself as an old man. If anything happened to you,
I—Oh, God, I don't know what I'd do."

She was sobbing and Joshua could only pull her into his
arms, hold her small person tight against himself. "Susan,
don't, you mustn't. There's nothing to cry over. You're
just tired. All the work of creating this wonderful house.
And the worry of Caleb being such a stiff-necked ignora-
mus. Ssh, it's all right. I'm here. . . ."

When did it change? When did the emotion wracking
his body become something other than paternal. He didn't
know. Only that one moment he was kissing the top of her
head, comforting her as he would Jessica when she cried
over a broken doll, and the next their mouths were locked
and they were drinking of each other's essence as if they
could never get close enough.

"Joshua, oh, my darling Josh. I've been so hungry for
you, for so long."

The words that would end it rose in his throat, choked
him. He had a momentary vision of Emma and he almost
pushed Susan away. But all such instincts were stillborn.
Joshua did not speak, his mouth and his tongue were
occupied with tasting her, sucking her lips, the soft skin of
her neck, the hard little nipples that somehow were exposed to him in seconds. And his arms weren't forcing her

from him. They were lifting her, noting that she weighed nothing at all, that carrying her to the bed and depositing her on it took no effort and was accomplished before he realized his own intent.

She fumbled with his clothes, with her own . . . and he helped her, because he could not make himself do otherwise. When they were naked and lying side by side, he felt the silk coverlet and it was as if his skin had more than its normal quota of nerve endings. It was as if all sensuality, all desire, everything he'd ever felt or wanted to feel, was here and now.

Susan moaned. "I can't wait. Take me! Oh, God, take me, Josh!" She didn't wait for him to roll over, she moved on top of him, feeling for his hardness, guiding him inside her. There was no further calculation. Whatever her motives, they had no part of this moment. This was the secret dream she'd nurtured ever since she first saw Joshua Morgan, the fantasy that had sustained her numberless times when she lay beneath Caleb. "Deeper," she whispered. "I want you deeper." She rose on her knees, her body arched back, linked to him in only that one place where all sensation and meaning lodged.

Joshua stared up into her face. Her blond hair tumbled over her shoulders and her eyes were shut. He shivered with the sensations she was causing as she rocked back and forth, up and down—but he kept looking at her. When the final spasms came, when he was gasping with a pleasure so intense it was almost painful, he still looked into Susan's face. Only it wasn't just her he saw. He saw Betty and Billy-Jo and Morgan. The four of them were astride his loins; the two women with whom he'd been unfaithful, his dead daughter, and his daughter-in-law—his body was emptying itself deep into the belly of each one.

He left Susan alone in the bedroom afterward. She listened to him descend the steps and heard the front door close behind him. They hadn't spoken. She didn't need words, neither did he. There was only this exquisite sense of relief, this sated hunger that had existed unappeased for so long. And there was triumph.

"I'm pregnant, Caleb. You have what you wanted." She said the words aloud into the empty room, then laughed softly. That's all she would say at first. It would be enough.

It would placate him, diffuse his anger. They would move into this lovely house and life would be very good. She would endure this pregnancy as she'd endured her previous one. No, this one would be better. Because she would have her precious secret. The thing she wouldn't tell Caleb just yet, but which would remain always in her arsenal. "I'm not quite sure, Caleb dear, but I have every reason to believe that Joshua is the father of our second child."

It was nearly five on a winter Sunday afternoon in Boston, no one was about. The streets were dark, silent, cold. Joshua walked through the Public Garden, across the Common, down Tremont Street, his route led to Scollay Square, to Billy-Jo's old house—the one where everything began between them, where Morgan was conceived. It had a sign in the window, "Rooms One Dollar a Night." He stared at it for a few moments, then walked on.

He walked without knowing where he was going or why, moving in a fog in which time had no meaning and thoughts were incoherent. Billy-Jo, Betty, Emma, Morgan, Jessica, Susan, death, incest. . . . The words were a litany that his shoes pounded into the pavement.

As he had so often these last months, Joshua tried to examine the thin line between murder and accident. He couldn't get it clear. And he tried to take hold of the concept of incest. Was it incest? What did the Bible say about the carnal knowledge of thy son's wife? Perhaps nothing. He didn't know. He'd never been much for the Bible.

The wind picked up, biting cold across the sea, and he realized with a shudder of revulsion where he was, sitting on a bollard on Pier One. Like in books. The criminal always returned to the scene of the crime.

"Hello, Morgan." Those had been his first words as he faced her where she stood across from his home.

She'd stared at him for some seconds before she said, "Hello, Papa." The word was a weapon she wielded with skill.

"You know, of course," Joshua said. "I thought you were so little that you'd forget."

"I never forgot. I know everything."

"Why are you coming here like this? I've seen you, night after night. Just standing here."

"I'm tryin' to decide," she said in the soft Arkansas drawl that was so painfully like her mother's. "I been tryin' to make up my mind what would hurt you most. Tellin' doesn't seem like enough."

He'd reached out to touch her then, and she drew back with a small hiss of revulsion that pierced his soul. He dropped his hand. "We have to talk. Please, let's walk a little."

She led the way, striding through the night as if with purpose, letting him hurry along beside her. When they got to Scollay Square, she stopped and pointed to Billy-Jo's former house. "She lived here, didn't she? This is where it started."

"Yes. Apparently she told you the whole story. Why are you so angry? Your mother and I cared for each other, she must have explained that. But I was married, there was no hope. . . ." The inadequate words trailed away.

Morgan had looked at him and she'd laughed, a harsh sound without mirth. "You cared for her, is that what you're tellin' me? Me, too. I suppose you cared for me?"

"Yes."

She turned away then, her shoulders heaved and he didn't know if it was with laughter or sobs. Some men came out of a nearby bar. They were drunk and raucous, possibly even dangerous. "We can't stay here," Joshua murmured.

They walked some more. Dumb with pain and anger, her hostility bristling in the night, almost a palpable thing. When they reached the docks, the moon came out from behind clouds and he saw that her cheeks were streaked with tears. "I'm sorry,'" he said softly. "I'm so sorry I could never be a father to you."

"You think I hate you for that? You're wrong. It's the way Mama died. It's because she wouldn't come east and get the doctors to make her well. It's because after she was gone—and it wasn't quick, it took a long, painful time— after that I opened the envelope she left me and there was a letter sayin' you gave me five thousand dollars when she took me away from Boston. And the money was in a bank in Little Rock, just waitin' for me. Five thousand dollars and she wouldn't touch it to make herself well. What's five thousand to a rich man like you, Joshua Morgan?"

"It was all I could afford at the time. Why didn't you write to me? When Billy-Jo got sick, I mean. I'd have helped then. It didn't have to be like it was."

"No, it didn't have to. Only she made me swear I wouldn't do anything. 'Not while I'm alive,' that's what she said. 'Cause she knew and I knew that if you really cared you'd have come lookin'. Least once in all those years, just to see if everything was all right. Only you never did, 'cause you didn't care. But Mama had to make herself believe you did." She whirled on him then, suddenly flailing his chest with her fists. "You never cared a damn! Not about her or me!"

Morgan shouted the accusation into the night, and he was half-occupied with fending off her attack, half with being frightened that someone would hear. But there was no one, the docks were deserted. Not even a gull disturbed the night. Only the shouted curses of his illegitimate child. "Goddamn you to hell, Joshua Morgan! I hate you for what you didn't do!"

She raised her hands to claw at his face, and he realized she wore no gloves and that her nails would leave marks he couldn't explain and he grabbed her wrists and tried to hold her away. But she was a big girl, tall and huskily built, as Billy-Jo had been. She fought him, twisting her body to and fro, writhing in his grip, finally yanking away with the full force of her weight behind her.

Morgan's momentum pulled him forward. Joshua fell to his knees. There was a coating of ice on the splintered boards of the wharf, he skidded until he broke the motion with the heels of his palms, feeling the shock reverberate through his frame. "Morgan! For God's sake!"

For the briefest of moments she was there in front of him, swinging her arms to regain her balance, then there was a scream and a loud splash as she fell. Joshua hurled himself forward. He almost lost control again, and only grabbing the bollard and wrapping his arms around it prevented him from falling after her. Gasping for breath, calling her name, he looked down. She was struggling in the churning water below the pier, trying desperately to get a purchase on one wooden piling, but it was covered in

slime and algae, her fingers came away as if they had
grasped only air.

"Morgan!" He leaned yet farther forward, reaching one
arm down. "Take my hand!" She tried, but a wave knocked
her farther beneath the structure of the dock. Joshua
scrambled to his feet, intending to jump in after her.

And then it was as if the world were moving at quarter
speed. His fingers fumbled with the buttons of his coat,
his legs carried him to the edge from which he could
launch himself into the sea—but all so slow. He knew the
seconds were ticking by, he could hear her gasping struggle. *Go*, he told himself. *Jump. Get her out.* But he did
not.

"Papa, I can't swim. Papa . . ." And then silence.

The scene played itself over and over across the empty
horizon. Joshua could see it, hear it, but he could not go
back. Nothing on earth could change what he'd done and
what he'd failed to do. Again and again Morgan called out
to him, and each time he waited until it was too late to
save her. Sometimes the face of the drowning girl was
replaced by other faces. Caleb looking at him with trust
and respect and love. Susan smiling and laughing.

There was no salt smell on the air, it was too cold for
that. A snowflake settled on his shoe and Joshua watched
until it melted into nothingness. It had been trying to
snow all day without success. Nature was a failure, as he
was. He pushed stiff fingers into the pocket of his vest and
withdrew his watch. After nine. Emma would be worried.
Sighing, he rose and began to retrace his steps.

Commonwealth Avenue was not entirely dark. There
were streetlights, and the glow of lamps behind drawn
drapes. He looked up at his home; lights in the library and
the living room. Next door the first four floors were black,
his office was closed and empty, but lights showed in the
windows of the upper floor. Caleb and Susan and their son
were at home.

For a moment he hesitated, looking from Caleb's windows to the trees across the street, examining his choices;
then he took the key ring from his pocket and mounted
the half-dozen steps to the impressive front door of his
office.

*   *   *

"No, Mom, I'm sorry. I don't know any more than that. Dad met Susan this afternoon for a tour of the Dartmouth Street house." Caleb swallowed hard, tightened his grip on the telephone, and tried to make his voice normal. No point in letting his mother know how he felt about that damned house. He turned to his wife, "Susan, what time did you say Dad left you?"

She was engrossed in a home-decorating magazine and she didn't look up. "A little after five, near as I remember."

Caleb repeated the information to his mother, then listened to her expressions of concern. Finally he asked, "What time was it when you last called the office?"

"Around nine-thirty," Emma said. "There was no answer. He hasn't been at the hospital either."

Caleb lifted his wrist and looked at his watch. "Well, it's nearly ten now. He could have come in, in the meantime. Or maybe the phone's out of order. I'll run down and have a look, okay? Call you right back."

Joshua sat at his desk. The large mahogany expanse was almost bare. The only light in the room was a small lamp that made a yellow puddle near his right hand. It illumined the prepared hypodermic needle lying neatly on a square of sterile gauze. He had removed his coat and his jacket and his left shirtsleeve was rolled up. Everything was ready, but he did not act.

Something was bothering him, some small, surface concern which overshadowed all his despair and his guilt. That distraction held him in thrall, it stayed his hand. A lifetime in medicine, forty years of caring and carefulness. That was it. He did not wish to betray his profession at the end. It was the one good and fine thing, his only remaining source of pride. He didn't want to soil it and he would not.

Joshua rose and carried the hypodermic to the sink in the examining room. He expelled the lethal contents down the drain, then flushed them away with copious amounts of water. After that he left the needle and the syringe in the sterilizer. They would be attended to in the morning when his nurse came in.

In his office he stood for a moment, staring upward at the heavy brass chandelier. He unbuttoned his suspenders, testing their strength and give between his two fists.

Satisfactory. Joshua secured one end around his neck, the other hung free over his shoulder. He carried a chair to the spot below the light fixture and climbed up on it. It took only a moment to fasten the free end of his suspenders to the strong central post of the chandelier.

He felt no urge to pray, no sorrow, no fear. Only intense exhaustion. Soon it would be over and he would rest. Taking one deep breath, Joshua kicked the chair away.

At that precise second he heard the door to the outer office open and his son Caleb calling to him.

Daniel's shoulders were stooped, his eyes red rimmed with exhaustion and grief, and his clothes rumpled. He did not look as if he belonged in his mother's elegant drawing room. "Why?" he asked his brother. "That's the thing I can't get my mind around. Why?"

Cal shook his head. "I've been asking myself the same question all this week. If there's an answer I can't come up with it. I think Mom may know something, but she's not telling."

"Shit!" Daniel pounded one fist into the soft, brocaded cushion of the sofa. "It's such shit. Not just for him, for her." He stared out the window at the wintery Boston evening, avoiding his twin's eyes. "I keep wondering if it would have been better if you hadn't cut him down."

"Jesus," Cal muttered. "Don't lay that on me."

"I'm sorry. I'm not laying anything on you, except maybe my nightmares. Of course you had to do it, I would have too. Instantly. So would anyone else. Don't look like that, old buddy. I've got a big mouth, that's all."

Cal shrugged. "Don't think I haven't thought of it." He turned to the double doors of the drawing room. "You're sure Mom's all right?"

"The same as she's been right along. Absolutely controlled, a steel rod for a backbone. I told her you'd be here about now, but she wanted to have a bath and change when we got back from the hospital." He half-rose from his chair. "Maybe I'd better go see if everything's okay."

Cal raised a restraining hand. "Give her a bit more time. We can't start acting as if she's likely to do something crazy too."

"No, I guess we can't. Cal, what are we going to suggest she should do?"

"Go on living as normally as she can," Cal said at once.

"Of course, but I don't mean that."

"You mean about Dad."

"Yeah, about Dad."

Cal sighed. "As far as I can see, there's only one thing to do. He's going to need full-time care for God knows how long, they won't keep him at Memorial. It will have to be a nursing home."

Daniel nodded. "That was my idea too."

They were quiet for a few moments. Eventually Cal got up and refilled their glasses from the bottle of scotch he'd carried in from the library. He handed Daniel the freshened drink. "I wish I'd seen more of Jessica these last few days. Trying to keep things on an even keel at the office has been a hell of a hassle. I don't see how you've managed to get so much time away from your practice."

Daniel didn't look at him. "I've got a partner, it's different." He switched the conversation back to Jessica. "Jess seems okay, but she's young. She's putting up a hell of a front. In her way Jess is as tough as Mom, but I don't know what's really going on in her head."

"Maybe she should move back here for a while, be with Mom," Cal said.

"I suggested it. She doesn't want to come. They've never been close, you know that."

"Yes. Listen, am I crazy, Daniel, or does Jessie blame Mom for all this?"

"Maybe a little, around the edges so to speak."

Cal shook his head. "Poor Mom, that too."

Emma came in on the last words. "What too?" She went to Cal and kissed his cheek. "How are you, darling?"

"Fine, Mom. I'm fine." He hugged her. She didn't feel like steel to him, she seemed fragile, as if she'd break if he squeezed too hard. And she looked terrible, her eyes were dark circled and her face gaunt. She was wearing a severe black tea gown and no jewelry, it didn't help.

Emma disengaged herself. "What too?" she repeated.

"We were talking about Jess," Daniel said.

"Oh, I see." Emma patted Daniel's shoulder as she moved past him to her customary chair beside the fireplace. "I know Jessie blames me for your father's condition, if that's what you mean. But right now I can't worry about her. My only concern is Joshua." She settled herself in the chair and folded her hands in her lap. "Now, I want you two to tell me exactly what is the prognosis. In simple, clear language, with no attempt to spare my feelings. But first, Daniel darling, I would like a very large one of those." She gestured to the drink he was holding.

Daniel poured a generous whisky and added soda and a lot of ice and brought it to his mother. Emma pressed the frosted glass to her forehead before she drank. "That's better," she said after the first sip. "Now, tell me."

Neither man spoke. She looked from one to the other of her sons, then fixed her glance on Caleb. "Tell me," she repeated. "Nothing you say will be worse than what I've been imagining."

Cal took a deep breath. "There's been a great deal of spine and brain injury. We don't know how long Dad was oxygen deprived before I found him, but it was long enough to—" He hesitated. His mother's beautiful blue eyes were unwavering. "To do a lot of damage," he finished weakly.

"Yes," Emma said quietly. "I've been told that much by the doctors at the hospital. But damage and injury are vague terms. What I want from you is something more specific."

Daniel took a long swallow of his drink, then set down the glass. "The paralysis is probably permanent," he said. "It's unlikely Dad will ever move again." He saw her wince, but he knew this was the only way. He went on. "The loss of speech is probably permanent too. As to his mind, nobody can say. Since he can't communicate, and is probably still in shock, it's impossible to know how much of his mind is left."

Emma turned to Caleb. "You agree with this analysis?" Cal nodded. Emma drank down her whisky without pausing for breath. She coughed a bit when it was gone, but apart from that the alcohol seemed to have no affect. Her voice was steady and her words distinct. "What you're telling me is that Joshua will be a . . . a vegetable for the rest of his life. Am I correct?"

She read agreement in both faces. "I see. Thank you. I needed to know." Emma stared at her hands for a moment, clenching and unclenching them in her lap, then looked up. "One thing more, how long is he likely to live?"

Cal closed the distance between them in two strides and put his hand on her shoulder. Emma patted it, then gently pushed him away. "Please, I must have all the facts. Tell me."

"There's nothing life threatening in his injuries, Mom. He could go on for years. There are certain dangers that accompany paralysis, but good nursing can minimize them."

Emma rose and went to the window, staring out into the night. The grandfather clock struck nine times. "It's late," she murmured. "You should go home. Both of you. I'll see you at the hospital tomorrow."

"Mom," Daniel said, "listen, I'll start looking into nursing homes. There are some good ones. Cal and I will vet them and give you two or three to choose from."

Emma turned to face them. "There is no need for an institution. I will not consider such a thing. I intend to care for your father here, in his own home. Marya will help me, and we'll hire whatever additional nursing or other staff that's needed."

"You can't," Cal said. The words were an anguished cry. "You can't bury yourself like that. What about your life? Your work?"

"Your father is my life, and I've already told Celia I won't be returning to the lab. Oh, there is one thing, we should have a proper hospital bed, and I suppose other equipment. Will you two see to that, please?"

"Why?" Daniel demanded. "Why should we help you become a martyr? Look, something snapped in Dad's mind. Neither of us knows what, maybe you do. But that's not important now. It's a fact, it happened. Technically he's still alive, as we just got through explaining. But for all practical purposes he's dead. Why do you have to turn your home into some kind of tomb for both of you? What is this, Mom, your American version of suttee? You throwing yourself on the burning pyre?"

"No," Emma said softly, "it's nothing like that. You don't understand, do you? Either of you? Very well, I will try to explain."

The pale beige window drapes framed her slim form, accentuated the thin, black-clad line of her body, and the unswept red hair with its wings of gray. When she spoke, there was an almost majestic quality to Emma's voice and her words. "I am fifty-two years old. I have been married to Joshua Morgan for thirty-two of those years. I have loved him even longer. It hasn't always been easy, but it has been a life, for the most part, a very good life. Now there is a new set of circumstances. There are new demands. As you've just pointed out, Daniel, it doesn't matter why they've come about, only that they have. And that Joshua is my husband and I am his wife. I am not about to turn over my responsibilities to an institution."

Emma waited, but neither of her sons spoke. "If you don't understand," she added softly, "then I fear for the marriages of both of you. Perhaps that's what you ought to be worrying about, not me and not your father. Now, it's getting late and I'm very tired. I'm going up to bed and I suggest that you boys go home. Both Ruth and Susan have been given short shrift this past week."

Cal watched his mother leave the room. When he turned to face Daniel he knew he was looking at a mirror image of his own white-faced horror. "I know the answer to the question now," he said in a hoarse whisper. "Now I'm sure I should have let him hang there and die."

"Jessie, can you talk to me?" Shama poked her head in the door of Jessica's bedroom, but she didn't go in. "If you want, I leave you alone."

"No, that's okay. Come in. But I don't feel like talking much."

"Okay, we just sit."

Jessie was sprawled on the bed. Shama knelt on the floor, then dropped her weight onto her heels. Jessie had been trying for months to copy the posture, she could never hold it for more than a few seconds. "I don't know why I can't sit like that."

"Because you are not Moroccan. You are born in America where are chairs for everybody. Jessie, when my mother and father were killed by the bomb I cried a lot. I am big crybaby for days and days. Afterwards I feel better. So I think is okay to be a crybaby."

"Sure it's okay, sometimes."

"So, why you don't cry?"

"I can't cry. I think I'm just too mad."

"You are mad at Doctor Josh. I know. I think you are mad at your mama too."

Jessie shook her head and her heavy chestnut hair half-covered her face. "No, I'm not. Everybody thinks I am, but I'm not. I can't talk to her about it. She doesn't understand me, she'll say I'm being selfish."

Shama shrugged. "Okay, so maybe you are selfish. I think I would be too mad."

"He was the one who was being selfish. He never thought of us, of me," Jessie said through clenched teeth. "He went and did it for some crazy reason of his own, and he never thought of what was going to happen to the rest of us. How could he, Shama? How could he be so mean?"

"I don't know. Maybe people get mean when they get old. Me, I'm not going to get mean. I'm going to remember how is it to be young."

Jessie pulled her knees up to her chest and buried her face in them. "Shit," she murmured. "I feel like shouting that out the window. Shit, shit, shit."

"Don't do it. Better you say *merde*. That's shit in French. No one in Brookline can understand."

Ruth came in carrying a tray. "Many people in Brookline speak French. You should teach Jessie to curse in Arabic, Shama. Then she really could say whatever she wanted and no one could understand."

"Good idea, I do it. What do you bring?"

Ruth set down the tray. "Milk and *ma'amoul*, for Jessie because she didn't eat any supper. Not for you, you're getting too fat."

"I don't care, I love *ma'amoul*." Shama took two of the date-filled cookies. "Hurry up and eat, Jessie. Otherwise I finish all of them and get fatter."

"I'm not hungry, but thank you," she added, looking at Ruth with a wan smile.

Ruth sat down on the bed and put her arms around Jessie. "You must eat something, *ma petite*. Maybe some soup, I have made the chicken soup with lemon and egg that you like. I can heat it."

"I can't eat anything now," Jessie insisted. "Tomorrow I will, I promise. Is Daniel home?"

"Not yet. He is with your mama."

Jessie made a face.

"Listen," Ruth said softly, "I don't think what Dr. Josh

did is Emma's fault. I think whatever he was so unhappy about, Jessie, it was something apart from the family. It's not your mama's fault or yours, or Daniel's or Caleb's."

Jessica began to tremble, her whole body shook. "We must have done something," she whispered, her face pressed against Ruth's breast. "Something. Otherwise how could he do that and not care about what would happen to us?"

"Jessie, listen to me. During the war it was terrible in Morocco, not as bad as some other places, but terrible. Everything we knew, everything we were used to, it all changed. The whole world was different. I used to think about the Germans, about Hitler, and I couldn't understand how they could do it, make everybody so miserable. Then I realized I wasn't ever going to understand it, so I stopped thinking about it."

"How could you stop? The war was all around you."

"Yes, it was. I don't mean I stopped thinking about the war, just about Hitler. I am never going to know what he is thinking, what made him do this, I told myself. So I am not going to get crazy trying to figure it out. I am only me, Ruth Morhaim. I can be responsible only for me."

She pulled back and looked into Jessica's eyes. "Do you understand what I am saying, *ma petite*? Nobody can be inside anybody else's mind. Even the people closest to you, the people you love, you can never know really what makes them do the things they do. So you can never blame them. But the most important thing is that you can never blame yourself, not for what someone else does or doesn't do. You must just be the best Jessica you know how to be. Only yourself, that's the thing you can control."

Jessica stared at her. At last two big tears rolled down her cheeks, and after a few seconds she was sobbing. Ruth hugged her very tight and Shama got up from the floor and sat on the other side of the bed. The three of them clung together and their tears mingled.

"You got Jessie to cry," Daniel said later. "That's a good thing, thanks."

They were getting ready for bed and Ruth stopped brushing her hair. "I didn't think you were home."

"I came in toward the end of it, heard you all upstairs. But I figured you were better off without me, so I didn't interrupt."

"I don't want Jessie to blame herself," Ruth murmured. "To imagine that somehow it's her fault."

"Yeah, I know what you mean. That's what we're all in danger of doing, isn't it? Taking the blame."

Ruth put down the brush. "You are thinking of Caleb."

"A little. And me. I was Dad's favorite. I probably should have gone into practice with him."

She turned and opened her arms to him. "Oh, Daniel, no. It's not your fault either. He didn't try to kill himself because you went to New York, he couldn't have. You must not think that."

Daniel drew her close and kissed the top of her head. "I don't think it. It's crazy, I know that. But the whole damn thing is crazy."

Ruth clung to him. The feel of his body was intoxicating, filling her with a fierce joy she could never get enough of, a hunger that was never completely satisfied. "I love you," she whispered. "I love you so much, Daniel. Why are we not happier? I mean us and not right now. Now it is different because of your father."

"I thought we were doing okay." He stroked her back, letting the sexual energy build as he knew it would, as it did. "I figure we're still able to make a little magic." His right hand went to her breast and the nipple hardened under his touch. "Take your nightgown off," he murmured. "And I'll show you."

She moved away from him just long enough to slip the gown over her head, then pressed herself back into his embrace. Daniel put his thigh between hers and his two hands on her buttocks and lifted her. "You're like a feather. My little foreign feather." He moved her up and down a few times and the friction increased her excitement. Her breath was coming in short gasps when he carried her to the bed. "Tell me what you want," he whispered. "I know, but I like to hear you say it."

"I want you to be inside me. I want to feel you deep inside."

"Like this. This is what you like, isn't it?"

"Yes, yes, yes. I love you. Oh, *mon Dieu, mon Dieu* . . . Daniel! Daniel! Daniel!"

She called his name in a rising crescendo of passion, not loudly, not so anyone else could hear. It was a secret shout, with her lips pressed to his flesh and the word-making a bond between them that seemed unbreakable—until they finished together and the ecstasy ended and she felt him leave her once more.

"See," he said softly, "I told you we were okay."

"This way, yes."

Daniel rolled over and propped himself on his elbow and looked into her dark eyes. "Ruthie, I heard what you were telling Jess, about each of us only being responsible for ourselves. I am the way I am. I can't change."

"I don't want you to change."

"Yeah, you do. You don't think so, but you do."

"No, it's not true. I love you the way you are. I love you for what you are—"

He pressed a finger over her lips and cut off the words. "You love me for what you think I am. That's not exactly the same thing. Ruthie, listen. What's happened, it's made me think about a lot of things. You and me for one. The way I see it, we're going to be okay as long as we give each other a little breathing space. Do you understand?"

"I think so. I have never wanted to choke you, Daniel."

"I know. But I don't want to choke you either. I've been wondering if you shouldn't go to school full-time, honey. Not just take these night courses at the high school, get a proper degree. You're a smart girl, you can do it."

"Ben Porter thinks so too."

"The teacher? See, I told you it was a good idea."

She did not want to be a student, she wanted to be a wife, and a mother. But she didn't say that. Nights like this, when they made love and were really close, were rare. She wouldn't spoil this one. "I will think about it," she promised, and drifted into sleep feeling happy despite everything—because Daniel was beside her, his hand still lightly on her breast.

The private-duty nurse looked up from her place beside Dr. Morgan's bed. She had been caring for him ever since his first day in the hospital, three weeks now, and she knew all the family members. The pretty blond visitor in the mouton lamb coat didn't come often, but the nurse recognized Dr. Caleb Morgan's wife. "He's resting comfortably, Mrs. Morgan. But there's no change."

Susan stared at Joshua for some seconds. She knew he was alive because everyone said so, but to her he looked like a corpse. Beneath the white sheets Joshua's body seemed to have shrunk, and his face was a pale blur that blended into the colorless pillow, even his silver hair had lost its sheen.

There was a tube taped to his face which entered his right nostril, where it went from there Susan neither knew nor cared. Another tube led from a needle in the crook of his inner arm to a bottle of colorless liquid hanging from a stand beside the bed. Everything was either colorless or white, the only relief was the green linoleum floor and the black band around the nurse's organdy cap. "Is he sleeping?" Susan whispered.

"Not exactly," the nurse said in a normal tone of voice. "He's conscious and awake I think. But he can't speak to us and we don't know if he can hear." She fussed with the clamp around the intravenous tube, the droplets of solution flowed at a slightly slower rate. "There, that's better."

Better for whom, Susan wondered. Whatever the nurse had done didn't seem to make any difference to Joshua. She moved closer to the bed. "It's me, Susan, Josh," she said softly. She waited but there was no sign that he understood. The green eyes stared straight ahead, the face remained immobile.

"Mrs. Morgan," the nurse said, "since you're here, could I go down the hall for a moment? My mother's ill and I'd like to telephone her. It won't take more than a minute or two."

"Yes, of course." Susan took the chair the nurse vacated and watched her leave the room. "There, Josh," she said when the door had closed. "We're alone. Are you going to turn to me now and say it's all an act, that you can hear and speak perfectly? No, I guess you're not. What a stupid thing to do, Joshua, try to kill yourself. Why should you feel guilty? I don't. I enjoyed it. And Caleb need never know, as long as he behaves himself."

Susan glanced toward the door, but there was no sign of the nurse. She turned back to her father-in-law. "There's one other thing, Josh dear. I'm going to have a baby. It's not yours. It's Cal's. I knew I was pregnant before you came to Dartmouth Street. But only just. So, if I ever want to tell Caleb that the baby is yours, I can and no one will be able to challenge my word. I have it all worked out, Josh. I wasn't quite sure how I was going to handle you, but you've taken that out of my hands, haven't you?" She leaned forward and let her lips brush his forehead. Suddenly she drew away. "Joshua, I could swear you shuddered just now. But you couldn't have, could you? You can't hear me and you don't know a word I've said. . . ."

The door opened. "That's done," the nurse announced cheerfully. "She's fine. Thank you so much, Mrs. Morgan, I do appreciate it. How is our patient?"

Susan looked from Joshua to the nurse. "He's exactly the same. Our dear Doctor Morgan is just the same. Isn't it a tragedy?" she murmured.

"A terrible tragedy," the nurse agreed as she plumped the pillows.

"Sorry about your father-in-law," Ben Porter said. "How's the family holding up?"

Ruth shrugged and shifted her books to her other arm. They were leaving the high school after an evening class on the Constitution. It was the first one Ruth had attended for a month. "We are all very sad. But everyone reacts in a different way." She thought of Daniel's return to New York, how he'd not said when he would come home next. "Some reactions are very hard to understand."

"That's natural. Tragedy gets each of us in our weak spot, whatever that may be."

Ruth paused by the door to the street. "Ben, tell me how it is."

"How what is?"

"Living with a really sick person. Having nurses in the house night and day."

He grimaced. "It's terrible, but you get used to it."

She touched his arm lightly. "If you're very strong and brave, like you, yes, I'm sure you get used to it."

"Is that what they're going to do with Doctor Morgan, bring him home and have nurses around the clock?"

"That's what my mother-in-law wants. My husband and his brother tried to convince her to put him in a nursing home, but she wouldn't give in."

Ben nodded. "I understand that too. Ruth, listen, you'll want to help as much as you can, I know that. But don't get sucked in, will you? Try and live a normal life, you and your husband."

She stared at him a moment, something flickered, then died in her eyes. She nodded and walked away.

Ben watched her going down the stairs. He'd yet to meet Dr. Daniel Morgan, but he already knew the guy was a first-class horse's ass. Imagine having a girl like Ruth in love with you, crazy about you, and not even trying to make her happy. Ruth wasn't a demanding woman, he knew her well enough to know that all she wanted was a home and a family and a husband who cared about her. He also knew her well enough to guess that she wasn't getting what she wanted.

A month later they brought Joshua home from the hospital and installed him in the specially equipped bedroom that had been arranged on the second floor in what had been the library. "We're home, Josh." Emma leaned over him and kissed his forehead. Joshua didn't move or respond in any way, but then, he never did. Emma ignored that and went on explaining.

"I'm going to take care of you now. Marya will help me. And we have a nurse who will come in during the night. See, I've put you in the library. It's always been our favorite room in the house. We can have long chats here together, just like we used to do. And I'll read to you from some of the books you've never had time for. Oh, and I've put a new Victrola in here, darling, so we can listen to music. Everything's going to be fine, Josh. I promise."

Emma turned from him for a moment, glanced around. As she had said, this room was somehow at the heart of their lives together. When she looked back on their marriage, she saw three places—Joshua's first office on Main Street in Gloucester where they'd met, the cottage in Annisquam where they'd begun to forge that bond which had withstood so much, and this library. God, how overjoyed she'd been the day they moved in, and how hard it had sometimes been, how many terrible problems they had discussed in this very room. . . . But they had survived, what was between them had survived. It was alive still, whatever Joshua's reasons for doing what he'd done.

"We've come a long, long way together, darling," Emma murmured, returning to the side of his bed. "We're going to make the rest of the journey together too." She kissed his forehead, allowing her lips to linger a moment against

his cool flesh. "Whatever the future holds, we'll be together. We banked a large fund of hope that first day in
your office, my love. Some of it's still there to draw on."

Downstairs Nora Marsh was once again marking the
calendar. This time she chose to do so in black. "February
fifteenth, 1947," she said. "I'm markin' it special, like I did
twenty-eight years ago when the twins was born. Like I
always do when something unusual happens."

"Don't seem like much of a red-letter day to me,"
Tessie muttered. "Seem's like a bad day. Madam is going
to wear herself out lookin' after him."

"I know," Nora agreed. "She's buryin' herself. I heard
Mr. Daniel say so. That's why I put a black circle around
the day. Seems to me this house is goin' into permanent
mourning."

SHAMA &
JESSICA

16

*P*aulhurst College for Women was housed in a cluster of mellow brick and granite buildings nestled in southeast Vermont, a few miles from the small town of Wilmington. Since its founding in 1802, the school had held its graduation exercises out-of-doors. It was a natural choice; in late spring the campus was breathtakingly beautiful, a paradise of dark purple azaleas and pale pink dogwood set against the backdrop of mountains clothed in fresh green pine. But on the morning of June third, 1954, the sky was black with thick, threatening clouds.

"I suppose it's stupid to ask if there are contingency plans." Shama leaned on the windowsill of her dormitory room and studied the weather.

"It's stupid," Jessica confirmed. "There can be no break with tradition. Didn't you hear Hayman say so?"

"I heard, but four years in this place hasn't convinced me that Frederick W. Hayman is God. I'm still laboring under the delusion he's a mere college president."

Jess moved to the window and stood beside Shama. "Not a ray of sunshine in four days, and it looks like it's finally going to pour."

"I suppose everybody will arrive, whatever happens."

"Sure they will. I talked with Daniel yesterday, they're coming in two cars. The family won't let us down." Jessie slipped her arm around Shama's waist. "Stop worrying, we've got hours yet. Maybe it will improve if we pretend we don't care. Meanwhile help me do something with my hair. Once I put that thing on my head I look like a fugitive from darkest Africa."

"I, if you will recall, come from Africa. And what you don't know about it is disgusting. How could you live with me all these years and still think in such stereotypes?" Shama set the mortarboard on Jessie's shoulder-length curls and stepped back a few feet.

"Well, what do I look like?"

"A fugitive from darkest Africa."

They collapsed in laughter, the small joke seeming outrageously funny. "It's only because it's today," Shama said, wiping the tears that streamed down her cheeks. "We're close to hysterics anyway, anything can set us off. And now I've ruined my makeup."

"To hell with your makeup, what about my hair? I can't go through the day looking like a—"

"No!" Shama shrieked. "Don't say it again. We'll never get out of here. Sit down, let me see if I can do something."

She shoved Jessie into a chair and picked up a brush. "I'll put it in a chignon so it won't bush out at the sides. Something regal like your mother always wears. Hand me those bobby pins."

"Shama, you know what's funny?"

"No more jokes."

"This is funny peculiar, not funny ha-ha. For years I had to teach you things, now you're the expert and I'm clumsy and awkward."

"I'm only an expert about foolish vanities. Like the fact that you need more mascara if you're going to have your hair like this. And I seem to remember that it's you not me who is valedictorian of the graduating class. That doesn't sound particularly awkward and clumsy." She rubbed a tiny brush over a cake of dark brown mascara. "Look up at the ceiling."

"I still think you've come the longest way," Jessica said. "You even speak perfect English now."

"Terrific, I'll tell that to Daniel. He spent a small fortune on eight years of private education so I could learn where the verb goes in a sentence."

"I think it's where in a sentence the verb belongs."

"Shut up. If you don't I'll smear this all over. Speaking

of telling the family things, when are you going to drop your bombshell?"

"Later," Jessica said. "Much, much later. After it's all over."

The Daniel Morgans kept two cars in their garage on Carrington Avenue, a Buick sedan and a Studebaker convertible. They also owned a Chevrolet station wagon which was usually parked outside the house. During the week Ruth drove the wagon; when Daniel came home from New York he usually used the convertible. Today, in deference to his mother, he'd chosen to take the Buick.

"Comfortable, Mom?"

"Very, but I still think I should be in the back and Ruth up here."

Daniel smiled. "You know Ruthie would never stand for that."

Ruth leaned forward, putting her head between the shoulders of her mother-in-law and her husband. "I'm fine in the back. But I'm nervous."

Emma reached up and patted her cheek. "I expect the girls are more nervous than you are."

"Is that supposed to help?" Daniel asked.

Emma laughed. Her laugh was more tentative these days, Daniel thought. Softer and less hearty. Perhaps because she didn't use it as often. What was there to laugh about when you spent all day, every day with a living corpse? He felt the stab of ineffectual pain with which the past seven years had made him familiar. And the anger. Goddamn his dad. Why wouldn't he die and set her free? That thought made him feel guilty, as always.

Ruth and Emma were chatting now, ignoring him. Ruth was saying something about the shop. She'd made a big success of it, no denying that. He'd suggested she go to college to occupy her time, instead she'd opened Le Petite Morocco a short distance from the house in Coolidge Corner, and turned it into a winner. "I am from a long line of shopkeepers," she'd explained. "It's something I know about." That was true, and she still had family in Morocco, so importing the clothes and cloths and leather goods from Africa had proved relatively easy. Why then did he clench his teeth when he heard her discuss her business?

He searched his mind for a comment to change the

subject. "There's the sign for Wilmington. We'll be there
in about fifteen minutes."

Emma rolled down the window and sniffed the air.
"Wonderfully fresh, but chilly. And it smells like rain."

"How can they have the ceremony outside if it rains?"
Ruth asked.

"Beats me," Daniel said, "but I'm told by Jess that it's
always outside, and this year is not to be an exception."

"Let us hope God has been informed." Emma rolled up
the window and watched the lovely Vermont scenery roll
by. "Is Cal still behind us?"

Daniel glanced in the rearview mirror. His brother's car
was not in sight. "I think we lost them about forty miles
back. I got bored with moping along like a tortoise, Cal
drives as cautiously as he does everything else."

"He has the boys with him," Ruth murmured.

For Ruth that was explanation and excuse for everything, Daniel thought. Cal could be thirty-five going on
seventy and Susan could be the prize bitch of all time, but
they had two sons, so their marriage was good and right
and holy—and his and Ruth's something less. "Yeah," he
murmured. "He's got the two kids. Too bad that's all he's
got."

Neither Emma nor Ruth replied.

"Such a tiring trip," Susan complained. "And my dress
is wrinkled, heaven knows what I'll look like by the time
we get to the college. I don't know why we didn't come up
a day or two ago and stay at a hotel."

Caleb negotiated the hairpin curve of the mountain
road, then increased the pressure of his foot on the accel-
erator. The big Lincoln Continental shifted into higher
gear. "I couldn't get away from the office for that long. I
did explain, Susan. You could have come up with the boys
whenever you wanted, I said that too."

He spoke with quiet patience, that was always the best
way with his wife. Not best for her perhaps; Susan quite
enjoyed arguing with him, she felt so powerful when she
won. But it was much better for him not to become angry.
Controlling his emotions had become a major occupation
in Caleb Morgan's life.

Susan made a face of distaste and turned to the backseat.

"Dav, sit up straight. And do stop sucking your thumb, John."

"Leave them alone," Cal said. "They're being remarkably good, considering." He glanced quickly over his shoulder. Both his sons were looking at the picture books he'd given them before the trip began. Susan never thought of things like that. Her solution to keeping two boys aged seven and eight content during a three-hour car ride was to leave them home. Caleb would never agree to that, and when it came to the boys she didn't fight him, she knew better. "How are you doing back there, guys?"

"Fine, Dad. But are we almost there?"

"Almost." Cal glanced at the clock on the leather dashboard. "About another half an hour. Who can tell me how many minutes there are in half an hour?"

"Thirty!" both boys shouted at once.

"Right. And in an hour?"

Susan turned and stared out the window. Caleb and his sons would play question games all the rest of the way. None of them expected her to join in. "Terrible weather," she murmured. "They can't possibly have the graduation outside."

Cal shot her a quick sideways glance. He could swear there was a small smile of satisfaction playing about her lips.

At exactly eleven A.M. a great crack of thunder echoed off the mountain tops and rolled down the hills and bounced from one to another of the college buildings. Shama ran to the window. "Oh no, it's going to pour."

Beside her a number of other windows opened, a series of heads poked out. Many of them were decked with curlers, a few were studded with pin curls, one or two already had their caps in place. There were muttered curses and incantations.

Jessica moved to stand beside Shama. "Look, there's Hayman."

The elderly president of the college was walking briskly along the path beside the dormitory building. He wore a dark blue pin-striped suit, but neither cap nor gown yet. He paused and took a gold watch from his vest pocket, glanced at it, then up at the assorted young women watching him. "Do finish your toilets, ladies. There is just one hour until the procession begins."

"What about the rain, Doctor Hayman?" someone shouted.

He held out his hand, palm upwards. "What rain? It is not raining. It will not rain." He snapped the watch shut and walked on.

"He's nuts," Shama said, slamming the window. "I can't tell you how glad I am to be getting out of this place. You stay here and you get crazy."

"I'm not glad to be leaving." Jessica barely whispered the words. "Once we're graduated I may never see you again."

"See, that proves it. You must be crazy if you think that."

"It's true. I'll be in Boston and you'll be in New York."

"May I remind you that commuting between Boston and New York is an honorable Morgan tradition. Besides, you'll be too busy to miss me."

"Never that busy. Shama, listen, I know we've been all over this, and the magazine job sounds great, but are you sure you're doing the right thing?"

"Dead sure. And you're right, we've been all over it. You'd better concentrate on how you're going to tell your news, everyone's had time to get used to mine. Let's finish dressing, okay?"

"Okay."

The rain began just then. The skies opened and loosed floods of water. "So much for crazy Hayman," Shama said.

At precisely seven minutes before noon the rain ended, the clouds parted to reveal a rainbow that shimmered as it spanned the mountaintops, and an army of undergraduates appeared to dry the six hundred chairs awaiting guests. The visitors had taken shelter in their cars. Now they began to take their places, thumbing through the programs they found waiting. "Look," Emma exclaimed in amazement, "the guest speaker is Celia Howard!"

Daniel chuckled. "I see the fine hand of the Morgan-Morhaim team."

"But Celia never told me, she never even mentioned it."

"Obviously we were supposed to be surprised. Maybe—"

It was noon, his words were cut off by the pealing of the three great bells atop Sloane Memorial Hall. They rang for a full minute, then stopped. Before their echo died away the music of the "Triumphal March" from *Aida* poured from the loudspeakers placed around the large expanse which was officially known as Chancellor Green, and which the students called pig meadow.

The faculty processed onto the green from the administration building, the new baccalaureates were assembled some hundred yards away in the gym. The music was fainter there, but they could hear it. "Here we go," Jessica murmured. She had the highest four-year average of anyone in the college, and just one of the honors accorded her because of those grades was leading her classmates. "No crinolines I hope, ladies," she mimicked the dean's final instructions. "They do so distort the fall of the gowns."

A few people heard her and giggled, the fashion for enormously full skirts supported by crinoline petticoats had been worrying the dean for months. The girl immediately behind Jess poked her in the back. "Come on, Morgan. Let's get this show on the road."

Jessica listened to another half bar of the music and counted the rhythm silently to herself. One . . . one, two, three . . . one, one. On the next long beat she put her left foot forward and led the two hundred and sixteen members of the graduating class into the brilliant sunshine bathing pig meadow.

Emma had discovered the Red Mill in Wilmington on earlier visits to Paulhurst. It had a large dining room but only five rooms for overnight guests, she'd had the foresight to reserve all of them the previous September.

"Very nice, Mom," Cal said when he carried Emma's small suitcase into one of the bedrooms. "You've done us proud. I suppose you don't need me to do a thing about dinner either."

"No, it's all arranged. That's fine, darling, just leave the suitcase on that rack. It was a lovely ceremony, wasn't it?"

"Great. Celia was marvelous."

"Yes, I thought so too. Fancy Jessie and Shama keeping that a secret. It makes me realize that they've both really grown up. I still think of them as children."

Caleb snapped open the locks of his mother's suitcase

and didn't look at her. "Yeah, I guess we all have to get used to the fact that they aren't. You need anything else, Mom?"

"Nothing, darling. I'm going to rest for a bit."

He let himself out of the room. It was on the corner of a low, Japanese-style building facing a stream. He and Susan had the room at the other end, and one adjoining it for their sons. The remaining two were for Ruth and Daniel, and Jessie and Shama. It was all quite conventional, well organized; Emma had lost none of her efficiency since she buried herself alive. Cal shuddered. He still did that every time he thought of how, in a manner of speaking, he'd been the one to erect her tomb.

The food at the Red Mill was excellent. They had a wonderful dinner, they chatted and laughed at family jokes and repeatedly told Jessica how well she'd spoken, how proud they all were of both her and Shama. How normal all looked, Cal thought. How secure and sure of themselves and safe. Nobody would believe what was going on under the surface.

He glanced at Daniel and Ruth. That marriage was almost as miserable as his own. Did his mother know? Yes, she probably did. Emma didn't miss much. Nobody else would guess though. Ruth hadn't stopped smiling since they sat down. Why shouldn't she smile? Look how far she'd come, how far she'd brought her sister. He didn't want to look at Shama, but he couldn't help himself.

God, she was beautiful. He'd thought her hair was curly when she was a kid, now it was straight and dark and if fell like a curtain either side of her lovely face, accentuating her prominent cheekbones and winged eyebrows and big dark eyes. The dress she wore was in some sort of dark brown-and-gold print. The material had clearly come from Morocco via Ruth's shop, with cap sleeves and a scoop neck and a tightly fitted bodice that swirled into a full skirt. Shama put every woman in the room in the shade. But she wasn't a woman, she was a kid just out of college, like a sister to him. Caleb pulled his gaze away and pretended to eat his strawberry shortcake.

There was a lull in the chatter and laughter. Daniel stood up. "I think it's time for another toast. Does everybody still have plenty of champagne? Good. Ladies and gentlemen, I give you Jessica Morgan and Shama Morhaim.

As a team they're unbeatable, they've proved that. Now I'm sure we're going to see Shama burn up the magazine world in New York. And as soon as Jessie makes up her mind what field she wants to conquer, she's no doubt going to do so in style."

Jessie waited until they'd all drunk, then she spoke. "I think that's as good a cue as I'm going to get. Listen, everybody, I wanted Celia to be here, but protocol says she has to be with old Hayman tonight, so I have to do it without her." She paused and sipped her champagne.

"Do what, darling?" Emma asked.

"Make an announcement." She looked around the table, her eyes finally came to rest on Daniel's face. "I want to tell you that I've decided to follow the Morgan tradition. I've been accepted to Harvard Medical School."

Ruth was the first to speak. "But, Jessie, you never said you wanted to be a doctor. Never once."

"I didn't know it until this year. I've been seeing a lot of Celia, she helped me make up my mind. The most marvelous things are happening in women's medicine." She turned bright red and grinned at her brother. "I mean, of course Cal knows a lot more about this than I do, and I don't want to put you out of a job, old buddy. But Celia says it's about time women got themselves into the act and took charge, and I think she's right."

"Isn't it extraordinary about Jessica?" Susan removed the second diamond ear clip and laid it beside the first on the small dressing table. "How did Celia Howard get her clutches into Jess without your mother knowing about it?"

Cal loosened his tie and pulled it off. "Jessie's grown-up, she can pick her own friends. Besides, I don't think my mother would see it as being in Celia's clutches."

"No? I'm not so sure. What are these wonderful advances in medicine that Jessica's talking about?"

He watched his wife removing the pins that held her blond hair atop her head. It fell loose to her shoulders. Once upon a time he'd found that exciting. Once upon a time, like a fairy story. "A number of things are on the brink of happening in gynecology." He thought of the secret clinical tests he'd heard about only recently. Celia probably knew about them, too, but Susan wouldn't be interested in the details. "Have you been in to the boys?"

"They're fine. Unzip me, darling, will you?"

She rose and presented her back for his attention. Cal released the zipper on the smoke-blue crepe de chine dress. She was lovelier than ever, a woman at the height of her beauty, why didn't that move him? He trailed one finger down the skin of her back, stopped at the closure of her blue lace bra, felt her shiver. "Undo it," she whispered huskily.

Caleb hesitated, made a mental effort to feel desire. It didn't come. It almost never did anymore. He snapped open the hooks with a quick movement, then stepped away from her. "I'll have a look at the kids."

Susan remained where she was, her whole body rigid. "Are you coming back?"

"Maybe I'll take a little walk first. You go to bed, don't wait up for me."

He stepped through the connecting door into the room where his sons slept before she could answer.

Dav lay very still and composed, the way he usually did. The child was like his father: Quiet, self-contained, a little shy, he even had red hair. Cal leaned down and kissed Dav's forehead and the child stirred once, then settled back into sleep. John was on his belly, arms wrapped around his pillow, three teddy bears sharing the bed. He'd kicked off his covers, and Cal grinned and pulled them back up, knowing the boy would kick them off again in minutes. John was the other kind of Morgan, he had dark hair and green eyes. John looked like Daniel, or like Joshua before— Cal shook his head to drive away the memory of his father before that inexplicable act of self-destruction.

He stood for a moment, studying his sons in the dim glow of the night-light, then let himself out by the door that led to the long porch which fronted all five rooms. He locked the door carefully behind him.

The night was very cool, almost cold. He thought of returning to his room for a sweater, then rejected the idea. Susan would still be awake. His white shirt made a bright spot in the darkness when he strode down the steps and onto the path that bordered the stream. The only sounds were of water rushing over rocks, and crickets performing their midnight symphony. No traffic, no sirens, it was blissful. He walked on, the path bent away from the stream and into deeper woods. The wind made a new sound as it stirred the pines. The scent was sharp and pungent and wonderful; beneath his feet fallen needles created a springy cushion for each step. He could walk forever, just keep going until he came to the end of the earth.

"Hi, it's cold. I brought you a sweater."

The voice startled him for an instant, then he stopped walking, but didn't turn around. "Hello, Shama, what are you doing out here at this hour?"

"The same thing you're doing. Enjoying the peace of the country. You'd better put this on, it really is cold." She slipped the heavy, fisherman's-knit cardigan over his shoulders.

Cal had to turn to face her as he negotiated himself into the sweater. She was wearing one of equal weight but another color. "How did you know to bring an extra?"

"I saw you go. I followed you."

"That was very thoughtful, thank you."

"Oh, Cal, what an ass you are."

"A college education hasn't done much to make you a lady, has it?" He grinned at her, he couldn't help it. He always had to smile when he looked at Shama.

"Not much. I don't think that's what it was supposed to do."

"No, I guess not. Do you know what I was thinking while I watched you up there today?"

She shook her head. "No, tell me."

"I was remembering the way you looked when I first saw you. You got off that train at South Station in that funny straw hat and that shapeless dress, so skinny you could almost blow away, and you curtseyed. We all thought you were angelic."

"Sorry I turned out such a disappointment. Fat and definitely not angelic."

He chuckled. "You're not fat. Hasn't all your education taught you the difference between fat and curvy?"

"I didn't think you noticed."

"Yeah, I noticed." He put one hand beside her cheek, then snatched it away. "Let's walk a bit, if you're not too cold."

"I'm fine."

They strolled along the path side by side. "I suppose you'll miss this place," he said. "I certainly would."

"I'll miss Vermont. But not college. I don't think I'd have gotten through if Jessie hadn't pushed me every step of the way. I'm not really the academic type."

"New York's going to be a big change," he said.

"Yes."

"That's all you've got to say about it? Aren't you going to tell me how the big city is where you belong and you're going to lick the magazine world."

She put a hand on his arm and stopped their forward movement. "I'm not a career girl, Cal. Not in my heart of hearts. That's not why I took the job with the fancy magazine in the sophisticated big city."

He looked into her dark eyes, they glowed in the moonlight. "Why then?"

"Oh, Caleb, don't you know why?"

He shook his head.

"Yes," she murmured. "You do. You just don't want to know. I took it because I cannot bear to be near you, my love. I cannot bear to go on knowing that I love you so desperately and that you love me— No, don't shake your head and don't say anything. You do love me, my Caleb, I know you do. And I have loved you since that first moment I saw you in South Station. And if you were a happily married man, it wouldn't have happened as it has. So I don't feel a bit guilty."

"Shama, listen to me. Nothing has happened. You're young and beautiful and you've had a remarkable life. I'm just the guy you're fixated on because you haven't met Mr. Right yet."

She giggled. "Mr. Right. Only you, Cal Morgan, would say something so idiotic. And if your scenario were accurate, it would be Daniel I'd have the crush on. Psychology one twenty-two. I took the course in my junior year." She reached up and put her hands at either side of his face. "I don't know why I love you so much, just that I do."

He put his hands over hers intending to disengage them, and somehow wound up holding them instead. "I love you, too, Shama. But not the way you mean. I'm an older man, a married man with two sons."

"You're thirty-five and I'm twenty-three, two years older

than Jessie, remember, and what the hell are we talking about? What has age got to do with anything?"

Suddenly she stretched upward and pressed her mouth to his. He could have moved away, but he didn't, not right away. He let the kiss go on for some seconds before he broke the contact between them and turned back toward the hotel. "It's late," he said gruffly. "We'd better go back."

"There's no going back, darling," Shama said softly. "I learned that years ago. The only place you can ever go is forward. It's that or you die."

He took three steps, then realized she wasn't following him. He couldn't leave her alone out here in the woods, and he stopped. "Shama, there's no point. There's nothing to be gained by torturing ourselves." The words were torn out of him, out of the subconscious depths where he'd already formulated them because he'd known for years that someday this conversation must take place. "I'm married and that's that."

"You're married to the prize bitch of all time," Shama said quietly. "Everybody knows, even you. Divorce her, Cal, for God's sake, divorce her. You don't love Susan, you love me."

"I love my sons," he murmured.

"I know." She moved up behind him, wrapped her arms around his waist and pressed her face to his broad back. "I know you love Dav and John. They're great kids. But, Cal, can it possibly be good for them to grow up with a mother and father who hate each other, who live in some kind of stony truce? Wouldn't it be better if at least part of the time they saw their father happy, lived with him in a house where there was love and laughter?"

"It's not that simple," he said softly. "And we have to go back." This time he was firm about disengaging her hold on him, but he kept a grip on her arm and pulled her along the path after him.

Shama didn't say anything until they reached the stream, only a few feet away from the inn. "Cal," she whispered. "Caleb, my love, are you sure? Can you look at me and say you want to throw it all away?"

He turned to face her. Even with the tears streaming down her cheeks she was beautiful. "I can't throw it away

because I never had it," he said. "And I never can have it.
Good night, lovely Shama. Please be happy."

Emma stood at the window and watched them return.
An owl hooted and it sounded to her like the most mournful sound in the world. Poor Caleb, poor Shama. She
wondered if she should go outside, intercept the girl, try
and talk to her. She put her hand to the knob of her door,
then let it drop.

What would she say? What could anyone say? Jessie was
probably awake. The two girls were so close. Jessica must
know all about it; Shama would get more comfort from her
daughter than from her. But she was the one who was old
and supposedly wise. She should have something consol-
ing to say to Shama, or to Cal for that matter. But she
knew she didn't. Because of the boys. Dav and John were
the hostages Caleb had given to fortune, and she knew no
way to ransom them back.

Emma pressed her forehead to the wood of the door. It
felt solid and eternal and somehow comforting. She heard
another door open and in the seconds before it closed she
heard Susan's voice. Such a Boston Brahmin voice, but so
full of venom. The door closed and she could hear nothing
more, but she could imagine the purgatory to which her
son had returned. Emma took a handkerchief from the
pocket of her robe and blew her nose. She would not again
weep over Caleb. It was too late, it had been too late since
she stood in Trinity Church and heard him say he wanted
Susan Davenport to be his wife. Maybe she could have
stopped it before then, but she didn't really try.

The Saturday following the graduation, three days after
they returned to Brookline, Shama came down to breakfast and announced that she was leaving for New York that
afternoon.

It was seven-thirty. Always an early-rising household,
everyone was up and Ruth was standing at the stove
cooking pancakes. She turned to her sister with the spat-
ula still in her hands. "But the job doesn't start until
September."

"I know. It's okay. I'll get a room in the Y and find a
waitress or a sales job until then."

"But why?" Ruth was puzzled rather than angry. "You have already made all the arrangements for your summer."

"I've decided to change them. It's not important anyway, just charity stuff. Somebody else can read to the blind."

Daniel looked up from his newspaper. "That sounds pretty irresponsible, Shama."

She stared at him a moment. "Let's not have a discussion on the subject of responsibility, Daniel. I think it's better if we don't."

He held her gaze for a moment. He was convinced that after more than eight years Ruth remained unaware of the abortion clinics, the nature of his private practice in New York, or the existence of Kitty Donnely or her many successors in the role of mistress. But sometimes he had the uncomfortable feeling that Shama knew it all. It was impossible, she couldn't. But he always suspected she did. "Okay," he said easily. "Wait until tomorrow and you can go back with me."

"No. I'm going this afternoon. I'll take the bus." She crossed to him and put her arm around his shoulders. "I'm not very good company at the moment. And I'm sorry about that bitchy remark."

Daniel hugged her quickly, then released her. Whatever she knew or guessed, it was all right. He and Shama understood each other, they always had, and they loved each other. "Okay, princess, have it your way. But don't worry about taking some schlock job for a few weeks, I'll see you through until you start at the magazine."

"No, I've cost you enough, Daniel."

"Don't be ridiculous. Money is for spending, I've always told you that."

Ruth turned off the gas jet and carried a platter of pancakes to the table. "Now you two have settled everything, do I not get to express an opinion?"

"Sure you do," Shama said easily. "As long as it agrees with mine."

Ruth still wore her hair severely drawn back from her face, when she frowned every thoughtful crease showed. "I don't think you are being very adult, Shama. I don't think it's nice to promise people you will help them, then disappear."

Shama put a single pancake on her plate, turned, and

lay a hand on her sister's arm. "Look, Ruthie, this is something I must do. I can't stay here right now. It has nothing at all to do with you. Don't be hurt, please."

"I'm not hurt. Only it's not right," Ruth insisted stubbornly.

"Ruthie, forget it. Just forget it. Please."

The sisters looked at each other for a moment; Ruth was the first to break the eye contact. She had a pretty good idea what Shama was running from, and there was nothing she could do about it. "I'll help you pack," she said finally.

"Thanks. That would be great. Where's Jess?"

"She left at the crack of dawn," Daniel said. "Something about helping Celia at her lab."

"On a Saturday?"

He shrugged. "Apparently so. These days your sister and I are pretty much in the dark about what you and Jess are doing, or why."

Jessica never remembered Celia Howard looking any different from the way she did now. The woman she'd known since she was a child had the same unevenly cropped white hair, the same lined face, the same square stub-nailed hands. She knew Celia was ninety-one years old, but she couldn't believe it. Now, in the lobby of the Ritz-Carleton Hotel on Arlington Street, she kissed the seamed cheek and thought that Celia even smelled the same. The scent of chemicals had always clung to her, it still did. "Good morning," Jessie said. "I've been thinking that you're immortal, one of the gods. Do you always get up at this hour? It's not even eight yet."

"Most days I do," Celia admitted. "The result of a strict upbringing and a lifetime habit. You look lovely, my dear. Your mother was your age when I first met her, and you remind me of her."

"Thank you, but I don't think I look anything like red-headed, gorgeous Emma. I wish I did, but I don't."

"Your coloring's different, of course. And you're not tall, but you remind me of her nonetheless. Something in the set of the mouth I think. And your speaking voice."

"My speaking voice is pure quiver this morning. I al-most wish you hadn't told me I was actually going to meet the great lady."

Celia chuckled. "I had to tell you. Gladiators should

have a chance to prepare themselves before they enter the arena. Ready?"

"Ready as I'm going to be."

"Fine, then let's go up. Margaret has arranged breakfast in her suite."

The elevator carried them to the fifth floor; they walked down a thickly carpeted corridor to a room with a dark mahogany door and a brass bell. Celia rang it. Almost before she removed her finger the door was thrown open.

"My dear, it's wonderful to see you. And this is Jessica Morgan, of course. Come in, both of you. Katherine arrived a few minutes ago. Thank God for this hotel. The coffee is piping hot and the orange juice is cold." Margaret Sanger stepped aside and waited for her guests to enter.

Jessica was thrown completely off balance. She'd looked up Margaret Sanger in *Who's Who*, so she knew the formidable lady was seventy-one, and God knew Emma had told her often enough about Sanger's battles for birth control. But this was a tiny, pretty woman with blue-rinsed hair and sparkling eyes, wearing a softly feminine blue silk dress and fluttering a lace-trimmed handkerchief. The other one, the millionaire society matron, was nearly six feet tall, dressed in rusty black that looked as if it had first appeared when Teddy Roosevelt was president.

"Katherine," Mrs. Sanger said, "you've met Celia Howard, and this is her young friend Jessica Morgan."

Katherine McCormick nodded to Celia, then studied Jess. After what seemed like forever she extended her hand. "Good legs, sturdy. You'll do. Pleased to meet you, Miss Morgan."

Jessie felt as if she should kiss the woman's ring, or at least curtsey. She merely shook her hand and sank gratefully into the chair Mrs. Sanger indicated with another flutter of the lace handkerchief.

Katherine McCormick poured Jessica a glass of orange juice from a tall, frosty pitcher. "So you are entering the lists, child. Glad to hear it, we need young blood. Look at the three of us." She waved a hand to indicate Margaret Sanger and Celia Howard and herself. "We each have at least one-and-a-half feet in the grave."

"You've done all the pioneering," Jess said weakly. "I hope my generation can live up to you."

"I'm not a pioneer now, I gave that up in 1904 when I

married." Mrs. McCormick added three fat lumps of sugar to her coffee. "Now I'm just rich." She grinned wickedly. "Very rich."

Jess knew the story—how beautiful Katherine Dexter was from Chicago, had graduated from MIT with a degree in biology in 1904, and shortly afterward had married a millionaire. When he died tragically, she inherited a very large fortune.

Jess ran the story over in her mind and again looked from Margaret Sanger to Katherine McCormick. It was all wrong, the devoted wife and wealthy widow should be the tiny woman with the tinkling laugh, the crusader for the rights of women should be the hulking figure in black. Suddenly the incongruity of it all struck her as hysterically funny. She could just see Shama's face when she told her about it. Jessie raised a cup of coffee to her mouth to hide her laughter.

"Now," Margaret looked at Celia, "you'll want a report on the latest progress."

"I'm fairly well up on what's happening," Celia said. "I've been in regular touch with Pincus in Worcester and Doctor Rock here in Boston." She turned to Jessica. "Did you know that years ago Cal almost joined Pincus and Chang in their research?"

"Cal? No, I didn't know that. I can't imagine him as anything but the society lady's favorite obstetrician."

"Doctor Caleb Morgan is Jessie's brother," Celia explained to the other two women. "When he was a resident at Memorial in the forties everyone thought he had a brilliant future in research. Pincus asked him to join the work at the foundation in Worcester. He didn't, of course." She turned to Jessica. "That was the year Susan got pregnant, the year Dav was born."

Katherine McCormick set her cup down hard. "There, that's it, that's what always happens. Poor girl, we're a decade too late for her. But we shall save the others."

"Poor girl, my foot. Susan's never done anything she didn't want to do." Jess spoke the words under her breath, more for herself than her listeners. They were unlikely to be interested in Morgan family dramas. She turned to the matriarch in black. "I'm told the research team is on the edge of a breakthrough, Mrs. McCormick, and it's all thanks to your generosity."

Mrs. McCormick leaned forward and fixed Jessica with her gaze. "Yes, child, I decided that what Margaret had always said was right. We must have a safe, simple, cheap contraceptive. I ordered it. I paid for it. I mean for us to have it."

Jessica could think of nothing to say. It had never occurred to her that you could request a scientific miracle as if it were a special cake the bakery could produce on demand.

"Jessie," Celia said, "I haven't told you the form that Pincus believes this new contraceptive will take. It's to be a pill, my dear, a perfectly ordinary looking pill that a woman need only take every morning. And once she does she won't be able to conceive."

Jessica looked at her in astonishment. "A pill? That's all?"

"That's all," Margaret Sanger said triumphantly. "No fiddling rubber caps or diaphragms, no messy jelly . . ."

"No waiting while the man has to pull on one of those ridiculous rubber overshoes," Mrs. McCormick added gleefully. "My solution will be an ordinary pill, like an aspirin. Once a woman takes it she can do what she likes with whom she likes—and for the first time in five thousand years she's not going to be left holding the baby."

The three septuagenarians looked at each other in triumph. Jessie stared at them. She was awestruck, but she was also choking with laughter. Shama simply wasn't going to believe that this conversation had ever taken place.

The Greyhound bus pulled into the Port Authority depot on West Forty-second Street at a few minutes past five. Shama lugged her two suitcases to the main concourse and stood staring at the bustling scene around her. Suddenly she felt very alone and very vulnerable. She'd been in New York before, on visits to see Daniel with Ruth. They'd stayed in Daniel's apartment on the East Side, and gone to the theater and shopped in the enormous and wonderful department stores. Those visits had not prepared her for this arrival.

People of every color and size were moving in all directions, a loudspeaker blared unintelligible information, and the smell of spicy hot dogs and greasy french fries wafted

from under an orange sign that said Nedick's. It was
unbearably hot. She felt perspiration streaming down her
back and knew that her green linen dress must look like
wilted lettuce. To make everything worse, she felt guilty.
She'd made up her mind at midnight, told Daniel and
Ruth at breakfast, and left at noon—all without a word to
Jessie.

She looked around and spied a bank of telephones.
Carrying one suitcase and kicking the other ahead of her,
she went toward them. She had to wait nearly five minutes for a booth to become available, but finally it did and
she went inside and dialed the number in Brookline.
"Ruthie, it's me. Yeah, I'm fine, but I want to talk to
Jess."

"She's not here. She came home a while ago, but she
went out again."

"Did you tell her I'd gone?"

"Of course," Ruth said. "She asked for you, I had to tell
her. She was very surprised, Shama. And a little hurt, I
think. You didn't tell her your plans?"

"No, I didn't see her after I made up my mind. Listen,
do you know where she's gone?"

"To her mother's, I think. You can call her there. Are
you at the Y?"

Shama said she wasn't yet, that she was going now, that
she'd speak to Ruth again in a couple of days. Then she
hung up and looked for enough change to make another
call. She only had a nickel and two dimes left, it wasn't
enough. She could call collect, of course, but she found
the idea daunting. Even after so many years she was still
intimidated by Emma. And struggling to get her suitcases
to someplace where they would give her change, then
back here to the telephones was just too much. She'd go to
the Y and call Jessie from there.

Somehow she managed to get the luggage and herself
out to Forty-second Street and into a taxi. "The Ninety-
second Street Y, please."

"On Lexington Avenue?"

"Yes, I think that's where it is." She'd never seen the
YM&WHA, hadn't even known it existed. But Ruth did.
"You're a Jewish girl, Shama, why should you stay at a
Christian place?"

"Y's aren't sectarian. Besides, I'm not Jewish, not the

way you are. I haven't been in a synagogue since I was six." Ruth had looked sad and a little surprised. "Okay," Shama had said. "I don't care which Y I stay at. I'll go to yours if it makes you happy."

So they had telephoned and reserved a room, and now she was on her way through the crowded Manhattan streets in this appalling, sticky heat to her very first home in the big city. It was just like Hollywood, she told herself. But she did not feel a bit like Doris Day or June Allyson, or the heroine of any other movie she'd ever seen. She felt terrible. She had been traveling for hours, was still traveling, and each minute of the journey was taking her farther from the man she loved, the man she was sure loved her. "Caleb," she whispered aloud in the back of the yellow cab. "Caleb, how am I going to live without you?"

The tears came then, they rolled down her cheeks in a silent, unstoppable stream. She fished in her bag and found some tissues and blew her nose loudly. The cab-driver looked at her in the rearview mirror. "You got hay fever, lady? I get it myself. It's awful this time of year. Comes from the ragweed."

She nodded and didn't say anything and blew her nose again.

Jessica found her mother sitting beside the window in her rose-and-gray bedroom. There was a tea tray on the small table beside her chair.

Emma looked up and smiled. "Hello, darling, you're a welcome surprise."

Jessie kissed her mother's cheek, then dropped to the floor beside her, ignoring the second chair. "Mom, do you think it's possible that women could avoid getting pregnant by taking a pill?"

Emma drew her elegant eyebrows together and thought for a moment. "Is this an academic question?"

"I suppose it is, for the moment."

"Very well, let me think." Then, after a few moments, "Theoretically I suppose it is. If for instance the pill contained some substance that killed the sperm, a sort of spermicide. But even if such a chemical existed, how fast would it be? How long before relations would one have to take this pill? I can think of a dozen other objections."

"You're on the wrong track. It's supposed to be a pill

you take very morning, like a vitamin or an aspirin. And you can never get pregnant as long as you keep taking it." Jessie put her fingers on the violet-sprigged china teapot and found it still warm. "Is there another cup around here?"

"I'll get Nora to bring you one."

"Don't bother, I can't imagine how the poor old dear continues to climb these four flights of stairs. I'll use your tooth glass." She went into the bathroom and returned carrying the glass. "Well, what do you think about the contraceptive aspirin?"

"It sounds fantastic. Unbelievable. Where did you hear about it?"

"From Celia, and Margaret Sanger and a millionaire witch lady named Katherine McCormick. A rich witch. She's footing the bill for all the research. It's a big secret, because of the law, but a doctor named John Rock is actually doing some clinical testing right here in Boston."

"My, you're moving in rarified company, Jess. I've heard of Mrs. McCormick." Emma settled back in her chair, watching her daughter. Jessie had turned out to be such a lovely young woman. She reminded Emma of her own mother. "Does Celia think this miracle pill is possible?"

"Yes. Definitely. She says that, simply put, it's going to stop women from ovulating, and if they don't ovulate they can't conceive."

Emma clapped her hands together. "No, of course they can't! It's so obvious, once you think of it. If they actually have a substance that can do that, if they're even close to it, then yes, Celia's right, it's highly possible."

"I thought so too. It all makes sense when you hear Celia and the other two explain it. But I wanted your opinion." She sipped the tea, it was lukewarm, not very good. She set down the glass. "Mom, if you hadn't stopped working to take care of Dad, you'd be involved, too, wouldn't you?"

"I suppose so, yes."

Jessie wanted to ask if Emma regretted her decision, if she hated the fact that this house had become a kind of prison for her. She couldn't find the words. They were closer now than they'd been when she was a child, her moving into Daniel's house in Brookline had somehow, paradoxical as it might sound, drawn them together. But her father's attempted suicide and its awful result was a forbidden place where neither dared to venture.

"Darling," Emma said quietly, "is your interest really research? If it is, maybe medical school is a roundabout way of going at things. You don't have to go to medical school, you know, just because you are Joshua Morgan's daughter."

Jessie winced. Hearing her father's name always made her wince. "It's not that. I'm not cut out for the laboratory, Mom. I want to work with people, with women. I suppose this sounds corny, but I want to carry the same torch you and Celia and those two women today have carried."

"It doesn't sound corny to me." Emma lay her hand on her daughter's head. "Let me play devil's advocate for a moment. Do you think this pill may be just a little too easy? May make us all a wee bit . . . well, perhaps the word is uncaring."

"You mean promiscuous. Will we all kick up our heels and become as raunchy as men? I don't know. I suppose it could happen like that." She looked up, meeting her mother's clear-eyed, aquamarine gaze. "If you'd had such an easy and certain form of birth control, I'd never have been born, would I?"

Emma was startled. She leaned back in her chair and considered the question. "No," she said finally, very softly, "no, I suppose you'd not have been born."

Jessie grinned. "That's what I figured. I've always known I was an accident."

"You mustn't think that means we didn't adore having you, darling. I mean, it's true we hadn't planned or expected another child, but there you were and—"

"It's okay, Mom. I'm a big girl, I understand such things. It's only that talking with those three this morning made me think of it. I went back to the house full of all of it. I was dying to tell Shama how extraordinary it was. There were those three old ladies, one of them a spinster, discussing sex the way they'd talk about a new hat. But Shama wasn't there. So I came here instead."

"Where is Shama?"

"She's gone to New York." Jessie studied her sandals and her white pedal pushers, anything to avoid looking at

Emma. "She decided to go early, and she left without saying a word to me about it."

"Jess, listen darling, you mustn't be hurt. I think Shama has a bit of a problem at the moment, some special unhappiness in her life. It may make her a little thoughtless."

Jessie looked up at her mother. "So you know about her and Cal?"

"There's not much to know, is there? She has a mad crush on him, has had for years."

"It's not a crush, Mom. She's in love with Cal. And he loves her."

"Jessie, it's impossible. Caleb is a married man with two children. And he's a great deal older than she is."

"Cal's married to a shrew, a bitch. The best thing he could do is divorce her."

"Jess! You mustn't say things like that, what about the boys?"

"If Cal could get rid of Susan and somehow get custody of Dav and John and marry Shama, it would be the best thing that ever happened to those two kids."

"Those are a great many ifs, and I know it's old-fashioned to say so, but I can't see how people can just divorce whomever they wish, whenever they wish. Marriage vows have to mean something or we have no basis for an orderly society."

"Nobody should have to live a whole life in as miserable a situation as Cal's in."

Emma didn't answer immediately. "I think we'd best agree to disagree. But I admire Shama taking herself out of it. It was the best thing she could possibly do."

"There wasn't any 'it' to take herself out of. She and Cal weren't having an affair, Mom. You shouldn't get that idea."

"My dear, such a thought would never occur to me."

Jessie smiled. "No, I guess it wouldn't. You are old-fashioned, as you've said."

Emma narrowed her eyes and tilted her head and studied her daughter. "Jessica, are you a virgin?"

"My God! Mom, that's none of your business."

"Isn't it? Well, nonetheless, I'm asking. Are you?"

"Why? If I'm not, will you lecture me on the sanctity of

marriage? Or are you going to tell me that nice girls don't and he won't respect me in the morning?"

"Neither," Emma said tartly. "I'm going to tell you—I *am* telling you that this pill is still pie in the sky as far as I know, and no birth control method is absolutely safe, and if you become pregnant, you as the woman will carry all the responsibility, at least in the practical sense. Nothing is worse, Jessica, than a marriage entered into because there's going to be a child."

"Is that why Cal married Susan?"

"I almost wish that were the reason," Emma said frankly. "But he adored her when he first met her, there's no denying it. And Dav wasn't born until they'd been married nearly two years." She glanced at her watch. "Now, that's enough chatter. Marya's with your father and it's time for me to relieve her. Don't leave for a moment so you can see her, darling. She stayed here with Daddy so that I could go to your graduation, but I know she was disappointed to miss it."

Jessica stood up, stretching her arms over her head and tossing back her heavy chestnut curls. "Yes, I will. Mom, Marya's the same age you are, isn't she? Fifty-nine?"

"Yes. Why?"

"I was just thinking that you're still beautiful, but she never was."

"Marya's beautiful inside, where it matters. Come with me, darling. You can say hello to Daddy too."

Jessica dropped her eyes and shook her head. "There's no point in saying hello to him, Mom. He doesn't hear us or see us or know whether we're dead or alive. He doesn't know if he's dead or alive."

"Jessie, you can't know that, no one knows it for sure, not even the specialists. For my part, I'm convinced he does know."

It was on the tip of Jessica's tongue to say in that case her mother should ask him how he could have done this to her, but she didn't. She never would. And even though she hated her father for what he'd done to his wife, she couldn't help but admire the courage with which Emma had shouldered the burden. "Okay, Mom, maybe you're right. But tell Marya I'm in the kitchen. I'll take this tray down while I'm about it."

It was when she got to the door Emma was holding

open for her because her hands were full of the tea things that Jessie paused. "Mom, about that question you asked me, just for the record, I am still a virgin. At least for the moment," she added with a wink. "Who knows what tomorrow might bring?"

"Now, Josh darling, I've had my little rest and I'm back. Shall we read some more of Mrs. Woolf? I know you didn't care much for the novels, neither did I. But these essays are quite wonderful, don't you agree?"

Emma picked up Virginia Woolf's *The Common Reader* and waited, as if Josh might actually turn to her and smile and offer an opinion one way or another. He didn't, he lay as he had lain for seven years, unmoving, staring into space. "No," she said, "perhaps you're right. It is rather warm this evening, and I'm feeling a bit too tired to read. We'll listen to music, and I'll knit a bit and tell you about Jessica. She came to see me," Emma continued as she selected a record and put it on the phonograph.

The sound of the overture of *The Mikado* filled the room. "Gilbert and Sullivan will cheer us both up. I was telling you about Jessie, she had an extraordinary morning. She actually met Margaret Sanger."

Emma picked up a blue sweater she was knitting for John and went on chatting, explaining about the birth control pill and what she'd said to her daughter about it, and Jessie's story of the incongruity of the three old ladies talking about contraception and sex. "She was longing to tell Shama all about it, but Shama's gone. She went to New York quite suddenly today. It's a good thing, I think. Very wise. She does have this awful crush on Caleb, and of course that can't ever come to anything. He'd never leave Susan and the boys, I'm sure of it."

Emma stopped speaking and stared at her husband. For a moment, for just the briefest part of a second, she'd have sworn that Joshua had moved a finger. No, of course he hadn't. She returned to her knitting, softly singing the words of the operetta along with the record. "My object all sublime, I will achieve in time, to let the punishment fit the crime, the punishment fit the crime. . . ."

17

*T*he bell rang over the door of Ruth's shop on an unseasonably raw and bleak October afternoon. She looked up and smiled. "Ben, how nice. It's a long time since I've seen you.".

"Too long, Ruth. I would have come before, but I didn't have an excuse." He lifted the clipboard he was carrying. "Today I've got one."

She came from behind the counter and stood on tiptoe to kiss his cheek. It seemed to her that Ben Porter had grown taller since his wife died two years before. Maybe it was only that he didn't stoop so much. "You don't need an excuse to visit me. Come, sit down. It's very quiet today. This kind of weather keeps everyone at home. I will make some tea."

When Porter first saw Le Petite Morocco, he'd called it an Aladdin's cave, and the impression was stronger than ever today. Bolts of cloth were stacked on the counters and had overflowed to most of the floor space by the door. He had to pick his way around the fabrics to follow her to the rear. "Where did you get all these wonderful things?"

"A shipment from my cousin in Marrakesh. They are nice, aren't they?" Ruth ran her hand over printed cottons in jewel colors and pastel silks.

"The colors are great. This one would make a lovely dress for you." He paused at a length of ivory-colored wool, gossamer sheer.

Ruth smiled. "That is the traditional wedding cloth of the Berbers. It's handwoven from bleached camel hair, and so thin because the tribeswomen make yards and yards of it into a special dress for the bride." He looked at her and didn't say anything. Inexplicably Ruth found herself blushing. "Sit here," she said quickly, pointing to an area marked out by a worn kilim carpet on which stood a red leather hassock worked in gold. "This is very old, it was made for the tent of an emir."

Ben looked doubtful, but did as he was told. The hassock was surprisingly comfortable. He waved his clipboard again. "I'm collecting signatures for a petition."

"Wait! That is very impolite, Ben. In Morocco you must not talk business until you have been social for a while. Especially in the tent of an emir. And first I must bring tea, or I am being impolite."

She disappeared into the back and returned almost immediately with a brass tray holding two glasses of steaming mint tea and a plate of little cookies. He took the tea and sipped it, watching her over the rim of the glass. "You look beautiful."

She blushed again. "I do not feel beautiful today."

"Why not?"

"I feel old. It's my birthday. I'm thirty-one."

"That seems pretty young to me. I'll be forty this year. Happy birthday."

"Thank you."

"Is the family taking you out to celebrate?"

"No, not until the weekend. Both Shama and Daniel are in New York, and Jessie is very busy at the medical school."

"So, your girls are grown up and out of the nest," Ben said. "You did a great job with them, Ruth. You should be proud."

"I did nothing. They are wonderful girls."

He smiled. "That's like you, even if it's not true. And not many ladies can point to two grown-up children when they're only thirty-one." Suddenly her eyes were full of tears. "Hey, what did I say? I'm sorry, Ruth, I didn't mean to upset you."

"It's not your fault. What I have been thinking all day is that I've never had a baby. And soon I will be too old. I love Shama and Jessie very much, but they are my little sisters, not my children."

He put down his glass and leaned over and took her

hand. "Look, it's none of my business, but did you and Daniel ever plan to have children?"

"I planned. Daniel has always said no."

He didn't think he should ask why. "Life's like that sometimes," he said softly. "But you've achieved so much, Ruth. Look at this terrific place." He waved his hand. "When you were a kid growing up in Morocco did you ever think someday you'd own a thriving business in Brookline, U.S.A.?"

"No. And if it were not for Daniel Morgan, I would not." She had answered yet again the question that was always unspoken between them: Why did she stay with Daniel when she was obviously unhappy? "I owe him everything, Ben. Me and Shama, God knows what would have happened to us if Daniel had not come into our lives."

He was still holding her hand and he squeezed it, then let it go. "I understand. Can I tell you about the petition now? It's that derelict building on South Street they're planning to pull down, some of us think it should be saved and rehabilitated. It has historical interest and it would make a great community center."

"You are still teaching me citizenship, Ben." She took the clipboard from beside the hassock. "Show me where I am supposed to sign."

"Good girl. Listen, I've got an idea. Will you have dinner with me tonight? That Italian place near your house maybe. To celebrate your birthday."

"You are very kind, Ben. But I am embarrassed. I did not mean to be asking for attention. . . ."

"You don't need to ask, my dear. And I don't often have the chance to take a lovely and interesting woman to dinner. Don't look so uncertain. I'm an old friend of the family, it's perfectly all right, Ruth."

She smiled and her whole face brightened. "Yes, you are right. Thank you, I would love to have an Italian dinner to celebrate my birthday."

"There's just one more patient waiting, Doctor, Miss Francis."

Daniel didn't glance up from the notes he was making in a thick file. "Fine, show her in."

Kitty Donnely didn't work with Daniel any longer, she

was far too wealthy, and too busy overseeing the vast empire which Nile Import & Export, renamed Nile Enterprises had become. The nurse who tiptoed out of the office was called Miss Clark and she had been with Daniel for five years, since he moved his private practice to this prestigious building on upper Park Avenue. She was sixty some, lived in the Bronx with her aged mother, and kept a small carving on her desk—the three monkeys depicting see no evil, hear no evil, do no evil. Miss Clark knew exactly how Dr. Morgan liked things. She'd left the syringes and the hypodermic needle ready on a sterile tray.

The reception room was paneled in bleached wood and had a pale cream-colored rug on the floor. The chairs were comfortable and covered in yellow-and-white chintz. There were fresh flowers on Miss Clark's desk and the magazines scattered about were all current editions. It was a very nice place to wait, but the patients left it willingly when it was their turn to enter the private office. No one who came here dreaded a visit to the doctor.

"Doctor will see you now, Miss Francis."

Mimi Francis stepped eagerly through the door the nurse held open, waited until it had closed behind her, then leaned over the desk and kissed Daniel's mouth. "Hello, you darling man. Are you ready for me?"

"Always ready and willing, Mimi. How have you been feeling?"

"Wonderful. Whatever you're giving me is absolutely marvelous. I've lost four more pounds, Daniel. And I feel great."

He smiled. He heard a variation on that theme every day. Like many of his patients, Mimi Francis was in show business, and she'd come to him because she was gaining weight and feeling depressed. "I know you've helped other women with similar problems. I only hope you can help me." There had been more than a hint of desperation in her voice on that day four months ago when she first consulted him. "If you can't, I'll never get another part, and I'll probably kill myself. I know that sounds melodramatic, but it's true."

Daniel thought it quite possibly was. They were pure ego these women, their only measure for personal success was how they saw themselves reflected in someone else's eyes. Daniel could make them thin by suppressing their appetites, and raise their spirits in the bargain. That made him God. "I can help you," he'd promised. "The vitamins I use will change your life."

He'd kept his promise, more or less. Mimi was twenty pounds lighter than when he'd first seen her, she'd just landed a part in a new Broadway musical, and she was so full of energy she hardly ever slept more than four hours a night. "Shall I weigh you?" Daniel asked. "Or are you past needing that reassurance now. You look terrific."

"You have to weigh me, there's no scale quite like yours, Daniel." She smiled and drew her tongue over her lips. "I'll just go behind the screen and get undressed."

Daniel remained where he was, watching her shadow as she stripped. He wasn't sure he was quite up to Mimi today. He'd had a hell of a lot to drink last night. On the other hand, she did what she did better than any woman in New York. He stood up and walked to the scales.

She came naked to meet him. A sheet was provided for his patients to wrap themselves in, but once they'd lost a few pounds almost none of the women bothered. Even the few who didn't want anything but the injections got a kick out of showing their bodies to handsome Dr. Morgan. Mimi went beyond that.

"How do I look?" She spun around so he could admire her.

"Delicious." It was true. She had a small, compact body, a bit too thin now, but still a pleasure to look at. "Let's see what you weigh."

She jumped on the scales; he manipulated the weight. "One hundred and two pounds and two ounces," he said. "That's as thin as you should get, Mimi. I'm going to cut you back to two pills a day." He would have preferred to stop them all together, but he knew that wouldn't work. He'd tried it before with other patients and it never worked. Not cold turkey. His judgment was confirmed by the look in her eyes.

"I can't manage without the pills. I'll get fat again."

"No, you won't. Not if you're sensible." He put his hand beside her cheek. "Trust me, Mimi."

"I do," she murmured. "But I can have the shot, can't I?"

"Yes, of course. The vitamins are good for you."

She took his hand and guided it to her left buttock. "You're going to put it right here, aren't you?"

"Yes," he kneaded her flesh. "Right here."

"Oh, good, I want it so much."

"You have to earn it, Mimi," he whispered. "If you're not a good girl I can't give it to you."

"I'll be very good," she promised as she sank to her knees and put her fingers on the zipper of his trousers.

In the outer office the telephone rang. "Oh yes, Miss Morhaim, doctor was expecting your call. But he's with a patient now. He can't be disturbed. Can he call you back?"

"Sure," Shama said. "Tell him I'm at the Y and I'll wait." When she hung up she thought again about Daniel's devotion to his patients. She'd been struck by it when she moved to the city four months earlier. Her brother-in-law never for any reason allowed a consultation to be interrupted by a telephone call.

Shama looked over the lunch menu. "I'd love the chicken Kiev, but it's so damned fattening. I've put on a few more pounds, Daniel. I think I'd better start coming to you for treatment."

His face darkened. "Don't be ridiculous. Have a salad. Just take in a few less calories each day and get some exercise."

"Running up and down the stairs to that new apartment will be plenty of exercise. Four flights and no elevator, I think maybe I'm crazy."

She had located a three-room apartment on the corner of Seventy-fifth Street and Third Avenue. The area had improved dramatically since the El had been torn down, but the building was old and there was no elevator. "It will be good for you," he said. "When do you move in?"

Before she could answer a waiter appeared. Shama ordered a chef's salad and a Coke, Daniel said he'd have a tuna sandwich. "And bring me another one of these, please." He gestured to his empty glass.

"Another Johnnie Walker on the rocks, right away, sir." The waiter moved off.

Shama looked at Daniel, but didn't comment. "I move in the first of next month," she said instead. "But I have to get some furniture before that."

"Go to Altman's and pick out whatever you want. Put it on my account."

"No, I won't do that, Daniel. There's no need. I'm earning a hundred dollars a week at *La Vie*, I can manage."

"A hundred dollars a week doesn't go very far in New York these days."

"I can manage," she repeated. "A dollar down and a dollar when they catch me. No, don't argue," she held up a forestalling hand. "Look, I'm delighted to be asked out to lunch, but I really called to remind you that it's Ruthie's birthday. Have you called her?"

"No, I forgot. I'll do it this afternoon. She'll be at the shop, I suppose."

"Sure, on a Wednesday where else would she be?"

"At a bridge club maybe, or at home, or at the hair-dresser's."

"Daniel, Ruth's not cut out for that kind of life. You know she isn't. Why do you resent her business?"

"I don't resent it."

"Yes, you do. It's obvious in every word you say, and you never want to talk to her about it."

He shrugged. The waiter brought his fresh drink and Daniel took a long swallow. "I don't know why it's been my fate to be surrounded by career women. Starting with my mother when I was a kid."

Shama settled back in her seat and eyed him. "Yes, that's really at the bottom of it. Emma *la formidable*. She's a great lady, but pretty intimidating. I suppose it was worse when you were a kid and she worked."

"Spare me the fruits of your psychology course. Tell me what they have you doing at that magazine."

"What I was hired to do. I translate articles from French and Arabic into English." Her salad came and she poured dressing liberally on the greens.

"You've just defeated the whole value of ordering a salad and not chicken Kiev," Daniel said. "And who in America wants to read articles translated from Arabic?"

"Salad without dressing is boring. I won't have dessert. And I've been wondering about the articles myself. Some of them are pretty stupid diatribes against American foreign policy. Ali says the purpose of them is just to show people here what the other side is thinking."

"Who's Ali?" He caught the waiter's eye and gestured for another drink.

"My boss, Ali Fatah. He's from Kuwait. His father sent him to Oxford, then gave him a few billion to play with.

Ali used some of it to start *La Vie*. Daniel, that's your third scotch, don't you have to work this afternoon?"

"This Ali sounds like a jerk, a spoiled playboy type. And don't tell me how much to drink. You've never seen me drunk in your whole life, have you?"

"No, of course not."

"So forget it. I have a high tolerance."

They spent the rest of the lunch talking about Shama's apartment, and when they were ready to leave and Daniel paid the bill, she didn't comment on the fact that he hadn't touched his sandwich. "You'll remember to call Ruthie, won't you?"

"Sure. Take care of yourself, kid. I'll see you at Grand Central Friday night."

When he got back to his office, Daniel put his hand on the telephone, then hesitated. A moment later he buzzed his nurse instead of picking up the receiver. "Call Penn the Florist in Boston, will you? Have them deliver two-dozen roses to my wife. Make sure they do it this afternoon, it's her birthday."

Two days before Christmas Mimi Francis appeared at Daniel's office without an appointment. "I have to see Doctor Morgan right away."

"I'm not sure he can see you, Miss Francis. Doctor is leaving for the holiday in a little while. I can give you an appointment early next week."

"I have to see him now," Mimi repeated, her voice rising on a shrill note.

The nurse went in to Daniel. "It's Miss Francis. She looks terrible, and she says she has to see you. I tried to put her off, but she wouldn't buy it. I think she's very upset about something, Doctor."

Daniel had already taken off his white coat and cleared his desk. He hesitated, then sighed. "Okay, send her in."

The nurse was right, she looked awful. Her hair was disheveled and her skin had a sickly-green palor. "What's the trouble, Mimi?"

"I'm a wreck, Daniel. A bundle of nerves. Ever since you cut back my pills it's been getting worse. Now I don't have any left."

"Why not? I gave you a three-month supply in October, Mimi. You shouldn't need any more until January."

"It was only a three-month supply if I cut back the dosage."

"The way I told you to."

"Yes."

She didn't look at him, simply stared at her hands. Daniel followed her glance, and noticed that the nails were all bitten to the quick. "You didn't cut back, did you?"

"I couldn't. Jesus, Daniel, I'm in a new show, I couldn't." She raised her face to his. Puffy, he noticed, as well as pale. And her eyes were dull. And when she spoke there was a tremor in her voice as well as the threat of imminent hysteria. "I couldn't get to rehearsals or keep going unless I took three or four a day. I'm very low on vitamins, Daniel. You know how I am. I took the last pill a week ago and I've been a wreck ever since. C'mon, just give me a shot now and a new prescription, then we can both go and enjoy our Christmas."

He stared at her. It was hard to imagine this shattered woman enjoying anything. "What are you doing for Christmas?" he asked softly. "Do you have family here in the city?"

Mimi shook her head. "Not here, I'm from Minnesota. Haven't been back in years. But don't think I'm going to be all alone." Her smile was so broad it looked like a grin painted on a doll, an enameled grimace. "I've got a million friends. I'm going to invite lots of them for Christmas dinner, get a turkey, do the whole thing. . . . If I can get my act together, that is." She leaned forward, extending both hands to him across the desk. "Please, Daniel. If you want, I'll even—"

He felt a sudden wave of nausea. "There's no quid pro quo, Mimi. It's never been that."

"I know," she murmured. "Sorry, I'm a little crazy today. Help me, Daniel. For God's sake, help me."

He stared at her a moment longer, then got up and took the key ring from his pocket and unlocked the drug cabinet.

He thought about it all during the train journey. He and Shama were in the club car, the atmosphere was joyous and convivial, awash in Christmas spirit, but he couldn't get Mimi Francis out of his mind.

"What's wrong?" Shama asked. "You haven't said a word to me in an hour."

Daniel took a long swallow of scotch, he wasn't sure if this was his fifth or his sixth drink, and set down the glass.

"Sorry, I'm thinking about a patient. I'm not sure about the best treatment for her."

Shama accepted that, she turned back to a conversation with the woman sitting at the table behind theirs. Daniel watched them, but what he was seeing was Mimi's distraught face. He knew the best treatment for her—she had to be weaned from amphetamine dependency, but he wasn't sure how to effect it, or how to get her to admit she needed it. What was wrong with being dependent on vitamins? she would ask. He had to get her away from her usual environment, some place where she could be watched and controlled. They should have a clinic of some sort, in the country maybe, a place where he could put patients like Mimi Francis. Yeah, that was a good idea, a great one. He'd talk to Kitty about it right after Christmas. Hell, it might even be a big money-maker.

Boston was at her best during Christmas. The lampposts of the cobblestoned streets around Louisbourg Square and Beacon Hill were hung with garlands of fresh greenery and there were candles in very window. The trees in the center island that bisected Commonwealth Avenue were strung with tiny white lights and there was a lovely crèche on the Common. In 1954 nature made the picture complete; on the night of the twenty-third it snowed just enough to frost the world white.

"I always liked this time of year best of all," Daniel said and reached for Ruth's hand. They were walking along Newbury Street, looking in the windows, buying a few last-minute gifts. It was Christmas Eve, almost five o'clock, Ruth had closed Le Petite Morocco just a few hours earlier. Now she let him hold her hand for a moment, then took it away.

Daniel was acutely conscious of the gesture, then chose to ignore it. "Look at that little cat." He pointed to a china Siamese one in a shop window. "Jessie would like that."

They went in and bought the cat. "That's it for me," Daniel said when the package had been added to the load he already carried. "Do you need anything else?"

Ruth looked at him wordlessly a moment, then shook her head. "No, I have everything."

"Good, we'll go have a cup of coffee then."

He took her arm, this time she didn't pull away, and he

shepherded her across the road to a small café that sold fancy teas and special coffees and little pastries. The crowd was rapidly thinning as everyone finished their last-minute shopping. Daniel spotted a free table in the rear and they took it, piling their purchases and their coats on an extra chair. Ruth said she'd have espresso and he ordered it, and a cappuccino for himself, and waited until the waitress had gone to say, "I always think you're a great sport about the Morgan Christmas carryings-on, Ruthie. I know it's hard for you since you're not a Christian."

She shrugged. "It's a family holiday, I see it from that point of view."

They'd had this conversation a number of times over the years. He nodded and didn't say more. The coffees came, Ruth dropped a lump of sugar in her tiny cup and stirred it thoughtfully. She was lovely, he decided. The cold had put roses in her cheeks. But her big, dark eyes seemed sad. "What are you thinking?" he asked softly. "What's bugging you, Ruthie?"

"Nothing." She spoke so quietly he almost couldn't hear her.

"There is something. You seem worried, so it's not nothing."

"I meant nothing new. The same thing is 'bugging' me, Daniel. Always the same thing."

The cappuccino suddenly tasted bitter and he set down the cup. "You and me? That's what you mean, isn't it?"

"I suppose. I was thirty-one in October, Daniel. I guess it's too late for me to have a baby now."

"Not necessarily," he said quickly. "Plenty of women have babies late in life. My mother was thirty-eight when Jessie was born."

She looked up at him her eyes searching his face. "I don't want to wait until I'm thirty-eight. There's no reason for me to wait, is there?"

"No . . . Yes . . . Oh, shit, Ruthie. I just don't know."

The waitress brought the check. "Hope you folks don't mind, we're getting ready to close for the holiday."

Daniel paid and they gathered up their things and went outside and walked to where he'd parked the Studebaker. On the drive back to Brookline he started to say something about having a baby, but Ruth stopped him. "Not now, Daniel. We have to go to your mother's and there isn't time. We'll talk after Christmas."

*   *   *

Many rituals attended Christmas Eve at 165 Commonwealth Avenue, most of them had been inaugurated years
before. Emma had always given Tessie and Nora the evening off, so there was a cold buffet supper spread out on
the dining room table and everyone helped himself while
trimming the tree. "Have some more ham, Cal," Emma
urged her son. "Dav, darling," she told her grandson,
"that little soldier has always hung just there on the left.
Yes, it's perfect now."

As usual there were massed poinsettia plants and a
single white candle in each of the drawing room windows,
and carols on the radio until the live carolers arrived on
Commonwealth Avenue. Emma wore the same bright green
silk gown she'd worn every year since her family could
remember, and the rest of them were dressed in finery to
suit the occasion. One thing was different, however. One
ritual had come into being only since Joshua entered his
living death.

Emma put a small tree on a table at the foot of his bed.
During the evening they all went one by one upstairs to
the former library and put an ornament on that tree and
wished Joshua a merry Christmas.

"Have you been up to see your father yet?" Shama
stood beside Cal at the small Sheraton table that held the
cut-glass bowl filled with eggnog.

"Yes, I'm always the first. How are you, Shama? How's
New York?"

"It's fine, so am I. You?"

"Fine, fine."

She filled a small glass cup with pale yellow eggnog, but
didn't drink. "You're not," she murmured. "Neither am I.
It's a lot of crap."

"Shama, don't. Please."

"Not tonight. I know. Cal, meet me someplace over the
weekend. Just so we can talk."

"I can't. There's no point."

"Caleb." Susan's voice came between them. She was
standing across the room by the windows, but her words
sliced the air as if they were a whip. "Caleb, would you
get me another drink, please?"

He looked at Shama, their eyes meeting for a moment
before he turned abruptly and walked away.

Emma had been watching. "Your turn to go upstairs, Shama," she said brightly. "Then John and he's the last."

Shama was given a small golden bell trimmed with red velvet ribbon and she carried it up the stairs. Marya was sitting beside Joshua's bed. Shama smiled at her, and looked at the Christmas tree and hung her bell on a branch, then stood staring at it for a moment. Finally she turned and let her eyes rest on the man for whom this whole charade was played.

He was as he'd been for so long now that she couldn't remember him as anything but a shrunken, unmoving figure. For Shana even the sense of tragedy had gone. She simply felt sorry for Emma. Joshua had died years ago and she'd stopped mourning him. "He doesn't know a thing, does he?" she asked Marya. "It's really for Emma's sake that we act out this comedy."

The older woman was crocheting, her needle continued to fly even as she spoke. "Maybe he knows more than we realize," she said placidly. "It's no harm to think so."

"Yes, it is." Shama was suddenly passionate. "It's harmful to the living to concentrate on the dead."

She turned and ran from the room. Marya stopped crotcheting and leaned over and smoothed the pristine sheet on the bed. "Don't mind her, Doctor Josh, she's young and full of life and she doesn't understand. Now, here comes little John. I can tell because always he runs, never walks. Just like Daniel used to do."

The child dashed into the room. "Merry Christmas, Marya. Merry Christmas, Grandpa. I'm the last one so I have the angel for the top!" He reached up and put it in place. None too gently. There was a dangerous moment when the tree tottered and swayed. Marya sprang to catch it, but there was no need. The tree settled and the papier-mâché angel smiled brightly from the topmost branch.

When Marya turned back to the bed, John was standing beside his grandfather, staring at him. "Isn't he ever going to talk to me? Never in his whole life?"

Marya put an arm around the child's shoulders. "He can't, my pet. There was an accident and he can't speak. But I know what he'd say if he could."

John turned his face up to hers. "What?"

"He'd say, 'Merry Christmas, John. I love you very much.'"

The little boy nodded, then turned back to his grandfather. "Well, if he could understand me, I'd say I love him too. I mean, I would if he could talk to me." He tore himself from her grip and ran from the room.

Marya smiled at Joshua. "You heard him, Doctor Josh. I'm sure you did. And I think maybe your fingers twitched again, the way Mrs. Emma says they sometimes do."

Christmas day they all spent in their separate homes. Ruth made a wonderful meal as she did every year. A turkey, of course, but stuffed with couscous and raisins, and she served spicy Moroccan pickles and cooked the sweet potatoes in coconut milk. Last year Ben Porter had been with them Christmas day. She'd invited him this year, but he'd refused.

"If the store ever starts boring you, open a restaurant," Jessie said, helping herself to more of everything. "You'll make a fortune."

"You and Shama ought to be writing down all Ruthie's recipes," Daniel said. "So the tradition gets carried on."

Ruth stared at him for a moment, but she didn't say anything until later. Not until sometime after four when Shama and Jessica went out for a walk because it was a bright, sunny day, and she and Daniel were alone and had carried their coffee into the den. She watched him lace his liberally with brandy, then she asked, "Daniel, do you want to divorce me?"

He looked at her and opened his mouth, but no words came. He took a long swallow of the coffee and it burned his throat. Ruth was still watching him, waiting for him to say something. "What in hell gave you an idea like that?"

"You don't want to have a child with me, you only come home a few days each month. Why should you want to stay married to me?"

"Because . . . because you're my wife. Why does anybody stay married?"

"Because they love each other. At least that's how it should be."

"The world isn't often the way it should be, Ruthie," he said softly. "I think you know that better than most."

She nodded, her dark eyes grave and her small form very still and composed. "Yes, but sometimes circumstances change. We don't have to go on doing what we had to do before."

Daniel ran his fingers through his hair and stood up and fussed with the logs in the fireplace. "You're talking riddles. I'm not good at all with this Eastern inscrutability."

"It's not a riddle, Daniel. It's very simple really. You married me and took Shama and me out of misery into a wonderful new life. You've done everything anyone could ever expect. You've been heroic, but you don't have to be anymore. Shama and I can both take care of ourselves now."

He poked the embers savagely and didn't look at her. "You're talking a lot of horseshit. You and Shama are my family. I love you."

"I know you do. But it is not the love of a husband for a wife, Daniel. I have known that for some time, but I told myself you needed me and it was my duty to say nothing, to be what you wanted me to be. But I've failed in that, I thought you wanted me to be independent, so I opened the shop, but you hate it. I thought I pleased you in bed, but you haven't wanted that from me for months and months. So now I realize you stay with me from a sense of duty, and I don't want it."

Daniel flung down the poker and went to the bar and poured four fingers of whisky into a glass. "This is all because I don't want to have a baby, isn't it?"

"Not the way you mean." She rose from the couch and went to him but they didn't touch. "I am trying to understand what is behind your not wanting a baby."

"Shit," he said again. "Ruthie, listen to me. My life hasn't gone the way I expected it to. It never has, tides keep coming along and sweeping me up and I find that I can swim pretty good, so I just go on doing it. Do you understand?"

She shook her head.

"No, I know you don't. Listen, my practice—" He broke off. There was simply no way on earth he could explain to her about his practice or what had preceded it. "If we had a baby, and if there was some kind of trouble later, that would be awful. A father should be someone like my father was. I've never been like him, an upstanding pillar of the community, a legend in medicine."

"I would not want you to be like Joshua." She lowered her eyes. "In the end he could not face his life, Daniel. I don't think that is such a thing to be admired."

"We were grown up by then, it didn't matter."

Ruth shivered and walked to the fire and stood beside it. "You're cold," Daniel said. "Shall I get you a sweater?"

"No, Daniel, I can't go on."

He stood very still, closed his eyes, then opened them. Nothing had changed. She was still standing there with her back to him, the words had not been retracted. "That's what this is about, you're the one who wants a divorce." She didn't answer. "That's it, isn't it?" he repeated.

Her reply was a tiny whisper. "I think so. Yes."

"Because I won't have a baby."

"Because you don't need me. I need to be needed, Daniel, to be loved. I need to have a purpose in life."

He knew what he wanted to say, the sentences were all formed in his mind, he had merely to open his mouth and speak them and everything would be set to rights. *I need you, Ruthie. I need you so damned much it's untrue. You're my anchor, my life jacket. You keep me sane, you make me know that there are honest, decent people in an honest, decent world, and that when I'm with you I'm part of that world* . . . He could not make himself say any of it, because if he did she would drop any notion of leaving him and stay. And he could not add that to his catalogue of sins. Without another word he set down his glass and went into the hall and grabbed his jacket and walked out of the house.

He walked for hours, all the way to the river and then along it, unaware of Boston on his right or Cambridge on his left, miles and miles. At some point he turned away from the Charles and eventually he came to South Station. It was after midnight by then and he went into the terminal and found a bar that was open despite the hour and the holiday, and he sat drinking a long time. Until the guy behind the bar said, "Don't you think you've had enough, bud?" And Daniel agreed that he had, and he got up and realized that his legs were rubber and he had to sit down for a while, maybe sleep.

The all-night movie was running, so he found a quarter and bought a ticket and went inside. Newsreels and cartoons and what they called "short subjects" flashed before his eyes in grainy black and white and gray, and he slouched in the seat in the comfort of the dark, and for a while he slept.

It was after six A.M. when he staggered out of the

theater, bleary-eyed, unshaven, a sour taste in his mouth. He still wasn't entirely sober, but he needed to be. So he could think it through. So far none of it made any sense, not the kind of sense he wanted—the kind that would be some justification for maintaining things the way they were. The Rexall Drug Store in the station was just opening and he went in. A pimply-faced kid behind the counter was pouring ground coffee into a huge machine.

"How long before that's ready?" Daniel asked.

"Twenty minutes maybe. You want some juice meanwhile?"

"Yeah. Orange juice."

The boy poured it from a large glass bottle. "I got the grill lit, you want some eggs?"

"No thanks. Just this, and coffee and toast."

"Okay. I won't make the toast until the coffee's done."

Daniel nodded agreement and sipped the orange juice. There was a mirrored wall behind the fountain, but he avoided looking at himself. The kid slouched against the counter and read the morning edition of the *Record*. It was pretty thin, day after Christmas, not much news. Not that the *Record* was big for news out of Washington or Europe.

"Should be done now," the kid said, laying the newspaper down beside Daniel as he reached for a cup and saucer.

Daniel's eyes scanned the page automatically. The story was at the bottom. There was even a picture of Mimi sprawled half-naked on her bed. ACTRESS DIES OF LONELI-NESS the headline blared. "Mimi Francis was found dead in New York late yesterday afternoon. Neighbors summoned the fire department when smoke began pouring out the door of the actress's apartment. They broke in and found the source of the smoke, a turkey cooking in the oven. The table had been set for Christmas dinner, but apparently no one who was invited had shown up. Miss Francis was already dead when the firemen found her, and while the first impression was that she'd succumbed to smoke inhalation, this reporter has learned that an empty pill bottle was found beside her . . ."

"Hey, mister, don't you want your coffee?"

Daniel ignored the shout and ran from the drugstore.

He still had a key to his parents' house. No one was around when Daniel let himself in. He heard some noise from upstairs in his father's room. The night nurse getting him washed no doubt. He stared up the stairs, then turned and went into the drawing room.

Nora found him there about an hour later. He was sitting in a chair that he'd pulled over by the window, staring into the street. There was a half-empty bottle of scotch beside him.

"Mr. Daniel . . . I'll bring some coffee, you just wait right here."

"No coffee, Nora. Can you please tell my mother I'm here and I'd like to talk to her."

Minutes later Emma came in. "Daniel, what's wrong?"

"Everything. I don't know why I've come here to put it all on you."

"Why shouldn't you?" Emma crossed to him and stroked the hair back from his forehead. "You look terrible, darling. And you smell worse." She reached down and retrieved the bottle. "And you've had enough of this for a while. Nora is bringing some coffee."

"I told her not to."

"Well, I told her to ignore you. Here she is now. Thank you, Nora. Just leave the tray there. I'll take care of it."

Emma poured strong black coffee into a cup and stirred in two sugars and brought it to her son. "Drink this, and when you can, tell me what's happened."

He swallowed the scalding liquid in one gulp. Emma took the cup and refilled it. "Ruth wants a divorce," he said tonelessly. "I don't blame her. It's been a pretty empty marriage from her point of view, but I can't think how I'm going to live without her."

"It doesn't seem to me you've exactly lived with her for some time." Emma spoke quietly, there was nothing judgmental in her tone. "No doubt, that's why she wants a divorce. Ruth is extremely loyal, Daniel. And she does love you, at least she did. I think you could fix things if you made some changes."

"Move back to Boston, you mean. Close the practice in New York. Start a family."

"That sounds like a good prescription." Emma sipped her own coffee and watched her son. "It would be an excellent start, Daniel. Are you going to do it?"

"I can't."

"Why not?"

"I can't simply up and walk away from the setup I'm in. It's not that simple."

"I repeat, why not?"

"I have partners for one thing."

Emma was surprised at how clear his words were. He wasn't slurring them, though she'd thought he was drunk as a lord. But he wasn't looking at her, he still stared out the window. "Partners can be bought out, Daniel. If it's a question of money, I can help."

He shook his head. "I have plenty of money." He hesitated. "Maybe you're right. Maybe Kitty and Abdul would have a price."

"Who are Kitty and Abdul?"

"My partners."

Emma took a deep breath. She knew what question she had to ask, and that she didn't want to. But she made herself say the words. "Partners in what, Daniel?"

"In the abortion clinics we've been running since just after the war." He heard her gasp but he didn't stop. "And all the side businesses they've led to. Most of them are legitimate, import and export of one type or another, but they were all financed by a special sort of D and C, issued on demand."

For a moment she buried her face in her hands, then she steeled herself. "I'm not entirely surprised, darling. I had some suspicions many years ago. But I preferred not to confront you with them. I think your father suspected, too, and chose, as I did, not to question you."

"Sorry," he said softly. "Not exactly acceptable behavior for the son of Emma and Joshua Morgan. I know that."

For a second her glance flickered toward the sickroom upstairs. "I'm no longer sure exactly what is acceptable behavior. Daniel, why have you told me all this now?"

"Because somebody has to understand why I can't do what Ruth wants. How the hell can I bring a child into the world when its father is under a cloud like that?"

She shrugged. "I'm not sure, but people do."

"I can't. It's not just the abortions, I even think they're justified whatever the law. It's more than that."

Don't tell me, she wanted to shout. *I don't want to know. I can't cope, Daniel. I can't help you. I haven't any more strength for anyone.* Instead she said, "What more?"

"My practice. I don't treat sick people. I minister to

neurotic women who think if they can just lose a few pounds their whole world will change."

"That doesn't sound so terrible."

"That's what I told myself for years. What the hell, if they feel better about themselves and look a little better, what's the harm? But there's only one painless way to do it. Amphetamines. They suppress the appetite and give a lot of temporary energy. But they are addictive, of course."

"Of course," Emma agreed. "And that's what you give some of your patients, amphetamines?"

"Not some, all of them." He turned to her. She was wearing a tailored, blue flannel bathrobe and her hair was in a single braid down her back. It was still mostly red, except for the silver wings at the temples, and she was still a beautiful woman. "Those ladies are the only patients I have, Mom. I haven't practiced real medicine since I got home from the war. So, I can't just say, sorry, I took a wrong turn somewhere, and do an about-face and come back to Boston and hang out a shingle and live happily ever after with my wife and the child she wants so desperately. It's too late."

Emma took a step toward him. "Maybe it's not, darling. It's never too late."

"Yes, it is. One of my patients died yesterday. I saw it in this morning's paper. They don't have the coroner's report yet, but believe me, I know exactly what it will say. She overdosed on Benzedrine. They found an empty pill bottle beside her bed. I gave her a prescription for sixty tablets four days ago. The newspaper didn't say so yet, but it's my name on that bottle."

Emma was frozen, rooted to the floor. "What are you going to do?"

"I'm not sure yet. But I've got to go back to the city and get a lawyer. I wanted you to know because it's going to make a hell of a stink. Ruth's going to need help. The rest of the family too. I'm sorry, Mom. It doesn't make anything better, but at least I wanted to say it. I'm so damned sorry."

The news reached Ruth at two-thirty on the afternoon of that same day after Christmas. She was downstairs in the house on Carrington Avenue when the policeman came to the door.

"Mrs. Morgan?"

"Yes."

"May I come in a moment, ma'am?"

Ruth stepped back and opened the door wider. "Yes, of course. What is it, Officer?"

"Is there anybody with you, ma'am?"

She shivered, and told herself she was being ridiculous. Years ago both Ben Porter and Daniel had taught her about the police in America. They weren't anything to be afraid of unless you'd done something wrong. And she hadn't. She glanced at the stairs. "Just my sister and my sister-in-law, they're upstairs. My husband went back to New York this morning. He's a doctor, his practice is in Manhattan."

She looked at the policeman and thought about Daniel. He'd come home about ten and not said a word to her, even though she tried to talk to him, to tell him she hadn't meant what he'd thought yesterday. Of course she'd stay with him if he wanted her to. But Daniel didn't want to discuss anything. He showered and changed and took the Studebaker and said he was driving back to the city. She'd begged him not to go, but it hadn't stopped him.

"It's about Doctor Morgan I've come, ma'am," the policeman said. He spoke very gently, as if she were a child. "I'm afraid there's been an accident. On the Merritt Parkway."

"Oh no! Where is Daniel? No, don't bother to explain. Wait, I'll get my coat. You must take me to him . . ."

"There's no hurry, ma'am. I'm sorry, there's not anything you can do now. It was a head-on collision. Doctor Morgan died instantly."

18

"*I*s this everything, Miss Clark?" Caleb glanced from the pile of files on the desk to the nurse.

"Everything as far as I know." The woman was twisting a handkerchief in her fingers and her eyes were red. "I didn't write the patients' notes, you understand. Doctor Morgan always did that himself. I only kept the records of appointments and billings."

"Yes, I understand. Thank you, and look, wouldn't you like to go home? I won't need you any longer and I can lock up when I'm done."

"Thank you, Doctor. That's very kind. I am rather upset. It's such a shock. He was always so nice to me. . . ." She sniffled into the handkerchief, "When did you say the funeral was?"

"Tomorrow afternoon at Trinity Church in Boston."

"Boston, I see. I'm afraid I won't be able to go. I live with my aged mother, she's not well."

"I understand. I'll mention the circumstances to my mother and to Doctor Morgan's wife. Now, go on home, Miss Clark. I'll be sending a check in a few days, six months' salary since this was so sudden."

She murmured her gratitude and left him alone with the pile of folders. Cal sat down behind Daniel's desk, in Daniel's chair, and stared at him. Once or twice he reached for the topmost file, but each time he pulled back. He did not want to read the history of his brother's treatments.

But he had to, before the police did. That's what his mother had said, and she was right.

Emma had phoned him yesterday afternoon at a few minutes past three. "Cal, you must come here at once. It's an emergency."

He'd thought it was his father, but she'd told him it wasn't, and nothing more until he was facing her in her rose-and-gray bedroom. "You've been crying, Mom. What's the matter?"

"Your brother is dead. He was killed in an automobile accident a couple of hours ago."

Just like that, the bald words. They hit him like a blow to the midsection, and he'd gasped and sat down hard. It was a long few moments before he could speak. When he did, he asked all the usual things. "How did it happen? Does Ruth know?"

"The accident occurred on the Merritt Parkway," Emma said. "Daniel had been drinking very heavily, and he took it in his head to drive back to New York today. And yes, Ruth knows. She's the one who telephoned me."

"Oh, God, Daniel . . ." He wanted to mourn his twin, to think about the fact that he was never again going to see the other half of himself. He wanted to tell his mother that she need not be so controlled, to put his arms around her and ease some of the rigidity from those determined shoulders, but there were others whose need for comfort was greater than his or hers. "I'd better go over there, Mom. I'll bring Ruth and Jessie and Shama here."

"Yes. That's my idea, too, but I had to see you alone first. There is something more that must be done, Caleb, and you're the only one who can do it. I have a very unpleasant story to tell you."

And she'd told him the things her other son had told her just that morning. She did it the same way she'd announced Daniel's death, without fanfare or any attempt to soften the truth. "I have suspected for some time that there was something not quite ordinary about Daniel's practice in New York," she'd said finally. "Perhaps you have too. No, don't say anything yet, I'm not finished."

Emma didn't continue immediately. She walked to her dressing table and picked up a silver-framed picture of her twin sons, aged eight; she studied it for long, silent seconds. The grandfather clock in the front hall struck five times. Daniel, Caleb kept thinking, Daniel. How could Daniel be dead? It was so unreal, so impossible. But he was. Cal had only to look at his mother to know it was true. Daniel was gone, he had ceased to exist except in their minds.

Emma allowed herself a small sigh and turned back to him. "What matters now is that the press mustn't be allowed to get hold of this story and make a great scandal out of it. Daniel is beyond the reach of justice or scorn, but Ruth and Jessie and Shama and the rest of us are alive. I will not have this family dragged through the mud, Caleb."

"I don't see how we're going to avoid it."

"I think we can. We're lucky in one respect. We are in the middle of a long holiday weekend when the wheels of the law turn a little more slowly. We can drag our feet too. We won't bury Daniel until Monday. Tomorrow is Sunday, I want you to go to New York, Cal. Go to Daniel's office. Find anything there that may be incriminating and burn it."

He'd taken a long breath. "I think that's subverting the law."

"Perhaps, But it makes no difference. As I said, Daniel has already paid for his crimes. The rest of the family are guilty of nothing."

He'd wondered if that were true, if they hadn't failed Daniel somehow. Perhaps none of this would have happened if years ago he or his mother or his father had recognized certain truths they preferred to ignore, accepted them, dealt with them. It was too late for that now. "How will I get into Daniel's office? Does Ruth have a key?"

"I don't know, I doubt it. But fortunately I have the home telephone number of Daniel's nurse. He gave it to me years ago, in case there was some emergency with your father and I couldn't reach him. I propose that you call her and break the news and ask her to meet you at the office. Doubtless she has a key."

And the acquiescent Miss Clark had a key, and she'd agreed to meet him, so now he was staring at the history of his brother's misdeeds. Cal reached for the topmost file and began reading.

As case notes went, these were extraordinary, written

not in terse medical jargon as such things customarily were, but in something Cal thought of as blank verse. They were a long, rambling reverie on the fear and loneliness that drive Daniel's patients to seek the kind of help he gave, and on his own motivations for giving it. Daniel had poured his soul onto these lined sheets of paper meant to record height, weight, and vital signs. "Sylvia's eyes never meet mine," he'd written. "She's so afraid. There's a bird trapped somewhere inside her, and what I see and hear is the mad beating of its wings against the cage. I can't release the bird, but I can give it peace for a time. Dosage of Methedrine increased to thirty grams daily . . ."

A procession of women passed before Cal's eyes: Sylvia and Elaine and Maria and Karla and Leona and Fay, and dozens more. He saw them all through the prism of his twin's perceptions, wounded creatures whose needs Daniel could not deny. Three hours later he closed the last file and realized he'd read Daniel's elegy, written by his own hand.

There was an incinerator in the building. Tenants had access to it through a chute next to the elevator. Caleb ripped each page of the files into many small pieces, then carried them to the hall and fed them slowly and carefully into the incinerator. When the last scrap had fluttered into the steel maw, he slammed it closed and stood there a moment and leaned his head against the wall. Finally he made his way back to Daniel's office and carefully tidied everything before he left, locking the door behind him.

Probably the police wouldn't ever ask about the case notes, why should they? Daniel hadn't been breaking any civil law in this skewed practice of medicine. If a patient chose to use a drug to commit suicide, that wasn't the doctor's fault. Besides, cops didn't have time to waste chasing guys who were already dead. And there had been no evidence in the office of abortion clinics, or any of the other things his mother had told him about. Daniel's partners, whoever they might be, would take care of protecting all that since obviously it was in their interest to do so.

Cal walked down Park Avenue. For the first time he cried. He could do that in the cold, half-deserted street where he was a stranger among strangers and no one paid him any attention. He was dry-eyed by the time he came to Grand Central Station. He checked the train schedules, then called his mother. "It's okay, Mom. I've taken care of everything."

"Thank you, Caleb. Are you coming home now?"

"Yes. The train leaves in twenty minutes."

"Everyone is here, except for your boys."

"How are you all?" he asked.

"How are we?" Emma repeated. "I don't know. How can we be? Numb, I suppose. Cal, was there anything incriminating?"

"Not really. But I burned all the medical notes. I don't think anyone's going to look for them anyway."

"Thank you," she said again. "Come home, darling. We need you."

Six hours later, in the house on Commonwealth Avenue, he was sitting close to Jessie, holding his sister's trembling hand, looking at Emma and Ruth comforting each other on the sofa, watching Shama who was curled into a ball of misery on the carpet at Jessie's feet. Susan sat a few feet away, staring out the window, separated from all of them by more than physical distance. In the shadowed room his wife's profile seemed carved in marble. Maybe Daniel had the best idea after all: Do what seems right to you and the devil take the hindmost. He would do the same . . . if it weren't for Dav and John.

"I can't," Cal told Shama a few hours after the funeral. "I can't do anything different from what I'm doing. I'm sorry, I just don't know any other way."

They were alone in his office. She'd begged him to meet her here, and this time he hadn't the strength to refuse. She was wearing a black knit dress and her long dark hair hung free, and she looked pale, but very beautiful. He wanted to touch her, longed to touch her, but he didn't give in. "We've got to get over to the house," he said. "The others will be wondering where we are."

"You mean Susan will be wondering."

"Yes, I suppose that's what I mean."

"Cal, you can't just let her ruin all our lives. You can't."

He sighed. "We've already had this conversation, Shama. Nothing's changed."

She whirled and faced him, her breasts visibly rising and falling with the intensity of her emotions. "Damn you, Caleb Morgan! Everything has changed. Daniel's dead.

He was alive one minute and dead the next. At thirty-five years old. Doesn't that make you think? Doesn't that make you realize that life is a bloody crapshoot and if you don't dare you never win?"

"It's not about daring, Daniel did plenty of that and it never made him happy. It's about responsibility and doing what you have to do."

She shook her head in wordless disagreement, then flung herself at him, wrapped her arms around his neck, pressed her body to his. Of course he kissed her, he couldn't do otherwise. He kissed her and held her and caressed her, and in minutes they had slid to the floor, to the elegant carpet in the elegant office which once had been Joshua's; and he was almost inside her, had almost taken that possession of her which she longed for him to take, when he pulled away. "No. Dammit to hell, no! I won't do this. I can't."

She lay where she was, not saying anything. Cal stood up and straightened his clothes and ran his fingers through the red hair he still wore in a crew cut, though it was no longer fashionable. A minute went by, then another. He stretched out his hand to help her up, but she refused it and scrambled to her feet on her own. "Let me tell you something," she said. "You're not a hero, Cal. You're an emotional coward. And that's a damned shame for both of us."

Ben Porter called at Ruth's on Tuesday. "I didn't know if you'd be here or at your mother-in-law's," he said. "I was at the funeral, but I don't imagine you saw me. I'm so sorry, Ruth."

"I saw you. Thank you for being there, Ben. Come into the kitchen. I'll make some tea."

Shama was there, she kissed his cheek. "Hi, Ben. Nice of you to come."

"I wanted to. How are you?"

"We're holding up. Here, sit down."

Ruth poured three glasses of mint tea and they looked at each other, old friends suddenly uncomfortable in each other's company. "I'm going out for a walk," Shama said. "If you two don't mind."

They said they didn't, and she pulled on a ski jacket and

a knitted cap and left by the back door. Ben watched her go, then turned to Ruth. "Where's Jessie?"

"With her mother for a few days."

"Oh yes, of course. I find it strange, how goyim do this kind of thing. I'm not used to it. I don't mean that in a critical way, only that to me it seems odd that you're not all together."

Ruth nodded. "I know what you mean. It's not like sitting shiva. They don't have any rituals for after the funeral. It's too bad. Doing things that are prescribed, that have always been done, helps."

Ben leaned over and took her hand. "I'm really so sorry, Ruth. I wish I knew something else to say."

"There isn't anything else. Daniel was a complicated man, both a very good and a very bad man. They all think I don't know, but I do. Not the details, I never wanted to know them, but once years ago my mother-in-law told me that Daniel always had to be a saint or a devil, that for him there was nothing in between, and she was right."

"Okay," Ben said. "I understand. But what about you, Ruth? What are you going to do?"

"Live," she said. "I've been through this before, Ben, losing the people closest in the whole world, I know all about that. And I know that the only thing you can do is go on living. Daniel would want us to do that."

He smiled.

On Wednesday afternoon, two days after the funeral, Cal went to the hospital. He'd canceled all but the urgent appointments at the office, moved them to the following week, but he couldn't neglect patients in the hospital. He did rounds for two hours, accepted condolences with a quick nod of his head, then went home.

The house on Dartmouth Street seemed somehow different at four in the afternoon on a weekday, he so seldom saw it then. There were white poinsettias in the foyer, a dramatic contrast to the midnight-blue walls and the guilt console and matching mirror. The flowers reminded him that for most of the world it was still Christmas, time of joy and laughter.

"Good afternoon, Doctor Morgan," the maid said.

She was a young Irish girl who had come to work for them a few weeks before, he couldn't remember her name.

The help was constantly changing because Susan was never satisfied—or they were never satisfied with her. "Where is everyone?" Cal asked as he took off his coat.

"Mrs. Morgan's out, sir. The children are upstairs with Miss Carlisle."

Miss Carlisle was the governess. And there was no place she and her charges were likely to be except upstairs. This was not a house in which two young boys could run free.

He went up to the third floor and opened the door to the playroom. It was empty except for a couple of ladders and a slew of drop cloths and cans of paint. Apparently the room was being redecorated. He hadn't known, but then he seldom knew much about the domestic arrangements.

He heard John's laughter from down the hall and moved on to the door of the boys' bedroom. "Hello, Miss Carlisle. Hi, guys. What's up?"

"Dav thinks his car can go faster than mine. But it can't." John held up a miniature car for his father's inspection. "See? Mine's a Cadillac, and that's going to beat a Buick any day."

Cal examined the expensive toys and listened to Dav's explanation of why he'd lost the last two races across the small space between the twin beds, but was sure to win the next one. The governess sat in a maple rocking chair by the window. There was a pile of knitting on her lap. She reminded him of Marya. "I see the playroom's being spruced up," Cal said. "How long before you get back in there?"

"It's not for the children, Doctor." Miss Carlisle pursed her lips and tugged at an errant stitch. "Mrs. Morgan says it's to be a guest room."

Cal stared at her a moment, then turned back to his sons.

He confronted Susan after dinner, over their ritual cup of coffee in the library. It was supposed to be a warm, private time for the two of them and wasn't, hadn't been since they moved into this house and John was born. "What's this about the boy's playroom being turned into a guest room? We have two guest rooms."

"Yes, but we need a third. More coffee, Caleb?"

"No thank you. Why do we need three?"

"I'm chairman of the hospitality committee of the Horticultural Society this year. I'm expected to put up visiting celebrities."

"What the hell is a horticultural 'celebrity'? And if you need an extra bed for a night or two you can put one in here, or in the playroom for that matter. You can't cram two growing boys into one small room in this huge place. It's unfair."

Susan adjusted the position of a stack of books on the table beside her. They were elegantly bound, but he doubted she'd ever read them. "The boys can't run our lives, Cal. That's silly."

"They're not running our lives. Not yours, by any stretch of the imagination. You hardly see them. But they need a place to play. The playroom stays."

"That's absurdly indulgent. You're spoiling them rotten."

He put down his cup, setting it carefully on the mahogany table beside his leather chair. "That's my final word, Susan. Get rid of the painting paraphernalia tomorrow."

"Caleb, you're being pigheaded. It's so unnecessary."

"Tomorrow," he repeated as he left the room.

The following day he called the house on Carrington Avenue. After a few words with Ruth he asked to speak to Shama. "I hoped you were still here. I mean, that you hadn't gone back to New York."

"Not until next week, I want to spend some time with Ruthie."

"Good. Listen, will you meet me someplace later? The Public Garden, maybe. On the Charles Street side of the pond. About four."

There was a pause, then she said quietly, "I'll be there."

She arrived before him. She walked along the path and thought about the first time she'd come here, nine years before. It had been with Cal, not with Daniel. It was Caleb who had taken her to ride on the fabled swan boats that first summer of her new life in the New World. Now the boats were in storage for the winter and the trees were all bare, but the old spire of Trinity Church and the new one of the John Hancock Building rose in the distance above the branches, and the place seemed to her as miraculously beautiful as she'd thought it then.

She saw him coming from the direction of Beacon Street, from the hospital most likely, wearing a tweed overcoat and a scarf, but no hat. His red hair glinted in the westering winter sun. Shama went to meet him and he took both her hands in his. "Hi. Thanks for coming."

She wore blue woolen gloves, Cal's were leather lined with sheepskin, but she could feel the warmth of his flesh through the layers of fabric between them. "You knew I'd come."

"Yeah, I guess I did. Shall we walk?"

He slipped her arm through his and they moved along the broad path. The dusting of snow that had fallen before Christmas was gone now, but it was very cold today, and it felt as if another storm were on the way. "I couldn't let it end like that, the way it did the other day," Cal said.

"It shouldn't end at all. Do you remember the first time you brought me here?"

"Yes, of course, I do. You could barely speak English and you were as stiff as a little wooden soldier, then you saw the swan boats and you laughed. It was the first time I heard you laugh."

"That's part of it, isn't it? You still think of me as a kid. Poor little Shama, the refugee who needs looking after. Another baby sister."

He chuckled. "You're wrong. I stopped thinking of you as a sister a few years ago. Otherwise I had to imagine myself some kind of monster, and I'm not. Just an ordinary guy who is in love with a beautiful woman who's too young for him. A guy who already has a wife. It's not an unusual story."

"I'm not too young for you. As to the rest, no, I suppose it isn't unusual. But if you were happily married, I'd never have allowed it to get even this far. You do know that, don't you, Cal? I'm not a home wrecker."

He squeezed her arm. "I know you're not. This particular home was wrecked years ago, long before you were a factor."

She waited, but he didn't say anything else. Shama's high spirits began to fade. He'd only wanted to apologize, to make sure they were still friends. She felt the tears starting again, little prickles behind her eyelids. She'd cried so much this past week. For Daniel, and for Ruth, and for Jessie who was still locked dry-eyed into her grief, and for herself and Cal. A river of tears for all of them.

"How's Ruth holding up?" he asked when they rounded

the bend and began walking along the short southeastern end of the pond.

"Better than I hoped. I think she and Daniel had come to some sort of impasse. She grieves for him, but not for herself. That wasn't a great marriage either, you know."

"Yes, I know. That's one of the things I've been thinking about these last few days. Shama, do you understand about Daniel?"

"As far as I'm concerned there's nothing to understand. I loved Daniel. I don't care about anything except that he saved my life and Ruthie's. He rode into our lives in an army jeep, but it could have been a white horse. Daniel was our knight in shining armor, Cal. That's the way I'm always going to remember him."

He didn't say anything because the lump in his throat wouldn't permit it.

"I talked to Jessie this morning," Shama said. "Jess can't cry, she never can when she should. But your mother's not crying either. Jess says she's very calm."

"I think . . ." he hesitated.

"Go on, what do you think?"

"I think Mom knows that Daniel may have wanted the accident to happen," Cal said very softly. "And she understands that. Maybe it was the best way out for him. And for Ruth."

She didn't answer for a few seconds. "Cal, if there's something specific behind all this, do I have to know about it?"

He stopped walking and put his gloved hand against her cheek and turned her face to his. "No, all you have to know is that Daniel loved you. And that I love you, in a different way. I want us to be together, Shama. I've been thinking about it all for days. Daniel and the way he was, the way his life was. A lot of it was because of things that happened years ago, maybe even before we were born. But I don't want to be a prisoner of that kind of destiny. I want to laugh and be happy and have love in my life. I want my sons to see what love is."

She pressed her face to his chest, inhaling the warm, particular scent of him which was barely there behind the winter smell of cold and oncoming snow. "We deserve that much," she murmured. "Oh, Cal, surely we must deserve it. God knows, Dav and John do."

"Yes. I'll speak to Susan tonight."

"What earthly difference can it make to you? You can have this mausoleum you call a house. You can have all the money you want." Caleb paused and took a deep breath. "It hasn't been a real marriage for years, Susan. I should think you'd be glad to be rid of me."

"And the boys?" She was very quiet, very controlled. They might be discussing the weather. "I presume you also mean that I'd be rid of my sons."

"Yes. You don't want them, Susan. You never did. You can have visiting privileges, of course, but I want custody."

Susan crossed her legs, her exquisite ankles showed beneath the long black velvet skirt she often wore for evenings at home. "And where would you take Dav and John? Since according to you I would have this house, just what do you have in mind for the children?"

He didn't look at her. "I'll make a home for them. Somewhere in the country perhaps, where they can have a place to play, a garden—" He shrugged. "All the things you hate."

"Ah, how idyllic it sounds. Caleb and his boys having barbecues in the backyard, and nice suburban neighbors who drop by to drink beer. Just what they need, obviously." She reached for a cigarette from a chased brass box at her elbow, waited for him to light it, then did it herself when he merely continued staring into the fire. "You won't need a housekeeper, will you, Caleb? A young woman of Shama's sort will doubtless be quite willing to do all her own scrubbing and cleaning. As long as you take her to bed regularly. She's been lusting after you since she was barely pubescent."

"Shama has nothing to do with this."

"Don't take me for a fool, Cal." Susan exhaled a long stream of blue-gray smoke. "That fugitive from the African ant heap has everything to do with this."

"Stop!" He whirled to face her. "Do you have to poison everything with your evil tongue? Just let me go, let me take the boys. You never wanted them," he said again.

Her voice was a contrast to his, still low and cultured and calm. "You're quite right about that. I hated the notion of having children and I hated the process. But they don't bother me that much now. They're the price I had to pay, Caleb. And I paid it."

"For what? Jesus, what have you bought? A husband who no longer loves you, an empty sham of a marriage. Why should you cling to such a charade?"

"Because it suits me. I am Mrs. Caleb Morgan, wife of the most successful gynecologist in Boston. I bought that and paid for it, Caleb, as I said. And I have no intention whatever of exchanging it for the role of a divorcée whose husband has run off with a little whore from the jungle."

He made half a motion toward her and she pulled back. But he never really meant to strike her and she never really thought he would. The moment of incipient violence passed.

She was the first to recover. "Such passion astounds me, Caleb. Having endured your fumbling inadequacies in the bedroom for all these years, this great feeling quite astonishes me."

"You're a bitch out of hell. But I don't care what you say, I mean to have a divorce. I'll do whatever I have to do to get it."

"Oh, it won't be that difficult. There's always Reno or Mexico, I'm quite sure you can have your divorce, Caleb. But you'll get it without my cooperation, and what you will never get is the custody of those two boys you so idolize. I shall see to it that you don't even have visiting rights. As the woman wronged, I'm sure I can achieve that."

She rose from her chair and went to the small bar and poured herself a drink. He watched her, trying to decide if she meant it, if she'd really try to cut him off from his sons. "I can understand your torturing me," he said finally. "But how could you be so cruel to them?"

"But I don't wish to be, Caleb. I want to keep my marriage intact, to provide Dav and John with a stable home. That's not surprising, I'm their mother. Of course, I have their best interests at heart. That's why I've kept the truth from John all these years."

"What truth? What the hell are you talking about?"

She cocked her head and studied him. The cornflower-blue eyes were unwavering. "Yes," she said, more to herself than to him. "I think it's time." Then, in a louder voice, "You'll never leave me, Caleb. Forget this whole mad plan. You may bed the little Jewish whore until the two of you are sick of the sight of each other, but legally and publicly and in every other way that matters, you're mine for as long as I wish to keep you."

"No," he whispered the word first, then shouted it. "No! This time you're not going to have your way."

"Oh, yes, I am." She laughed. The sound was incredible to him, but it was real. Susan laughed again. "I am going to have whatever I want, Caleb. Because if I don't have it, if you don't give it to me, I shall tell John the truth."

He opened his mouth to ask again what truth, but the words wouldn't come. There was a cold place in the pit of his stomach and the icy chill was spreading.

"No idea what I mean, Cal? Can't you guess? Where was your father for those few hours before he hung himself? Come now, surely you can remember. He was here, darling. With me. We hadn't moved in yet, but the bedroom was already furnished. And that's where we were, Joshua and I, upstairs in that bed. Nine months before John was born. Joshua was a wonderful lover, by the way. Magnificent."

"I don't believe you." It was all he could say and it came out in a hoarse whisper. "I don't believe you."

"Don't you? Well, it really doesn't matter whether you do or not. John will believe me when I tell him that Joshua is his father, that Joshua tried to kill himself because he felt so guilty about doing those naughty things with his son's wife. He'll believe me most of all when I tell him he isn't your child. That father whom he so adores isn't his father at all. Too bad, John, I'll say, but that is how life is sometimes, darling."

He did lunge for her then. He grabbed her and the sherry glass she held flew from her hand and splintered unheeded on the hearth. "Bitch! You're a lying bitch! I won't let you do this, I'll kill you first. I swear it."

He was shaking her, and her pale gold hair came loose and fell around her shoulders. Susan didn't resist him. She stayed limp and waited until his burst of fury had spent itself. She was not frightened. Joshua might have killed her if the circumstances were reversed, but never Caleb. A moment later he flung her to the couch, and turned and hung onto the table to keep from collapsing under the weight of his rage and disgust.

"There," Susan said softly. "That part of it's done with. Now we understand each other, Cal. And you know me well enough to know I'll do exactly what I say, don't you? Oh, and something more, I'll tell Emma the truth too. In fact, I'll probably tell her before I tell John. And Jessica, of course. I think the whole family should know what kind of man is lying in state at 165 Commonwealth Avenue, what kind of man a devoted wife has wasted her life on."

"No." He didn't shout the word this time, he whispered it in pleading tones. "No. You can't wreak such havoc, you mustn't."

"But, Cal, I don't want to. I won't. Unless, of course, you make me."

"Shama, can you meet me at the Brighams in Coolidge Corner in half an hour?"

"Brighams, Cal, are you sure?"

"Yes. Half an hour, at two, see you then."

Shama heard the telephone click and stared at the receiver. She'd been waiting for this call since she woke at six this morning. "I'll talk to Susan tonight," that's what he'd said. All day she'd heard the words over and over in her head, with alternating ecstasy and despair. What if he didn't do it? What if Susan wasn't home? What if one of the boys had some need that distracted him? But he would do it, he'd said so, and the whole rest of their lives depended on it.

Had he? And if he had, why meet her to discuss it in a place as public as Brighams? She went slowly into the kitchen, dark brows drawn together in concentration.

"Who was that?" Ruth asked.

"Cal." Shama opened the refrigerator, poured herself a glass of milk and stood beside the counter staring at it.

"What's wrong?"

"Nothing, Ruthie. I'm going out, I don't know when I'll be back."

"Are you meeting Caleb?"

"Yes."

"Shama, listen, I know how you feel but—"

"Ruthie, I can't talk about it now. I'll explain later if I can. And don't worry, please, everything's going to be fine. Wonderful in fact."

Ruth watched Shama take a heavy red wool jacket from

the hook beside the back door and slip it over her black slacks and sweater. How beautiful she was, the little sister who had been the child she never had; how beautiful and how vulnerable. She knew that Shama loved Caleb, knew it wasn't the love a girl feels for a big brother, not anymore: Shama was a woman, and Caleb was the man she wanted. Ruth also knew how Caleb felt, she had read it in his face a dozen times. But he was married to Susan. She ached for them. "Shama, be careful, darling."

In that instant Shama made up her mind that everything was perfect, that she was imagining some problem boded by Cal's choice of meeting place. Her smile was radiant. "Don't worry. We'll talk later, okay?"

"Okay."

Ruth watched through the kitchen window as the red-and-black figure practically skipped down the driveway.

The crowd at Brighams was thin, the main lunch rush had passed, but there were a number of people about. It was still the holiday week, many people had not yet returned to their workday lives. Caleb paused in the door, looked around, and spotted Shama at the rear. He made his way to her, taking off his overcoat as he walked. "Hi," he said as he slipped into the chair facing hers.

"Hi yourself, my love." She whispered the words, a caution left over from the bad days before everything had been made clear and certain between them.

Caleb dropped his eyes. "Have you ordered?"

"Not yet. No one has paid any attention to me."

He turned and summoned a waitress. They both ordered hot chocolate. When they were alone again, Shama stretched her hand across the table and waited for Cal to take it. He didn't move. The little knot of fear that had formed in her stomach earlier grew tighter and larger. "Tell me," she said.

"Not much to tell." He still hadn't once looked directly into her eyes.

"There must be. Did you talk to her?"

"Yes."

"Well?"

"She won't let me go."

Shama drew one long, painful breath, fought back the panic rising in her throat. "You knew she wouldn't just roll

over and play dead, darling. Not Susan. You must have
known that."

"Yes, but . . ." He stopped speaking while the waitress
put the cups of hot chocolate on the table.

"But what?" Shama clasped her hands around the steaming cup, but she felt no warmth. "You have to go, Cal.
Move out. She can't hold you against your will."

"It's not that simple."

"The boys, I know. Darling, listen to me, we'll fight her
for custody. I know it won't be easy, but if we can show
the way she is, the way she treats them, we're bound to
win. The other day I was reading about how there's always
a social worker appointed to interview the children in
custody suits. What the kids want carries a lot of weight.
You know what Dav and John will say if they're asked who
they want to live with."

"Don't," he said. "Don't torture us both. It won't work,
it can never work. I'm sorry I let us live on false hope for a
few hours, but I was wrong. I can't do it, she won't let me
do it."

Shama wanted to scream, to shout his name and pound
her fists on his chest and keep on doing it until he saw
reason, until he broke away from the evil spell cast by that
bitch he was married to. But she couldn't, not here in
Brighams. She understood now why he'd chosen this meeting place.

"Are you going to let this happen?" she whispered
hoarsely. "Are you just going to allow her to wreck our
lives and the lives of your sons? Because that's what she's
doing, Cal. She's no kind of a mother, and someday when
they get older both Dav and John are going to despise you
for never trying to end the hell the three of you lived in."

He shook his head. His hands were balled into fists on
the marble-topped table. "Please, there's nothing you can
say that I haven't already said to myself. But I have no
choice, absolutely none."

He leaned forward now and grabbed her hands. The
contact traumatized them both, for a moment they clung
to each other and didn't say anything. Cal lifted her
palm to his lips and kissed it briefly, then broke away.
"I have to go. Forgive me, my beautiful, beloved Shama. I'd
have given almost anything if it could have been the way I
dreamed it, the way I hoped."

"Almost anything. What was it that you couldn't give? What price did she ask that was too high to pay?"

"My son's sanity."

And that was it, he was gone and she was sitting in Brighams staring at two untouched cups of hot chocolate. The waitress came back and picked up the dollar bill Cal had left on the table. "Get you something else, miss?"

Shama shook her head. "No, nothing else. There's nothing else I want."

Cal went back to the office, he saw patients, he went to the hospital and saw more patients. He looked normal, he sounded normal, he prescribed and cautioned and examined and cured as he always did. There was no outward sign of what raged inside him.

At six he was finished at Memorial, preparing to go home, telling himself he had to do it, to walk again into that house where she lived—because of the boys. A voice came over the loudspeaker. "Doctor Morgan, will Doctor Morgan please call reception. Doctor Morgan." Cal picked up the telephone.

"It's Mrs. Watkins, Doctor. She phoned your office and was sent directly here."

Cal always knew all his patients. "Jane Watkins?"

"Yes, Doctor. It seems she's in labor."

"She's only six months along. Damm it." He pulled his white coat back on and hurried down the hall.

It was after eleven when he left Memorial. In the end he'd had to perform a cesarian to deliver Jane Watkins of a stillborn baby boy. It was heartbreaking, because she'd been thrilled about her pregnancy. But there would be other children. He'd used his father's technique, the one everyone used now. Thanks to Joshua cesarian sections no longer endangered future childbearing. Thanks to Joshua.

The night suddenly had turned mild. He left his car in the parking lot and walked to Back Bay. His footsteps echoed in the darkness. He came to Commonwealth Avenue and stood looking at the two adjoining houses where almost all his life had been lived. And in one of them his father lay in a living death. He still had keys to both.

He let himself in to 165. It was almost midnight and very quiet, undoubtedly his mother and Mayra had already gone to bed. The night nurse would be with Joshua now. Cal climbed the stairs to the former library. A night-light cast a dull glow in the hall and there was a sliver of equally dim light from beneath the door of the room where his father lay. He opened the door.

The nurse looked up, startled by this intrusion into her shadowy and lonely world. "Oh, it's you, Doctor Morgan. Is something wrong?"

"No, nothing's wrong. I was just passing and thought I'd look in. Go down to the kitchen and have a cup of tea, why don't you? I'll sit with him for a bit."

"That's very kind, but really there's no need—"

"Go on," he repeated. Accustomed to obeying the commands of doctors, she went.

Cal stood for a moment beside the bed, then sat down. He didn't take his eyes from Joshua's face. His father's eyes were open, but then they always were. They never knew when he was awake and when asleep. That was one of the most repugnant symptoms of his condition, the one the children could never hear of without shivering, those eternally staring green eyes.

Cal looked into them. "John's eyes are green too," he said softly. "Just like yours. But so are mine. So that doesn't prove a thing. But *this* does. You're the proof, Dad. I know everything now—why you tried to kill your-self and locked us all into this nightmare. Susan told me you slept with her, with my wife. She says that John—" His voice broke and he began to sob.

The sobs lasted only a minute, then the tears ended and he was trembling with rage, with a fury so monumental he thought he might split into countless atoms and just blow away. "You bastard, you filthy rotten fake. All that moral rectitude, all that fatherly love and concern. It was a lie. A goddamned, fucking, son of a bitch of a lie . . ."

He didn't shout, he whispered, because despite everything he could not forget his mother. This burden she must not also be made to bear. But he could free her from the rest. It would be so easy.

He hesitated only a moment, then lunged forward, pulled one of the pillows from beneath Joshua's head, and pressed it over his face. "Die, you bastard, die. It's what you deserve."

The impulse lasted only a few seconds. He took the pillow away in less than half a minute, Joshua's breathing

was not in the least affected. "I can't," Caleb murmured.
"The sins of the fathers will not be visited on the children.
I won't make Dav and John a murderer's sons. And they're
both mine, do you hear me? Mine. Susan can think what
she likes, and I'll do whatever it takes to keep her from
saying it to anyone else, but I *know* they're mine. John as
much as Dav. And someday you'll die. And then I hope
you rot in hell."

He heard the nurse's step on the stair, and by the time
she came into the room everything was as she'd left it. The
silent, caring son sitting beside the tragically afflicted father.

Three days later Cal made up his mind yet again,
another turn taken in this week of cataclysmic change. He
couldn't go on living with her. The sight of her made his
skin crawl, her voice came to him like the permanent
squeak of chalk on blackboard, the smell of her perfume
made him gag. It was impossible, he could not spend the
rest of his life sleeping beside the wife he hated, waking
beside her, seeing her across the breakfast table, and
coming home to her each evening.

"I'm leaving," he told her on Sunday evening.

It was late, the children were asleep, Susan was preparing for bed and he was standing in the doorway of the
bedroom, still fully dressed. She'd been brushing her hair,
now she put down the brush and turned to him. "Again,
Cal? I thought we already had this conversation."

"Not a divorce, not even a legal separation. You can
have the sham marriage you're so intent on preserving. I
just don't want to live with you. I don't want to have to
touch you ever—even accidentally."

"We both know the girl you want to touch, darling.
That's not going to happen. I meant what I said, Caleb. I'll
tell the whole story, and don't think I care in the least
what it will make me look like, because I don't."

"I never thought you did. And this isn't about Shama.
She went back to New York yesterday. I'm never going to
see her again. But I'm not going on with this horror show.
I've taken an apartment on the other side of town. I'll live
there."

She set down the hairbrush thoughtfully, considering
his words. "I see . . . Well, perhaps that's a good idea,
Caleb. You're not exactly terrific company, and I've al-

ready told you what I think of your performance in bed. There are certain things I need you for, however."

"I'll pay all the bills, as I told you I would."

Susan laughed. "I know you will, that's one thing you're very good at, earning money. I meant that I'd need you to appear at dinner parties occasionally, and take me places. You're an excellent escort, Caleb. Superior, to give you your due. Always so attentive and gentlemanly."

He couldn't look at her, he turned and stared up the stairs toward the room that held his sons. "The apartment's on West Cedar Street, it's walking distance for the boys. Miss Carlisle can bring them there after school."

"Sometimes," Susan said distinctly. "That will be fine as long as it's all kept discreet. We'll both promise to be that, won't we, Caleb? We'll both be discreet?"

"Yes."

"And if she moves in with you, if I ever hear that the Moroccan whore has her Jewish claws into my husband or my sons, then you'll have no one but yourself to blame for what happens. Do we understand each other, Caleb?"

It took him a long time to force out the words. "Yes, we understand each other."

"Good. Go whenever you like, I shall quite enjoy having you and being rid of you at the same time. I'm quite astounded by your cleverness, Caleb."

Caleb had rented the top two floors of a lovely bowfront house on West Cedar Street, just off Beacon Hill. There were six spacious rooms with high ceilings and large casement windows that let in the sun. The old hardwood floors creaked, the bathroom belonged in a museum, and the heating system made an incredible racket—but it was an island of peace, and walking distance to the hospital. Now he need only go to Back Bay to see his mother.

Dav and John went to the Lenox Academy for Boys near the hospital. Two days after he moved he gave Miss Carlisle a key to the apartment. "I've taken a place close to the hospital," he said, not meeting her eyes. "It's convenient when I have to work late. And I'm moving my office to that new medical center they're building across from Memorial. So I thought you might bring the boys there after school, to the apartment, I mean."

"Yes, Doctor Morgan, I understand." She put the key in

her pocket. "Have you spoken with Dav and John about these . . . new arrangements."

Cal shook his head. He knew he had to do it, but he wasn't sure what he could say. How do you tell two young boys that for all intents and purposes you're leaving their mother?

"They won't be shocked," Miss Carlisle said gently. "Forgive me if I'm overstepping my bounds, Doctor Morgan, but children are much more perceptive than most adults give them credit for. We'll just tell them very simply, shall we? Without a lot of explanations they don't need. Make it all sound like an adventure."

He took her hand, almost overwhelmed with gratitude. "Thank you, Miss Carlisle. You make it sound so simple."

"It can be, Doctor. At least for the children."

She brought them to Cal's most afternoons after school. They'd wait for him to come home, then they'd all have supper together, either something simple cooked by the governess, or a treat in one of the nearby restaurants.

By the time he'd been in the new apartment for about three months, Cal had set aside a bedroom for his sons and one for Miss Carlisle. Frequently Susan would receive a telephone call around eight to say that the children and their governess would be spending the night on West Cedar Street. She didn't object, as she'd said, she was quite pleased to be rid of him, and of her sons, too, apparently.

It was a life of sorts, allowing him to survive as a man and to thrive as a father; but there was a huge, gaping wound in his life where Shama should have been, a wound that bled and ached. Caleb told himself it would be okay because it had to be.

Ali Fatah was short but brawny, dark, and good-looking in a way that was bound to turn coarse as the years passed. "*Kaifal-hal?*" he asked perching on the corner of Shama's desk.

"I'm fine, and don't speak to me in Arabic. I don't like it. I've told you that."

"There are a lot of things you don't like—me for instance. And that's silly, since I'm handsome and charming, not to mention that I'm your boss."

"I do like you. I just think we should speak English

since we're in America. Here are those translations you asked for this morning."

He took the papers she handed him and didn't look at them. "Shama, it's a beautiful day, the first sunny day in ages, come have lunch with me. We'll go to Rockefeller Center. They always give me a table near the window, so we would be able to watch the skaters."

She glanced out the window at the early February day. It was nice. She'd been so numb these past five weeks she hadn't noticed the weather. "Why not?" she said, more to herself than him.

Ali grinned. "Yes, very wise. Why not?" He got her coat and held it for her. "You should have furs," he said. "A beautiful woman in New York in winter should wear furs."

"You don't pay me enough to afford a fur coat."

He frowned as if he hadn't thought of that. "No, I suppose I don't. Okay, you get a raise. Starting now you're earning a thousand dollars a week."

"Don't be ridiculous," she said as she buttoned her coat. "Nobody pays a translator a thousand dollars a week. Besides, you don't really need me at all. Your English is fine, and you could translate the articles yourself."

"Why should I? I'm the boss. And if I want to pay you a thousand a week, I can do it."

She smiled and shook her head. He wasn't serious, of course, but there was no arguing with Ali, he was a spoiled child accustomed to doing exactly what he wanted. A very rich spoiled child. This magazine was a plaything for him, she realized that now.

They walked out of her tiny office to the reception area. A pretty little blond girl sat at a desk so large it dwarfed her. "We're going out to lunch," Ali told her. "To talk business. We may be gone for hours. If anyone calls, I'll get back to them tomorrow."

The other girl looked hurt. Damn. Ali must have had something going with the receptionist, Shama thought. She'd been so wrapped up in her own misery, she hadn't noticed. Now she'd made hard feelings.

As they got out of a taxi at Rockefeller Center she asked him about it. "Have you been seeing your receptionist? Socially, I mean."

"Socially? Yes, I guess you could call it that." His grin said everything.

They entered the Promenade Cafe and were seated right away.

"That's shitty," Shama said as soon as they were settled at their table.

He stared at her in surprise. "What did you say?"

"I said that's shitty. Not you and the girl, but your smirk when you admitted it. You're no gentlemen, Ali Fatah."

"And you're no lady. Besides, all Arabs are attracted to blondes. Haven't you heard that?"

"I never said I was a lady. Underneath I'm still a Moroccan street urchin. And I didn't know about the blondes. She's a nice girl. You shouldn't ignore her feelings like that."

"I wasn't ignoring her feelings. It's over, been over for a week. And it's not always true about blondes." He reached forward and flicked one finger through her long, dark hair. "In the end we go back to the Arab ideal of beauty."

"I'm not an Arab."

"No, you're a Jew. I know, but it's okay. We can declare a private truce, you and I. I told you that when I hired you."

"Yes, you did." She picked up the menu and glanced at it and said she'd have a chicken sandwich.

"Have a steak. You've lost a lot of weight these past few weeks, I like you better plump and juicy."

She refused the steak and stuck to her first choice, but when the food came she only nibbled at it. On the other side of the glass, skaters in multicolored finery dipped and swooped and glided across the ice. They made patterns of color and form that reminded her of a kaleidoscope she'd had when she was a kid.

"I hate eating alone," Ali said.

The words summoned her out of her reverie. "What?"

"I said I hate eating alone. You're not here with me, where are you?"

"Nowhere, I was just watching the skaters."

"Shama, I want to take you to bed."

She stared at him. A giggle bubbled in her throat. She couldn't remember the last time she'd laughed, but the baldness of the statement, the total inappropriateness of it, struck her as extraordinarily funny. "You're crazy."

"No, I'm a Kuwaiti, an Arab. A sheik, if it comes to that. When we want a woman we tell her and take her."

"Just like that?"

"Sometimes, yes." He got up. "Come."

They hadn't finished their coffee, and his mood seemed suddenly to have changed. Shama stood and shrugged into her coat before he could hold it for her.

He took her arm when they got out onto the street and hailed a cab and murmured something she didn't hear to the driver and half-shoved her inside. They'd gone a couple of blocks before she realized they weren't going back to work. The magazine's office was on Twenty-second Street and Third Avenue, the cab had turned uptown on Third, not downtown. Oh, God, there was going to be a scene of some kind. "Ali, listen, I didn't mean to make you think—"

"Ssh, don't say anything. I have a surprise."

She shrugged and leaned back against the seat. He wasn't trying to wrestle with her or anything like that. It was okay.

The taxi let them off on the upper East Side, Third Avenue and Ninetieth Street. "I lived near here when I first came to the city," Shama said. "At the Ninety-second Street Y."

He paid the taxi and it sped off, and he turned to her. "This isn't the Y. Come inside." She hesitated. "Shama, it's all right, really it is. I'm not a rapist."

Of course, he wasn't. Rapists didn't wear suits and ties and cashmere overcoats and have degrees from Oxford University. She followed him up a few steps to a double front door that he unlocked and opened for her. It was a whole house, she realized with a shock, not an apartment building. She didn't know anybody else in New York who lived in an entire house. "Don't tell me you own this place?"

"Of course I do. Why wouldn't I own it?"

Because it must have cost hundreds of thousands of dollars, that's why. But money was not a problem for him. "No reason. It just surprised me."

"I have a bigger surprise. Will you let me play my little game? It's harmless, I promise."

"What game?"

He smiled at her. "Don't sound so suspicious. Go up those stairs and go into the first room on the right and wait for me. Go on, it will be nice. I give you my word."

She hesitated again, then climbed the stairs. The upper hall and the doors looked perfectly ordinary. Nice dark wood paneling and a beige carpet on the floor. She turned the knob and went into the first room on the right, exactly as he'd instructed—and gasped.

It was a tent. The walls and the ceiling were draped in cured hides. The floor was strewn with woven carpets in jewel colors. There were low brass tray tables and mountains of cushions. But it was the smell that assailed her and made her dizzy with remembrance. The place smelled like the souk in Casablanca. The odor, like that of the Moroccan bazaar, was a medley of spices and incense and the tang of camel. She took a deep breath, let it out slowly, wanted to laugh and to cry at the same time. The music began then. Part of her mind knew it came from a loudspeaker she couldn't see, but another part believed that somewhere behind her a man sat tapping rhythms with long brown fingers and chanting an Arabic love song she had known all her life.

She didn't feel like Shama the American girl who spoke perfect English and had a college degree and a nice, respectable family. She was a child again, and the world around her was both terrifying and ripe with promise. She was the Shama who had darted around corners and scurried from stall to stall in the marketplace, the Shama who had grown so suddenly wily and wise when her parents were killed and there was no one but her and Ruth, and they had to fend for themselves.

She sank to her knees on one of the piles of cushions and closed her eyes and just let herself feel and remember. When she opened them, Ali was standing there. He wore a white jellaba. "Welcome home," he said softly.

19

*T*he airplane touched down in a perfect landing. "Welcome to San Juan," the stewardess announced over the loudspeaker. "Please remain seated until we have come to a full stop in front of the terminal, and be sure to take all your hand luggage with you when you leave."

Jessica peered out the window. The wintery New York she'd left behind might not exist. Everything here was golden sunlight and palm trees. She turned to Celia, already free of her seat belt and busy gathering her magazine and handbag. "It's incredible to think we were practically snowbound hours ago."

Celia smiled, she knew this was the first time Jessica had flown, but they had not come to Puerto Rico to marvel at modern transportation or admire the scenery. "We've no time to be tourists, my dear. It's into the trenches for us."

In this winter of 1958 Celia Howard's trenches were located in two places on the island. Twenty-two months earlier, in April of 1956, the first field trial of the pill known as Enovid began in Rio Piedras, a suburb of the island capital of San Juan. Less than a year later the second was started some fifty miles to the southeast in the small town of Humacao.

Both locations had one overriding recommendation: A woman doctor enthusiastic about birth control. It was to speak with those women that Celia had come to Puerto Rico. John Rock trusted her intuitions and her yankee honesty as much as her professional skills. "Go down there, Celia," he'd said. "See what they're doing, and come back and tell me what you think. The more of us who stay in contact with them, the better it's going to be."

"How about my taking Jessie, John?"

"Jessica Morgan, the young intern whose been doing so much volunteer work in my lab?"

"The very same. I've known her since she was born," Celia had explained. "And she's the future, John. A representative of the generation that must take up the torch, one of the best." Rock didn't answer immediately. "Don't you like her?" Celia asked.

"I like her quite well. But she's Joshua Morgan's daughter, isn't she? And Caleb Morgan's sister?"

"Yes. What does that have to do with anything?"

"I'm not sure," he looked perplexed. "It hasn't bothered me having her know about our laboratory tests, but field trials . . ." Rock sighed. "Of course Joshua's been retired for years. He's dead now, isn't he?"

"As good as dead." Celia explained.

"Awful, a dreadful story. But Caleb Morgan's taken over his father's mantle as Boston's most beloved society obstetrician."

"Ah, I see," Celia said. "You're worried that Jessie will say something to Cal about the field trials, and he'll let the cat out of the bag."

"The work is still a matter of great secrecy, my dear, despite all the rumors flying around. Did you hear that Parke-Davis has made a public announcement to the effect that their company would never become involved in the marketing of anything so sordid as a contraceptive pill?"

Celia snorted. "Goodyear does a multimillion dollar business in condoms, John, but what they advertise is tires. The world is simply going to have to adjust to reality. And if Cal were a threat to the work, I'd never have involved Jessie, as I have from the first. But they can both be trusted, take my word for it."

John Rock had learned to rely on Celia Howard's word. "Very well, take the girl," he said. "You're no youngster and may need her help. And the experience will be good for her. I'm glad I thought of it."

So they were here, staying at Humacao, and a few hours after they landed Jessie got her first real look at the conditions and the patients of the trial. While Celia rested,

a young social worker showed Jessie around. "I suppose
our arrangements will seem quite primitive to you," the
social worker said. "Doctor Rock must have a wonderful
facility in Boston."

"Not really." Jessie walked on toward the low adobe
building of the clinic; it gleamed with whitewash, as the
red tile roof reflected the sun. "The Free Hospital gave
him space to continue his research when he retired from
active practice a couple of years ago, but it was a hovel
until Mrs. McCormick paid to have it remodeled. It's not
all that magnificent now."

The social worker was Maria Asuncion de Vega, a dark,
pretty girl who had insisted that Jessica call her Asuncion,
but who persisted in calling the other young woman,
doctor. "Ah, Doctor Morgan," she said now, her black eyes
growing misty with emotion. "You say those words so
easily, but to me and to many of us here they are like
words from the Bible. Rock, Pincus, Chang, McCormick,
the Free Hospital for Women . . . They have changed our
lives." She opened the door of the building. "Please, come
in."

Jessie looked around. The clinic was ordinary, much as
she expected, but the women lined up in the waiting room
astounded her. "They're all so old," she murmured.

They were wizened and gray and garbed in black, and
they sat patiently waiting to be given a week's supply of a
pill which taken daily would "regulate their menstrual
cycle." That was the purpose for which the Food and Drug
Administration had licensed Searle Pharmaceuticals to make
Enovid in 1957, to treat menstrual disorders. The fact that
it also prevented pregnancy was never publicly discussed.
But it was hard to imagine that these old women weren't
long past the age when either problem concerned them.

"Are they getting the drug for their daughters?" Jessie asked.

Asuncion shook her head. "You misunderstand, Doctor.
It's not surprising, you do not know our circumstances
here in Puerto Rico. Not one of those patients is over
thirty-five."

Jessie gasped. "I don't believe it."

"It's true. Most of them have at least six children, and
that's only counting the ones that are alive. They have all
been pregnant ten, sometimes twenty times. They had

their first child at fourteen or fifteen. Is it any wonder they look old before their time?"

"No, of course, it isn't. Obviously I have a lot to learn, let's get started, shall we?"

She was a lowly intern at the Free Hospital and her only role here was an an observer, Jessie had no delusions of grandeur. But she knew her volunteer work with Dr. Rock, and her association with Celia and Mrs. Sanger and Mrs. McCormick had given her a ground-floor introduction to a remarkable change in the way the world worked. She planned to make the most of it.

She sat beside Asuncion and listened to the social worker interview patients after they had seen the medical missionary, Dr. Adeline Satherwaite, and received a further seven-day supply of Enovid. "Are you well, señora?" Asuncion asked each patient.

"Sí, señorita."

"And does your husband know about the medicine?"

A smile would light the tired face, usually displaying numerous missing teeth. Calcium deficiency, Jessie guessed. All those damned pregnancies. But it hadn't sapped their spirit. "Ay, que va! Ni mi marido ni el cura, pero estoy muy feliz, muy libre. . . ."

Thank God she'd had four years of Spanish at Paulhurst. Jessie could understand the reply that was repeated over and over, "Don't be silly. Neither my husband nor the priest knows, but I'm so happy, so free. . . ." She'd specially wanted to observe this part of the process, the social results of the pill. What Jessie had seen at Dr. Rock's facility had given her a full understanding of the medical effects. Now she wanted to know what it meant in the lives of real women.

"It's a miracle for them," she told Celia later that night. "A miracle."

"Of course. Did you ever doubt it would be?"

"Not really, but I wanted to see with my own eyes. It seems so incredible that all this is happening in this little village in Puerto Rico, and nine-tenths of the world doesn't know a thing about it."

"You know why they chose Puerto Rico, Jess? Precisely because this is a Catholic island and always has been. There are no anti-birth control laws on the books here because no one has ever felt it necessary to make any. No legislator has had to insure that women remain chained to their biology, the Church has done it for them."

"I still can't make myself believe that John Rock himself is a Catholic."

"A deeply committed, devout Catholic," Celia confirmed.

"Then how can he be doing this?"

"He has a brain, that's how."

They were in the sitting room of a simple guest house known as La Residencia de la Santa Cruz. Celia was nursing the small cup of thick, sweet coffee that had ended their meal of fresh fish and boiled potatoes. Jessie sipped something stronger. "John's not your garden variety sort of Catholic," Celia continued. "He's been studying human reproduction all his professional life, and he's better informed on the theological positions regarding it than most priests. He's convinced that preventing ovulation is a natural means of birth control, because it doesn't kill anything. Since there is no ovum for the sperm to fertilize, there isn't even the potential of human life."

"Will the Vatican buy it?"

"God knows." They both laughed. "I suppose I'd mean that literally, if I believed in God," Celia added.

"It still seems crazy. We're here in this most Catholic of Catholic countries at the request of a Catholic doctor, studying birth control. Amazing."

"I suppose it is, but to the extent that Puerto Rico is part of the United States, it's the only place in the country where a woman is not required by statute to spend her life as a brood mare."

"But that's just what they have been. Asuncion says some of them have been pregnant twenty times, that most of them had their first child when they were still children themselves."

"Exactly, but that situation was so firmly entrenched that the wretched men who make the laws never thought about it." Celia grinned wickedly. "Aren't they in for a big surprise?"

Jessie was leafing through a stack of locally published magazines and newspapers she'd been given at the clinic. "It's not a surprise anymore, apparently. This stuff is full of dire warnings, not just that a woman who takes the pill will go straight to hell. They say there are disastrous side effects, that the women will lose all their hair and get God knows what, and any children born later will be cripples and idiots. It's not true, not any of it. We've clocked almost seventy woman-years of experience with the pill by now. We know it's not true. How can they print this slander?"

Celia shrugged. "Rats who've been cornered, they'll do anything to get out of the trap. That campaign has been going on for months. But the women flock to the clinics." She made a disparaging gesture toward the pile of literature. "The lies have had no effect."

"They would at home though." Jessie frowned. "No matter how brave the women are, the damned men make the laws and this kind of thing would just give them another excuse for resisting change."

"Exactly. So we're in Puerto Rico." Celia glanced at her watch. "I'm very tired, my dear. I shall go up to bed if you don't mind."

"No, of course not. I'm going to finish this delicious thing," Jessie lifted the glass that held a chilled piña colada, "and gaze at the moon for a while."

"You do that," Celia said softly. "Gaze at the moon, dear child, and tell yourself that womankind can do anything when they set their minds to it."

Jess watched Celia climb the stairs. What an amazing person she was, in her nineties and she still ran her lab, still worked for the cause she so deeply believed in. But her back was very stooped tonight, and her shoulders sagged. More tired than she had admitted, no doubt. She'd have to take special care of Celia for the rest of their stay.

There was a wide veranda running along the front of the building for which Jessie headed, taking her drink along with her. She ignored the oversized rocking chairs in favor of a perch on the wooden railing. The wind sighed in the palm trees, crickets hummed, tropical scents she couldn't identify filled the night, and soft, balmy air caressed her skin. "It doesn't feel like I'm in the midst of a revolution," she murmured. "But I think I am."

Caleb and Jessica had grown much closer in recent years. It wasn't just that they had medicine in common now; their new intimacy was also the result of the painful gap Daniel's death had left in their lives. Both Caleb and

Jess had come to terms in their separate ways, but they clung to each other as the only sibling each had. And Cal's situation underlined the reality.

He was still not a free man, and he'd accepted that he could never have Shama; she had gone a great distance both physically and spiritually, moved out of his reach. But as he'd told himself two years earlier, he had a life and had made one for his sons. It was the best he could manage, and it seemed better after Jessica had moved in. She came in 1956, soon after beginning her internship at the Free Hospital, when Ruth married Ben Porter. It was decided that Jessie would make her base at Cal's, sleep there on those nights she wasn't on duty. The newlyweds were going to live on Carrington Avenue, obviously they needed their privacy.

Closeness to his sister was balm of sorts when Caleb needed it most. It wasn't just that Ruth's marriage put a kind of seal on Daniel's death—they were all happy for her and liked Ben—but Caleb had been shattered by the brief sight of Shama at the wedding. He hadn't spoken to her, she didn't give him the opportunity, just came and left before anyone could question her about her extraordinary new life. But that fleeting contact had torn open the wound.

She was stunningly beautiful, exquisitely dressed in Paris clothes. In a sense she was as exotic and foreign as she'd been that day in 1945 when she arrived as the castoff of war. This new Shama had left them all behind, left her old love behind, too, it seemed, she had not once met his eyes.

The next day, helping Jessie move her stuff into one of the bedrooms of his apartment, Cal had been conscious of his sister as an anchor to a world he could understand.

As the months passed he learned to delight in her enthusiasm for medicine. Jess had none of the usual cynicism of interns. Two years later she hadn't developed any, she still bubbled and he still loved to listen to her. Cal was the one who heard the story when she returned from her ten days in Puerto Rico.

"It's fabulous," Jessie told him over coffee and donuts in the living room at ten on a Saturday morning.

Cal didn't have office hours on Saturdays, and he'd already been to the hospital and picked up the donuts on his way home. Unless the telephone rang with the news that one of his patients was in labor, he had a whole day to spend with his sons and his sister. He took another jelly donut and listened to Jessie enthuse. "The pill works, Cal. And it's changing people's lives."

"Bound to," he agreed. "That's probably why there's so much opposition. Have you seen this?" He passed a copy of *Fortune* magazine across the coffee table. Jess looked questioningly at him, then took it. "In the back," he said. "I turned down the page."

She flipped to the dog-eared corner and quickly scanned the article. "I don't believe it. They object on both moral and economic grounds. How did they find out, and how can they be so self-righteous?"

"They found out because almost everybody who matters knows now. You can't keep news like this secret from the movers and shakers, Jess. And *Fortune*'s moral argument is the same one you hear everywhere. All birth control, and particularly a method as easy as this, is an attack on motherhood and the stability of the family. It's going to make every woman a whore. It's an invitation to free love and wholesale seduction."

"Bullshit."

"Thus speaks the emancipated woman. Rudely. But you're right. Have you noted that they also predict that the FDA will take years to approve the pill, if it ever does?"

She was still scanning the column. "Yes, they say it's only been tested on five hundred women. That no drug firm would dare market it for long-term use, only as a treatment for illness." She glanced up. "They don't know about Puerto Rico, about the hundreds of women taking the pill there."

"Apparently not. But they're just expressing the attitude most people share, Jess. Birth control is immoral."

"Bullshit," she said again.

"I agree, I already told you that. Their other argument is more logical, at least from *Fortune*'s point of view. Babies are big business. You have to buy clothes for them, food, furniture, appliances. . . . Hell, sometimes even a whole new house. Your pill threatens the economy of the nation.'

"So women should be slaves to turn the cogs of the capitalist machine."

Caleb guffawed. "Since when did you become a communist?"

"I never thought I was, but garbage like this might turn me into one."

Dav came in just in time to hear Jessie's last words. "Turn you into what, a garbage collector?" Twelve-year-old Dav didn't know why his father and his aunt thought that remark so funny. He decided to ignore their laughter. "Are you guys talking or can I turn on the tube?"

"My square-eyed son," Cal said. "I begin to regret buying the damned television."

"It's educational," Dav said. "Mr. George, my English teacher, said so."

"Oh, I see. And what educational thing are you going to watch? And where's your brother?"

"John's still doing his homework, but he'll be down soon. It's Saturday morning. Cartoons are on."

"Of course, how could I forget? Okay, turn it on and we'll all be educated by Bugs Bunny."

Dav pushed the button that switched on the television, then rummaged in the donut box. There were none left. "Too late, sport, sorry," Cal said. "Tell you what, to prove my heart's in the right place I'll make some popcorn." He got up and started for the kitchen, grinning a little because this is what he'd always wanted, a happy, unpretentious house, kids who were relaxed and could sprawl on a couch if they felt like it.

A flickering image appeared on the screen and halted his progress. Caleb sat back down and stared. It wasn't quite time for the cartoons. A weekly news magazine was on the air. An Arab man was being interviewed.

"Why's he got that funny kerchief on his head?" Dav demanded.

"It's called a keffiyeh," Jess explained. "They wear it to protect against the sun and the sand in the desert. Now, be quiet for a minute, Dav. I want to hear this."

Obviously Caleb wanted to hear it too. He was hunched forward, listening intently while a reporter questioned Ali Fatah about the role of the newly formed Arab Friends of Peace. "But you have almost no followers here in Kuwait, for that matter very few in the entire Arab world," the interviewer said. "Surely your movement has no future, Sheik Ali."

"If it hasn't," Ali said with quiet dignity, "then neither has the Middle East. We have to learn to live with Israel or we will die together, Arab and Jew alike."

The scene faded and was replaced by one of the reporter alone in a studio. "Shiek Ali Fatah's noble gesture is seen as just that by most observers here. Nearly everyone believes that the generous funding he has given to his new foundation cannot make up for the lack of enthusiasm among his fellow Arabs. It's rumored that as well as his western education and his generally liberal outlook, the sheik has been influenced by his constant companion of these past few years."

A picture of Shama seated by a pool in a caftan and dark glasses flashed on the screen. "Hey! That's Aunt Shama," Dav exclaimed. The camera panned to show a uniformed servant carrying a tray and descending from the terrace of a magnificent house. "Boy, that's some joint. Is it hers? I didn't know Aunt Shama was rich."

"Ssh," Jess and Cal said simultaneously.

". . . palace in Kuwait and the villa here on the French Riviera," the reporter was saying. "Although an American citizen, Miss Morhaim is originally from Morocco. She's also Jewish, a fact which has made the sheik's life difficult among his fellow Arabs, and no doubt played some part in his decision to give five million dollars to the cause of peace between Israel and her neighbors."

The program switched to another topic, Jess turned to her brother. Cal had leaned back in his chair, eyes closed, an expression of such misery on his features that she could think of nothing to say.

Emma had been the first member of the family to know that Ruth was going to marry again; she couldn't be the first to know the latest news, but Ruth was determined that she'd be the second. She called and invited her former mother-in-law to lunch.

Incredibly, on this late day in March, spring seemed suddenly to have arrived in Boston, at the Coolidge Tea Room in Copley Square when they met. The place was an institution, few men were brave enough to enter its sacred precincts. This was where Boston ladies met for lunch. Emma had taken Ruth there for the first time many years ago. "If you want to understand the natives," she had said, "you must study them in their habitat, my dear."

Today Ruth wasn't interested in observing Boston society. All her attention was on Emma. "I spoke with Jessie yesterday," Ruth said. "She had a marvelous time in Puerto Rico."

"Yes, I talked with her too. She says the weather was wonderful."

Ruth smiled. "I don't believe for a minute that Jessie and Miss Celia went to Puerto Rico for the weather. No, don't say anything. I know they're working on some miracle medicine that no one must know about yet. I will wait, but Jessie's going to make us all very proud of her someday, I'm sure of it."

"She's very young," Emma said. "She's not really doing anything remarkable yet, just watching other people do it. But I'm sure you're right. She will do something extraordinary one day. Jessie's always been unique."

"Ben says every person is unique. That's why he enjoys teaching."

Emma reached out and patted Ruth's hand. "Your Ben is a fine man, my dear. And you're happy, aren't you?"

Ruth's smile was radiant. "Very happy. We . . ." She dropped her eyes.

Emma studied her in silence a moment, then asked, "Ruth, do you have something to tell me? Not that you have to, of course, I'm not even your mother-in-law anymore."

"You are always my family," Ruth said simply. "Always. And I want to tell you. I'm going to have a baby. I went to see Caleb and he told me for certain two days ago. We were trying, but I thought I was too old and when it didn't happen right away I thought it was too late. But Caleb says it's true.

"My dear, if that's what you want, it's marvelous. When?"

"In the fall, the first part of October, we think. Caleb says I'm very healthy. He says there won't be any problems as long as I do exactly what he tells me."

"Of course there won't be any problems. Is Ben pleased?"

"Oh yes! He always wanted children too. But with his wife so ill—"

"Yes, I understand." His wife was an invalid, she thought, and your husband was a tormented man, but now you have each other, and you're to have a baby. Emma couldn't be anything but joyous for them; there was no point in thinking that this should have been her grandchild, the child of her dead son. It was Daniel who had made things as they were, not Ruth. "I'm thrilled, Ruth dear. Who else knows?"

"Only me and Ben and you and Caleb, so far. I will tell Jessie the next time I see her."

"And Shama?" Emma asked softly.

Ruth simply looked at her food. She'd ordered the dish the Coolidge was famous for, creamed chicken on a buttered biscuit. "Caleb says I must follow a strict diet. He doesn't want me to put on too much weight. This isn't diet food, is it?" She didn't wait for an answer. "Never mind, I'll begin tomorrow." She hesitated, and when she spoke next her voice had grown grave. "I'll tell Shama when I can. When she calls me the next time."

"Does she phone often?" They'd none of them seen Shama since she had flown home for her sister's marriage. On that occasion she had stayed in the country only a few hours, just long enough to stand beside Ruth under the traditional Jewish wedding canopy. She'd come alone, without her Arab boyfriend, and left before the reception. Emma knew why, they all knew why. Because she didn't want to be with Caleb. Still, it was hard to accept Shama's present behavior; this mad partying with the international jet set was not at all a Morgan-type thing. "Do you speak with her often?" Emma asked again.

"She calls me every few weeks, perhaps once a month. I want her to come home, Emma, but I don't think she ever will."

"It's hard to know where home is for someone like Shama." Emma spoke softly, hoping she wouldn't be misunderstood. "She's such an intense young woman, so full of . . ."

"She is full of love," Ruth supplied.

"Yes, I know." Emma had been going to say passion, but perhaps Ruth's term was more accurate. She looked up and smiled. "But I'm sure she'll come home to meet her new niece or nephew when the time comes."

"I hope so." Ruth looked pensive for a moment, then her mood changed again. "I cannot worry about Shama now, she's a grown-up. And I can't be unhappy when I'm so happy. That's not good English, is it?"

"It's fine English, my dear. Just fine. And I'm happy too. Ecstatic."

"Emma, I have been trying to figure it out, when Jessie was born you were thirty-seven?"

"Thirty-eight."

"Yes. And when this baby is born I will be almost thirty-five. I don't think that's too old to be a good mother."

"What nonsense, of course it's not. Listen, Ruth, all this pressure on women to get married and have a baby almost the minute they're through with school, I went through that too. It's a throwback to the Middle Ages. And the idea that a woman is too old to have children after thirty is the same thing. I'll tell you something I've never told a soul, I was mortified when I was pregnant with Jessica, really beside myself with shame. It ruined my whole pregnancy and it almost—"

She broke off, there were things about that she couldn't discuss even now. "Never mind. What I want to say is if you want a baby and can have one, then it's the perfect time. Savor every minute of the experience, my dear. Caleb will keep you well, and you must just enjoy it all."

"I plan to," Ruth said. "I'm going to sell the shop."

"Oh, I see. You want to be a stay-at-home mother, do you?"

"Yes. I don't think every woman must do that, Emma. Not in America. I don't believe all these things they write in the ladies' magazines about, what do they call it? 'togetherness.' But for me, yes, I want to stay at home."

Emma leaned forward and gripped Ruth's hand. "Then do it, my dear. Do exactly what seems right to you and Ben. Now let's have apple pie and ice cream for dessert. We won't tell my son, and you can begin being sensible tomorrow."

Interns worked appalling hours, there was almost no time for any social life. It was rare that Jessica had a date, but, incredibly, she was off duty for two whole consecutive days this glorious week in June. And she had a date tonight, which was why she was standing in the creaky old bathroom of the apartment on West Cedar Street holding a small bottle of pills.

Her period had finished yesterday. She could not now be ovulating, therefore she had no need to worry about getting pregnant. Besides, she was still a virgin. Why should she imagine something was going to happen tonight that had never happened before.

Because she wanted it to.

Timmy Michaels was a nice guy, nothing more, a tall, slim blond man who was a surgical resident at the Free Hospital, and whose time off this month coincided with hers. He'd asked her out almost as an afterthought when a casual conversation in the hospital canteen revealed that coincidence. So there was no reason to think . . . But there was, he'd try, he was bound to. Every guy did. And this time she just might give in.

"Why?" Jessie asked her reflection in the hazy bathroom mirror? "Why Timmy when you've crossed your legs for every other guy you've ever known?" *Because I'm twenty-five*, she told herself. *Because it's about time I discovered what all the fuss is about. Because I may never meet anyone I want to marry, I'm not even sure I want to get married. But I can't be a gynecologist who hasn't a clue what the whole thing actually feels like.*

She turned on the tap. There were nothing but gurgling sounds for a moment or two. Finally a thin stream of water issued from the ancient faucet. Jessica filled a glass and swallowed a pill. Even if this turned out to be a one-night stand, or a no-night stand, she had to inaugurate the new dispensation with the proper precautions. For better or for worse, from now on she was on the pill. But she wasn't going to start keeping clinical notes to add to Dr. Rock's data. He'd be sternly disapproving. Too bad the people who thought the pill was an instrument of Satan didn't know what a stern, old-fashioned moralist John Rock was. It might take some of the wind out of their sails.

She'd arranged to meet Timmy on the Esplanade at seven. He was waiting for her, a canvas bag slung over his shoulder. "Hi, I brought a blanket, but we can get chairs if you prefer."

"Lying on the grass sounds much more appealing. Let's find a place before the crowd gets any thicker."

The free summer concerts on the Esplanade were a Boston tradition, had been since the park area beside the Charles and the band shell were built in 1931. A lot of musicians from Symphony played with the Pops, and the lesser God known as conductor, Arthur Fiedler. Fiedler seemed to know exactly what kind of music delighted an audience relaxing outdoors on a summer evening.

Timmy and Jess sprawled on his blanket. They drank Cokes which Timmy bought from a street vendor and doctored with splashes from a hip flask full of rum. The easy, undemanding notes of Chopin floated along the river, followed by a medley of Gershwin show tunes, then a pastiche of Gilbert and Sullivan overtures. He had his hands in her underpants by the time they played the famous four bars from *Pinafore* which everyone knew as "Rule Britannia." Which was what she'd expected when she rejected pedal pushers in favor of a full cotton skirt.

"Mmm, you're delicious, Morgan. You feel wonderful. I think I'm in love."

"Don't be an ass, and call me Jessie. Morgan makes me think I'm working. Oh!"

"Like that, do you? So do I." He took to biting her neck, little sucking nibbles, while his busy fingers kept pushing all the right buttons. A long, sighing moan escaped from Jessie's lips. "Hey, did you come?" he whispered in her ear. "As fast as that?"

"I don't know."

He pulled back and stared at her. "I don't believe it."

"Why not?"

He didn't answer because a man a few feet away turned and made hissing sounds that meant shut up. Fiedler led his musicians into the last selection of the evening, Tchaikovsky's *Capriccio italien*. The cymbals clashed, the percussionists hammered out rhythms made for sex. "Let's get out of here," Timmy whispered.

Jess got to her feet, she was shaking all over. She wasn't sure she could walk. Timmy bundled the blanket back into the bag and took her arm, pressing his body close to hers. "It's not far, come on."

What wasn't far was his room, a small cubbyhole a few blocks away on Cambridge street. It smelled musty and there was clutter everywhere, but he'd obviously prepared for this evening. The bed was free of litter, a pristine raft in a sea of junk. He'd even had the foresight to change the sheets.

"Why won't you marry me?"

"Timmy, I don't want to get married. I've told you that over and over." Jessie sat up in the bed and pushed her hair back from her face. "God, it's hot."

He lay staring up at her. She knew he was looking at the curved underside of her breasts, and that her chin was jutted out at a defiant angle. "You're afraid of commitment, but you love me, I know you do."

Jess didn't know what to say. How could she tell this nice, sweet guy who was convinced that he loved her that she did not love him? Particularly in light of the fact that they made wonderful, passionate love at every opportunity and had been doing so for two months, ever since that June night on the Esplanade. "I thought it was supposed to cool off tonight," she said instead.

"Jesus, I propose and you talk about the weather. I don't understand you, Jessie. I don't think I'll ever understand you."

She lay down and put her head on his chest, stroking the matted blond hair with her fingers. "Leave it alone, Timmy. For tonight at least. It's too hot to argue. Can't we just enjoy ourselves?"

They did, until it was six A.M. and she had to leave to go on duty.

She thought about Timmy all during the subway ride to the hospital. Did he love her, or was he in love with love? And what difference did it make since she was quite sure she was not in love with him? Certainly, she didn't want to marry him or anyone else, at least not now. But she enjoyed sleeping with Timmy. She saw no reason why she shouldn't sleep with him. And that led her to thinking about the pill. If it were not for the fact that she had access to Enovid and was taking it regularly, this situation could not exist. She was the first of a whole new breed, Jessie told herself, a free woman, Free to have an affair the way a man always had with no fear of consequences. But surely that didn't mean she could ignore how Timmy felt, did it?

It was a whole new dimension of life, the responsibility of sexual freedom. It was one women had been able to ignore until now. She wished there was someone she could talk to about it, but the only person she might have trusted with such revelations was Shama, and Shama had cut herself off from Jessica as effectively as she had separated herself from everyone else.

As always, Shama felt unbearably sad the moment Ali withdrew and broke the link between them; while he was still shuddering with ecstasy, she felt herself starting to cry. She blinked back the tears as she usually did.

"Kam?" he murmured, reaching over to stroke her hair. "Was it good for you?"

He asked that each time, and inevitably she gave him the same answer, *"Naam, bijair."* She always told him it had been wonderful, in Arabic and in English, because an Arab sheik genuinely concerned with a woman's pleasure was a marvel. "It was great, Ali. For you too?"

"Perfect." He reached for the hot towels a servant always left beside the bed. They were kept in a brass container Ali had told her was traditional for the purpose. "Arab men have been practicing this form of birth control for hundreds of years, and it always makes a mess. So we've learned to deal with it in the nicest possible way."

Now he sponged himself and her with the steaming square of cloth, lingering over the tender insides of her thighs, making the gesture an act of love. Yet another remarkable thing, that he performed this ritual cleansing and didn't wait for her to do it. Shama knew that couldn't be traditional, but it was part of the whole thing, another indication of the strange bond that had united them for nearly two years. She was a treasure, a departure from anything he was accustomed to or might have expected to possess, and it was as a rarity that she was precious. For Ali she was foreign and thus exotic—American and Jewish— but because she was also Moroccan, familiar enough to be understood.

His hands caressing her with the steaming towel were a kind of lovemaking, she suspected he wanted to begin again. But she did not, she never did. Shama feigned sleep, and in a few moments he left her alone.

September mornings at the villa in Roquebrune were always magnificent. They breakfasted on one of the terraces, with the Riviera and the blue-green Mediterranean spread before them. The coffee was strong and thick and sweet, the croissants buttery, everything should have been perfect. Shama tried to act as if it were, but apparently she wasn't much of an actress. "What's wrong, Shama?" he asked. "You're very quiet this morning."

"Nothing's wrong. I guess I'm just tired." What else could she tell him? The things that were wrong were beyond his power to alter. It wasn't his fault her period was three days late. Ali was always very careful, if there had been an accident, it wasn't really his fault. And he couldn't turn himself into Caleb, or make her forget him. "Nothing's wrong," she said again.

He looked at her a moment, then shrugged. "Okay, perhaps you're tired. I have a meeting in Cannes this afternoon. I was going to suggest you come and do some shopping. Maybe you should stay here and rest instead."

"Yes, I think I will. What kind of a meeting?"

Ali laughed. "A very American question. No Arab woman would ask her husband about his business."

"I'm not an Arab, and you're not my husband."

Something in her tone alerted him. "Shama, listen. I think my father will see reason if we just do it. I think we should get married and tell him after it's done."

"No, not like that." She shook her head. The opposition of Ali's family to their affair was a safety valve, a protection. She wasn't prepared to give it up. Which was why she wasn't prepared to have a baby, that would make Ali all the more determined to marry her. If she didn't get her period in the next few days, she would make some excuse to leave him and go to Paris. Surely she'd be able to find a doctor in Paris who did abortions. She thought of Caleb. The notion was too painful and she pushed it away.

"Actually my meeting in Cannes is with some Israelis," he was saying. "Representatives of a peace group, intellectuals."

"That's wonderful, Ali." This time her enthusiasm wasn't false. "A little progress at last."

He shrugged. "We're not making progress yet, just talking about making it. But I suppose it's a start."

He rose and kissed her and left. Shama continued sitting on the terrace, staring at the sea, wondering about her life and about the ties she had severed so abruptly, but could not forget.

"I saw Ruth yesterday," Emma said. "She looks marvelous, Josh. Blossoming. And I mean that literally. She's in her ninth month now, the baby's due in a few weeks. She's enormous, but Cal doesn't think it's twins."

Emma adjusted the pillow beneath Joshua's head as she spoke. He didn't move, he never moved, but she was conscious of a change. "Do you want to tell me something?" she asked. "Yes, you do."

She could always tell. No one would understand, no one would believe the communication between them, the uncanny way she could read his mind. She had never tried to explain. How could she when only she knew that there *was* a mind still trapped in that motionless shell? The rest of them, even Marya, still thought Joshua was a vegetable, a living corpse. Only Emma knew the full horror of the truth, that he was as he'd always been, but trapped in a body that could not be made to do his will. Except for one little finger.

She took a pad of paper and a pen and perched them on her knee, then slipped her left hand under his right. "Whenever you're ready, darling," she said softly. "There's no hurry."

Slowly, painfully, with exquisite exactitude the tapping began. His little finger against her sensitized palm. One tap for the letter *a*, two for *b*, three for *c*, and so on. They'd worked it out a year ago. Joshua made the one motion he had willed himself to be able to make, he moved one finger, and she wrote down the letters he indicated. Finally, after an hour, she had transcribed a six-word sentence. "R must do whatever C says."

She read the banal little message aloud, so he'd know she'd gotten it correctly. "Yes, darling," she said. "I'm sure Ruth is doing exactly what Cal tells her to do." All that exhausting effort, to say almost nothing.

Emma bathed the sweat from his forehead. These sessions were agony for Joshua, but she knew they were ecstasy too. However unimportant the things he had to say, communicating them was a triumph, a secret proof known only to the two of them that within the dead shell he remained a man and alive.

Shama was walking in the grounds of the villa when it happened. It took less than forty seconds. One minute she was standing beside the fountain in the rose garden, the next three figures in jellabas and keffiyehs had sprung from the top of the wall and surrounded her. She screamed just once, then something was clamped over her mouth and nose and there was a sickly sweet smell followed by unconsciousness.

Motion. Being carried, then deposited in a car. A brief moment when consciousness became strong enough so she thought she could make a sound and tried—then the cloth clamped over her nose and mouth again and the nauseating smell followed by more blackness. Then cold air, a wind that blew in her face and revived her, the sense of arms around her, carrying her, but not Ali's arms, a stranger's. He reeked of garlic and sweat and his face was so close to hers she could smell his foul breath.

Be still, she told herself, don't let on you're awake. She opened her eyes a little bit, just enough to see where she was. A big open space, very dark. It was night. She heard words in Arabic, but they were low murmurs and she didn't hear them clearly enough to know what was being said. The man carrying her hadn't spoken, the voices came from somewhere just ahead of them. She could make out only *gariban*, hurry. Then they started to climb.

Not a hill she realized after a second or two, they were going up some stairs. Through slitted eyes she saw a metal handrail and narrow metal steps. An airplane! Dear God, they were taking her into a plane. She knew it was now or never, and she opened her mouth and screamed as loud as she could.

If there had ever been a chance, she'd lost it, left it too late. The man carrying her had reached the top of the steps and he flung her forward into the cabin, then entered himself and turned to slam and lock the door. Shama was still screaming and another man squatted beside her, watching her and listening to her and laughing. Then, after a few seconds, he raised his hand and slapped her face. Three times. Very deliberately and as hard as he could. "Shut up, Jew whore," he said in English. "No one can hear you but us."

She tasted blood in her mouth and she stopped screaming and stared at him. He had a thin, dark face and a heavy beard and one of his eyes had a drooping lid below an ugly scar. She would never forget that face, she thought. Later she would be able to identify him for the police. Then she realized that if he'd intended there to be a later he would never have allowed her to see him. Kidnap victims held for ransom were always blindfolded. He seemed to see that realization and the terror it engendered dawning in her eyes, and he laughed again.

Someone she couldn't see said in Arabic, "We're taking off, better strap yourself in."

"What about her?" the man beside Shama asked.

"It doesn't matter, leave her where she is."

The one who had hit her grunted and got up and sat down and fastened his seat belt. Shama lay where she was, staring at his legs. He had jeans on under his jellaba, and American cowboy boots with elaborate markings on the leather. She wanted to run, almost tried to, then realized how stupid that was. The plane was moving quickly, gathering speed. There was no place to run to. She moved her head and looked around. There were eight seats, four on each side of a narrow aisle. There were two men with her, but she remembered three coming over the wall of the villa. The third must be the pilot.

The pair in the cabin spoke to each other in Arabic once more. "How long will it take to get there?"

"About four hours."

"Will we get paid as soon as we deliver her?"

"That was the arrangement."

"Good. I know a wonderful whorehouse in Al Kuwayt."

"Why bother paying for it? We have four hours with this one for free."

Shama did the first smart thing she'd done since the nightmare started. She did not allow herself to scream or shudder, she didn't even flinch. She listened to them discuss the prospect of raping her with an absolutely blank face, and when the attack began she fought and cursed and protested only in English. As horrible and unthinkable and terrifying as it was, as painful and brutal and degrading as it became when one after the other had used her body, she did not sacrifice her single advantage—the simple fact that apparently they did not know she spoke Arabic.

20

Word of the abduction did not reach Boston for nearly a week. When the call came, it was Sunday afternoon and Ben was home correcting papers.

"This is Ali Fatah, Shama's friend. With whom am I speaking, please?"

Ben felt his throat constrict. He could practically taste the bad news. It couldn't be anything else. Ali Fatah was not calling to talk about the weather in the various jet set playgrounds he and Shama frequented. "This is Ben Porter, Mr. Fatah. Shama's brother-in-law."

"Oh yes, she has spoken of you."

There was a long pause on the other end of the line. Ben carried the telephone to the door of the den and peered into the hall and the kitchen beyond. Ruth had gone upstairs to take a nap about an hour ago. He satisfied himself that she hadn't come down. "What's wrong, Mr. Fatah?"

The silence lengthened. Finally Ali spoke. "There isn't any easy way to tell you—" But he still couldn't make himself say more.

"Is Shama dead?" Ben asked softly. It was the worst thing he could think of, and if it was the truth he wanted to know now, immediately. If it was not, well, anything else was better. Probably.

"I don't think she is dead," Ali said. "I pray not. But she has been kidnapped."

"Oh, Jesus." Ben sat down hard on the chair behind the desk. "When? Who did it? Why?"

Ali explained as well as he could. It took only a few moments. Shama had been abducted by enemies of his who wished to use her to strike at him. He had received a letter telling him that much, but not where she was or what ransom was being demanded for her release.

"That's all you know?" Ben demanded.

"That's all. I'm sorry."

"You're sorry? That's all you can say? What kind of a crazy world do you live in, Mr. Fatah? What the hell kind of people do you run around with?"

"I'm sorry," Ali repeated. "You can't say anything I haven't already told myself. It's my fault entirely. I waited until now to notify you because I hoped . . ." He allowed the words to trail off, unable to express whatever it was he'd hoped.

Ben took a deep breath. "Listen, my wife is going to have a baby any day now. I can't let her find out about this without preparing her first. Where are you? Give me a number where we can reach you."

He wrote down the string of numbers Fatah recited into the telephone and hung up. Then he stared at the instrument for some moments before turning and climbing the stairs.

The room was filled with blackness and with a heat so intense it was like another presence, but Shama knew she was alone. She huddled in one corner, pressed against the stone wall, waiting, listening. She would know by the footsteps who was coming. The woman in the chardak, or the others, the ones who had brought her here. She couldn't stop shivering. She'd been doing it since those endless hours in the airplane when they . . .

Don't think about it, make the thought go away, she told herself. When she was a child in Morocco and the bombers had been overhead and she was terrified, but afraid to scream, she used to bite her fingers so hard the pain made her forget what was happening. She wanted to do that now, but they had tied her hands and her feet. She bit her lips instead.

Ben walked down the hall to their bedroom, the door was open and he stood and looked at Ruth. She was sleeping, her dark hair loose and spread over the pillow.

She lay on her side, knees drawn up and both hands cradling her enormous belly. Who was it who had spoken of being "surprised by joy?" C. S. Lewis he thought. It was a good commentary on happiness that came late in life, long after you'd given up expecting it. That's what had happened to them, they'd been surprised by joy.

He took a step into the room, stretched out a hand to touch her, then drew back. Joy now, but earlier so much pain, and all visited on her by forces beyond her control, like this new torment that waited for her when she woke. Some people made their own monsters, but Ruth's had come from outside.

He watched her a moment longer. A knitted yellow blanket hung over the back of a chair and he shook it out and spread it over her legs and the beloved bulge which was the wonderful promise of their child. Then he went back downstairs and picked up the telephone.

"Caleb? Thank God I got you. This is Ben Porter and I have to speak with you. It's an emergency and I just don't know who else to call. No, Ruth is fine. This is about Shama."

Three days later Jessie held tight to Caleb's hand while the Alitalia plane lifted into the air. It wasn't the takeoff that frightened her, and not the thought of flying such an incredible distance. She was so full of fear for Shama, so brimming over with it, that there was no room for more. She was clinging to her brother to keep at bay the demons of despair. Thank God they hadn't been persuaded by her arguments that she should go to Kuwait alone.

They had met on Carrington Avenue a few hours after Ali Fatah's call, all of them ignoring any other claim on their time, and assembled to discuss the impossible. "I'm the logical choice," Jessie had insisted. "I agree with Ben, one of us has to go and it has to be me. Whatever's happened in the past couple of years, no one is closer to Shama than I am. If . . . *when* she's released, I'm the one who has to be there."

Caleb shook his head. "I'm going. Stop talking about it. I can cover myself at the hospital and the office, and Miss Carlisle can manage the boys. If necessary even Susan can play mother for a few days." He turned to Ruth.

She had sat on the couch between Emma and Ben,

pressed against her husband for comfort and support. Despite her bulk she looked very tiny and achingly vulnerable. "Yes, please, Cal, if you can. She will want you there." It was true because of what they all knew, that Caleb loved Shama and that once she had loved him, and it needed to be acknowledged, but speaking the words seemed an enormous effort for Ruth. Her voice was a low whisper, and she was so pale and drawn, her eyes looked like two black saucers.

"It may mean I won't be here to deliver junior," Cal had said gently. "But don't worry. I'll arrange for a colleague to take care of you. A good man, I promise."

"About that I'm not worried, having a baby is something natural. What is happening to Shama, that is not natural."

No one contradicted her. The thought of Shama, of what she might be going through, was a palpable presence in the room, a horror so real it almost had a form and a taste and a smell.

It was for Ruth's sake that Emma was there. Emma had never been close to Shama and she hardly knew Ben, but she loved desperately three of the four people in this room and their anguish was hers. "What about the American Embassy?" she asked. "We do have one in Kuwait, don't we?"

"We do," Ben said. "I called them as soon as I spoke with Cal. I got a lot of diplomatic gobbledegook about being patient and waiting to see how the Kuwaitis handled the situation. I'm not sure they even believed me. That's when I decided one of us had to go over there."

Emma glanced at each of them, they were almost paralyzed by their terror and their grief. They seemed like zombies. She stood up and smiled her strong, beautiful smile. "Yes, of course. And two of us is even better, so it should be Jessica and Caleb." She waited, but no one contradicted her. "There, that's settled. I'll make some tea, Ruth dear, if you don't mind me poking around in your kitchen. Jessie, why don't you try and get the airline? See if you can find out how you get to Kuwait and make reservations. Then I think Caleb and Ben should both speak to this Mr. Fatah."

So now Jessie and Cal were flying east on a journey that brought them to Rome after eleven hours, and then, five hours later, to that six-thousand-square-mile piece of desert at the head of the Persian Gulf between Saudi Arabia and Iraq.

"Until Shama went to work for Ali Fatah I never knew this place existed," Jessie murmured as they deplaned.

Cal glanced around. "Neither did I, but that doesn't strike me as very odd for an American. I don't think we're going to run into anyone we know from Boston." The airfield of Al Kuwayt, the country's capital, lay like a square of shiny black cloth unfolded over the sand. Around it in every direction was nothing but a barren dun-colored land broiling under a merciless sun.

He took his sister's arm and drew her forward to the single building which had to be the terminal. It was a utilitarian space, simply a large room with a roped-off area that served as a baggage claim. Getting out of the sun was a relief of sorts, but the press of bodies generated almost as much heat and the stench was overpowering.

The place was full of people milling about and speaking a variety of languages, none of which Jessie or Cal understood. A few men in western business suits mingled with Arabs in jellabas and keffiyehs. There were a handful of women as well; most wore the black *chardak,* a robe that covered them from head to foot and allowed only the eyes to show. Until she spotted one stunning blonde in a red sheath dress, a ton of gold jewelry, and the highest heels she'd ever seen, Jessie believed herself the only woman wearing what she thought of as ordinary clothes.

She tugged at the skirt of her blue seersucker suit. The white cotton blouse which had been so fresh when she put it on in Rome was soaked in perspiration, and the toes of her navy-and-white spectator pumps were already dusty. "What do we do now?"

"I'm not sure. Fatah said he'd send someone to meet us, but I don't know how we're to recognize whoever it is."

That mystery was solved quickly. A young Arab appeared beside them and touched his forehead and his chest in the traditional salaam. He was dressed like all the others, in flowing white robes, but his English was perfect and very British. "The doctors Morgan, I presume?"

"Yes. I'm Caleb Morgan, and this is my sister, Jessica."

The boy salaamed twice more, once for each of them. "I am Anwar. Sheik Ali is my uncle. Please, if you will come

this way. Do not concern yourself with your luggage, it
will be attended to."

He led them back out into the brutal heat and glare, but
the discomfort lasted only a moment. In seconds they
were seated in the rear of an enormous gray Rolls Royce.
The car was air-conditioned and the cool air was a blessing.

Anwar unfolded a seat across from them and waited
until they were settled, then he tapped on the window
separating them from the chauffeur. The Rolls glided into
motion. "We are going to Sheik Ali's palace, it will take
about forty minutes to get there. In the meantime . . ."
He touched a button somewhere and a table appeared
beside him revealing a drinks cabinet. "I can offer you
scotch, or some white Burgundy. Or just club soda if you
prefer."

Jessie wondered about the Islamic prohibition against
alcohol, but she remembered Shama telling her years
before, when Ali Fatah was simply her boss, that the
Kuwaitis weren't rigid about their religion. Nonetheless,
she wasn't interested in whisky or wine. "Club soda," she
murmured. "Thank you."

Caleb said he'd have the same thing. "Very wise," Anwar
commented, handing them heavy crystal tumblers. "Our
climate is something you have to adjust to, and it's easier if
you don't drink spirits right away." He smiled, displaying
perfect white teeth that gleamed against his dark skin.
"I'm at Oxford, King's College. I tell my English friends
that the desert climate probably accounts for the Prophet's
views of strong drink. Maybe he'd have had a different
attitude if he'd done his preaching in London."

They continued chatting about inconsequentials; beyond
the windows of the limousine Al Kuwayt appeared as a city
in the act of creating itself. Everywhere they looked they
saw new buildings under construction. Cement mixers and
cranes were scattered across the landscape like locusts.
"My country has fewer than a million and a half people,"
Anwar explained. "And until very recently we were entirely ruled by our traditions and our past."

"And now?" Jessie asked.

"Now we are trying to find a way to blend the best of
our history and our culture with the advantages of the
twentieth century. That has become possible because where
once we were poor, we have become rich. This century

has discovered a use for that peculiar black sticky stuff which Allah in His wisdom put beneath our sands." He grinned again, a frank, open grin that showed once more those perfect teeth.

Jessie nodded, as she watched the women on the streets in their black robes.

"You eat nothing," the woman murmured. "You must eat." She held the bowl close to Shama's mouth, forcing a little of the stuff between her lips. Shama knew it was laban, *a kind of yogurt, but made from goat's milk and more strongly fermented than anything she'd ever tasted. She had bitten her lips so badly, they were raw and swollen, and the* laban *burned. Besides, she couldn't make her throat open far enough to swallow. The yogurt dribbled down her chin, and the woman cursed softly in exasperation. "Kama turid," she said. As you wish. Shama made no reply. She still clung to her single secret, the only chink in her powerlessness, that she could understand them and they didn't know it.*

Later, how much later she didn't know, a man came. He was old, but he looked strong. She could see his eyes below his headdress because another man was with him, holding a light. He played it over her body, and the one with the dark, powerful eyes studied her. "So much fuss over a woman," he murmured. "Not even a beautiful woman. Do you think she's beautiful, Tariq?"

"Not now, Excellency, but perhaps before they . . ."

"Ah yes, that was unfortunate. But what can you expect from men like that?" He shrugged. Shama watched him, her eyes fixed on his, but she made no sign. The man leaned forward, then drew back abruptly. "She smells. I thought I might find her amusing, I've never had a Jew, but those pigs ruined her." He turned and the man with the flashlight swung the beam away. They left and she was alone in the dark once more. She tried to summon Ali's face to comfort her, but it wouldn't come. Instead she kept seeing Caleb.

The Rolls left Al Kuwayt behind and headed west on a strip of black tarmac which cut a narrow swathe through the expanse of limitless sand. There were some low hills on the far horizon, and for a few moments a caravan of

camels appeared silhouetted against the fiery sun. Seconds
later they had disappeared. "Was that a mirage?" Jessie
asked.

"No, camels are still the transportation of choice for
much of our population," Anwar explained.

Cal shifted restlessly. "Look, don't you have anything to
tell us about Shama?"

Anwar held up his hand. "Please, you must forgive me,
Doctor Morgan, but I can't talk to you about that. I don't
know anything, really. We're almost there and Sheik Ali is
waiting for you. I'm sure he'll tell you everything he can."

The Rolls swallowed the road. They met no other cars
and saw nothing other than momentary glimpses of distant
camels. Without something to measure against, it was
impossible to know how fast they were going, but Jessie
was sure it was very fast.

"Over there," Anwar said finally. "On your left, that dot
is the palace."

It was just a speck at first, then it grew larger and they
saw that it was green. "An oasis," Cal murmured.

"Yes. No doubt when my ancestors decided to build a
permanent house they chose this site because of the existence of a spring. My uncle and my father, Sheik Hassan,
have added the latest methods of water conservation and
irrigation." He smiled again. "It's supposed to be a big
secret, but they brought in Israeli engineers."

They were close enough now to distinguish the tops of
palm trees behind a high wall that stretched as far as they
could see. Moments later they were passing through a
gate, and the world had been transformed. It was lush and
green. There were fountains and rolling lawns and flowers.
Jessie identified other flashes of color as birds darting
among the trees. It might have been paradise—except that
everywhere were men in jellabas with machine guns slung
over their shoulders.

The guards stood at attention as the Rolls passed. Soon
the limousine drew up before a magnificent facade of
intricate stone carving and hammered bronze doors. Ali
Fatah was waiting for them. He didn't salaam. He just
shook both their hands and drew them forward into the
palace. "Please, come this way so we may talk."

Fatah led them down a long passage. Jessie had a swift
impression of cool marble in a spectrum of colors from

beige to pink to carnelian red. She hadn't known marble came in anything but white. The woven carpets underfoot glowed like jewels. Waist-high brass vases were filled with roses that shed a heady perfume in the cool, sweet air.

They came to an open door at the end of the corridor. Another of the ubiquitous armed men stood beside it. Ali murmured something, then waved them forward. The room had an arched ceiling supported on carved pillars, and a still, square pool of bright blue water in its center. There were more of the gemlike carpets on the floor, and piles of silk cushions everywhere. Ali ignored the cushions and pointed to three small chairs beside the pool. "I think we will be most comfortable there."

He waited until they were seated, then clapped his hands. A servant appeared with a tray containing bowls of fruit and plates of cakes and a variety of bottles and glasses as well as three coffee cups. "What can I give you?"

"Do you have mint tea?" Jessie asked. It suddenly seemed the most important thing in the world to have what Shama would have had, what Ruth had taught her to love.

Ali looked at her, nodded in understanding, and murmured something to the servant. He went to the door, spoke to someone they couldn't see—the guard probably—then returned. "The tea will come in a moment," Ali said. "And for you, Doctor Morgan?"

"Look, you're very kind, but we didn't come here to—"

Ali raised his hand. "I know, Doctor Morgan, believe me. But we have our ways of doing things, and they're not so unreasonable. We'll all make more sense if we're comfortable and not thirsty or hungry while we talk. Will you have a whisky? Or coffee perhaps?"

"Coffee," Cal said gruffly.

"Qahhwa," Ali said. The servant poured a thick black liquid from a small brass pot into an exquisite china cup. Another man entered the room. He brought steaming mint tea in a glass cradled by a carved silver holder. Ali took a scotch and soda. Finally the ritual ended and the servants were dismissed and they were alone. "Now," Ali said, "I will tell you what I know."

"Everything," Cal said. "Tell us every detail. We're so much in the dark. This whole thing is so impossible to comprehend."

"For an American, yes, I suppose it is," Ali said. "I'll begin at the beginning. Ten days ago Shama was abducted from the garden of my villa at Roquebrune on the Riviera. She was there alone because I'd gone to Cannes on business and she decided to stay home."

He paused and for a moment pressed the glass he held to his forehead. He was in pain, Jessie realized. He really loved her. She started to reach out, then drew back, too shy to make any such gesture of sympathy. Ali recovered himself and went on.

"I have been able to determine that she was taken between four and five in the afternoon, and that there were three men involved."

"Arabs?" Cal asked.

"Thugs, hired hands, but yes, they were Arabs. At least the child who saw them, the son of one of the gardeners, said they were dressed as such, and it's a logical assumption."

Jessie leaned forward. "Why didn't this child get help, raise some sort of alarm?"

"Eventually he did, but by then they had her off my property. I wasn't there, you see, and the men who would have known how to handle it, my bodyguards, were with me in Cannes. The servants tried to reach me, but the call came after I'd left my meeting. It's a drive of nearly an hour from Cannes to Roquebrune. It was past six when I returned and learned what had happened."

"Jesus!" Cal exploded. "Didn't anybody think to call the police?"

Ali closed his eyes, then opened them. "Doctor Morgan," he said softly. "I've spent almost all my adult life in the West. I am at home in your world, in many ways I admire it, but I am an Arab, a Kuwaiti, the son of a man of great power in my country. The thing I have been most insistent on with my servants is discretion. No, no one called the police. That is a decision which could only have been made by me."

"Okay, what did you do?" Cal was still clutching the miniature coffee cup. He set it down and leaned forward, fixing the other man with his gaze.

"I made a number of telephone calls," Ali said quietly. "I was able to determine that Shama had been taken out of France on a small private plane. They had filed their flight plan as they had to do. It wasn't much of a surprise that they were coming here to Kuwait. I followed them."

"And came here to this splendid palace." Cal's voice was tinged with bitterness. "I take it that what you've been doing is waiting here with all the comforts of home until these bastards decide to tell you what they want."

"I have been doing a great many things," Ali said. "Everything that can be done, believe me."

"But whoever took Shama still has her."

Ali's silence was answer enough. Cal started to say something, but Jessie motioned him to silence. She leaned forward and this time she did put her hand on Ali's. "Listen, what do I call you? Mr. Fatah? Sheik Ali?"

"Please, just Ali, you are Shama's family. And I . . . I feel that we are not strangers."

"Okay, Ali. We're not blaming you, really we're not. We're just terrified and out of our depth. I've never been involved in anything like this before, neither has my brother. Please tell us as simply as you can. Why have they taken Shama? Do these thugs want money? Can it be paid?" She took a deep breath. "I guess what I, what we, want is your honest assessment. Are we going to get Shama back?"

He took a long time to answer. When he did his words were so low, they had to strain to hear him. "I don't know. I pray that we are." His voice grew a little stronger. "If it were a matter of money, it would be simple. But the pigs who took her were hired hands, as I said before. The person responsible is one of my countrymen, a very powerful man. He hasn't stated his terms. He's left me to figure them out for myself."

"And have you?" Cal asked.

"Oh, yes. I knew as soon as I found out who was behind this. I have been involved in a small effort to create some kind of bridge between Israel and the rest of us. Shama was taken to punish me for that."

"Then unmake your goddamn bridge," Cal exploded. "Let somebody else build it or try to build it. Tell this bastard whoever he is that you'll run around cursing every Israeli ever born if he'll let Shama go."

Ali stared at him for a long moment, then he stood up. "It's not that simple, Doctor Morgan. I wish it were, but it's not. Now, you must be tired after your long journey. I will show you to your rooms. I have taken the liberty of arranging that your dinner will be served there. We can talk again in the morning."

The desert night fell as it always did, suddenly and without warning. One minute it was light and the next dark. Ali stood by the window of his private suite and watched the stars twinkle into being in the blackness. After a while he looked at his watch, then he raised his eyes to the sky once more. A long time passed, finally the signal he was waiting for came, a light tap on the door.

He went and opened it, and the man came in without a word of greeting, slinging his rifle off his shoulder as he did so. "Well?" Ali demanded.

"Nothing," the other man said. "We did everything we could do, but we can't find out where he's holding her." He lay his hand on Ali's arm. "I'm sorry." Then, after a brief pause, "Ali, listen to me, I'm your brother, I love you. But you're being crazy. Forget her, the whole thing is insane. You can't let one woman change everything. You're making progress, you said so yourself. You're our only hope, Ali. If you can't do this, no one can. We'll be condemned to war for a hundred years. If it were just the Israelis, it wouldn't matter so much. We could beat them. But it's the Americans—"

"Stop. I know everything you're going to say. I've been telling myself the same thing for ten days. But I can't do it."

The man whose name was Hasan stared at his brother for a long time, then he turned away. "So what are you going to do?" he asked tonelessly.

"Talk to the chief."

"He won't see you. He's washed his hands of you."

"He'll see me. This is what he's been waiting for, for me to come crawling. He's probably behind the whole thing."

Hasan didn't reply, just watched while Ali pulled on his jellaba and wrapped his head in a keffiyeh. Then they left together.

The chief had a palace of his own, one more splendid than any of the ones he'd given to his six sons, but he was seldom to be found there. Sheik Mohammet al-Rashan Fatah lived in a tent like his ancestors, like the countless chiefs of the powerful Kuwaiti tribe who preceded him.

Ali squatted across from his father, a fire of camel dung smoldered between them. "Why do you come to me?" the old man asked.

"Because only you can help me."

"All your life I have helped you. I denied you nothing. I sent you to England to be educated so that someday you would be the kind of leader this country needs. I made myself understand when you became more like them than like us. And for all of this how have you repaid me?"

Ali did not speak.

"You lived openly with a Jewish whore and you spoke openly of giving in to our enemies." Sheik Mohammet shot his head forward on its scrawny, cranelike neck and spat into the fire. "Every day I beg Allah to forgive me for being the sire of such a son."

"The woman has done nothing evil," Ali whispered. "Whatever you think of me, she does not deserve what has happened to her."

"She is a Jew, if she suffers I take pleasure in it."

The words were cruel, but not the tone of voice, it was almost a ritual declaration. Ali felt the first flutter of hope. "It says in the Koran—"

"*Uskut!* Silence! You dare to quote the Holy Book to me? What have you come here for? Do you think I stole your whore? I would not waste my time."

"I know you didn't abduct her," Ali said. "We both know who did. Samal."

The old man's roar of rage filled the tent, it bounced off the hides and caused the flames of the fire to flicker. "Do not mention the name of that turd of a camel in my hearing. He is my enemy, the enemy of all of our line. Is it for this you have come to me? To speak the name I hate most in all the world." He grabbed his head with one hand and rocked back and forth, calling to Allah to witness the abuse heaped on him by his own son.

Ali waited a moment for the histrionics to pass. It was a sham, he was convinced of it. Samal wouldn't have dared such a move unless he had the old man's tacit understanding, but this was a drama that had to be played to the end. "He is my enemy because he is yours, Father. And now he has dared to do this thing which blackens our honor. He must be made to pay."

The old sheik leaned forward and grabbed the folds of

Ali's robe. His right hand had only two fingers, the others
had been shot off years before, and his left arm hung
useless by his side, injured in some battle he hardly remembered. Still the strength of him was overwhelming, it
came across the space between them in waves. Ali felt it
must force him backward, physically and spiritually back
to wherever his father wanted him to be. "For myself I
will deal with that pork-eating maggot in my own way, in
my own time, but that is not good enough for you, is it?
You want me to do something now."

"Yes. I want you to get Shama back. You can do it,
Father. Only you. I have tried and I failed."

His father snorted. "You sent Hasan, but you are both
like women. You have forgotten the old ways, and the
desert keeps her secrets from you. But you are right, if I
chose I could get her back."

"Choose," Ali whispered. "Choose to do it. I'm begging
you."

"And if I do, then what?"

"Whatever you say."

"No. You will take her back to that other life where you
are most comfortable. You will live with her openly again."

"Not if it displeases you. I swear it."

"I don't believe you."

Ali held his breath for long seconds before he spoke.
"Father, I swear to you in the name of Allah, if you will get
her back, I will do whatever you say. Whatever pleases you."

The old sheik leaned back on his heels and studied his
son. Many seconds passed before he spoke. "First, you
will disband this foundation of yours. You will make a
public announcement, saying that Allah has opened your
eyes, that now you know the Israelis are vermin who can
never be trusted, that we must make *jihad*, holy war, until
the last Jew has been forced into the sea."

He couldn't let it all die without at least a semblance of
struggle. "Father, what I have done has been for our
people, for Arabs everywhere. I don't care about the Jews
as such, only about peace so that we can use what we have
to make progress, make things better for ourselves. If we
are forever at war—"

"All this I have heard before," the old man said. "If you
are still singing this same song, my son, we have nothing to
talk about."

The fire flickered, the seconds stretched into minutes. At last Ali nodded. "It will be as you say."

"Good. Next you will sell the houses in New York and on the Riviera. You will come home to Kuwait and stay here. And you will marry your cousin Fatima as I have always wanted you to do."

"Yes."

Sheik Mohammet smiled for the first time since his son had arrived. "Good, very good. Allah has heard my prayers, praised be His holy name. I myself will lead my men to find her. *Inshallah* she will be free tomorrow."

Ali bowed his head. His suspicions had been correct. There would be no search, no fight. None was necessary. His father could not promise to free her so quickly if he wasn't party to the abduction. Mohammet had made common cause with Samal, a man he hated, to regain control of his son. Allah alone knew what Samal's motives had been, but in this convoluted political world they could be anything. Sooner or later he would know. It didn't matter. What mattered was only that Shama would be free—and he would never see her again, never touch her again.

He salaamed and stood up. "May Allah pour blessings on your head, my father. Thank you. Where will she be released?"

Mohammet shrugged and thought for a moment, then he smiled a broad smile that exposed his toothless gums. "The brother and sister who are with you now, the Americans, send them to Israel. Tell them the woman will be given to them there."

The woman came again, this time she was not alone. Two men were with her. At first Shama thought they were the ones who had taken her originally and she shrank back in her corner, baring her teeth and hissing defiance at them. The taller of the two reached down and yanked her to her feet and she knew she had never seen him before. Besides, they wouldn't do all those unspeakable things with the woman looking on. She went limp and did not struggle, but even after they cut her bonds she could not walk.

"She has no strength because she would not eat," said the woman.

"It does not matter. As long as she's alive when we give her to them."

Shama tried to make her mind work, to figure out who they meant, where they were taking her. She couldn't think. The man who had spoken slung her over his shoulder and carried her out of the darkness into the light. She had to close her eyes against the sudden glare of the sun, when she opened them she saw she was being carried across a courtyard to a gate. Armed men stood beside the gate, but they made no attempt to stop them. Beyond the wall were a line of camels. The man carrying her barked an order and one of the beasts was made to kneel. He flung her across the saddle, then mounted himself. "Remember, she must be alive when you put her on the airplane," a voice said. Her captor grunted and covered her half-naked body with the skirt of his robe. She could smell his skin and feel the heat of the sun beating on her flesh beneath that scant protection.

A great many diplomatic strings were pulled to allow Ali Fatah's private plane to land at Lod Airport in Tel Aviv. Air Traffic Control brought them down on a little-used strip far from the commercial runways. Armed Israeli soldiers surrounded them the moment the wheels touched the tarmac.

A man in a business suit came on board and inspected their passports. He didn't say a word until he'd looked at all their documents, then he grunted and started for the door, motioning them to follow. The three of them, Ali and Jessie and Caleb, were taken under guard to a shed about half a mile away. It smelled of motor oil and men's sweat, but it was empty.

There was a table with a telephone, but no other furniture. Obviously the Israeli didn't consider it part of his job to make them comfortable. "You can wait one hour," he said. "If they don't deliver the package you're waiting for by then, you'll all have to leave Israel." He turned to Caleb. "Officially you're not here. If you and your sister wish to come back you can enter through the usual channels."

Caleb nodded. There was no mystery about the man's attitude. This situation was no doing of the Israelis, but involving them like this could lead to a diplomatic incident if things didn't go as they should. "Thank you," he said. "Look, it's possible that Miss—"

"The package you're waiting for," the Israeli interrupted.

Caleb felt anger start to build, but he controlled it. "Okay, it's possible this so-called package will require medical care. My sister and I are doctors, but we may need a hospital."

The Israeli shook his head and turned away.

Ten minutes went by. Fifteen. Nobody spoke. From time to time one or another of them looked at a watch. Only ten minutes of their allotted hour remained when a jeep roared onto the tarmac. Caleb and Ali both started for the door, Jessica right behind them. "Wait," the Israeli said, moving to block their path.

They went back to the window. The jeep stopped some fifty yards away. One of its doors opened and something was pushed out. From the shed it appeared to be a bundle of old rags. Whatever it was, it lay motionless on the burning tarmac. Jessie caught her breath in a sound somewhere between a gasp and a sob. The jeep roared off. They all broke for the door once more. This time the Israeli didn't stop them.

She was breathing, but that was all they could say. It was Cal who lifted her into his arms. "We've got to get her out of this heat." He started back to the shed at a trot.

Ali and Jessica followed him. When they regained the relative cool of the shed, Caleb lay Shama gently on the floor. She was tied into some kind of burlap sack, it was knotted around her neck. Jessie flung open the supply kit they'd brought with them and handed Cal a pair of scissors. He cut the burlap away and they eased it off of her. This time Jessie didn't allow herself to gasp. It was Ali who moaned when Shama's naked body came into view.

She was filthy and covered with bruises and cuts and weals. Dried blood was clotted on the inside of her thighs and down her legs. Caleb pressed a stethoscope to her breast while Jessie tried to get a blood pressure reading. It was Ali who took a square of moist gauze and knelt beside her and sponged her face. It was into his eyes that Shama looked when she opened hers.

"Ali, is it really you?"

"Yes, it's me. Don't try and talk. It's all right, my sweet. You're going to be all right. We're in Israel. You're going to go home."

"Her heart's steady," Cal said to his sister.

"Cal . . ." Shama tried to lift her head when she heard his voice. "Caleb," she whispered, "Caleb."

He yanked the stethoscope from around his neck and flung it aside, pulling her into his arms as he did so, cradling her head against his chest. He didn't say a word, nor did she, but both Ali and Jessie pulled back, aware that for the moment they were utterly superfluous.

The Israeli was standing a few feet away, watching them with no expression on his face. After a few seconds Cal looked up at him, still holding Shama. "We have to get her to a hospital," he said. "Look at her. We need X rays, intravenous fluids. For God's sake, what kind of a place is this?"

The Israeli kept staring, then he grunted and went to the telephone. They heard him speaking gutteral Hebrew, but none of them knew what he was saying. A moment later he hung up and turned back to Cal. "An ambulance will be here in a couple of minutes. You can take her to Tzrisin Hospital until she's well enough to be moved." He shifted his gaze to Ali. "You have to go. Now."

"Yes," Ali said quietly. "I know that."

He stepped forward and put one hand on Shama's hair. "Good-bye," he murmured. "I hope someday you can forgive me for being the cause of so much agony."

She didn't turn her head. It was Cal who looked up and said over her shoulder, "Good-bye Ali. And thank you."

21

They left Israel after three days. At first they didn't tell anyone they were on their way home. "Better not yet," Cal said. "If Shama doesn't handle the trip well, we'll have to lay over in Rome." When they got to Italy they decided she was coping with the journey, but the country was in the midst of a telephone strike. "We can send a cable," Cal suggested, and Jessie did.

It was ten P.M. in Boston on the night of October sixth when they landed at Logan. They'd expected Ben to meet them, but he was nowhere to be seen. "Maybe they never got the telegram," Cal said. "We'd better call."

He was holding Shama's hand and obviously he didn't want to leave her, it was Jessie who went in search of a telephone. She found one and dialed the familiar number in Brookline. There was no answer. "It doesn't matter," she told her brother, "we can take a cab. I still have my key."

He glanced at Shama. She was staring straight ahead, paying no attention to their discussion. "Let's go," he said sharply. "I think the best thing is to get her there with no detours."

"Here's why nobody came to the airport or answered the phone," Jessie said as soon as they'd unlocked the door. "Ben's left a note, he took Ruth to the hospital at seven. She's in labor."

Cal glanced at his watch. It was eleven-thirty. "I'll call and see what's happening."

Jessie led Shama upstairs to her room, listening to Cal's

soft voice on the telephone meanwhile. "Who knows, maybe
you're already an aunt," she said brightly. "Tell you what,
five bucks says it's a boy."

Shama didn't answer. They'd come to the door of her
old room and she paused at the threshold and looked at it
as if she'd never seen the place before. Jessie felt a chill of
apprehension; she'd thought Shama had come through her
ordeal remarkably whole, now she seemed to be disintegrating while they watched. It was to distract herself as
much as Shama that Jess leaned over the banister and
called, "Cal, what's the news?"

"Nothing yet. Hang on, I'm coming up." He bounded up
the stairs and moved to Shama's side and slipped an arm
around her waist. "Welcome home, kid. Glad you made
it." It was almost a verbatim repetition of what he'd said to
her that first day when he met her at South Station.
Shama didn't reply.

He moved away, told himself that it was unrealistic to
expect Shama to respond to sentimental wisecracks at this
point. "I'm thinking I ought to go see Ruth. Will you
ladies be all right?"

"Of course, we'll be fine," Jessie said brightly. "Call us
the minute you know anything."

"Will do."

They weren't exactly fine. Shama remained unnaturally
silent, nothing Jessie said elicited a response. After half an
hour Jess left her in bed and went downstairs. Despite the
lateness of the hour she telephoned her mother.

Emma hadn't heard from them since they called from
Tel Aviv to say that they had Shama and she was alive and
would recover, now she was surprised to hear her daughter's voice. "Where are you, darling? How are you? And
do you know that Ruth is in labor?"

"I'm a little tired, Mom, but other than that I'm okay.
We're at Carrington Avenue. And we do know about
Ruth, since Ben left a note. Cal called the hospital and
he's gone over there, but as far as I know she still hasn't
had the baby."

"No, I thought not. Ben promised to let me know as
soon as she did. Jessie, how is Shama?"

Jess hesitated. "I'm not sure. Until we got here I thought
she was making excellent progress. But coming home seems
to have set her back some. Maybe she's just tired and it

will be better in the morning. Mom, we'd better hang up if we want to hear about Ruth's baby."

"Yes. But, Jessie, welcome home, darling. I'm very proud of you."

It was two A.M. when Cal called to say that Ruth had given birth to a baby girl. Jess had been nappping on the couch in the den and she was barely awake when she heard him say, "They're going to call her Rachel, Ben says that was Ruth's mother's name."

She mumbled something about giving Ruth and Ben her love, then went up to see if Shama was sleeping. She wasn't, she was lying on her bed, staring at the ceiling. "That was Cal. Ruth's had a little girl. Six pounds nine ounces. Mother and baby are doing fine. Congratulations, Auntie."

Shama didn't reply.

Jess sat down on the side of the bed and took the other woman's hand. "Shama, do you want to talk? About the details, I mean. You haven't volunteered any, and neither Cal nor I thought we should ask, but we already know quite a bit. The medical exam was pretty thorough."

The laboratory report had said only repeated sexual intercourse, it was Cal who had supplied the ugly word rape. Then he'd cursed softly for a long time and gone out and walked the streets of Tel Aviv. When he came back an hour later, he agreed with Jessie that there was no point in mentioning it unless Shama did. But now Jess wasn't so sure they'd made a wise decision. "Maybe it will help if we talk about it," she murmured. Shama merely shook her head.

"Okay, but if you want to, you know I'll always be around to listen. Oh, there's something I forgot. Ruth and Ben are calling the baby Rachel. That was your mother's name, wasn't it?"

This time Shama actually looked as if she'd heard, and though she still didn't say anything, Jessie saw a single tear course down her friend's cheek.

It wasn't a good night for getting over jet lag. Jessie slept badly before and after Cal's call, and the doorbell rang at seven-thirty. When she stumbled to the door half-asleep and disoriented, she found Marya. "I'm sorry I woke you up, honey. But your mama and I agreed I should come right away. I'm going to take care of Shama until Ruth comes home with the new baby, then I'll take care of her."

This speech was made while Marya marched into the front hall, set down her suitcase and a shopping bag, and removed her hat and coat. "Okay, you go back to sleep now for a while. One thing, I only been here a couple of times before, where's the kitchen?" She had picked up the shopping bag. It bulged with groceries.

"The kitchen's through there on the left. I can't go back to sleep. I have to go to work. I told the hospital I'd be gone a week, it's already ten days."

Marya cocked her head and made a face of disgust. "Yeah, sure, they would love it you should go now and take care of sick people, since you're so wide awake and would know exactly what you're doing. Back to sleep. Which room is Shama in?"

"Her old bedroom, second door on the right at the top of the stairs. My room's next to hers. Ruth left them both exactly as they were when we lived here."

"Good. Ruth is a smart lady." Marya put one fleshy hand on Jessie's shoulder and spun her around. "March. When you wake up I'll feed you something nourishing. *Then* you can go to the hospital."

Jess did as she was told, and chuckled to herself when she realized how much she enjoyed being bossed around by Marya again after all these years.

A few hours later, over eggs and sausages and Marya's special potato pancakes, it occurred to her that Emma would miss Marya a great deal. "How's Mom going to manage if you stay here for a few weeks?"

The older woman shrugged. "Lately your mother spends more and more time with Doctor Josh. I'm not much use to her. She won't miss me."

"Marya, that's not true. How can she help but miss you? And why is she with Dad more than before?"

Marya carried the pan from the stove and flipped another sausage onto Jessie's plate. "It's funny with Doctor Josh and your mother," she said thoughtfully. "She's always insisted on talking to him like he could hear every word, like inside he was normal. Now she talks about him the same way." She sat down and didn't meet Jessica's eyes, just stared into her coffee cup. "Once a couple of weeks ago we were talking about something and she said, 'Josh says—' Then she stopped, like she'd just remembered he couldn't say nothing, hasn't said nothing for eleven years."

Jess put down her fork, suddenly she wasn't hungry. "Marya, that's awful."

"Maybe. Maybe it's not so terrible. We're getting old, your mama and me. Sixty-three this year. I think she's doing what I do sometimes, living in the past." She reached out and took Jessie's hand. "Like sometimes I pretend to myself you're still a little girl and still need your Marya."

"I do, darling. I always will. And don't tell me you're old, I don't want to hear it." She glanced toward the hall and the upstairs. "But at the moment I think it's Shama who needs you most of all. She's been through a horrible time, Marya. She needs lots of tender, loving care. Be gentle with her."

"Care I know about, Jessie. Only you should tell me about the medical things."

She explained about the vitamin supplements and high protein diet that had been prescribed for Shama. "You understand that it's Cal who is in charge, Marya? He won't let anyone else take care of her, not even me." Marya nodded solemnly. "I'll give you one prescription though," Jessie added. "She needs to talk. Until she can, she's not going to get better."

Caleb appeared on Carrington Avenue every day. He went through the motions of making it a medical visit, taking Shama's temperature and blood pressure and holding her wrist to count her pulse. "You're not ill," he said after four days. "At least not ill enough to stay in bed. You've got to get up and move around, Shama. Take walks, the weather's terrific at the moment."

She shook her head.

Cal put his hand beside her cheek. "Staying in bed isn't good for you. Trust me, I'm the doctor, right?" He waited, but she didn't respond. "Okay, not until you're ready," he said softly. And later, sitting in the kitchen with Marya, "She went through hell, so we can't be too rough on her, but she's not doing herself any good physically just lying in bed. See if you can get her to walk around a little, even if she won't go outside."

Marya tried, but without success. They told each other maybe it would be better once Ruth came home from the hospital with the new baby. Shama and her sister had been very close until she took up with Ali Fatah.

The baby was perfect. "The best thing that's happened to this family since John was born," Jessie exclaimed, hugging the infant to her. "God, why didn't anybody tell me babies smell so marvelous."

"Depends on when you pick them up," Ben said, smiling at her over the top of the Sunday *Globe* sports section. "Sometimes they don't smell so marvelous. Haven't you handled lots of babies, Jess? I thought the Free was a hospital for women, doesn't that include babies?"

"Of course it does, but the nurses get to do all the cuddling. I haven't been on the pediatric wards for months, and when I was it was only to say increase this dose or decrease that. Anyway, it's different when it's your own family. Oh, you gorgeous little thing," she cooed, putting her cheek against the child's and kissing the tiny hand she held to her lips. The gorgeous little thing started to cry.

Ruth appeared instantly. "Feeding time," she said, taking the squalling bundle that was Rachel. "I'm going to nurse her up in Shama's room, I do that sometimes."

Jess hadn't been off duty for two-and-a-half weeks, this was the first she'd heard of that arrangement. "It's an interesting idea, Ruthie. Does it work?"

The other woman shook her head. "Not so far. She doesn't look at me and she doesn't talk. But Ben put a rocking chair in there, and Rachel and I just sit with her and I keep hoping it will help. Something alive and normal . . ." Rachel interrupted by increasing the decibel level of her demand for food. "We'll talk about it later," Ruth said as she fled the room.

Ben watched his wife disappear up the stairs, then put down his paper. "Jess, is there something we should know about what happened to Shama? I mean something more than we do know."

"I don't imagine you need it spelled out, and I don't know the details because only Shama does and she won't talk about it. But, put it this way, if you picture the worst things that can happen to a woman in such a situation, you'll be pretty close."

"I see," he said softly. "I thought it must have been like that."

"I keep wondering if any man can imagine what that's like," Jessie murmured. "It seems to me that it's an area of women's medicine that's been completely neglected, and I think that's because most of the gynecologists have been men."

"Going to do something about that?" Ben asked.

Jessie grinned. "You always were disarmingly perceptive. The answer is maybe, I still have to think it through. I'd planned to concentrate on reproductive work, because of Doctor Rock and Celia." She paused. "Do you know anything about that?"

"Only that you're working on some dramatic new kind of family planning."

"Of birth control," Jessie amended. "Let's call it by its right name. It's not approved yet, but mark my words, it will be. And when it is the whole world's going to change for women. But that wouldn't have altered anything in Shama's case. Except—" Jessie clapped her hand to her forehead. "My God, what an idiot I've been." She bolted out of her chair and up the stairs.

Ruth was sitting in the rocking chair singing a lullaby to Rachel, something in Moroccan Arabic that Jessie couldn't understand, though she'd heard it before. Ruth used to hum that same song when she worked around the house, all those years when she longed for Daniel to agree to have a baby. Jess looked at mother and child briefly, only long enough to think that it was the most beautiful sight in the world, and somehow a consolation for the loss of Daniel, then she turned to Shama. "Listen, something has just dawned on me."

Shama's face was to the wall and she didn't move.

"Look at me, dammit!" Jessie remembered Ruth and the baby and lowered her voice. "Shama, please, look at me." She sat down on the edge of the bed and put her hand on Shama's arm. Finally her friend turned her head and faced her. "There, that's better. Jesus, I haven't ever seen you this thin. Aren't you eating?"

"As much as I want, I'm not very hungry."

"That has to be the first time in our lives I've heard you say that." Jessie grinned but saw no answering light of humor in Shama's eyes. She decided to plunge on. "I've been awfully stupid, Shama. We all have. In the light of what happened we should have thought of it, but none of us did. Listen, are you worried that you may be pregnant?"

"No, because I'm not."

Jessie let out a long sigh. Behind her she heard Ruth stop crooning to Rachel and she knew the other woman was listening too. "You're sure?" she asked.

"I'm sure. I got my period a few days ago. I thought I was pregnant before it happened, by the way. I was going to have an abortion."

Ruth gasped, but Jessie didn't allow her shock to show. "Why? Because Ali wouldn't have wanted the child?" She was saying anything, without thinking about it, because this was the most conversation she'd gotten out of Shama since they left Israel.

"Because he'd have wanted it too much. He tried to talk me into eloping and presenting his father with a fait accompli. A baby would have been even better. A double fait accompli."

"But you didn't want to marry Ali?"

"No, I didn't want to marry him."

"What did you want, Shama?" Jess leaned forward and took both of those thin, trembling hands into her strong, capable grip. "What do you want now?"

She thought the answer was almost ready to be spoken, that the key which would unlock this debilitating depression hovered on Shama's lips. Then Rachel lost her hold on her mother's breast and howled in frustration, and the mood was broken.

The Church of St. Stanislas was near North Station, a squat red brick building sandwiched between the railway yards and huddled beneath a traffic flyway built later, with no regard for the church tower. Most people would find the church almost as ugly inside as out. There were garish, nineteenth-century statues everywhere, the kind with painted yellow hair and apple-red cheeks and saccharine smiles. The altar was an elaborate pastiche of gilt and plaster roses, and recently someone had festooned the pews with paper flowers. But for the Boston Polish community, St. Stanislas was home. Here the sermons were preached in Polish and they could confess in their native tongue. Marya Czerniki had gone to St. Stanislas twice a week since she came to America in 1912. Anna Turnovski the dressmaker went there too.

The two women often met on Saturday afternoons. They would sometimes spend a short time together and exchange gossip after they had each been to confession and finished their private devotions at the altar of one or another of the many saints. That is, Anna would gossip. Marya considered herself above tittle-tattle, she just listened and nodded. Nonetheless, she was very interested in what Anna had to say, because what they had in common beside their nationality and their religion was Susan Morgan. Susan had been one of Anna's best customers for years.

"So, you want a cup of coffee?" Anna asked on this last Saturday in October when they met in the vestibule of the church.

"Why not?" Marya shifted her eternal shopping bag to her other hand so she could take her friend's arm. "C'mon, we'll go across to the station."

There was a Rexall Drug Store in the terminal and it had a lunch counter. Coffee had recently gone up from seven cents to a dime a cup, but it was still cheaper than anywhere else in the vicinity. "Coffee regular," Anna told the tired-looking woman who took their order. "I'll have a slice of that apple pie too. Put a scoop of vanilla ice cream on it. A small scoop. You can charge me for half."

Marya ordered coffee and skipped the pie. She was accustomed to homemade baked goods made either by Tessie or herself. Of course Anna wasn't. She might be a widow like Marya, but she lived alone. Naturally she wouldn't bother making pies. That was one more thing that gave Marya a secret feeling of superiority. She had a family, even if it weren't exactly hers in the sense of blood relations.

The food came while Anna was talking about her landlord, how she'd had a big fight with him because he wouldn't fix the window in her kitchen that stuck so she couldn't open it. "So I tell him if he ain't gonna send somebody to look at that window, I'm not gonna pay my rent."

Marya was not interested in Anna's window. "You seen my Caleb's wife lately?"

If Anna was surprised at Marya raising the subject first,

she didn't let on. "Matter of fact I did, though she don't come to me so much anymore. I mean, she can afford to buy the originals now, so she don't need the copies, right? But she came in a couple of weeks ago with a picture outta *Vogue*. A gorgeous outfit."

"What kind of an outfit? A suit?"

"Nah, a nightgown and one of them fancy robes they call a negligee. Schiaparelli. It ain't on sale in America, just in Paris. 'Oh, Mrs. Turnovski,' she tells me, 'I have to have it. You can make it, can't you?' So I says sure I can make it. I mean, I don't do underwear usually, but if you make it with a needle and thread I can do it. Has to be very expensive I tell her, if you want it in real silk like the one in the picture. Course I tell her I can make it in rayon a little cheaper."

"Did she take the rayon?"

Anna through back her head and laughed. "Her? What, are you kidding me? Pure silk. She brought me the material a couple of days later. Beautiful. Like a rainbow. Dark purple fading to pale pink. Where she got it I don't know, but one thing I can say for sure, it had to cost forty dollars a yard." She smiled in triumph. "And you know what it took to make that set? Eight yards. Full, out to here . . ." She began describing the negligee set in exquisite detail.

"When did you say she got this?" Marya interrupted.

"A few weeks ago. I finished it end of September. Imagine, with the material and my work it cost her maybe four hundred dollars. To sleep in."

Marya knew quite well that Susan had not acquired the nightgown to sleep in.

Caleb visited every two or three days now; because, Marya knew, he couldn't justify a daily visit to a patient whose sickness wasn't physical. He arrived on the Tuesday morning following Marya's talk with Anna Turnovski. She waited for him at the foot of the stairs when he came down from Shama's room. "Is Ruth home?" Cal asked.

"She went for a walk with the baby. I sent her. She gotta make the most of this beautiful weather. Soon it's gonna be too cold to take the carriage out."

He pursed his lips. "I wanted to talk to her. Will you ask her to call me at the office, please?"

"Sure. Meanwhile come in the kitchen, I made fresh bread, and the coffee is hot."

"Marya, I'd love to, but I really shouldn't take the time. I have patients waiting at the office."

"Ten minutes only. Nobody's gonna die in ten minutes." She stood in front of the door, hands on her ample hips, barring his way.

It wasn't like Marya to be assertive. Suddenly it dawned on him that she'd gotten rid of Ruth so she could speak to him privately. "Okay, I never could pass up your bread. Besides, you're right, nobody's likely to die while I have a cup of coffee."

They went into the kitchen, and she poured it for him and added extra cream, the way he liked it, and slathered butter on a thick slice of her black bread. "You're always telling me I'm going to get fat, how come you're so generous today?" he asked, taking a large bite of the delicious bread.

"Maybe I'm just feeling kind. But it's true, you're gonna be thirty-nine next month, Caleb, you have to watch you don't get a potbelly."

His belly was absolutely flat and he was as lean as ever, but he looked grim. "Thirty-nine, it sounds pretty old. What have I done with my life, Marya?" he asked softly.

"You became a wonderful doctor, that's what. And you got the boys."

"Yes, thank God, I do."

"And if you weren't so pigheaded you could have a woman who loves you."

He was so shocked, he just stared at her. The remark was totally out of character; Marya hadn't spoken to him in that tone of voice since he was a child. She was always conscious of their different roles, more aware of that divide than he'd ever been. "I'm not sure I know what you mean," he said.

"You know." She sat down across from him. "Caleb, if I didn't love you so much since you were born, I wouldn't be opening my big mouth now. Only it kills me. There's that poor girl up there eating her heart out because she's been through so much and because she loves you and she doesn't think you love her. And there you are, loving her back and afraid to say so. Don't deny it. I know you like a book. I see the way you look when you go upstairs and the way you look when you leave."

He put down the cup of coffee. "I'm not denying it," he said quietly. "Marya, do you think that's what's behind Shama's depression, her refusal to get better? You think it's because of me?"

"I know it is. Sometimes when she thinks nobody is around I hear her crying. She's loved you for years, Caleb. And you've always been too stubborn to do anything about it."

Cal shook his head. "It's not the way you think. Once, a few years ago—" He broke off. "What's the point, I'm married to Susan, remember? She'll never give me a divorce."

"So forget a divorce. You ain't lived with her for years. What are you supposed to do, be a monk?"

"Sometimes I ask myself the same question," he said softly.

"Good, then maybe you've got some sense in your head. And ask yourself something else. Why would Susan go to Anna Turnovski the dressmaker and pay four hundred dollars for a copy of a Paris nightgown? You think she's being a nun all by herself in that big house? Take my word for it, Caleb, she ain't."

He was silent for a moment, then he shook his head again. "It doesn't matter. Whatever she's doing or not doing, I can't get a divorce. And I'm not prepared to ask Shama to be my mistress." Marya snorted derisively and Cal patted her hand. "Thank you for caring what happens to me, Marya dear. Don't forget to tell Ruth to call me, will you? I want to bring a psychiatrist to see Shama, and I think I should discuss it with Ruthie first."

Marya began clearing the table, making loud noises as she slammed things into the sink. "A psychiatrist. Sometimes you're the biggest fool I ever met, Caleb Morgan. That girl don't need a psychiatrist. She needs a man who loves her and can make her forget all the terrible things that happened."

Ruth called him later that afternoon but he didn't mention the psychiatrist, Marya's scornful derision of the idea had made him doubt his medical judgment. "I just wanted to know what you think about Shama," he said instead. "Is she making any progress toward returning to a normal life?"

"No," Ruth admitted. "Not that I can see. We're very worried about her, Cal. I haven't said much to you because Ben and I thought maybe we were exaggerating. We were hoping there was some medical explanation."

Cal evaded the implied question. "Thanks, Ruthie. I wanted to know your opinion because you're with her the most. Let me think about it a bit longer. I'll get back to you."

He was scheduled to take Dav and John to the Garden that night. The hockey season had started the previous week and he had bought tickets the month before. There was nothing Cal felt less like doing, but the boys were looking forward to it and he wouldn't disappoint them. He thought maybe the game would divert him, but no power play the Bruins mounted succeeded in making him forget the things Marya had said. It wasn't that he gave a damn about any affair Susan might or might not be having, it was the injustice. She could to what she wanted, damn her, she *had* everything she wanted. He was condemned to a life of frustrated loneliness.

"Hey, Dad, did you see that?"

John was tugging at his arm, Don McKenney was skating around the rink with his stick in the air acknowledging the roar of the crowd, the scoreboard marked up another Bruins' goal. "Yes, son, I saw it. Great play!" he added with as much enthusiasm as he could fake. He put his arm around John and hugged him. "A terrific goal. Best one so far."

Oh, God, he loved this boy so much, loved them both so much. He would do nothing to put them at risk. Nothing. But it was almost four years since Susan had made her horrible accusations, bludgeoned him with her terrifying threats. John was eleven now, not a baby anymore, maybe it wouldn't matter so much. *I can explain*, he thought. *I can tell him how meaningless it is, that he's mine in ways that have nothing to do with biology. . . .*

The boys were both eating cotton candy. John's cheeks were spread with sticky pink stains. They were pudgy cheeks, still puffed out with baby fat. And when he jumped to his feet to cheer another Bruin player pushing the puck across the ice with consummate skill, his voice still had the high-pitched tremor of childhood. Cal watched him, his throat choked with tears, and knew he couldn't do it. The whole thing was out of the question. As always, Susan held all the cards and he knew she wouldn't hesitate to play them.

The Bruins won by three goals, all scored in the last two minutes of play, and his sons were so dizzy with excitement, Cal couldn't help but be infected by it. They laughed and joked all the way home, then finished the evening with hot cocoa and marshmallows at the kitchen table. "I'd hate to do a blood count on you guys right now," Cal said as they washed the cups and saucers. "The sugar count would be off the scale. No sweets tomorrow, and God help us when you next go to the dentist."

He finally got them into bed, shushing them repeatedly because Miss Carlisle was already sleeping. They seemed too excited to fall asleep, but when he checked after twenty minutes both his sons were dead to the world. Cal stood a moment in their bedroom, watching them in the dim glow of the night-light, then he tiptoed out and closed the door.

He didn't feel like sleeping. Jessie was on duty tonight so he was alone in the living room with his thoughts. The whole thing rushed over him again. Shama, oh God, Shama. He'd thought she was brooding over what had happened, and over the end of her affair with Ali Fatah, of her jet set life. But Marya's words haunted him, made him remember the way she had turned first to him in that moment when her captivity ended.

He heard her voice again, saw her battered body and the way her eyes had looked into his when she whispered, "Cal, oh, Cal . . ." It had been affirmation of a love that had never died or changed. And it was when he'd made no indication that anything had changed that her depression began. But what could he do? Tell her he still loved her when—

The telephone rang. It was the hospital, one of his patients was in labor. "I'll be right there." He wasn't sorry to have his thoughts interrupted.

At a few minutes past seven A.M. Caleb delivered a fourth son to a woman who had been his patient for six years. "Another little guy, Linda," he told her. "He looks great and you were terrific."

"So were you," the woman murmured as she drifted, smiling, into sleep.

Cal changed his clothes and walked out into a morning of autumn splendor. The air was like wine and the trees that rimmed the parking lot were red-and-gold banners against a brilliant blue sky. Nobody should be lying in solitary agony on a day like this, not when it was entirely preventable and unnecessary. He turned the key to the ignition and headed his car toward Brookline.

Ruth let him in and he pushed past her with only a mumbled greeting. The smell of coffee and frying bacon filled the house, but the door to Shama's room was closed. He knocked once, then walked in. "I want to talk to you."

She looked at him and didn't reply.

Cal crossed to the bed and grabbed her shoulders. Jesus, she was skin and bones. "Listen to me, this has to stop. I'm not letting you do this, Shama. It's crazy. You're making yourself into an invalid, a psychotic, and for what? It's not because of those filthy bastards who raped you, is it? Well, answer me, dammit! Is it?"

"No." The word was a whisper.

"Is it Fatah? Are you killing yourself because he walked away from you? He did it because that was the price he had to pay for your freedom. Nobody spelled it out, but he told us enough so Jessie and I could read between the lines. We explained all this to you, we talked about it back in Israel. So is it because of him?" He was still holding her, shaking her. Her head was bobbing up and down like a rag doll's. "Is it Ali?" he demanded again.

Suddenly she pulled away from him. She jerked her body to the opposite side of the bed and pushed his hands from her shoulders. "No," she screamed. "No! No! No! You know why. Goddamn you, Caleb Morgan, you know!"

Now he too was shaking, trembling with rage and with love and with need. He couldn't stand up because his legs wouldn't hold him and he sat down on the side of the bed. "I know. I love you, so I know."

"Cal." That was her only response, his name. Just as it had been in the hot and stinking shed on the Israeli airfield. "Cal, oh, Cal."

He reached for her and they clung together for a long few moments, both weeping. "I have to explain," Shama murmured against his chest.

"No, you don't."

"Yes, I want to. I could handle it until we came home. Then it seemed to me that everything had come full circle. That I'd been running and running, and terrible things had happened to me, but it was all for nothing. You still didn't want me and I was right back where I started. Where we started."

"I want you. Sweet God, I've never stopped wanting you. But I was afraid."

"And now?"

"I'm sick of being afraid. I can't live with fear any longer. We'll have to take our chances, my darling. It won't be the way I wanted it to be, I still can't divorce Susan. But maybe we can steal a little happiness, around the edges so to speak."

"Around the edges is good enough for me," she said with a long sigh.

They stayed like that for some time, clinging to each other, then Cal stood up and lifted her to her feet. "Get up. You have to move around. We have to get some strength back into your legs. C'mon, you can do it, I'll help you."

He supported her and they walked together into the hall, then hesitantly down the stairs, taking one step at a time, Shama hanging on to him and to the banister.

Ruth and Ben and Marya were all standing below on the landing, watching them, summoned perhaps by their earlier shouting match, or simply by a telepathy born of their concern for Shama. She wore a short nightie, the kind he thought was called a baby-doll. Beneath it her thighs and her legs were like sticks. A few times they almost buckled, but she struggled on. When they reached the foot of the stairs, she smiled. "Ruthie, I'm freezing. Do you think maybe you could get me a robe?"

Ruth ran up the stairs. Marya turned and hurried into the kitchen, calling over her shoulder. "Come in here, I'll make toast. The coffee is hot." Ben stayed where he was and grinned at them.

Caleb grinned back, then led Shama to the table. Ruth appeared with a bathrobe, a blue chenille thing that had seen better days. "I'm sorry," she murmured. "This is all I found in your closet. It's from when you were in high school."

"I'd better get some clothes if I'm going to get up," Shama said. "I'm a little old for a return to bobby socks and pleated skirts."

It was Cal who helped her into the robe, then sat down

beside her again. Food appeared. Marya had produced one of her instant miracles, scrambled eggs and bacon as well as the promised toast. They each ate with one hand, because neither wanted to let go of the other. Ben left for school. Ruth said she had to feed Rachel. "I gotta go too," Marya said. "The butcher's saving me a nice roast. I gotta pick it up." Within minutes they were alone in the cheerful kitchen with its good, warm family smells and happy memories.

"This weekend," Cal said. "I'll cover myself at the office and the hospital and we'll go away."

"Yes, please yes."

For answer he leaned over and put his mouth on hers and they stayed like that for a long time.

When they crossed the border into Maine it was a little past eleven on Saturday morning. Welcome to Kennebunkport, a sign read, The Only Place in the World so Named. "It must be an Indian word," Cal said. To confirm that assessment the first motel they saw was called the Squaw Inn. He stopped the car. The parking spaces were almost all full.

"Did you make reservations?" Shama asked.

"No, I suppose I should have. Zillions of people must be coming to see the foliage. We can keep driving and go further north."

"No," she said. "Not if they have a room here."

The man in the office spoke with a thick Down east accent, and in customary Maine fashion he wasted no words. "Got one room. Double bed. You want it?"

Cal hesitated. They hadn't actually said anything specific about this weekend, and considering her recent ordeal . . . He felt as awkward as he had in those long-ago days before Susan.

"A double bed is fine," Shama said firmly.

Cal smiled at her and signed the register Dr. & Mrs. Caleb Morgan.

The room was small and simple, but there was a window looking out at woods and a stream. "It reminds me of that place we stayed for your graduation," Cal said.

"It doesn't remind me of anything. It's fresh and new and just ours." Shama sat in the room's only chair while Cal unpacked the few things they'd brought with them.

Her clothes were borrowed from Ruth, one dress and a pair of slacks and a cotton flannel nightgown and robe. "Not very glamorous," she said laughing. "I'm sorry, I'll do better once I'm able to get to a store."

"Shama, listen, I'm not pushing you. I didn't set this up as a great seduction scene. I only wanted us to be together. I know you must have horrible memories because of what happened."

She shook her head. "My love, I'm not likely to confuse you with any Arab terrorist." He still looked doubtful. Shama held out her arms. "Caleb, come here."

He dropped the shirt he was holding and crossed the room and embraced her. Still, his kiss was very gentle. He couldn't stop remembering what she'd looked like when he cut her out of that burlap sack, couldn't believe those terrible memories wouldn't overwhelm her.

Shama leaned back and looked into his eyes. "Take me to bed," she whispered. "Now, darling. We need to find each other. We've been lost for so long. Take me to bed."

He lifted her and took the two steps across the rag rug that brought them to the bed and put her down, then stretched out beside her. "I'm pretty much a novice," he whispered. "Which sounds crazy for a guy who has two kids and is almost forty, but it's true."

"My novice," she said as she unbuttoned her blouse. "That's all that matters."

She took the blouse off and unhooked her bra. He bent to kiss her breasts, but stopped. "I love you so much. I don't want to hurt you." Shama rolled onto her side and pressed her cheek to his, then she giggled. "What's funny?" he asked a little stiffly. "Me?"

"No, of course not you. Look."

Cal turned his head. There was a sign above the night table on his side. It said This Bed is Equipped with Magic Fingers, Insert Quarter Here for a Stimulating Massage.

In a moment he was giggling, too, and soon laughter carried them into love.

"Mom, do you think women's medicine is going in the right direction?"

Emma considered the question in that intent way she had. "I'm not sure I know what you mean, Jess."

They were once more in Emma's bedroom, the place

where lately they had shared so many of the talks that were healing the old breach between them. Jessie sat cross-legged on the floor in a pool of golden light made by the sunshine of this Saturday afternoon. "I've been thinking about it a lot," she said. "Shama's experience set me off, then I started looking at the whole thing. All gynecology has been going one way since Dad's day. The kind Cal practices, that I'm being trained to practice, it's more of the same."

Emma poured tea. She had come to cherish these snatched hours with her busy daughter. Sometimes when she reflected on it, it seemed a miracle. Without either of them planning it or working at it, closeness and mutual understanding had been born. She wasn't sure what had precipitated that change, but she was enormously grateful for it. "More of what?" she asked, handing Jessie the cup.

"Interference. I mean, look at the way we organize labor and delivery for a start. An episiotomy is standard these days, and we wouldn't dream of not shaving the pubic area, and no matter what a woman wants to do, whatever position might make her feel more comfortable, she has to be on her back with her legs in stirrups. But until a while ago women didn't do any of those things."

"Until a while ago the mortality rate for mothers and babies was appalling."

"Yes, I know that. But I can't help wondering if we're going a little crazy. A lot of what we do is wonderful and it saves lives, no question about it. But why does it all have to be so unnatural?"

"I'm not sure," Emma said. "Why did you say that what happened to Shama made you think of all this?"

"Well, it didn't exactly. I had been toying with some of these ideas before that. But when I saw her, saw what had happened to her, it made it all so much more real. We're so defenseless, Mom, so much at the mercy of men. Once the pill is approved, a lot of that is going to change. I think women are going to sense their own power and freedom for the first time. Maybe the medical profession will take another look at delivery techniques, too, but nobody has even considered how to treat women who have been raped." She stopped. "You do know what happened to Shama, don't you?"

"No one has spelled it out, but I guessed," Emma

said softly. "That poor child. No wonder she's been so withdrawn."

Jess shook her head. "It wasn't just that. It's all mixed up with Cal and the way they feel about each other and the fact that he's always refused to divorce Susan. Thank God he seems to have come to his senses."

Emma was startled. "Oh, why do you say that?"

"You mean you don't know? They've gone away together this weekend. Don't look so shocked, they're not kids. Besides, they love each other."

"It's not that. I'm really not very shockable, darling, whatever you think. But what about Susan?"

"What about her?" Jessie stood up and stretched. "As far as I'm concerned she can rot. Cal's just going to have to divorce her, that's all. He'll have to go to Reno and do it."

Emma leaned back in her chair and closed her eyes. God, she was so tired, so worn-out with all the currents of pain that had plagued her family for so long. "I don't think Susan will just stand still for that."

"Probably not. But in the end what can she do? Cal has custody of the boys, de facto if not de jure, and they have to be the only hold she has over him. No judge would give them back to her now, not after she hasn't wanted them for years." Jessie leaned over and kissed her mother's cheek. "Have to go, I'm on duty at three. Conversation to be continued at the first possible opportunity."

Emma remained where she was after her daughter left. It wasn't Jess who occupied her thoughts, she was thinking about her son and his wife and his children, and the young woman he loved. The grandfather clock in the hall struck four, time to go back to Josh. She had hired another nurse since Marya moved to Ruth's. This one came at noon and stayed until four, so Emma had a break in the long hours between the night nurse's departure in the morning at seven and her return at eleven in the evening.

Emma's limbs felt heavy when she stood up. Old. Ideas were buzzing in her head, suspicions and fears and griefs that she'd long buried. The whole thing made her dizzy, and once she stumbled as she descended the stairs and had to grasp the banister to keep from falling.

She didn't want to think about these things. She didn't want to open wounds that had healed after years of anguish. Not even for her beloved Caleb, the child she had always loved best of all. Besides, Cal wasn't a child any-more, he was a grown man, a father and a husband. He had gone beyond her influence, she couldn't help him now. No, that wasn't true. At least it might not be true. She'd not been able to help Daniel, but there was still time to do something for Caleb. With a deep sigh of resolution Emma opened the door to the old library which had become Joshua's prison.

"Mrs. Morgan, are you all right? You look so pale."

"Yes, Miss Cooper, I'm fine. Thank you for your concern, but you may go now."

Joshua was waiting for her. She sensed that, though no one else would have. Emma took her customary place beside her husband's bed. "Good afternoon, dear." She put her hand in his, felt the single tap of his finger against her palm which was a greeting.

Half an hour went by. Emma didn't move, she was as still and as silent as the man in the bed. Finally she took another of those long breaths which had marked each of the new paths her mind had led her down during this long and extraordinary afternoon. She leaned over and stared into the sightless green eyes of the husband she had loved so long and at such a price. "Josh, can you hear me? Are you sleeping?"

Her hand was still below his and she felt his finger move slightly against her palm. "No, you're awake. Good. My darling, we must talk. You and I are coming to the end of our lives, but Caleb has much of his left and so do our grandsons. Caleb loves Shama, Josh. He's loved her for years. But he has refused to divorce Susan. I thought at first it was because of the boys, but Jessie has just pointed out the obvious. He *has* custody of Dav and John. It would be all but impossible for Susan to get them back now."

She paused but Joshua didn't move his finger. "I have thought about this for a long time," she whispered close to his ear. "Even when I didn't admit I was thinking about it. I believe you know something, Joshua. I believe that your attempt at suicide had something to do with Susan, and that means you could know what terrible hold she has over Cal. What happened that day, Joshua? Please, you must tell me. We must redeem ourselves, my dearest. We must see that our children do not spend their lives paying for our sins."

Finally, after a long pause, she felt the slow tapping of Joshua's finger against her palm.

The night nurse had a key, that way she didn't have to ring the bell and disturb the Marsh sisters when she came on duty. At a few minutes before eleven that Saturday evening, she used it to let herself into the house at 165 Commonwealth Avenue.

The nurse hung her coat in the hall and climbed the stairs and tapped lightly at the door to her patient's room, then let herself in. Mrs. Morgan was sitting beside her husband. "Good evening," the nurse said brightly. "And how is our Doctor Morgan tonight?"

Slowly Emma turned her head and looked at the woman. "My husband is dead."

The nurse suppressed a gasp and hurried to the side of the bed. "His eyes, they're closed!" The exclamation was most unprofessional, but she couldn't help herself.

"I closed them," Emma said. "I did it when he died. It's funny how easy it was, death must have relaxed the muscle." Her voice was matter-of-fact and pitched low, but exhaustion marked every word.

"Mrs. Morgan, you must let me call the doctor. You must lie down."

"Oh, I will now. I just didn't want to leave him alone before you came."

The nurse waited while Mrs. Morgan stood up and gathered a stack of papers she'd been scribbling on. She wasn't surprised by that, the other woman always spent a lot of her time in this room writing, though she had no idea what. She waited until her employer had moved away, then stepped forward and leaned over her patient. There was no pulse.

"He's been dead over an hour," Emma explained. "As I said, I didn't want to leave him alone."

"I'll call the doctor," the nurse said.

Emma nodded. She knew it was the doctor's responsibility to determine the cause of death. She also knew what he'd find. Joshua's heart had given out. But no one but she would know that he had killed himself. For five hours without pause Joshua had made the enormous effort required to tap his finger on her palm. She had let him do it and she felt neither regret nor grief, because only in this way could Joshua right a terrible wrong. She had known exactly what that superhuman effort was costing him and so had he, and he'd done it willingly. Emma was content. It was not an ignoble way to die.

Cal looked around the drawing room. There was no one there but himself and Susan and his mother. "Mom, where are the others?"

Emma sat across from him in her customary chair by the fireplace. Considering that his father's funeral had taken place twenty-four hours before, she looked remarkably composed. She wore a black tea gown he'd seen her in countless times, and she was faultlessly groomed even if very pale.

"What others, Cal?"

"You said we were going to read Dad's will. I expected a lawyer. And Jessie, of course. Maybe even Ruth and Ben."

"Those legal formalities will be dealt with in due course." Emma picked up a stack of yellow foolscap sheets from the table beside her. "What I have here is your father's true last will and testament, Cal. It concerns only the three of us."

Susan sat on the sofa, separated from her husband and her mother-in-law by physical as well as emotional distance. But as usual she was careful about the external forms of things, she wore a black faille suit and black hose. She crossed her legs and the swishing noise of expensive fabric rubbing against silky skin made the only sound in the room until she asked, "Are you referring to those papers, Emma?"

"Yes, these papers."

"Then I assume they are something Joshua wrote before he became ill."

Emma shook her head. "No, it is a story he told me the day he died. I wrote it down exactly as he dictated it."

Cal caught his breath. "Mom, you're very tired, obviously overwrought. Why don't you let me give you something and put you to bed?" He half-rose.

"Sit down, Caleb. Stop looking at me as if I've lost my senses. I am tired, but I am not 'overwrought,' as you so delicately put it. Joshua and I communicated all the time. We'd been doing it for at least five years."

"But how?" Susan demanded.

"Are you telling me Dad could talk?" Cal asked at the same time.

"Be quiet, both of you. I'll explain, if you will listen. No, he couldn't talk. He was exactly as you knew him to be, except for two things. One, he could hear perfectly, and two his mind was completely unaffected by his physical disabilities. It was simply trapped inside a body that would not obey his commands. But after years of trying, Josh gained control of the little finger of his left hand. I would take that hand in mine and he would tap his finger against my palm. We worked out a code. Very simple really, he tapped one for *a*, two for *b*, and so forth. That way he could spell out words. I wrote the letters down as he dictated them."

Susan hadn't moved. She was staring at Emma in paralyzed shock. It was Caleb who murmured. "I don't believe it. I mean, it must be true, but I can't believe it. The effort must have been enormous."

"It was," Emma agreed. She gestured to the papers she held. "These three pages took five hours, without a break. That's what killed him," she added without any obvious emotion. "Telling me this strained Joshua's heart beyond its ability to survive."

Cal felt physically ill, he bent forward, head in his hands. "What must it have been like, a normal mind trapped in a body like that?"

"It was pure, unmitigated hell," Emma said softly. "Remember that when you listen to your father's story, Cal. Whatever he may have done, he paid. Oh, yes, he paid."

Susan still hadn't said a word, suddenly she stood up. "I don't think I want to hear any more of this fairy tale, Emma. There's nothing but your word for any of it."

"Sit down." Emma looked at her daughter-in-law and repeated the command. "Sit down." The eyes of the younger woman and the older locked in a contest of wills. After a few seconds Susan sank back in her seat.

Emma nodded in acknowledgment of her victory, then put on her reading glasses. "I have not edited this document in any way. I am going to read it to you exactly as Joshua told it to me, including things which were meant only for me. I believe you both have the right to know every word."

She glanced up for a moment, looked from Cal to Susan, then lowered her head and began reading. "I love you. Sorry. Never wanted you to know. Must for Cal, Dav, John. For Shama. Susan says John mine. Could be, slept with her that day." Emma's voice faltered only for an instant, then she went on. "Sorry. Sorry. Love you. John not my son. He is Cal's. Susan told me. Came hospital after tried kill myself. Gloating. Deserved it. Not Cal. Not John—"

"Stop!" Susan jumped to her feet. "Stop this at once. It's obscene. That crazy old man lying there and you telling us he told you all this in code. It's obscene." She reached for her black lizard handbag. "I'm not going to listen to any more."

Caleb crossed the room in one stride. "Shut your mouth or I'll shut it for you. Sit down." He shoved her onto the sofa, then turned to Emma. "Is there more, Mom?"

"There's more. But you know the basic facts now." She folded the papers and set them aside. "Your father begged your forgiveness, Cal, and mine. You may read the whole thing whenever you wish. What matters is that we all know the truth. Now it's my turn to ask a question. Joshua said that Susan told you some years ago that John wasn't your son, but his. He says that you came to see him one night and accused him, even though you thought he couldn't hear or understand. He says you told him she'd threatened to tell John the same story and that's why you never divorced her. Is that true?"

For a moment Caleb couldn't speak. The night he'd almost killed his father, Joshua had known. "It's true," he murmured finally. "She also said she'd tell you and Jessie the story."

"Yes, I thought it must be true." Emma stood up and took the few steps that brought her to the side of her son and his wife. "I blame myself in part for the havoc you've been allowed to create in this family," she said quietly. "I knew what you were years ago, but I was afraid to speak the truth to Cal because I loved him too much to risk his anger and rejection."

Emma took a deep breath and gazed at Susan for some seconds. Susan didn't look at either of them, she stared straight ahead as if they weren't there. "I helped kill my other son because I wouldn't face up to his weaknesses," Emma murmured. "You gambled that I'd make the same

mistake twice, and God help me, you were almost right."
She turned to Caleb. "Now, my dear, she can't hurt any of
us anymore. Poisonous snake though she is, Joshua has
drawn her fangs."

Susan's body jerked as if she had just come out of a
coma. She jumped to her feet. "You're wrong, both of you.
You haven't won. I still have a weapon you can never take
away. When I tell John that he's Joshua's son not Cal's,
he'll believe me."

"No, he won't," Cal said calmly. "You've lost touch with
the boys. You don't know them, I doubt you ever did.
John's smart as hell, Susan. And he's sound. You can tell
him your vicious story, and I'm not saying it won't hurt
him to discover his mother is a whore who hates him
enough to use him as a weapon. It will. But he won't
believe your lies. Not when I tell him the truth and he
hears his grandfather's story."

"She will tell John nothing," Emma said. "Listen to me,
Susan, and don't forget one word of what I say. You are
going to Reno. You are going to file for divorce. You are
not going to see either of my grandsons again until they
are adults who cannot be mortally wounded by you. If you
do not do exactly what I tell you, I will make this entire
affair public. Everyone will know that you were willing to
destroy your own son. Do not think I will hesitate to do
that for the sake of Joshua's memory, or for the rest of us,
or even for John and Dav. It will do them less harm than
you can do. The only one who will pay will be you. You
will not be able to show your face anywhere in this city.
You will be dropped from every board you serve on,
snubbed by every hostess. You will be a pariah, Susan.
The whole world will know you for what you are, and they
will despise you for it. Almost as much as I despise you."

Susan looked at each of them. Once she opened her
mouth, but she said nothing. It was Emma who had the
final word. "Get this creature out of my house, Caleb."

Shama and Caleb planned a June wedding. "We have to
wait because of all the legalities," she told Jessie. "You
won't be running off to Africa before then, will you?"

"Don't worry, I wouldn't miss it. Anyway, I don't go
until late August. The U.N. has a special training program
and I have to complete that first." Jess had recently an-

nounced that she'd taken a job with a relief program providing medical care for women in the underdeveloped world. "I'll be here to see you walk down the aisle," she added, grinning.

"It's not going to be exactly that," Shama said. "We're being married by some judge Cal knows. At your mother's house."

They were in the den on Carrington Avenue. Jessie reached for her friend's hand. "Remember how we used to sit in here and listen to Frank Sinatra records and dream that someday we'd get married?"

"Sure do. I wouldn't have told even you, but in my dreams it was always Cal who was the groom." Shama hesitated, then asked, "Jessie, do you still want to get married?"

"I'm not sure. Maybe someday, if the right guy comes along. But so far he hasn't turned up and I don't plan to hang around waiting."

"What about that doctor you mentioned."

"Timmy Michaels? He has his points, but I'm not going to marry him. I've finally managed to convince even him of that fact. The world's changing, Shama. The world for women especially. I want to be part of that change."

Shama started to say something, but Marya came in. She was still wearing her hat and coat. "Good, you're both here. I can't wait to show you this." She was brandishing a package.

"What is it?"

"Wait, you'll see." Marya turned to Jessie. "Remember that Christmas before Daniel came home from the war, how he sent us all presents from Morocco?"

"God, I haven't thought of that in years," Jessie said. "But you're right, that's exactly what he did. He sent us presents from Ruth's shop in Casablanca. I remember he wrote to me about them before they came."

Shama was staring at the brown paper-wrapped parcel. "Are you telling me that came from the old place on the Rue des Juifs?"

"Yeah, it did," Marya said triumphantly. "I never did nothing with it, too fancy for me. I just put it in the drawer in my room and forgot about it. This morning I remembered, so I went to Dartmouth Street and got it."

She was opening the package as she spoke, in that slow,

careful way of hers which preserved every bit of string and paper. Finally it was done and Marya lifted a length of pale cream-colored lace and shook it out for them to see. "All handmade, it's gorgeous."

She looked at Shama. Her cheeks were wet with tears. "Don't cry," Marya said. "Only I wondered if maybe you'd like to have your bride dress from this. I mean, since it came from your home country and all."

Shama wiped her eyes and smiled through her tears. "You couldn't know, but my mother made that lace," she whispered. "It was for Ruthie to get married in, then for me. I was furious with Ruthie when she sold it to Daniel." She picked up the cloth and stroked it lovingly, then held it against her.

It was Jessie who went to the kitchen and found Ruth and dragged her into the den. "You've got to see this for yourself," she said, refusing any further explanation.

Ruth stopped in the doorway, it was obvious that like Shama she had instantly recognized the cloth. "Mama's lace," she whispered. "I sold it to Daniel when I first met him. Because at that point the only thing that mattered was for Shama and me to survive."

The sisters looked at each other across the length of lace and a lifetime of memories. "We did more than that," Shama whispered. "Thanks to Daniel, and the family, and America, and you, we did more than survive."

Marya decided that she had to say something or they would all drown in tears. "Listen, you're gonna make a gorgeous bride for my Caleb, only see you don't spill nothin' on this lace. 'Cause after the wedding we're gonna put it away for Rachel when she grows up."

It was, however, Ben who had the final word . . . later, when he'd come home and been told the story. He insisted on opening a bottle of champagne. "To all of us," he said, lifting his glass. "And *L'chaim*, to life."

THE DELANEY DYNASTY

THE SHAMROCK TRINITY

THE DELANEYS OF KILLAROO

THE DELANEYS: *The Untamed Years*

THE DELANEYS II

NORA ROBERTS

☐ 28578   **PUBLIC SECRETS** $4.95

☐ 27283   **BRAZEN VIRTUE** $3.95

☐ 26461   **HOT ICE** $3.95

☐ 26574   **SACRED SINS** $3.95

☐ 27859   **SWEET REVENGE** $3.95

Buy them at your local bookstore or use this page to order: